THE LILAC PLAGUE

THE UNCHOSEN SERIES BOOK ONE

K. J. DAWSON

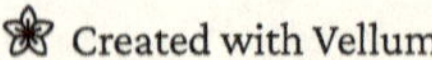 Created with Vellum

*to
The Unchosen
the passed by,
the last picked,
the overlooked.*

*with every quiet battle
and every unsung act,
you Become, you are
The Hero.*

THE UNCHOSEN SERIES

The Lilac Plague
The Rose Court
The Canina Thorn

MAP OF CORNARA

CHARACTER LIST

Nicoleta Aurelian, "Nikka": Azure, half-Getaen and half-Dacian, daughter of a scholar and linguist

Calvus Aurelian, "Papa": Azure daisy scholar, Nicoleta's father

Leila Aurelian, "Mama": Getaen, Nicoleta's mother

Rubia Bythesea: Getaen Healer, Leila's closest friend

Marcus Constantin: Clover farmer from the Rodnic Valley, Rufus' son

Otho Constantin: Clover farmer from the Rodnic Valley, Marcus' father

Emperor Cassus VII: Emperor of Dacia

Mystic Marianna: Poppy residing in Capidava

Lady Katalin Vulpe: Rose noble residing in Capidava

Tulia: Poppy servant in the Vulpe household

Master Elek Moldva: Lily merchant from Capidava

Lady Essa Redvalley: Getaen, adviser to the throne

High Judge Vasile: Lily noble, judge over imperial and Capidavan cases, and adviser to the throne

Captain Lucius: Thorn, Head of the Imperial Guard for Rupea Castle

Jamil Redvalley: Getaen Thorn, Imperial Guard

Commodus: Thorn, Imperial Guard

Historical Dacian Characters:
Trajan Caracalla, "The Blood Conqueror": brought all of Dacia and Getae under one ruler

Emperor Cassus Caracalla III: Descendant of Trajan Caracalla

CORNARA CLASS SYSTEM

Rose: Upper noble with a title. Often in an influential position of authority in the kingdom. Often oversee an estate, at behest of the crown.

Lily: Lower noble with a lesser title. Often in a lesser position of authority in the kingdom.

Thorns: All military, including the city watch, Imperial Guard, and Emperor's Own.

Azure Daisy: Scholars and artisans, including: astronomers, philosophers, painters, sculptors, and historians. No title. Often have small inheritance and dwelling.

Clover: Skilled workers, including: farmers, merchants, and craftsmen. No title. Sometimes own land or property.

Poppy: Laborers, including: miners and servants. No title, no property.

Lilacs: Desolate, poor, diseased, and slaves.

Reeds: The Getaens, magical and non-magical. A class unto themselves. Although technically may marry into other classes, own land, or have wealth, always considered Reeds.

*Individuals can move up the class system by marriage, by gaining wealth, or by doing something extraordinary; and conversely, they can be demoted.

TYPES OF MAGIC

Healer: Heals using herbs infused with magic. Can also use incantations alone or to strengthen the healing properties. Employed after someone is unwell.

Protector: Builds strength and resilience to injury or sickness. Three types of protection: mind, flesh and sinew, and/or blood and bone.

Illuminator: Infuses light into objects, primarily luminary orbs.

Sonus: Modifies sound — dampens or amplifies.

Sensitive: Senses emotions. Also known as "the truth teller."

Clarifier: Heightens experiences, or clarifies memories.

Mirror (also known as a "Ghoster"): Records messages, feelings, or memories for others. Embodied as a "ghost."

Bonder: Bonds people or objects with magic.

Seer: Sees possible futures (rumored to not exist).

Unspoken magic: Magic so dark and dangerous, Getaens renounce this ability and do not discuss.

PROLOGUE
THE LILAC PLAGUE

I hid outside the partially open door of Papa's study, listening to my parents' laughter. Could they hear my breathing, my heart pounding? I wasn't supposed to loiter outside their study, but my news would spoil their morning. I hated to disappoint them. I was back from my trip early and without an offer of apprenticeship. But, the Healer's path they had urged me down had never felt right.

And why would it? I didn't have magic.

I rolled the stem of the canina flower between my cold thumb and fingers, releasing the sweet scent from the pink petals. The cool dawn air still clung to the marama scarf draped over my head and shoulders, yet I was sweating.

I peeked through the crack between the carved door and the mud-caked wall. Papa studied a scroll with Mama perched on the desk next to him. Dust motes danced in the soft light streaming through the small windows high in the study wall, promising another day of sunshine for the many plants along the wall. Below the windows, a massive amphora, inlaid with intricate gold detailing, sat with distinction.

"The true," Papa read aloud, scratching his head, "cor

menus? Cor menus means 'true heir.' The true heir shall unlock the greatest treasure. And upon the head of the "cor menus," or true heir, shall fall the glory of the land. As the ruler, so the land. Health and life or ash and bone."

Ash and bone. The words echoed in my mind, making my skin crawl, but the scent of the canina calmed me.

Mama ran her hand gently across Papa's hunched shoulders before kneading up his neck. Mama's pale fingers were a stark contrast against his deeply tanned skin. Even if the sun hadn't darkened him from his latest research expedition, Papa was Dacian, and his skin had warm, copper undertones. Mama was his opposite, blond and fair-skinned, a Getaen. Somehow, despite the prejudices of both their people, my parents' marriage stayed strong and happy. My news would be yet another unspoken challenge to overcome.

Mama leaned over Papa's shoulder. "Almost right, my love, but look, 'cor menus' could also mean something other than 'true heir.' High Getaen sagas often use the pair 'blood' and 'heir,' 'cor capus och cor menus,' so this could mean, 'upon the head of the true heir, or true blood, shall fall the glory.'"

Papa reached up and patted Mama's hand. "I'd be lost without you, Leila. With your help, the pieces are starting to come together."

"Nicoleta," Mama said, "You know better than to lurk by doors and listen to things you ought not."

Her tone held no sting, but still, I cringed knowing she'd spied me through the crack. I pushed the door open, and Mama pulled me into a suffocating embrace.

I stepped back and handed Mama the flower. She looked into my eyes like she was reading my soul. She knew. And I knew she knew. I blinked and dropped my gaze to the delicate gold chain of her necklace. The disappointment on her face was more than I could bear.

"It's beautiful. And fresh from the mountains." Mama sniffed the flower, not remarking on the pulverized leaves. She didn't ask the question I dreaded, but the waiting only made it worse. She pulled her long, elegant scarf from her head. "Will you braid the canina into my hair?"

I wanted to hide in my room, to be alone in my misery. Instead, I combed my fingers through Mama's long, honey waves. Concentrating on weaving each strand, I appreciated her drawing me closer.

I ached with worry that my failure would disappoint them, but I'd never imbued herbs with magic and never would. Like my parents, I had no magic in my veins. But not all Healers had magic, and they hoped Rubia would offer me a Healer's apprenticeship. The skilled training would enable me to be a Clover, or even stay in our class as an Azure, instead of tumbling down to a Poppy, or worse.

I'd purposefully selected a canina for its long stem for hair-weaving, knowing it was Mama's favorite. I wove the stem in with the braid over her shoulder. In the Getaen tradition, mothers and daughters braided each other's hair until the daughter marries. It wasn't uncommon for girls in Moesia to marry by fifteen, but Papa promised I wouldn't ever need to. I wondered if his promises were more for his own peace of mind rather than for mine.

"How was your first overnight forage with Rubia?" Papa asked what Mama hadn't.

Rubia was renowned as the most talented Healer in Moesia, and she was also Mama's closest friend. They were closer than sisters. She was like a second mother to me though she was often as snuggly as a prickly zakres plant.

"She's young. No need to rush," Mama said.

"I'll be thirteen in a few days." My hands shook as I twisted the final strand of hair and secured it. Most of my schoolmates had already started their apprenticeships; however, my parents still seemed to see the 5-year-old version of me.

I stood back and inspected the braid and flower tucked behind Mama's ear, complementing her face. Mama's features weren't individually beautiful, but Mama's friendliness and confidence made her an undeniably pretty woman.

"Yes, you're almost a grown woman," Mama agreed with a quick squeeze of my hand. "Tell us all about your adventure. Were you able to gather the summer supplies Rubia needed?"

I took a deep breath, wanting to get right to the point. After all of my effort over the last year, Rubia decided to give the apprenticeship to someone else.

"Rubia said —"

The front door slammed against the terracotta wall, cutting off my words. Rubia shouted our names and burst into the study.

"Thank the stars you're all here." Rubia's piercing green eyes bulged, her face bright red. "It's here!" Rubia shouted. Tendrils of her ash blond braid were loose and disheveled. "We must go. Now!"

"What's going on?" Papa placed a calming hand on her shoulder.

Rubia shrugged him off, her attention focused on Mama as she fired off her words with rapidity. "Nikka is still packed from our journey. We can forage for food in the mountains." She nodded as if her directions should make sense to us. "Anything you must have in the next two weeks, grab it and follow after us." She grabbed my wrist. "We will meet you outside the gates. Hurry! There isn't a moment to spare."

My shoulders tensed. This wasn't like her. Rubia yanked me out of the study, past the hearth.

"What's wrong? Where are we going?" I asked.

Mama grabbed Rubia's shoulder. "Rubia, —"

Rubia spun around, her eyes full of intensity. "The plague. The Lilac Plague. It's here."

"No." Papa's voice was hushed. "It can't be."

Mama's eyes widened. She snatched up her satchel and shoved all the food on the table into it before bolting into their bedroom. I'd heard stories about the Lilac Plague wiping out distant villages — how could it be here?

Rubia shoved my still-packed bag into my arms. "Quickly, Nikka. Your parents will catch up."

She pulled me out of the house and into the street — her panic completely absent from our neighbors. The last of the miners walked down the street, and older children carried the day's water from the city well.

"See, everything is fine." Papa stood empty-handed on our stoop.

I *wanted* to believe Papa, but my heart thumped in warning.

"Stay if you want, but we're going before they close the gate." Rubia tugged me away from our home. I glanced back.

Mama had joined Papa and handed him a blanket. "Hurry, my love."

She pushed him forward. Mama, who had never been a bit aggressive with anyone — ever. Even more than Rubia's panic, Mama's urgency struck cold terror through me.

I alternated between running and walking to keep up with Rubia's brisk pace. The young children playing in the streets were blurs, and the yeasty aroma from bakeries chased us.

I slowed for Mama and Papa to catch up. A somber man stepped out of his house, a white canvas draped in his arms. Sweat stained the armpits and back of his linen camasa. He unfurled the canvas and then hung it from his door.

Time slowed, and he glanced at me — with glazed, reddened eyes.

The snap of the canvas drew my attention, and my stomach

dropped. The black X could only mean one thing. The look of horror on Papa's face confirmed it. Rubia tugged on my hand, but my feet were rooted, my eyes fixed on the X as I hyperventilated.

Someone cried out, setting off a cascade of chaotic motion and frenetic screams. Rubia gave another tug just as a throng of strangers rushed past us, and her hand slipped away. I was pushed to my knees, swallowed by the crowd. I cried out as someone tripped over me and landed on my back.

Someone grabbed my arm, yanking me to my feet. Mama. She pulled us through the crowd, dodging and weaving the converging mass, away from the black X, the harbinger of plague and death.

I'd been too slow to react, had almost been trampled, and it had cost us valuable time. I muttered my apologies, and Mama squeezed my hand with a quick pulse to let me know it was forgiven.

Rubia yelled over the commotion as we fled down the street. "I got a message soon after coming through the gate that three families needed me. One was on the way home, so I stopped in. The smell hit me before I crossed the threshold." She lowered her voice, and I almost missed her next words. "One never forgets that smell."

My feet were sore from the mountain trek, my boots pinching my toes. My bag bounced against my hip with every footfall. Yet, I ran as fast as my legs would carry me down through our hillside city. We passed blissfully unaware people still working and playing as if Moesia wasn't about to descend into madness.

As we rounded the corner, I could see the city gate below. It was still open with several Moesian city guards stationed around it. Hope flared in my chest. My feet moved so fast I was afraid I would lose my balance and fall, tumbling forward on the cobblestone in a tangle of limbs.

Four guards emerged from the guard tower with supplies in their arms. They dropped them outside of the gate.

They were abandoning Moesia, preparing to lock us inside.

"No!" Papa yelled though we were too far away to be heard.

"We can still make it!" Rubia cried out.

I put on an extra burst of speed. The guards moved to the gate, pushing it closed. We were within a stone's throw. My stomach lurched into my throat. What had I done? If only I could get back my moments of stupor when I stared at the X on the flag.

"Stop!" Mother screamed at the guards, her braid flying from side to side as she ran.

The guards either didn't hear or didn't care. We could climb the walls, but the pile of weapons with their supplies warned that would be a deadly choice.

The Lilac Plague was said to be a curse. What had we done to offend Zalmoxis?

The innocent laughter and movement of the city faded away around me. My sights focused on the shrinking slip of air between the two massive doors. If we didn't make it, it would be my fault.

The sliver of air grew smaller and smaller until the gate closed with a slam of wood and iron. A shock of dread went down my spine. Papa pounded on the gate, but it was no use. I pressed my palms against my temple, pulling at my hair. Mama reached out, fumbling to grasp Rubia's arm, her breathing coming in short, shallow rasps. Pulling out the pendant she wore every day, Mama's face went from open terror to grim determination. I didn't know what she was planning.

At this point, it didn't matter. We were trapped inside Moesia with the Lilac Plague, and it was all my fault.

This place is hollow and cold. I've tried to run away from Rupea Castle many times. Each time, my tutor is whipped in front of me, taken away, and replaced with a new one without a word. Once I hid on a ceiling beam, my latest tutor none the wiser. Her cruel face was scrunched up with worry. Later, I flinched with each snap of the whip.

It was luck that Hanna found me one day, covered in soot, crouching in the fireplace. I'm no longer forced to wear itchy clothes or learn their language. Hanna is married to someone powerful, the Blood Emperor.

Getae don't have Emperors. We have Clan Leaders appointed to protect us from Zalmoxis. But our Clan Leader must have done something terrible. Zalmoxis crushed my clan and my family using the bloody fist of a human army. The Blood Emperor's army. When he's near, I cling to Hanna's skirts and feel her legs tremble through the folds. I hold her steady. She protects me. As the Blood Emperor's wife, she's the only one who dares.

Hanna gave me blank pages for a journal and told me to hide my thoughts well.

— VAHID THE LAST OF THE SAGE HILLS CLAN

CHAPTER

ONE

THE TRUE KEY

Today, I would see Mama again. I'd longed for this day for three years. I hoped I would get the closure I wanted. Hope wasn't a simple, cheerful feeling of possibility. No, it had an undercurrent of dashed dreams and regret. I released my apron that I'd balled up in my fist and attempted to smooth out the wrinkled mess. Every stitch I'd embroidered was washed in tears, especially when my aching sadness swallowed me whole. But I'd cleaned my cantrinta aprons and dress as carefully as I had washed the ashes from my face.

I scooped up the food basket from the table and approached Papa's study, ensuring he was likewise prepared.

Clinging to hope required courage.

Before the plague, I had loved hovering outside Papa's study, trying to snatch bits of my parents' conversations. Their whispers once drew me to this spot. Now, I only came to deliver meals.

Like many other trays, last night's supper lay untouched on the floor. Left to his own devices, Papa would never leave his study, but today was too important.

11

We would both be reborn when we crossed our threshold, officially out of mourning. For the first time in three years, after bathing, I didn't re-apply the ritual ashes to my forehead. I took a deep breath and pushed the door open.

Papa was stooped over his faded tomes, his shoulders rounded, fingers black with ink. He had always been a wiry man, but now his cheeks were sunken, his skin waxy.

Several scrolls lay near the nub of a guttering candle. Fortunately, Papa didn't need its scant light with the dawn pouring through the high windows behind him. On the right wall, the shelves held what knick-knacks remained from my parents' travels, bottles of ink, and piles of innocuous notes. Dry, cracked soil filled the massive pots along the left wall, the plants long dead.

A bin sat next to his desk, and I blinked, wishing I was wrong about what I saw. But, no, it overflowed with scrolls. I gripped the handles of the basket tighter. After the plague, Papa had grown careless, leaving piles of scrolls out for weeks at a time.

I paused, letting my eyes wander to the side of the room. Near the planters, six terracotta tiles lay upended next to the chasm that extended seven feet into the earth underneath our home. The scrolls should be hidden below, the tiles in place. I fought to keep my breathing steady.

At least, lost in his parchments, Papa didn't see the strain on my face. I edged further from the chasm's maw just steps away and swallowed. As the years passed, I avoided the ghosts that haunted me here. The plague ripped out my heart hour by hour, day after day. But what came after the plague had blackened my soul: the raid.

Papa never spoke of the raid, the scrolls, or the plague. He'd stopped trimming his whiskers, tucking in his shirt, or meeting people's gaze. I wanted to shout that it hadn't been his fault;

the scrolls were harmless — simple studies of southern clans. I wanted to end the scorn of our neighbors, other scholars, and the city's university. Regardless, the swirling gossip over what the guards had discovered in the scrolls had done its damage. Besides, part of me feared the gossip was only an echo of the vile truth.

Fortunately, the guards, the Thorns, had only found a few scrolls — most had been shoved away, buried. I know because I'd been buried with them. The writings on most were still a mystery to me, but a hidden cavern meant hidden records. Hidden records meant secrets, and secrets could be treason. Treason led to death. The scrolls were dubious, at best. I shuddered at the thought of the soldiers discovering the scrolls underneath the tiles.

Even so, the fantasy of chastising words rolling off my tongue and forever silencing those who judged us lived in the back of my mind. But my tongue would never keep up with my whirling mind. Not anymore. My words, once as quick and nimble as an antelope, had disappeared completely after the raid, only to return with stumbles and stutters.

"Papa, it's time. I made Mama's favorite." I didn't stutter the well-practiced words, despite the tension in my shoulders. My fingers brushed the soft crust of the butternut bread, the lid on the jar of maple butter, the wax-wrapped honey cakes, and the fuzzy bundle of apricots, assuring myself every detail was perfect.

I held up the basket, but Papa continued to scrawl on his parchment, oblivious. This sweet meal was inappropriate for mourning but perfect for this day of celebration. It'd been years since Mama had made cakes. Before the plague. Almost three years since we had to burn the dead: the neighbor's boy, my great aunt, half the town. We had burned Mama. The stench still lingered if I inhaled deep enough.

Despite the ashes and tears, I'd sheltered the bright hope of today's promise — a chance to say goodbye and move forward. I was anxious to see Mama's message to us. It was the one happy thing I'd clung to: the blue vision.

Moesia was the largest city within a two-week walk of the southern clans, and we had plenty of magical Getaen customs to show for it, like the blue visions. I ached to see Mama, but it was bad luck to visit any sooner. No one wanted to tempt vengeful Zalmoxis into scourging Moesia again.

I touched Papa's shoulder. He twitched and blinked before breaking into a smile. It warmed my heart until the early morning light reflected off the scar that pinched an uneven line down his face. Guilt knotted my stomach.

"Oh, yes, Nikka." Ash clung to the wrinkled crevices of Papa's skin, and dark circles bagged under his eyes. He put down his parchment. "You startled me. How long have you been standing there?" He rubbed his thumb and forefinger across his closed eyes, leaving a smudge of ink similar to the bruise he'd suffered that night.

My throat tightened. The city gates. The plague. The raid. The darkness. The corners of my vision blurred. Memories threatened, and the basket handle felt slick under my chilled fingers. The urge to bolt thrummed through me. Instead, I set the basket at my feet, resolved to stay.

"What day is it?" Papa chuckled and stretched his back, seeming unaware of my terrors. "What is time, anyway? Perhaps time stands still while our present selves change; the past a misconception and the future undecided."

His words grounded me back in the moment. I relaxed, comforted by his usual philosophical musings.

"Notice anything?" I tucked a loose strand of my dark, honey-blond hair behind my ear. My face hadn't been free of ash since I was twelve years old, before Mama died.

"Still my bright, golden-eyed girl. You changed your hair?" He guessed.

How did he not notice my clean, ash-free face? Then again, he saw details in crumbling scripts yet forgot to eat for days.

"Did you smell the butternut bread?" After all these years, I didn't know if my tongue could handle the shock of maple-sweetness.

Realization dawned on his face. "It's today?"

"The dawn is an hour spent." I was anxious for Papa to bathe so we could cross our threshold, both clean and new. Perhaps washing the ash from his face would wash away some of my guilt, too. "We need to hurry so we don't m-miss well-wishers at Mama's g-grave," I added.

"You've done everything to prepare. Alone. I'm sorry, Nikka," he said.

"You've just been busy with your work," I lied. Papa did little work for the university anymore. He vacillated between pouring through his stockpile of research and staring into space. Only by the grace of his meager inheritance did we survive.

Papa stared past me, deep in thought. "This day has arrived too soon."

How could he say that when each day crawled by more slowly as today approached?

"I meant to talk to you weeks ago. I have something to show you." Papa stood up and walked to the shelves.

I lifted a hand to stop him and rush him to clean up, but reminded myself that I was still his daughter, not his minder.

Papa moved aside bottles, quills, and a clumsy sculpture I'd made as a child. He wriggled a stone out of the wall, revealing a single scroll hidden behind it. My heart thumped.

Papa slid the scroll out from the wall and placed it in my hands. His initials, C.A., for Calvus Aurelian, were stamped into the yellow wax. A claim; whoever found it would know who'd created it.

"When I first traveled south, the Getaens were kind but always guarded," Papa said. "After I married your mama, she traveled with me. Over time, her people welcomed us — at least the allied clans. They threw fantastic feasts and shared striking insight. I'm even an honorary member of the Antelope Hills. Many of my fellow scholars assumed this was why I married Leila. Some were jealous, but most others scorned me for marrying below my status."

I leaned forward, eager. My parents had shared much about Getaen customs but nothing about Mama's family or past. I didn't even know how she, a Getaen Reed, had married an Azure far above her status.

"My peers didn't see your mama as I did. She was more clever than all the stuffy Moesian University scholars combined. She opened my eyes to new concepts and deeper meanings of Getaen symbols. More importantly, she brought such joy into my life. My time with her was a gift." Papa's eyes glistened, but he swallowed his emotions.

I savored his words of deep affection. Perhaps more so because I knew no one would ever say anything like that about me. I'd heard the whispers — no one wanted to marry someone with a cursed tongue. There was no use moping about it, though, especially not today. I cleared my throat, ready to spur Papa along, but he continued before I could stutter a word.

"Forgive an old papa his faults. I should've shown you this before now." Papa gestured for me to break the seal. "We worked on this for over a decade."

The seal snapped under my fingers as his words registered. I unrolled the parchment, my hands shaking with excitement or dread, more likely a combination of both.

Precisely-inked symbols marked the scroll, but the illustration in the center demanded my attention. I traced the distinct orb, round on one side and flat on the other. The rush of blood pulsed in my ears, drowning out everything else.

I know that pendant.

"M-Mama's necklace? You were studying it?"

Mama had worn the pendant every day of her life until the plague. When the gates slammed closed and we found ourselves trapped, Mama instructed me to recite strange, ancient words and then placed the orb in my hand. Sometime in those hazy days of despair after Mama's death and the raid, I'd given the orb to Rubia. It seemed odd now, but Papa insisted that Rubia keep it until I was older.

Papa swallowed, the lump in his thin neck bobbing up and down. "The orb is part of a legend, both Getaen and Dacian, from the time of Emperor Trajan Caracalla."

My mouth was suddenly dry. Emperor Caracalla, the Blood Conqueror. Over two centuries ago, the brutal ruler had expanded Dacia's boundaries on all sides, particularly on the east where he drove to the sea, claiming all the Getaen lands along the way. His descendants still held the Dacian Empire, every single territory, in their grip.

I leaned forward, my angst making my sentences less even. "W-why didn't you tell me about this sooner?"

The moment stretched as my mind whirled. The open cavern practically screamed from behind me in warning and anticipation.

Papa pressed his fingertips into the desktop. "Your mama asked me to delay as long as possible."

Tension crawled up my back. They'd always kept their research from me, and today, the day I wanted to celebrate Mama, I learn *she* was the one keeping me in the dark? A knot formed at the base of my neck. Didn't she trust me?

Of all the days to tell me, why ruin this *one?*

He placed the ink bottle at the top of the scroll, the weight keeping it from furling. "This is an illustration of the True Key. It's made of yellow gold, and see —" His hand hovered over the scroll, not touching it, as if it was too sacred to breathe on. "— the imperfect sphere has indentations and markings. To the casual observer, it's meant to look like a trinket. Nothing special, especially here in Moesia with all our gold mines. But the True Key is an artifact of incredible worth."

Papa dropped his voice, despite the closed, thick glass windows, placed too high to peer through. "It's said to open a Dacian treasure so immense that it will change the course of the entire kingdom. It has the power to topple rulers." He pointed to symbols below the illustration, and he lowered his voice. "A new emperor will rise."

He searched my face, imploring me to understand the importance of this revelation.

The knot in my neck grew roots, making my stomach twist as I tried to make sense of Papa's words. But I couldn't. I kept calm, but my worry mounted. Since Mama's passing, Papa had retreated into his own head. He'd missed meetings with the scholar's guild. He'd stopped traveling, bathing, or eating regularly. Had Papa's poor self-care and grief pushed him to create this fantastical tale?

"Papa," I said, reasoning with him. "It's unlikely that a D-Dacian artifact of such worth b-belonged to an unknown d-daughter of a Getaen clan." I held out my arms. The ridiculousness plowed through me, leaving anger behind. Couldn't he honor Mama without trying to cast her as a mysterious owner of ancient lore? It was madness to think she had a priceless relic linked to an infamous emperor.

He leaned forward. "I assure you, I too had doubts. But Leila's wild stories intrigued me, and I loved her enough to research her claims. I found a record of a 'first key' in the university, but it was tied to a curse, not a treasure. Even so, the description of the key matched, and we continued to search. We found whispers and crumbling records scattered throughout the kingdom. Soon the research on the key, the treasure, and the possible curse became our shared passion."

Papa pointed to the parchment's illustration. "I created this record, a compilation of my research."

Was this scroll proof of madness? The stuffy air in the study made me lightheaded.

"This is a lot to t-take in." I struggled with the words, desperate to leave.

I missed Mama so much it hurt, but now I was angry with her, too. I'd spent years mourning, only to have my wounds ripped open again just when I'd begun healing enough to move on.

No, Mama was not a dreamer like Papa. She and Rubia were focused, driven by a shared past, not delusional. Perhaps she'd told Papa not to tell me this because it was nonsense, and she wanted to protect me. Perhaps when Papa saw her today, it would bring him back to me.

He needed to see Mama. I needed to placate him, then get him to the gravesite. I took a calming breath. "The orb is a special k-key that opens a mysterious treasure?"

"Perhaps the treasure of knowledge," he said.

"Isn't love the greatest treasure?" I tried to direct the subject back to Mama.

Papa cleared his throat and rolled up the parchment. "You must be excited to get your mama's final wishes for you."

Regret pricked my heart. Papa must have sensed my doubt.

"Rubia kept the blue vision safe. You're lucky it wasn't damaged in the raid," Papa said, changing the subject.

"We're lucky. This is a chance for b-both of us to see Mama again."

Papa swirled a sealing wax stick over the weak candle flame. Silence stretched between us while he resealed the scroll with his stamp. He set the scroll down and took both my hands in his.

"Your mama asked me to delay these truths because they're a burden," his voice thickened with emotion. "I've shown you a mere grain of sand in the desert of information you'll need to learn. However, this grain will help prepare you for whatever your mama's message may be."

He squeezed my fingers just like Mama used to. His touch was deliberate, his eyes full of depth and knowledge. Doubt crept into my heart. What if he wasn't delusional?

"You'll help me understand and remember her words," I said.

"Your mama and I said our goodbyes before we were sequestered from each other. I remember her healthy, glowing, and strong. You didn't have that luxury. With your immunity to the plague, you saw too much. She said the blue vision was for you alone." His eyes welled. I didn't know what to say. He rarely showed strong emotions.

I blinked back my confusion. It felt wrong for him not to see Mama one last time.

"Run along, my dear child. You've indulged your old papa enough for one day." Papa released my hands. "Besides, I have many records to put into storage. It's not wise for me to keep them out for long." He glanced at the stacked tiles.

I barely felt floors under my feet as I moved to the door, the upended tiles and piles of scrolls blurred in my periphery. Papa was sending me to the graveyard alone.

I miss my family. Darkness surrounds me in this cold castle. Hanna says it is important for me to find my place. She keeps a protective hand on her growing belly when she moves about the castle. The other servants poke me and say that the Empress Consort will not favor me for long.

— *VAHID OF GETAE*

CHAPTER

TWO

SHATTERED BLUE VISION

The sun lingered at the apex in the sky, waves of heat making images in the distance dance. Laughter and chatter filled the air. The city of Moesia spilled down the hillside in layers and layers of houses. The fine manors of the Golden Lily sparkled atop Moesia's hill with the lower classes of Azures, Clovers, and Poppies, each tiering down toward the Lilacs in the Fissure.

The graveyard curled around the southern edge of the city. Graves were in loose family groupings, and Mama's was on the outskirts of the Aurelian family plots. A winding line of oaks cut through the high desert, long ago pampered until their roots reached the aquifer deep below.

Several families clustered under the protective shade of the nearest gnarled oak, greeting friends, and sharing food and wine. Like many others, I wore a crisp dress with elaborate, yellow embroidery running down the sleeve and wrist. The patterns were incredible as everyone had been like me, cooped up in mourning each evening. Over the top, women wore front and back matching catrinta full-aprons, tied together at the sides. Mine had nubby, yellow borangic silk ribbons, gifts from Rubia.

As I scanned the road to the cemetery, I tugged at my marama, the scarf loosely wrapped around my shoulders. I scolded my vain hope of seeing Papa's limping gait. He wouldn't come.

Well-wishers, neighbors, and people who claimed to be distant relatives visited me at Mama's grave. I'd plastered on a pleasant face, recited my rehearsed phrases as they shared stories, and offered honey cakes, apricots, and wine. All the while, my thoughts whirled with Papa's secrets. I told myself he was delusional, but as I contemplated everything I knew of him, I had an uneasy feeling that there could be truth to his tale.

I fiddled with my fingers, anxious for Rubia's arrival. I knew she was saving Mama's grave for last when she could let her façade of smiles fall.

To most, Rubia was a butterfly of Moesia, beautifully fluttering through a crowd, creating laughter and lightening spirits. More than one man had tried to catch her, but I could never imagine her with a marriage scarf pinned in her hair. Besides, her colorful wings were a distraction. Those who spent time with her came to realize she had a stern, practical nature. She wasn't a dreamer like Papa. Rubia always told me the truth, no matter how difficult it might be for me to hear.

An old acquaintance of Mama's approached. I remembered his name, Gallus, just in time to greet him. I retreated to my blanket and basket under the oak tree to give him privacy. Gallus knelt, dirtying his fine linen trousers. A wide, embroidered leather belt strained to hold his ample waistline. Tucked at his hip was a fashionable dagger, typical of the ones carried by Lilies and the few Roses I'd seen.

My head ached from regurgitating the social niceties I had rehearsed for moons. The more I practiced, the less I stuttered.

It would've been an easier task if Papa's words hadn't fought for attention in my mind.

Wiping his eyes, Gallus stood and walked toward me.

"Greetings, Gallus." I placed a honey cake on a napkin as he sat down.

"Thank you, Nicoleta." His hand shook as he accepted the food. I hadn't seen him since before the plague, and I sat in an awkward silence across from the nobleman I barely knew. He continued, his voice almost dreamlike. "I still remember the first time I met Leila. She'd just escaped a Getaen clan war and was selling medicinal packets she and Rubia had concocted. That was before Rubia had proven herself, back when they were both just more faces in a crowd of newcomers. But I noticed Leila's intelligent eyes behind the dirty face." He lowered his voice. "Not many people know this, but your mother had only learned a bit of Dacian in the south. I was the one who taught her our language."

I leaned forward. Mama hadn't spoken much about her early days in Moesia. I had always wondered how Mama met Gallus, but like so many things, now I'd never have the chance to ask her.

"That was k-kind of you."

Lost in his memories, Gallus didn't seem to notice my stutter.

"Leila's smile could warm all of Dacia on a cold winter's night." Gallus beamed for a moment before his brow furrowed. He crumpled the cake in his grip.

"I would've married her. Me, a Lily, marry her, a Getaen Reed from the Fissure."

The tone of his words crashed down on me, like Getaens were polluted refuse.

Some of the people around me quieted. I shifted my weight, imploring him with my eyes to stop. Mama was a private person, and I knew she wouldn't want her past loudly shared.

"If he hadn't interfered, Leila would have married me. And she'd have lived in the Golden Lily above the disease, not the putrid Commons. She never would've gotten sick," Gallus said in a sonorous voice. The eavesdroppers started to whisper. My chest burned with shame.

Despite Gallus being a Lily and my elder, I cleared my throat, determined to stop his emotional tirade.

"I blame myself for Leila's death," he spat. "I should have stopped Calvus when I'd had the chance."

"S-stop." My throat could barely eke out the word. I wanted to sooth Gallus' temper, but a single syllable was all I could muster.

A hand gripped Gallus' shoulder, and I looked up to see Rubia looming over him. Without the layer of ash on her skin, I barely recognized her radiant face.

"Hello, old friend," Rubia said, her voice like a splash of cool water on a scalding stone. She strolled between us, breaking Gallus' concentration and shielding me from his vitriol at the same time. "How often old regrets threaten to bubble to the surface. Only moments ago, I cried thinking about the silly tricks I played on two children who once lived next door to me. It's funny, the things we remember."

Rubia's musical voice caused the others nearby to nod before returning to their own stories and desserts. I was in awe of Rubia's ability to smooth over even the most awkward situation.

"Forgive my outburst, child. You had no control over the past," Gallus said to me.

Rubia sat down, her back to the oak tree and the crowd beneath it. Her face was serene, but she jerked her loose scarf from her head down to her shoulders, her fingers tense.

"You have no right to come here and spew your sadness," she said, her whisper sharp and cutting. "This is a sacred day of rebirth for the living, not for doling out regrets."

Gallus' face tightened. I held my breath, waiting for him to chastise Rubia for berating her betters. But then looking at me, his eyes softened with his exhale. He had a strange paternal look that made me squirm.

"It is a day of healing. I'll do better in honor of your mother's memory in the years ahead," he said.

I watched, dumbfounded, as he strode toward his horse and led it to the main road.

"Looks like a hundred people are still here, despite the heat," Rubia said, as if she hadn't just confronted a Lily.

I wouldn't drop the past so easily.

"W-what was G-Gallus… " My eyes scrunched then bulged, trying to get the words out.

"Breathe, Nikka. It only gets worse when you're flustered," Rubia said.

Her advice grated. Of course, I needed to stay calm. I rubbed my hands on my arms, trying to brush away my irritation. I took a breath and tried again.

"People in the Golden Lily d-died as well." My body quaked from the exertion of the words as I wrapped Gallus' unfinished cake, saving it for the birds in the city square. "The p-plague knows n-no status."

"Gallus pursued your mother, but to the utter rejoicing of his family, Leila married Calvus. But Gallus never stopped caring about her. Unfortunately, his wife and child died in childbirth, and many of his friends and family died in the plague." Rubia brushed two fingers over the gold chain around her neck. "Grief can make one do terrible things."

I wanted to press her for more of the story of Mama and Gallus, but she was my elder, so I respected her silence. Besides, there were more important questions. What could she tell me about the orb?

Before I could ask, Rubia pulled out the tip of a blue vial from her pocket, and my heart stopped. My fingers itched to hold it. She was diverting my frustration from Gallus. Clever, but I saw through her ploy. Still, she held a blue vision — Mama's blue vision, the very thing I'd dreamed of for three years.

Rubia knelt next to me and placed the blue, glass vial in my hands. She cupped my hands in hers, the façade she wore gone, replaced by love and loss in the sheen of her eyes. In her unguarded moment, I had an opportunity; a minor but uncouth manipulation. But if I was ever going to be able to read her face, it was now.

I leaned closer and dared whisper. "Papa told me your necklace is Getaen. But it is also Dacian. He also told me a few other interesting things."

Rubia clenched her jaw, and her expression closed off. That was all the confirmation I needed. She knew the rumors of the treasure, curse, and the Blood Emperor. But was any of it true?

"This isn't the time," Rubia hissed. "I must check on my apprentice." She scurried away before I could object.

I disliked confrontation, but I had to know more about the pendant Mama had given me — the one Rubia now wore. In the meantime, Mama's blue vision, her final message, meant more than emotional closure. It might hurl me down new, troublesome paths I hadn't known existed.

THE FIRST STAR sparkled faintly overhead and pink streaked the skyline. The sun was disappearing past the western scrublands. In the distance, a few blue-hued ghostly wisps lit up for overeager families. It was the first time I'd ever seen a blue ghost. My heart thumped in my chest, wishing Papa or Rubia were here to explain how all this worked.

The blue vial was slick in my sweaty palm.

I tried not to be jealous of Rubia's apprentice. I told myself that it was for the best that Rubia hadn't selected me for the position. Moesia needed a Getaen with magic. And the boy from the Fissure she'd selected needed the training. Still, Rubia's rejection stung.

Rubia said I was destined for something more important. Her vague promises were cold comfort, especially when she refused to say what my great destiny might be. Perhaps she envisioned me caring for Papa all his life?

I stood rigid under the oak tree as visitors left before the curfew grew too close, leaving the dead their twilight discussions with their living loved ones.

Glass shattered the night. A faint blue vision rose like smoke near the feet of two, silhouetted figures in the distance. They were too far away to see their faces or guess their ages, but my heart squeezed at observing them huddled together. I hated that I glanced up the road again. He wasn't coming.

As the color in the sky darkened and a million stars dotted the firmament, several more blue spectral visions lit up like comforting lanterns in far-flung areas of the graveyard.

No one had explained the intricacies of what to do or what to expect. No one spoke of it as Zalmoxis was said to twist the lives of anyone who spoke of the blue visions except during ceremonies or death rites. My hand trembled. Should I rip open the sealed cork top?

Quick footsteps sounded on the dry dirt behind me; I turned to see Rubia rushing forward. My heart lightened, even though Rubia risked skirting near a mourner, intruding on the last tender words from their loved one. It was rude, and she risked someone calling upon Zalmoxis to curse her. Still, I was grateful.

Rubia gripped my shoulders, the fruity scent of wine on her breath. "I'm sorry. Your questions took me by surprise. Your father was so long in telling you any crumb of truth, I assumed it would be my responsibility to teach you about the key when you were of age. But, I understand why he chose to tell you about the orb now. There is so much to explain, I'm not sure where to begin."

"So Papa isn't misguided? The orb really does open a treasure?" I whispered.

Rubia put a finger to my lips. "He had acquired more truth than any Dacian in many generations. Whatever he told you will help prepare you for your mother's message."

My heart pounded.

"Smash the glass on the ground and listen. It will be difficult to understand. Your papa is expecting you to stay with me tonight. It's all been arranged. I'll wait up for you." She pulled her scarf up over her head before leaving me alone at Mama's gravesite again.

What information was so overwhelming that I'd have to turn to Mama's closest friend for support? Was it something Papa couldn't face? My fist tightened around the blue vial. Was I holding the answers?

The packed earth was silent under my feet. At Mama's headstone, I sunk to my knees and closed my eyes. I clutched the vial to my chest, savoring the delicate strands of hope gripped between my fingers. Distant cries carried on the warm breeze. People in the graveyard were shedding tears of joy, peace, or sadness at seeing their loved ones for the last time.

I checked over my shoulder to confirm my solitude. Spectral blue lights dotted the graveyard, bathed in stars and a sliver of the moon hanging in the sky.

I hefted my blue vial in the air and brought it down on the marble grave marker. Shattered, the glass shards tumbled into the dirt.

From the vial, a wisp appeared. Small at first, but it grew. I stumbled backward, awestruck as the wisp twisted and transformed into a blue, transparent form of Mama.

It was only a recollection. She couldn't see me, but I pretended she was there. Her hair was braided with a canina flower tucked in behind her ear. I sucked in a breath. The day we tried to escape the city came flooding back. The heat, my too-tight shoes, the crowds, and Mama's firm grip as she pulled me to my feet after I'd fallen. Details I'd forgotten. I touched my hand to my chest, remembering the weight of the orb, remembering the interesting bumps and etchings on the surface.

Mama's voice from the blue vision pulled me from my memories back to the cool evening in the graveyard. "Nicoleta, our beloved golden child. I once wished to give you many brothers and sisters, but it was not to be. You received the love destined for many children. I hope I did not suffocate you with my attention."

My heart swelled, and tears pricked my eyes. Mama's voice was as I remembered, only softer, as if faded by the years. "There were many things I hoped to share with you before I was taken to Zalmoxis. If Rubia delivers this vision, it means I didn't accomplish my duty. I failed as have so many before me. The mantle of this burden falls to you and Rubia now."

"Duty? What burden?" I reached out to touch her, but my hand glided through her dress as if it were nothing but smoke.

Without pausing, Mama said, "When I was a girl, I lived in the southern, Getae lands. We were happy, and although my clan no longer exists, I planned to introduce you to our past allies when you were older."

I leaned in closer. I'd known Mama's and Rubia's clan was gone, but they never spoke about what had happened.

"When I was fifteen, our village was destroyed. It was a slaughter. Rubia, myself, and one child, Mehr'd, escaped the village purge." Mama looked to the side at something or someone in the room where she recorded the vision. "Mehr'd died of a snake bite on the journey. Leaving his little body in a shallow grave was one of the most difficult things I'd ever done."

My hands flew up to my mouth, trying to imagine Mama at my age, living through such horrors.

"When we arrived in Moesia, we found shelter in the Fissure. It might seem like a terrible fate to you, but it was a sanctuary for us. I was fortunate to find work with a wealthy family in the Golden Lily, and Rubia sold magic potions," Mama explained. "Calvus was seeking a Getaen translator, and I was recommended. We worked together, and soon we were smitten. Honestly, his nose was always in a dusty scroll, so I don't know how he noticed I even existed." Even in the vision, Mama beamed. "I was afraid to tell him the truth about the pendant I wore, but a secret like that would destroy us eventually. So I told him. It was the best decision I ever made. Though, Rubia was upset."

Mama paused, "Rubia is a Guardian, one of two. I became the second Guardian when I was fifteen, when our clan was destroyed. Today, I passed my responsibility on to you."

A Guardian? Her words were like thunder. My toes and fingers tingled, my head spinning.

Mama continued. "So much of what this kingdom believes is a lie. Only a few of us know the truth, and we dare not speak it openly."

From outside the soft, blue glow of Mama's memory, more cries pierced the night air. I leaned closer to hear Mama better, but up closer, the blue vision looked more like unformed smoke than defined facial features. I stepped back, wanting to believe Mama was truly with me, not an echo carried in a blue vial.

Mama dropped her voice to a whisper. "The wrong heir is on the throne."

I shook my head, not sure I heard her words correctly. Thankfully, Mama paused to let her words sink in. Another cry rang behind me. In the recesses of my mind, a warning sounded. Those weren't the cries of mourners. That was a cry of fear. My belly knotted as I remembered the timbre of the screams when the city erupted the day the plague broke out.

"Seven generations ago," Mama continued.

I spun and scanned the graveyard.

"... twin princes Cassus and Odon, sons of Emperor Trajan Caracalla," Mama said behind me.

This would be my last chance to see Mama, to hear her words from her lips, but I couldn't shake the crawling sensation of danger, a feeling I'd hoped never to feel again after the raid. I tried to convince myself the cries were simple loss and pain, rage or disappointment at some revelation from the blue apparitions; deep inside, I knew they weren't.

"Over two centuries ago, the Getaen clans struggled to unify. Trajan Caracalla took advantage, defeating all of our clans and bringing our people under his rule," Mama said.

Then I saw it. Distant shadows moved through the graveyard, the glint of metal in the moonlight. Dread consumed me. I couldn't move a muscle.

"On his deathbed, Trajan made a pact with his sons, sealed with the magic of a powerful mage," Mama continued.

I couldn't tear my gaze from the shadows around the graveyard, moving from one blue vision to another. Another voice cried out, caught unawares, and stopped short by dull thumps. The air thrummed with violence like a storm.

"To avoid a divisive war, Trajan created a way for his twin sons to share the power. Cassus' line would rule the country for five generations and then switch to Odon's line. Then, the lines would unite through marriage and continue to rule."

I was rooted, unable to run.

"The mage sealed the pact with a complex spell that grows in strength over time."

The shadows moved again to another blue vision. Closer. *Thump.* The night closed in around me, suffocating me. Soon the shadows would be here.

"Many of the details of the spell and the pact have been twisted over the generations... "

Despite the cooling air, my hands were clammy. The shadows disappeared; the thumps stopped. My body relaxed enough for me to move. Though I hated to be robbed of Mama's words, her voice, her secrets, I knew she wouldn't want me to suffer an attack.

I balled my hands into fists. I dropped to the ground and crawled to the foot of the oak tree.

Mama continued, but I could only hear snippets above the sound of rustling clothes and gravel crunching under me as I scrambled away. "The mage created... power... the line of Cassus... not trusting... "

I yanked off my scarf and created a sling, shoving my boots and socks into it, and looped it over my neck. I braced my bare soles and dug my fingers into the bark to shimmy up the tree. The first branch was high enough that I'd probably never walk again if I fell. But I continued to climb. Once in the canopy of leaves, Mama's words were lost.

I sat on a stout branch, pulled two acorns from between the leaves and waited, my body quivering. I hoped I hadn't selected a rotten section of tree. In the quiet of the night, my heart beat so loudly I feared it would echo across the graveyard.

I imagined Papa hunched over his scrolls right now. Could he have climbed this tree? I shuddered, grateful he was safe at home.

Two figures, dressed in the color of night, crept beneath me, straight for Mama's vision.

"No one's here," a man hissed.

My throat threatened to close.

"This one's talking about the plague. About Cassus," another said in a nasally voice.

Part of me relaxed, hearing their local accent, not rough like the one-time raiders of the north. They were dangerous thieves, but not from the Emperor's Imperial Guard.

"That doesn't mean anything. Getaens created hundreds of these ghost-magic-things when the plague broke out," the first man said.

I shifted for a better look through the leaves. I spotted their green half-cloaks. My breathing quickened, realizing they were the city watch, trained Thorns, not common thieves. They stood steps away from Mama and her treasonous revelations. She'd get Papa and me hung.

"This is the vision the captain alerted us to. I can feel it," the nasal voice said.

I threw the acorns as far as I could toward the main path to the city. Though, to avoid hitting the branches above me, I couldn't throw them as hard as I would've liked.

The Thorns rushed toward the sound, their soft leather boot footfalls quickly fading. I counted to fifty then climbed back down the tree. Mama's blue vision had faded to a wisp, but she was still speaking. I couldn't return to her grave. The soldiers would be back soon. I crawled on my elbows into the darkness, bitterness and fear balling in the back of my throat. I moved away from where I'd thrown the acorns, alert to any movement around me. I feared that a soldier would leap out of the darkness at any moment.

I paused to listen for footfalls.

The blue vision continued, barely loud enough to hear. "Rubia and I made the decision on your behalf, one that you may despise us for later. But, I'm desperate to protect you from this plague. I couldn't bear to watch you die when I could prevent it. However, the orb's protection comes with a terrible responsibility."

Protection? I pressed my hands against the cooling earth, horrified and angry that I'd missed some of her final message.

"A responsibility you didn't understand when you repeated the ancient oath."

The words I'd spoken — I'd lumped that experience in with the many others about magic I didn't completely understand.

I crawled a few paces. Blood thrummed through my trembling body. The lies I'd been told all my life battled for my attention. I pushed them aside, focusing on escape. Without the wide, main road back to the city, I'd have to find my own, unmarked path.

"For that, I am deeply sorry." Mama's ghostly impression faded to a smoky vapor, the blue color all but washed away. "Now you must take my mantle of finding and protecting the true heir who can end the curse, a descendant of Odon. Because you are the second Guardian."

The Blood Emperor has negotiated with the Northerners to send me an arcane master of magic. She is as cold, tall, and old as the ice mountains that birthed her. She says my mind is mediocre at best, but the corner of her lip twitches when I demonstrate Binding. My specialties are creating amulets of health, calm, and uplifting the spirits.

Hanna tells me I must impress the Emperor's councilor, Dragan, who makes my skin crawl. Every amulet I create makes his eyes shine with greed, and he demands more. I've tried and tried to impress him, not just to avoid his barbs but to gain a single nod of approval.

— VAHID OF GETAE

THREE

GUARDIAN PROMISE

Despite the chill, my blood was on fire. I assured myself that, logically, Thorns couldn't be looking for Mama's blue vision. She was a simple Getaen with no resources. Whatever lore her clan taught, it was long forgotten. Or never known. The soldiers were an unfortunate coincidence, gone before they heard anything incriminating.

Rubia's home wasn't far up the hillside, but it was past curfew. I raced up the narrow cobblestone streets. If I could reach her without getting caught by a night watch Thorn, she'd get everything sorted. Rubia, the other Guardian. Rubia, the one who knew what the title meant.

I checked over my shoulder and tapped on Rubia's peeling red door, glancing at the neighbors' shabby entrances on either side. Once, the doors of this community had been painted in vibrant colors. I wasn't sure if it was the plague or the raid, but people moved slower. Tongues were sharper, tempers shorter. Drinking deepened. Portions of the city had yet to be rebuilt and maybe never would be.

Rubia flung the door open, her eyes glittering with excited

anticipation. Her face fell. "What happened to you? Did you fall?"

"I was a-attacked," I said flatly.

Rubia gasped. In a fluid motion, she pulled me inside. The candlelight revealed gashes on my dirty palms and rips in my dress.

"A-almost attacked. I got away. They... They never saw my f-face." I was bubbling over to ask Rubia about Mama's vision, but I couldn't brush off the soldiers' attack.

Rubia grabbed a cloth and one of many tinctures from shelves filled with well-worn bowls and chipped cups. In front of me, on the thick slab table in the center of the room, she poured water into a bowl, steam curling into the air.

I stumbled as my words fought for their turn on my tongue, explaining the screams and my clamoring up the oak tree. "They said they were s-sent by their c-captain to find a p-particular blue vision and they —"

"Their captain?" Marigold oil spilled from the tincture. "The two people were Thorns?"

"They were hunting for someone in the g-graveyard. But, it couldn't have been me. I mean, it's me." Memories surfaced of the last time Thorns burst into my life. Then, I had initially thought they'd come to help. I was wrong. A shudder went through me.

Our family had many secrets; what if one spilled out?

Rubia backed away from me, panic rising in her voice. "They saw your Mama's blue vision?"

"Only a s-snippet of it," I said. "About the p-plague."

She nodded.

"And Cassus," I added.

Rubia frowned.

"I threw an acorn. D-distracted them. They... they d-didn't

see much." But why were they in the graveyard at all? "It's impossible for them to know... "

Rubia silenced me with a glare before mixing the marigold water in spastic movements.

"Even if they stumbled across your mama's blue vision by accident, it's foolish to assume her words didn't alert them to something more. It won't take them long to identify the Aurelian family grave markers. They'll be looking for your papa soon."

"P-papa. He has scrolls out. Everywhere!" I took a deep breath, trying in vain to calm my twisting stomach. "B-but he said he was c-cleaning them up so they'd never find anything."

"We must warn him. They'll descend on him like locusts by first light if they suspect anything." Rubia dunked the cloth into the water and scrubbed my hands. I was almost glad for the pain; it sharpened my focus. "This will have to do for now. Fetch the linen, and bandage your hands. We must leave."

I frantically wrapped my hands and wrists while Rubia snatched items from her trunk and stuffed them into a satchel. Bags of herbs were haphazardly bundled before being unceremoniously tossed into a second satchel.

I held up my hands; the linen bunched in some places and was too sparse in others. "I'm ready."

"Patience," Rubia snapped. With a quick sweep of the broom, she brushed the embers away from the hearth. Rubia used the handle of a long spoon and pried up one of the floor bricks.

I stopped pacing long enough to see her snatch bronze coins from where the brick had been. A bigger piece, a gold nugget, she placed in a pouch.

"One more thing." Rubia slid one of her recipe parchments out from a locked box and turned it over. With her back to me, she scrawled with a quill. I balked at the desecration of one of her Healing recipes. With her carving knife, she stabbed the note onto the table. I sucked in a breath, waiting for Getaen curses or at least an explanation. Instead, Rubia blew out the candles, and the room was plunged into darkness.

"Now we can go." Rubia opened the door, letting the scant starlight into the room.

In the open doorway, Rubia thrust her light suman cloak and one of the satchels into my hands. She gazed into her home, sighed, and closed the door with a soft click.

"Pull the hood up and stay close. Listen to the sounds of the night; sudden scurrying of little paws is a signal that someone is coming," Rubia said.

Some regularly disregarded the curfew, but I obeyed it, avoiding Thorns whenever possible. We were exposed on the street, but I nodded. Better to be caught by city watch than not warn Papa, just in case the Thorns from the graveyard decided to investigate. Rubia tucked the orb out of sight under the thick shawl she wrapped around her neck and pulled over her head.

In the narrow alleys, I followed Rubia's lead, stepping over rotting garbage and debris. As we moved, my eyes adjusted to the semi-darkness.

The plague, the death, and the raid — each a terrifying event was like a hammer crashing down, shattering my life. I dreaded those memories. I stumbled, feeling like I couldn't breathe. But I needed to remember every detail so I could make sense of this mess.

In the quiet, I let the memory of the Lilac Plague creep into my mind.

Three years ago, we weren't the only people who had run for the gate. The screaming, yelling, pounding on the doors made my ears ring. Papa pulled me against him and used his body as a shield as we pushed our way back up the street we had just raced down. We found shelter in an arched doorway.

"Calvus!" Rubia's voice rose above the growing noise. Her dress was torn, her hair falling free of her usual braid. Behind her, Mama stood, clutching her pendant, tears on her face.

Mama embraced me and kissed Papa then pulled away, lifting the pendant off her neck.

"Leila, what are you doing?" Rubia asked.

"The plague is here. We must protect our daughter," Mama said.

"She's too young to be a Guardian," Papa protested.

"She's too young to die of plague," Mama said fiercely. She took me by the shoulders and looped the necklace over my head, holding the pendant away from my chest. My heart fluttered like a hummingbird.

"I'm so sorry, my golden child. There's no time to explain. You must trust me and repeat what I tell you."

I looked from Papa to Rubia to Mama. A strange silence hovered over us as if nothing mattered outside the small circle of our family.

"Yes, Mama," I whispered.

The words reminded me of the Getaen I'd heard in the markets, but they were different, more like a song or a poem. Mama spoke each phrase slowly and I repeated after her. When it was done, Mama dropped the pendant. It fell lightly to rest on my chest.

I was jerked out of the past when I bumped into Rubia. We paused by a barrel, my feet in a puddle I hoped held only water. Rubia was next to me and had the answers I was determined to get.

"Am I a G-Guardian? What d-does that even mean?" I blurted. I hadn't repeated a poem all those years ago. No, my words had bound me into a magical oath. How could I begin to understand the promises I'd made? How could Mama tie me to the dangerous games of emperors and traitors?

Rubia didn't flinch. "I'm sorry, but your Mama and I were only trying to protect you. Hopefully, you'll understand someday."

"Why would I look for Odon's f-family?" Someone descended from a wicked traitor? The traitor whom bards strummed harsh songs about that drove little children into their parents' arms?

"What do you know about Prince Odon?" Rubia asked.

My jaw tightened. I didn't want to recite a history lesson. "He was the son of the B-b-blood Conqueror. He wanted the throne for himself, so he tried to m-murder his b-brother. His p-plot was uncovered. He f-f-fled and no one heard from him again."

"To understand what it means to be a Guardian, you must understand the past. You know half-truths and twisted history." She peered around a corner, grabbed my hand, and guided me across the street and into another alley.

My heart thumped as I scampered behind Rubia, willing her to move faster. The alley widened, and I strode next to her.

Rubia whispered, "Once Emperor Trajan died and Cassus inherited the throne, things improved for Dacians, but the terror increased for the Getaens. Cassus needed our people under his control. The Blood Emperor defeated our armies, but his son, Cassus I, broke our will to fight. Cassus demanded that the Getaen clan leaders turn themselves over to his armies. If clan leaders refused, Cassus wiped out their entire clan." Rubia's grip on my wounded hand tightened as she continued. "Many of the leaders surrendered to Cassus to spare their clans. They realized, too late, that Emperor Cassus didn't just want the leaders. Cassus slaughtered their entire families. The emperor aimed to annihilate any hope of a Getaen leader's child returning to threaten his rule. It was a dark time."

Rubia shook her head, loosening her grip on my bandaged

hand. "Almost overnight, the Emperor installed his own Getaen leaders. He murdered all warriors he perceived as a threat and replaced them with religious leaders. If the religious families kept the clans at peace, the clans would be left alone, not at the receiving end of his wrath."

"Religious families?" I asked.

"Families with magic in their bloodline," she added, guiding me around a barrel in the shadows.

At the edge of the lower Commons district, Rubia slowed as we approached a window with light flooding through. A woman sang a Getaen lullaby but with Dacian words, so the lyrics were slightly disjointed. I knew the original verse from Mama, but many people didn't.

Many Moesians were like me, a mix of both Dacian and Getaen. Though people with more Dacian blood liked to emphatically remind those of us with less. But I'd have gratefully traded my Dacian blood for Getaen. Only Getaens carried magic.

"Wait. Since y-you have magic. Does, does that mean... " I trailed off, trying to picture Rubia as anything grander than a Poppy.

Rubia pressed up against the wall, half her face lit from the candlelight streaming through the window, the other in shadow. When she spoke, her voice was husky with a bitter edge. "Since the time of the great Getaen migration from the far north a thousand years ago, my family's veins ran thick with magic. Emperor Cassus appointed my family to be the new leaders of our clan. Yes, I was born a Getaen of privilege. For seven generations, Dacia has been ruled by Cassus' descendants." Her face screwed up. "My family ruled our clan while under the Emperors' thumb. Until we didn't."

We crawled under the window ledge, and the Getaen

melody faded behind us. How large had Rubia's clan been? Did she know Mama before they journeyed here?

We waited at the edge of the main cross street into the upper Commons where Papa and I lived. I held my breath, listening as a set of marching footfalls faded. Finally, Rubia signaled for us to scurry across the wide, cobblestone road.

Rubia continued as we climbed the hill. "While Emperor Cassus III ruled, the women in our family started passing down something more important than magic; a secret right under the Emperors' nose. The Guardianship." Rubia rested against a wall, breathing hard. She didn't carry water up and down the hill like I did each day. She had an apprentice for daily chores. "It began with Dacians, but it has been a Getaen responsibility since my great grandmother. The Guardians protect the True Key. Ironic, isn't it? A Getaen holding the key for the true heir to the Dacian throne?"

She grasped the chain around her neck and pulled out the orb hidden under her dress. For the first time since I'd given it to her, she removed the necklace and placed it in my hands. The weight, the way it fit in my hand, the memory of wearing it came back to me in a rush. I wrapped my fingers around it, feeling in my very core that I needed to keep it safe.

"The orb opens a treasure meant for the true heir? One of Odon's descendants?" I said, putting together what Mama, Papa, and Rubia had told me.

Rubia squeezed my arm, excited. "My dear child, to be able to finally share these truths with you... I'm overjoyed. Your papa and I have so much to teach you."

Rubia slipped the chain back over her head. She trudged forward, winding along a narrow street toward my home. "It's deadly for anyone other than a Guardian or the true heir to touch the pendant. Even for those with good intentions, like your papa, they'll die if they carry it.

I tried to soak up her words, but my worry about Papa battled for my attention.

"The key protects the wearer just like the wearer protects it. If you wore this pendant and the soldier in the graveyard grabbed it, the pendant would attack them."

"What do you mean?" I asked.

"Honestly, I'm not exactly sure. My grandmother said whoever touched it was cursed. Unless they release the key, they'll turn to ash," Rubia said.

Rubia never admitted to not knowing anything. She'd change the subject or redirect the question to hide her lack of knowledge. Hearing the unknowns about the orb made me feel both more grown-up to be in her confidence and at the edge of a dangerous precipice at the same time.

In the distance, shouts rang out. My stomach dropped. I should have gone home first.

As we drew closer to home, a horse brayed. More shouts cut through the night. We sprinted. The only time we heard such noises after curfew in the Commons was when there was a terrible illness, menace, or alarm. Always something bad.

The Emperor wants me to do terrible things. I know it's only because of Hanna that he hasn't asked more wicked things of me, yet. She spends most of her days with her twin boys and on occasion she'll have me tell them stories of Getae. What little I recall of the sea and the hills are simple but happy times.

The Empress has dark circles under her eyes, and she strains to smile. I quietly presented her with an amulet of protection. She sewed it into her belt, and it looks nice with the other decorative coins.

— VAHID OF GETAE

FOUR

AN IMPOSSIBLE CHOICE

Dread washed over me. In the alley across from my house, Rubia pulled me behind a stack of crates. We crouched, hopefully hidden from view.

Rubia peeked first. "Your house is crawling with Thorns. They got here fast."

I pushed myself up. Soldiers or no, I had to find Papa.

"Wait." Rubia grabbed my wrist, her hand a vice that left my fingers tingly. She muttered under her breath about the timing. "Thorns must have gotten here first and *then* went looking for you."

I pulled away enough to peek around the crates myself. Twilight obscured the guards on the street, too many to count. As they marched past torches, I realized what the Thorns were carrying.

"They f-found the scrolls!" I hissed. "W-we…" must help Papa! My words balled up in my throat.

"Hush, child." Rubia scolded. "You think you'll parade over there and demand to see your papa? They found the scrolls and then dispatched soldiers to find you at your mama's grave. It's fortunate that you came to my home first or you'd have been caught in this net."

I slumped to my knees, unable to take my eyes off the macabre sight, unable to feel my fingers in Rubia's grip. On our home's stoop, two soldiers held luminaries for a third to inspect a scroll. Their words were inaudible, but their movements were sharp and brisk.

"Gallus. It had to be." Rubia dug her nails into my wrist. "He pointed the soldiers in your papa's direction. Gallus always suspected Calvus was trouble. He probably thought he was doing your mama a favor, getting your papa locked up and freeing you. Imbecile! He had no idea what he was getting involved with. He'll be questioned, too. Information this disruptive will taint everyone associated with it." Rubia threw her back against the mud wall of the alley in frustration. "They probably arrived here before you even smashed your blue vision."

"W-we can't l-leave him!" My jaw muscles tightened as I started to hyperventilate.

"It's a hornet's nest right now, Nicoleta. If you approach them, you'll end up in a dungeon next to your papa. The best thing you can do is stay free to continue his mission."

"I can't l-leave. P-papa needs h-help."

"You think he cares about his own life?" Rubia's tone could've chipped diamonds. "He would rather die than see you harmed, which is assuredly what will happen to you if you attempt to come to his rescue. Believe me, nothing will make him happier than knowing you escaped. That you live."

I yanked my arm from Rubia's grip as I spun around, my back scraping against the crates. I squatted in the mud and hugged my arms around my knees. My instinct was to run into the house, screaming for Papa. But past that impulse, deep down, I knew Rubia was right.

"The last decade of your papa's work is being confiscated right now. The Emperor will likely thank him sincerely for rounding up the rare documents and the meticulous notes on Odon's genealogy." Rubia crouched down and gripped my shoulders. "Nicoleta, Calvus knew the risks. The Emperor will likely burn the records along with your papa on a pyre. There's nothing we can do."

"No!" I tried to push Rubia away, but her hold on my shoulders tightened. I'd have small bruises, but I didn't care. Papa was a gentle scholar whose only crime was a thirst for knowledge.

"Shh!" Rubia adjusted her weight, pinning me. "This is much bigger than Calvus. He is one man. We are trying to save the people of this kingdom from a horrible fate. You must choose: try to stop the curse or die trying to rescue your papa."

I turned my head away, refusing to answer the impossible question.

Rubia took a deep breath and relaxed her hold, her hands more soothing than restraining.

I selected my words carefully. Rubia was always direct, making it easier to predict her reaction to my bargain and prepare a counter argument.

"A deal, then. I'll help you find the true heir and the treasure. I'll be the G-Guardian as Mama was b-before me. However, you must help me with something, first."

Rubia grunted but nodded.

"Help me find out what happened to Papa," I said. "I won't be able to sleep at night or focus during the day if I don't know his fate." Surely, another opportunity would arise to save his life.

Rubia tilted her head, seeming to read my thoughts. But I knew her powers, and mind reading wasn't one of them.

"Papa has been looking for the t-true... for the true heir for years. What will a few w-weeks matter?" I ask.

"Fine." Rubia released me and slumped against the wall. "Then we must travel to the capital. The local Thorns will soon realize the importance of Calvus' knowledge. They'll transport him to the Emperor to be questioned." Rubia's voice softened. "He'll be killed as soon as they get the information they want from him. I know your papa wouldn't want you to carry such a burdensome memory."

I knew Rubia carried dark memories from her youth and then from the raid. I appreciated that she wanted to protect me, but I couldn't let her past stop me.

"I must know the truth." I repeated what I'd rehearsed in my head.

"I agree to your terms; now we must go. The Thorns will be at my door sooner than I'd expected, if not already. They'll find the note on the table and realize we're planning to leave the city." Rubia helped me to my feet. We fled from my home, leaving the soldiers and Papa's research — a lifetime and more. Papa would weep to see his precious records haphazardly thrown into the back of a wagon.

Fury and disbelief battled inside me. Mama and now Papa had been taken from me. I stumbled after Rubia in the alleys. If I had any chance of saving Papa's life, I needed to know everything he and Rubia were going to teach me, and quickly.

When we paused at a corner, I whispered my first questions. "What was on the note you left on your table? How did you know we would be fleeing the city?"

"When you've been through what your mama and I have been through, part of you is always ready to run," Rubia answered simply. "The note was for my apprentice, giving him my home and all my belongings. If I returned, I could just remove the note. If not, well then... " Rubia's voice trailed off. She checked around the corner and waved for me to follow her.

We were headed toward the merchant district of the city. Soon that area of Moesia would be bustling with pre-dawn activity.

"Why does it matter who the Emperor is?" I asked.

"Nikka, I need to think. We need a caravan and —"

I grabbed Rubia's sleeve, "Why do we need a 'True Heir?'"

"It's tied to the curse, Nikka. Without the proper heir, the curse will continue." Rubia spun around, her features swallowed in the darkness of the alley.

A weight settled on me, something Mama had probably explained in the blue vision but I'd missed.

"The curse," I whispered. I dreaded the answer I already knew was coming. "What is it?"

The burning, burning, burning flashed in my mind.

Rubia's voice rumbled with intensity. "The Lilac Plague *is* the curse."

The truth of her words punched me, and a thousand questions swirled in my mind. But one inevitable conclusion demanded my attention — one that both shocked and horrified me.

"So unless this mysterious true heir is found," my stomach roiled, "Cassus VII will rule a kingdom of ashes."

My northern master is impressed with my progress. Binding is my specialty. In my mind, I envision bringing elements together that are meant to be. Like love within a family.

Though my magic does so much good, the servants avoid me. I've long since given up hope I'll find a friend. My master said I'm superior to them, and they're frightened of me. I ask her how many Getaens are in the kingdom, and she looked at me, surprised. "All of them."

Councilor Dragan demands that I create amulets of darkness. It terrifies me, so I hold back. Even so, my skill has warranted a formal presentation at court. I stand tall and silent. I know Hanna is proud of me even if she doesn't show it. She saves her smiles for rare occasions with her sons. Instead, she touches the amulet I gave her and her shoulders relax.

My master says my magic will be famous throughout the kingdom, and I can use fear to my advantage. I like the idea of the Emperor fearing me, but not the princelings. I want them to love me like a brother.

— VAHID OF GETAE

CHAPTER

FIVE

APPLES AND OATS

Before the sun rose, the first caravans started lining up at the main gate. While we waited, concealed in an alley, I dusted off my dirty dress and aprons the best I could. I re-folded the linen on my hands and then assessed the satchel Rubia had given me charge of, finding an extra camisole, socks, and the dried herbs wrapped in cloth.

Merchants shuffled around in their tents, a few opening the flaps.

Rubia handed me two herb packets with scents of eucalyptus and lavender. "Trade these to Jolan's daughter. The eldest son's bones ache from the work in the mines. She'll buy at a fair price. Get a heavy cojoc cloak — you'll need warmth where we're going — and meet me by the gate. I'll make our caravan arrangements."

I pulled my hood up and made my way along the row of merchants setting out their wares. The merchants cast furtive glances at the extra soldiers milling in the space between the market and the main gate. I'd never seen so many Thorns in one place before.

Were they looking for me? Though I'd cleaned up a bit, my

dress certainly had remnants of someone who'd crawled through the dirt. The air was still cool, and I used the excuse to clutch my scarf tight against my chin.

Instead of Jolan's daughter, an elderly woman sat at their tent. She traded my herbs for her own cloak and pointed out the sturdy stitching. I argued the bottom of the cloak was worn from dragging on the ground and was able to bargain for water gourds as well. It wasn't the finest cloak, but my cojoc was impossible to retrieve.

By the time I finished preparations, the square was full, and merchants were already leaving the city. Near the front gates, Rubia waited in an alley. Before she even touched the heavy cloak in my arms, she pursed her lips. She rarely approved of anything I purchased alone, especially because she knew I hated to verbally barter; she always thought I overpaid.

"It was an excellent p-price." I argued against her silent displeasure.

"You'll soon see why," was all she said.

"And water gourds." I held up two gourds with straps that I'd already filled with water from the city well.

"They'll do," Rubia said. "You didn't get any apples, did you?"

"What?" I asked, confused. I shrugged off her loose-weave cloak, the cool morning air permeated my dress. "No."

"Good. We'll have plenty of them on this trip," Rubia said, taking back her cloak that she'd lent me. "And oats, too, on our ride to Patridava. Follow me."

Rubia threw on her cloak and pulled the hood over her head. I copied Rubia's movements, and the foul stink of long-past-stale tobacco smoke hit me like a wall. The undertones of mold and mildew unfurled, demanding attention. I choked back a gag just as Rubia raised a brow, assessing me. I decided breathing through my mouth without complaint would be better than admitting Rubia was right.

Weaving past carts and wagons, I acted casual, even though sweat beaded my forehead. Every glance weighed on me. I feared the soldiers realized Calvus Aurelian's daughter was nowhere to be found. The soldiers had already interrupted Mama's blue vision, searching for me. Were they at Rubia's home this morning? Asking the neighbors when they'd last seen me?

We stopped in front of an old farmer who was feeding his two horses bright green apples. He was a lean, wiry man with a few sunspots on his deeply tanned hands and wrinkled face. He wore a wide-brimmed hat, and his gray and brown hair was pulled back into a low ponytail. A round guild crest pin with a wagon wheel crossed by a scythe clasped his moss-colored shoulder cloak around his throat. His beard was stained red from tobacco, which he had tucked in his cheek. Papa always said tobacco was a sign of an undisciplined man, but I kept my expression pleasant.

"Constantin, this is the daughter I said would be traveling with me." Rubia waved to me, and I nodded my head.

The farmer looked at my face and then spit into his cup, which didn't bode well for his first impression of me. I wanted to shrink back in on myself, but before I could step back, he turned to Rubia.

"Our route to Patridava is slower than taking the Emperor's Highway. I suggest another caravan," the old farmer said, a dribble of juice at the corner of his lip.

"Traveling a little slower and off the Emperor's Highway is agreeable for us," Rubia said.

"We'll be two days slower than most caravans." Constantin started to turn away, but Rubia quickly stepped around to face him again.

"Two days is agreeable. Do we still have an accord?" Rubia pressed.

Constantin rubbed his bearded chin. "Being a cautious old man, I would require that you wear your hoods up the entire duration of the trip."

I frowned. The midday summer heat would be miserable enough without my heavy leather cloak, let alone with my hood up. Not to mention the rancid smell of death. Rubia gave a terse nod of agreement.

"Also, you'll need to wear trousers," he added.

We had no trousers. We'd have to go back to the market to find them. And the farmer's wagon was near the front of the gate. He'd be gone long before we could purchase men's clothing and return.

A young man shouldered his way through the crowd and put a hand on Constantin's shoulder. "Everything in order, Papa?"

The young man was only a few inches taller than me with broad shoulders and olive-copper skin. His gray eyes were the color of ribbed clouds before a summer storm. The young man's gaze swept over Rubia and me quickly as if dismissing us with a glance.

I fidgeted with the cloak. Why did it suddenly feel so shabby? Moments ago, I hadn't cared. Now I was conscious of my un-braided hair, the sweat on my back, and the dirty linen wrapped around my hands. I chastised myself. I had a mission ahead of me. Papa needed me. And I shouldn't care a bronze bit about my appearance. I forced my tense shoulders back.

"I was just telling these ladies that our caravan will be too slow for them," Constantin said.

"You agreed to take us," Rubia argued.

A traveler left through the gate, and the line moved forward. There were two guards at the gate, asking questions and rummaging through the wagons. Usually, Thorns hastily evaluated wagons and generally ignored those traveling on foot. Today was different. The soldiers must have realized I might attempt to leave the city. Perhaps they thought I would try to find my uncle in the mines. Papa would have been silent about Rubia, but it was only a matter of time until our neighbors suggested her name. Either way, this was bad.

"We come to Moesia regularly. More soldiers are milling about than usual," the young man said, "Perhaps you should stay home until whatever trouble is brewing passes by."

"This is my son, Marcus Constantin. He knows everything. Just ask him." The old farmer snorted and spit. "He doesn't talk much, but when he does, he always has gems to share. Probably because instead of talkin', he's always thinking." He pointed to his head. "And we all know how dangerous thoughts can be."

Is he joking or serious?

Marcus turned his back on us and hopped up into the wagon seat. I watched the way his shoulders moved and the bend in his wrist as he held the reins of the horses.

Rubia shot me a glare. I flushed with embarrassment and wanted to tell her I was studying him to glean information as I did to everyone. Wasn't I?

A wagon left through the gate and we moved forward again. Rubia kept pace with Constantin and his wagon.

"We will be no trouble," Rubia said. "We'll pay you double what we agreed."

Double? My heart thumped.

Two Thorns in their green half-cloaks marched past us and spoke to the guards at the gate. A flash of worry crossed Rubia's face, but she replaced it with a smile. Papa said Rubia could charm the rattles right off a snake.

"Only a fool would remove a rattle. They were the warning."

Rubia had shot back. Then everyone had laughed. Now Rubia's charms could be our salvation.

My gaze drifted back to Marcus in the wagon. He looked like many other Dacians with his chestnut hair and his summer tan. His clothing was not fine but sturdy and well cared for. His wavy hair was clean and trim. They had enough income to stay in boarding houses in the cities, but not enough for paid protection.

"You agreed to let us travel with you." Rubia reminded him, keeping her smile. "And here we are. Are you not a man of your word?"

Constantin shrugged, but Marcus' shoulder twitched.

"What is your business in Patridava?" Marcus asked.

"Our business is our own just as yours is. We merely need the company of trustworthy traveling companions for the road." Rubia's voice was like a honey drop. "Your papa has already accepted our offered fee. I thought him to be an upstanding man, but he seems to want to go back on his word."

Rubia nudged my arm. I jerked my attention away from Marcus and followed her gaze. A group of Thorns lingered less than twenty paces away, conversing.

I held my breath and shifted, putting my back to the soldiers. Were they gossiping about the raid on my house?

"We'll wear our hoods day and night if we need to. We're prepared for our journey and don't want to delay our departure." Rubia put on a sweet smile and played with a strand of her long, blond hair. "We are just simple people who wish to travel north."

Marcus waited quietly as if he expected me to add something.

I wanted to say something. Something pleasant so they would let us travel with them.

I look forward to the journey. I'm excited to see the kingdom.

Anything. But I would stumble over my words, embarrassing myself and revealing my stutter — more than enough reasons to convince the farmer and his son to refuse us. Instead, I looked away, knowing my face would give away the lies in Rubia's story. We were dangerous passengers to carry.

"Do we have an arrangement?" Rubia asked.

Constantin spat into his cup as we arrived at the gate. The farmer looked to his son. Marcus was frowning at me. Why? Did I look that awful?

The old farmer's eyes took on a mischievous glint as we pulled forward to the gate. Was he going to tell the soldiers that we were pestering him?

The two Thorns on either side of the gate looked us up and down as we approached.

"What is your business?" the guard on the left asked.

"Merchant farmers. Apples and oats," Marcus said.

The guard on the right frowned at Rubia and me. He leaned forward, his hand on his sword.

"And are these women leaving with you?" the guard on the right asked, a wolfish grin on his face.

For a horrible moment, I envisioned Constantin pushing us into the arms of the Thorns, a cruel laugh on his lips.

"Yes," Constantin said. "Yes, they are."

Was the old farmer agreeing to take us? Only a few steps separated us from freedom.

"There's a missing girl. Maybe you've seen her?" The guard pointed at me and Rubia. I wanted to bolt, but Rubia stilled.

The guard pointed at the farmers, "You two may go."

In my mind, the gate was closing. My vision blurred.

"But we cannot leave without my sister and niece," Constantin said.

The guard raised a brow. "This is your family?"

I inwardly groaned. Rubia and Constantin couldn't look more different.

"Ah, yes, we traveled here from the northern orchards. This is my son." Constantin nodded at Marcus, a younger version of the farmer.

The guards didn't look convinced as they scrutinized our faces.

"My niece is even wearing my cloak," Constantin added.

I stood taller. This rancid cloak might be the best purchase I'd ever made.

"My wife's Getaen, and this is her sister. She often returns to Moesia to visit their family. Don't you recognize her?"

The guard studied Rubia closer. I tensed. I was sure his appraisal would haunt us later. Perhaps his exact description of Rubia's aprons and cloak later would save him from the disgrace of dismissal.

I cleared my throat to keep the guard's attention on us instead of noticing how Marcus was grinding his teeth and gripping the reigns as if he were choking the life out of them.

"What's the holdup? Is she the girl or ain't she?" shouted a guard from the gatehouse.

"Go on." The guard flipped his hand, signaling us to go ahead. It was all I could do to keep a normal pace instead of sprinting away.

Rubia slipped something back into her bag and then grabbed my hand, our sweaty palms clutched together as we walked through the gate.

The wagon slowed, and the farmer waved for us to ride in the back. "I'll get you to Patridava, but you'll pay us triple."

A terrible illness has Capidava in its grip. The Empress Consort and her son, Cassus, are both in bed with fevers. Servants who've ignored me for years now beg for magical remedies for their loved ones. I tell them herbs are not my specialty, which is true, but my magic is better than none. I am angry with the Dacians for all their laws against magic. How dare they turn to us now?

I've tried to see the Empress, but the guards keep me away. Even with their fear rolling off them, they're loyal to her. How can I blame them?

My Norte master recommended a Getaen Healer. One was brought in; her clothing reeked of hay and swine, but her reputation was impressive. Dragan allowed me to watch the procedure as part of my training. I smelled the bloodroot. Poison for the royal family. She didn't even try to hide it from me, so sure I would keep her secret. I hated that I was forced to choose between those who care for me now and a people who did long ago.

I reported the Healer's treachery and threw out the tea. The Healer was put in chains. My master was sent away for her ill advice. I've surpassed her skills in Binding, and I won't miss her cold nature, but part of me is lonely. I'm the only magical person in the castle.

—*VAHID OF RUPEA CASTLE*

CHAPTER

SIX

A BINDING OATH

Rubia and I huddled together on the back of the farmers' wagon as it bumped down a packed, dirt road. The sun was dropping lower in the sky, and my body ached from the constant jostling. Cloying fermentation wafted around us from spoiled apples, smashed under the half-empty barrels.

I fiddled with the edge of my satchel, re-living my last conversation with Papa.

"Don't fret. Eat another apple." Rubia grinned.

I groaned but was grateful for Rubia's distraction. "After three days of apples, I'm sick of them."

"Just imagine how you'll feel after another four more." Rubia laughed.

I longed to take off my stuffy hood, but as promised, Rubia and I had kept our faces hidden.

"I think the old man who owned this cloak probably died in a cloud of smoke." I hoped the fresh air would kill off the mildew.

"So you admit that your leather cloak wasn't the wisest purchase." Rubia pinched her nose, teasing. "Oof! The stench is even greater in the sunshine."

In the heat of the day, with my body sweltering underneath, the cloak emanated stale smoked tobacco strong enough to kill an alley cat. I wondered if this cloak had been handed down for generations with strict instructions to only smoke while wearing it.

Rubia pulled out a fried pastry from her satchel with a triumphant grin. "For you. I'd save it for your birthday, but it'll be dried out by then."

"How did you…"

Rubia handed me the pastry, and my memory jumped back to the cakes I'd abandoned by Mama's grave — enjoyed by nighttime critters, no doubt. It seemed like a lifetime ago.

"Thank you," I said, breaking off a chunk for Rubia.

Constantin, or, as I'd learned, Otho Constantin, sat up front next to his son, who held the reins. Marcus had remained quiet through most of the trip and that was for the best. I might have lost myself in his cloudy gray eyes and embarrassed myself as I stumbled over my words. I was pretty sure that Zalmoxis created Marcus to torment me.

Mama said falling in love was easy if you let your heart be open. In all the years I'd known Rubia, I'd seen her flirt and smile, but never in love. Without a word, Rubia communicated that love was a weakness. So, I'd kept my gaze firmly on the scenery.

Unlike his son, Constantin seemed pleased to have new ears to talk to. His initial reluctance to our presence vanished. He'd already told us *multiple* times about his wife's baking. Reportedly, she made the most delicious warm bread, the top perfectly browned and crusty. My stomach rumbled, so I was glad when he turned to the subject of his horse.

"Velos is the fastest horse in the Rodnic Valley." Of his two horses, he pointed to the dark bay steed on the left. "A captain of the Capidavan army made me an offer of purchase just last year. Said our family would have the honor of having Velos serve the Emperor. I told him that Velos is a spoiled horse, raised on oats and apples; he was too finicky for the army and would soon be a sickly burden. Even if the captain suspected it was a lie, a small part of him must have feared it was true. Who would want to be stuck on a long, dangerous journey with no horse? The captain let Velos be, gratefully. We farmers depend on our horses to transport goods. Can't lose good stock to the soldiers or we'd be dragging our carts around ourselves and getting nowhere."

I held my breath, waiting for Rubia to remind him that he'd told us that story twice already, but she merely pursed her lips.

Before Constantin could regale us with another tale of his wife's glorious cooking or the joys of grafting varieties of apples, I hopped down from the wagon.

"I'll walk a bit. I need to stretch my legs." With my daily hiking up and down the Moesian hill, fetching water and going to the market, my legs yearned to move.

"Good idea," Rubia said, joining me. She limped for several paces before finding her stride. She didn't complain, but she was used to mixing herbs or tending to the sick for most of the day, not arduous traveling.

The tracks cut through a meadow filled with spindly grasses and dotted with trees. A few clouds lazed in the blue sky. Dry dirt dusted up behind the wagon, so we stayed well behind, giving us the perfect excuse to talk outside of earshot of Constantin and his stoic son.

Over the last two days, as we had walked, Rubia reiterated the importance of being a Guardian. The secrecy. She taught me the incantation to pass on the orb to another, future Guardian. The words were in an ancient Getaen dialect, but every syllable had to be exact. According to Rubia, there must be two

Guardians at all times, but I struggled to memorize the tongue-twisting words.

"Did you practice the words again last night in your mind before you fell asleep?" Rubia asked, in Getaen.

"Of course," I said. Once I had the words committed to memory, it would be much easier to not stutter.

To bind the key with your soul
Va poltim o kaga met ditaveshi
To imprint duty on your heart
Va skalm taut epi dabaveshi
Protect the key while it protects you
Mezenai to kagareshi mezenzai veshreshidi
To strengthen your stride and to make plentiful/long your life
Va embalan naraveshi kai va emburim drigaveshi
To assist you in protecting the true blood/heir
Va gherm veshidi mezenai to cor menus

"I'll keep practicing." Would I ever get the words correct? I wished Mama had taught me more ancient Getaen.

"Good. Now, where did we leave off? Ah, yes, the pact between the Blood Conqueror and his twin sons, Odon and Cassus," Rubia said. "You've always been taught that Zalmoxis cursed Odon for his treason. But, the truth is, Odon and his children lived long, healthy lives in Rupea Castle and nearby estates. All was well with Odon's descendants until Cassus III; everything changed. Cassus III had no intention of turning over the throne to his cousin's grandchildren. He started assigning his cousins to dangerous border skirmishes or creatively poisoning them. Some cousins had married and moved to other city-states in the kingdom. No matter where they were, one by one, they died.

"Rumors spread about the line of Odon being cursed. Some

of Odon's descendants suspected it was Cassus III, not Zalmoxis, who was curtailing their lives. Others believed the original spell would somehow keep them safe. But, Cassus didn't believe in the curse. Whether he thought the magic wouldn't hold, or was a monsoon he could weather, or merely a ruse by his long-dead great-grandfather, we'll never know. But we *do* know there was a well-timed slaughter. Within the span of a single day, most of Odon's descendants were murdered."

I clutched the strap of my satchel. "But some escaped?"

"Obviously," Rubia continued, "No plan is perfect. A group escaped to the green valleys of the north. Plus, two sisters escaped to the south. Fifty years later, those in the north were hunted and killed. Your papa traveled to the northern valleys when you were a baby, about twenty years after the plague had attacked the same area. As far as he could find, none of Odon's descendants survived."

"And the sisters in the south?" My heart thumped. The south was the land of the Getaens. Rubia and Mama's land.

Rubia stopped on the road, lowering her voice, "They were harbored by my clan for almost four generations."

I gasped. Not only had Rubia's family guarded the key but, more importantly, the bloodline.

"Why didn't they claim the throne?" I asked.

"Some of them wanted to try despite knowing Cassus VI would murder them. Others had married into our clan and never intended to lay claim. But they all agreed, for the safety of their children, to remain in hiding until the time was right to return," Rubia said, her voice tight.

Ahead, Marcus pulled the horses off the road. It was only a few hours past high noon, so why were we stopping? Rubia and I hurried forward, continuing our hushed conversation.

"But the curse... " I was dumbfounded that any descendant of the formidable Blood Conqueror would huddle in fear.

"Between the fading memories and the scant records, much of the information about the curse was forgotten. They knew they were the rightful heirs, but not much about the oath or the curse. On top of that, they had no proof. No army. For all they knew, the mysterious curse would be upon Cassus' line, and they could return and reclaim the throne once Cassus' children were weakened or gone."

The farmers pulled the wagon behind cover from trees and foliage, camouflaged from passersby — the perfect spot reprieve for the night.

Rubia slowed her pace, lowering her voice. "Only after your papa gathered documents from around Dacia did we realize that the curse and the Lilac Plague were one and the same. The plague won't end until someone from the line of Odon fulfills the oath and sits on the throne."

"Am I... ?" My mouth went dry. Odon's family had intermarried with the Getaens. Was I a hidden descendant?

Rubia shook her head. "It would be so much simpler if you were the chosen one, born a true heir to the throne. But unfortunately, you are not. Neither am I. And now we must fight to save the Dacians and the Getaens from generations of emperors — lofty pigheaded brutes who have condemned us with their pride. I hope the Odon bloodline will be more protective of the kingdom's people."

"What if there are no descendants left?" I asked.

Rubia switched back to speaking in Dacian. "Then we're all doomed."

THE ROAD WAS BUILT near a stream that branched off the Dacian River. Without the wagon wheels and the clomping of the horses, the stream's burble tempted me. I longed to take a bath, but when I'd broached it yesterday, Rubia said we should wait until Patridava.

I'll die in my own stink.

Constantin and Rubia pulled blankets off the wagon and walked around, looking for comfortable places to sleep. Alone with my thoughts, I stretched. As I lifted up my arms, I knocked my hood back, the fresh air welcome.

"Removing your hood? Don't you keep your word?" Marcus asked.

I jumped and jerked my hood back in place, bristling. Marcus had barely spoken, but now that he did, he repeated the same accusation Rubia threw at Constantin when he tried to back out of his arrangement to take us to Patridava. The situations were completely different.

I scowled at Marcus' back as he unhooked Velos from the wagon. How did he still smell like soap, simple lye mixed with lemongrass?

"Sorry, I was trying to make a joke." Marcus pulled off the saddle, tossing it into the back of the wagon. "I'm impressed you'd wear your hood through the summer heat."

Was this his attempt at conversation? I should give him the benefit of the doubt. I should joke back with him, but what if my words started and stopped? Or just stopped? He'd think I was a fool or worse. I pressed my lips tight.

"Have you ever been to Patridava before?" Marcus asked.

"No." I inwardly celebrated not stumbling over my word. One word. Normally I was fine with a few syllables, but I was tense around Marcus. I didn't know him, and no matter how much the way his hair curled on his forehead intrigued me, his withdrawn demeanor hadn't set me at ease.

A slight breeze ruffled the side of my hood. My stench was probably choking him. Marcus paused his work on the horse's hoof. My chest burned as a blush crawled up my neck. Why did

Rubia insist we not bathe until Patridava? Marcus must be trying not to vomit. I took a polite step back.

He walked the horse to a tree, securing her for the night.

I stood rooted to the ground, gripping my satchel. I wanted to finish our conversation. I wanted to gush over the new and unfolding landscape. I wanted to share a joke about my reeking cloak. Ask him about his farm, his family. This was his attempt at friendliness, and I couldn't find my voice to reciprocate.

Marcus returned to remove the other horse from the wagon. He took two steps toward me. I could barely breathe. I looked around, hoping for inspiration from something compelling to keep his attention. Keep him talking so I wouldn't have to. Trees? Stream?

Marcus interrupted my frantic thoughts, his expression stony. "I didn't realize that farmers were so far beneath you. Don't worry. I won't offend you by talking to you further."

He unfastened the other horse from the wagon without a second glance at me.

What? I reached out to explain my silence even if I stuttered through it.

"Nicoleta, I need your help," Rubia called, interrupting me.

I looked from Marcus to Rubia, who was scrutinizing us with her arms folded. I shook my hands out and walked over to her, keeping my face deep under the cover of the hood. The last thing I wanted was for her to see me upset. She'd lash Marcus with her tongue or worse. I glanced at her satchel, knowing she'd likely come prepared with a potent vial or two.

"We found this spot to be the best place to rest within miles," Constantin called as he rolled out his blanket. "It's a short leg of the trip and we stop and fish."

I grinned. We would have time for a fire tonight.

"If you'll gather the wood, we'll share the fish." Constantin hefted two fishing spears from the wagon. "Unless you'd like to fish and we'll gather the wood."

Fresh fish were a delicacy in Moesia. Rubia was adept enough at catching them in the little streams in the hills around Moesia. I waited for Rubia to make the decision for us, though I hoped for fishing.

"We can gather firewood," Rubia said, dashing my hopes.

"We better get started then." Marcus took one of the spears from his father in one hand, a woven net in the other.

Rubia led me away from the river where the farmers were headed.

"I thought you enjoyed fishing?" I whispered, even though Marcus and his father were gone. "And I'd like a bath."

"This gives us a chance to talk without having to raise our voices over the river." Rubia threw off her hood and bent down and picked up a stick. The trees were denser than I'd ever seen even in the Moesian hills we explored. There were hundreds around us as well as shrubs and vibrant orange wildflowers.

"This place." I took a short breath. "Nature is so different after just a three-day ride."

"I've traveled to many places, mostly small towns around Moesia. All different in their own way." Rubia held out her branches. "Here. I'll stack the wood in your arms." She dumped her sticks, adding to the ones I'd gathered. "I have a plan, but you're not going to like it. Still, you must hear it." She put a heavy branch in my arms and met my eyes. "This is your chance to show me you're a woman. Not the girl you were in Moesia. When I tell you my plan, you will not beg to find another way. You will not cry. You will nod your head and say that you'll do what needs to be done."

Whatever Rubia had to say, I could hide my feelings in the long, fading shadows and the cowl that still covered my head. "Tell me your plan."

"When we arrive in Capidava, I will request to see the High Judge. Rumors are that he has a Getaen great-grandmother. You'll find, in the circles of Rupea Castle, Getaens are few and far between. We take what help we can. I'll tell him a scholar taken from Moesia, and I'll also 'confess' that I assisted the Moesian scholar in his research of a Getaen clan said to be the source of a golden orb — I know the legends, and I'm willing to share them for a price."

"You'll give them the necklace?" I searched for the golden chain, but it was hidden under her camasa.

"No. Of course, not." Her eyes flashed. "I'll give information about the necklace. Information they already have in the scrolls; they just don't realize it. Yet. It'll take a team of scribes and translators moons to comb through and decipher the records. I'll simply be speeding up their research."

If only I'd stayed home and cleaned up the scrolls myself. Maybe they never would've been found.

"And in exchange, I'll ask for money. I don't care about their coin, but it's a believable request. While I'm in the belly of the beast, there will be opportunities to find out what happened to 'my old master.'" She winked.

Papa.

I hated to think of Rubia risking her safety for the *possibility* of finding out what happened to Papa. There had to be a less perilous option. But, I'd promised her I would agree. Still, my mind clouded with dark futures. Rubia in the stocks. In prison. Vanishing, along with every shred of information about the True Key and the curse. I shuddered to think what they'd do to a person with that information. First Papa and then Rubia? Why throw another loved one to the dwolves?

"It'll be dangerous to go to the High Judge. Maybe another, lower judge w-would be safer?" I closed my mouth, seeing Rubia's eyes narrow. I had promised not to complain.

"He's the only one with the power to give me what I want." Rubia's voice was sharp. She dropped another stick to the growing bundle of kindling in my arms but didn't meet my eyes.

"I understand," I lied, but I wanted her to finish divulging her plan.

Rubia continued, "In addition to the information, I'll have one other important thing to give them. I'll offer you as a servant of the Emperor, to be a scribe to the clerics."

"What?" I gasped. "You would l-leave me in Capidava?"

Rubia stopped collecting branches, her stare penetrating into the darkness to the north. "You'll be in the one place Calvus could never enter, Rupea Castle. You'll have direct access to information tucked away in the secret corridors and forgotten chambers. If there's any forgotten lore or scrap of history about the line of Odon, you'll find it. You'll pass your knowledge to your children someday. Besides, there's no record of "the treasure" being moved or existing in any other place. There's a strong possibility the Emperor has it secured in the treasury or another location in Capidava."

"We can search through archives together," I suggested.

"It's possible they'll have us work together, after a time. I'm Getaen and can help with the interpretation. You'll be apprenticed." Her words were light, feigning ease.

Yet her words dredged up a memory. She had said I was destined for something greater when she denied me the Healer's apprenticeship.

"You had planned on something like this all along?"

"Not quite." Rubia sighed. "Your mama wanted you to have the Healer's apprenticeship with me. I considered it. Despite your lack of magic, you had a knack for finding herbs and making salves. You could memorize anything."

"Then why d-didn't you offer it to me?" I asked. "You merely hinted at my p-purpose."

"Nikka, speak from the pit of your stomach. You must minimize that stutter if we're to trick the clerics into taking you as an apprentice."

I frowned, the advice boring under my nails.

"Your mama did everything she could to prevent you from becoming a Guardian," Rubia said. "You were her only child. The last scion of our once thriving clan. She wanted to protect you from the dangers of Guardianship. The Emperor is still hunting for any of Odon's descendants and he's most definitely still looking for the key." Rubia angled a long branch against the ground and snapped it in half with a sharp stomp of her foot. "The plague changed everything."

All the talk of the Lilac Plague and the True Key caused more memories to bubble to the surface. Something in the shared look between Mama and Rubia the day the plague descended. Papa's grave expression. Mama promised I was immune.

"Only the wearer is protected," I whispered. My knees felt weak.

Rubia had told me the necklace protected me, but I didn't understand it. I hadn't wanted to understand. I'd pushed away the horror that Mama gave her life for mine.

"The plague is like a seed blown about by cursed winds. It settles in whatever part of the kingdom it chooses. Your mama died because of generations of royal selfishness." Rubia slammed a large branch into my arms.

My knees wanted to buckle, but I took a gulp of air and started back to our campsite.

"Why would clerics t-take me as an apprentice?" I wanted to talk about anything but the pain thrust into my heart;

Mama's death was my fault twice over. I dropped the sticks in the clearing.

Rubia set two large stones on the ground. "You'll be my Dacian master." She winked at me. "With a little hair dye, you'll blend right in. You will pretend to know nothing of the curse, and it would be to their advantage to apprentice the educated daughter of a scholar. They'll think all I want is some silver in my pocket and protection for the daughter of the master I was once loyal to."

"Too many things could go wrong."

Rubia's mood was a sudden dark storm. She guided me away from the pile of sticks, her thumb digging into my shoulder. "You promised."

"I'm not asking for another way. I'm clarifying. That's not against the rules," I said.

"You know how to dance on the edge of a blade, my child," Rubia said. "We'll both get what we want. I'll have planted a Guardian in Rupea Castle, preparing for Odon's descendant's return. And you'll find out what happened to your papa."

Rubia always planned ten steps ahead. There was more she wasn't telling me. Contingencies I hadn't thought of. *Isn't there a safer way?* I held the question inside my head, wanting Rubia's trust.

"We don't have a moment to waste," Rubia said. "For years, my grandma taught me about the orb and the Guardianship, long before I took the oath. You'll have to use that quick memory of yours, it's more important than ever before." Rubia took my hand in hers. "I know why you can't memorize the enchantment for passing on the orb. You're afraid of the reason you'll need to use it."

I opened my mouth to argue, but Rubia's eyes were filled with compassion and she earnestly continued. "It's understandable that you'd fear losing me. But, in your mind, you must let me go. There will be a time when I'm no longer with you. Embrace it, or you'll stagnate your progress. Your mental strength is not just vital for me or your papa. Not even for Moesia. You must do it for *all* of Dacia."

Her words threatened to crush me. After Mama died, I'd never let myself imagine my life without Papa and Rubia. Now, I'd lost Papa, and Rubia told me I had to embrace losing her as well. How could I lose the people who tethered me? Did I only have days before I'd be an orphan, completely isolated in my secrets?

Rubia kissed me on the forehead, something she rarely did. "Now, go find more stones while I prep the fire."

I bit my lip, holding back my tears. *No crying.* Rubia demanded it.

"When you get back, we need to talk about what happened last night," Rubia added. "Your nightmares."

"THAT'S THE SIXTH FISH. Well done, Marcus." Constantin's voice carried over the water.

With the thick layers of trees and shrubs lining the river, I hadn't realized I had wandered anywhere near Marcus and his father. Had they heard me smashing through the shrubs?

"Thick-snouted river fish, too. We don't often catch this fish back home," Marcus said.

"But we get red-striped lake fish, the best catch in the king-dom," the old farmer replied.

Before I could call out to them, I was interrupted by Marcus' sharp response. "I'll have plenty of time for the northern lakes in the future. There are other places I'd like to experience now."

"Son, we've discussed this. Your grandfather and I both

agree it's time for you to take your place in the Agricultural Guild. We've indulged you for far too long as it is."

I swallowed. I couldn't see Marcus or Constantin, but their voices sounded over the rushing river. I took a step back, a twig cracking behind me. I winced, but their argument continued.

"You've always shown promise. Talent," Constantin said. "Ability to understand complex things. But all that you've become, you owe to the guild. The old masters have spent a great deal of energy training you. You're expected to use those skills to help the Guild. It is a great honor to —"

"Is it honorable to take advantage of two women in distress?" Marcus said.

I gasped. Embarrassed, I searched for a place to sneak away without being overheard.

"Don't be ridiculous." The farmer brushed off the remark. "Two wealthy women of Moesia, needing my pity? They needed safe passage and were happy to accept my offer."

A narrow animal track squeezed between the bushes a few steps ahead — probably the path Marcus and Constantin had used to access the river. I spun around, scanning the opposite direction for the route with the least amount of dry leaves and twigs.

"I'll do whatever it takes to keep my family safe and provided for," Constantin rattled on. "When I was a boy, those of us who survived the plague and were lucky enough to stay in the valley, we lived off fruit, roots, and rodents for an entire winter. The following year wasn't much better. I never want my children to experience that. Ever." There was splashing at the river. They were on the move.

Debris from the trees and shrubs covered the ground. How did they not hear me approaching?

"Let's gut these fish. I'm starved," Constantin said, abruptly changing the subject.

I gritted my teeth and tip-toed away.

"It's more important for people to honor their word," Marcus said, "even if it's difficult."

Rocks cracked against each other, likely one of the farmers, finishing off the fish. I ran, ignoring the crunching under my feet. I dropped down behind the thickest shrub, tucking my white sleeves and the bottom of my dress under the brown cloak best I could.

"The Lilac Plague cares nothing for honor," Constantin scolded. "You need to learn to make hard choices in order to survive."

Leaves and twigs crackled as the farmers strode down the path. Marcus said something, but between the growing distance and my blood thumping in my ears, I couldn't hear him.

I counted to ten before peeking over the bush to make sure they were gone and then dashed away. Rubia would be wondering where I was. I walked the long way around back to camp so I would enter from a different direction than the farmers. When the camp was in sight, I grabbed a few more rocks and stowed them in my apron before strolling into the clearing.

"We're in luck tonight, Nikka. Thick-snouted river fish!" Rubia said, seeing me return.

I set the stones down next to the fire. Constantin was already gutting a fish, but Marcus was nowhere to be seen.

Rubia had created a thick pile of dried grasses and pine with branches on top. She reached into her satchel and pulled out a vial filled with a milky-white substance. I scooted back, watching Constantin's face for a reaction.

Rubia threw the vial next to the pine needles, the glass breaking against a jagged stone she'd placed in the center. The pine needles burst into flame.

"By Zalmoxis. You're a witch!" Constantin slapped the top of his head.

"I'm a Healer. A *mage*." Rubia's eyes narrowed. "Witches are old crones kept by the Emperor. Traitors to their Getaen blood."

Constantin laughed. "If you insist. Still, could you look at a sore on my foot? The darn thing won't go away."

"Healing treatments aren't part of our travel agreement," Rubia said.

Constantin rubbed his chin. "We usually catch extra fish and dry them for the road. How about we split the catch."

"If you split the dried fish and chop up that tree for firewood." Rubia grabbed an ax from the supplies in the wagon and pointed to a downed tree just north of our campsite.

I scurried forward, amid their negotiations, to place sticks in the fire pit. The elixir started the fire, but it needed fuel to keep going.

"Agreed," Constantin said. "Your Nicoleta can gut the fish while I'm gone."

My heart thumped. How did I get drawn into their negotiation? "I've never gutted a fish b-before."

I cringed at my stutter. I'd kept it hidden for all these days only to slip up now. Constantin's face softened and he gave me a sympathetic smile. I was used to people either judging me for my curse from Zalmoxis on my tongue or pitying me. I wasn't sure which was worse.

Gutting fish can't be too difficult.

"I'll do it." My face contorted as I spit out the words. I tugged my hood down further. "I can gut the fish."

"I'll show you how when I return." His words were strangely kind. I wish he'd go back to his gruff, talkative self.

He took the ax and strolled into the meadow. Rubia stood as if to leave, too.

"We'll burn through what we've gathered before

Constantin returns. Tend the fire, and I'll gather more." Rubia headed toward the river.

The shadows faded along with the sun, and my stomach rumbled. Rubia and I caught fish on our mountain trips, but she had never taught me to gut them. I had learned about herbs and medicine, but there were gaping holes in what I knew about surviving. I had to soak up as much knowledge as I could while I could.

From the shadows, loud, squishy footfalls sounded. Marcus emerged from the underbrush, his boots and pants soaked past his knees.

What should I say? Rubia would return soon, so I couldn't delay. At least the shadows were deep enough that Marcus wouldn't see my face contort with my cowl up. "The fire's warm. Come, dry your feet." I congratulated myself on my smooth words.

Marcus set his spear in the wagon before returning to the fire. He removed his boots in silence. When he said he wouldn't speak further, had he meant only in that moment or the rest of the trip?

"Nice to have the fire going. Thank you." He set his boots near the fire then pulled out his dagger with a masterfully carved ivory hilt and started gutting his fish.

I studied where Marcus sliced the skin, how he removed the guts, and which pesky little bones to look for. Only because I was *learning*, and not for any other reason, I told myself.

"Did you find any good sticks to cook with?" Marcus' head was down, intent on the fish. His deft fingers manipulated the tip of the dagger with ease, flicking the bones away from the flesh in smooth motions.

I dug through the dwindling pile and found a stick not too small to burn through, but not so thick it would destroy the muscle of the fish and fall into the flames. Handing him the perfect stick, his hand brushed mine. I pressed my lips together, wondering if he was aware of my every movement like I was aware of his.

"This wood is too dry. It'll catch a flame. I'll cut off a green branch." He rose and jogged off, leaving me alone.

I leaned forward, putting my head in my hands, telling myself the heat in my cheeks was from the fire.

Constantin returned and dropped four split logs next to me. "This should keep us warm for a while. After I show you how to gut and clean a fish, I'll fetch more."

"Let me try. And you can tell me what to do. I watched M-M-Mar... I can do it."

Using Constantin's knife, I sliced the fish as Marcus had done, my fingers mimicking the movements. Rubia returned with more firewood and tended to the fire while observing with an approving eye. Soon both fish were prepped for the fire.

Marcus joined us with two slender cooking sticks. I had to keep myself from laughing when I pictured the heavy fish precariously dangling in the flames on their too-thin branches.

"Time to wash up." I held up my fish-slimed hands.

Constantin wiped his knife. "Marcus, will you show her the way to the river?"

My stomach felt like butterflies were frantically trying to escape at the thought of standing alone at the river with the man who didn't like to speak to me, who couldn't stand being near me for even a moment. Maybe this was my chance to mend things. Though my concern with Marcus was small compared to what Rubia had in store, if I couldn't even talk with him and explain myself, how did I expect to survive as an apprentice in Rupea Castle?

"Don't worry about Nicoleta," Rubia spoke up, not looking at the farmers. Her words were meant more for me than for them. "My daughter will be fine on her own."

I'm now regularly invited to court, which I thought would bring me happiness. Today, the Healer who attempted to poison the Empress Consort and Cassus was sentenced to death. She called me a disgrace and a waste of magic. Her words pierced me more than any knife.

— *VAHID OF RUPEA CASTLE*

CHAPTER

SEVEN

SECRETS IN THE LIGHT

I pushed on the tiles above my head. They were heavy. Too heavy. Terracotta tiles were usually cool, but these were warm. Too warm. Cracks of light showed between the tiles, but not enough. Not enough air. I couldn't breathe. I cried out, but no one could hear me. I pounded my fists overhead. The tiles grew warmer. I pushed until my strength failed. I screamed for Mama. Where was Papa? The tiles grew hot. Scalding. They burned my flesh. Ash fell. Down, down, down. It filled the space around my feet. Dust in my eyes, in my mouth. Scrolls tumbled, disappearing into the ash.

Pick them up. Pick them up. They cascaded, never-ending. They slipped deeper as ash filled the cavern around me. I was choking on the dust, fighting for air. I was drowning in ash.

Someone called my name. Mama? I cried out for her. No, she's dead. The boils, the ravished skin. She's dead! I tried to scream, but my voice was gone. The ground itself trembled. My soul was consumed. Suffocating. Someone called me again, her voice clawing at me.

"Nikka. Nicoleta." Hands gripped my shoulders, shaking me. "It's just a dream. Wake up."

91

A fire crackled. The cavern fell away. The ash faded. Cold air wrapped around me. I opened my eyes to a sliver of the moon and bright stars above. I wanted to cry with relief, but the tears wouldn't come. They were stuck in my dream where I couldn't access them. Rubia stopped shaking me and wrapped an arm around my shoulder, pulling me into an embrace.

Across from me, the fire lit Constantin's face. His moods were increasingly soft, which I hated. He rubbed his eyes and lay back down, wrapping his blanket around him.

Next to him, Marcus rose. "I'll fetch her water."

The nightmares roared back every night since we left Moesia. Marcus had fetched my gourd from the wagon last night. They probably wished they'd never agreed to bring along a cursed young woman with sleep terrors.

"No need. I have it here." Rubia handed me the gourd that rested next to my bedroll. The water was refreshingly cool.

Marcus slumped back down. A few leaves clung to his hair, practically begging for someone to brush them out. I dropped my gaze and took another sip of water, pushing ridiculous thoughts of Marcus out of my mind.

I drank another sip and let the cool water wash away the nightmare. Rubia waited until Constantin was snoring before she whispered to me in Getaen. "You need to tell me about your nightmares. They're getting worse."

"I have these memories. D-details I'd f-forgotten until I learned about... " I glanced at the two men across the fire. The word 'Odon' was the same in both languages. I dreaded discussing my nightmares, the complicated dance stomping around in my head. "The raid."

After three years, I still avoided thinking about the raid. Papa had insisted on hiding me, but he didn't have much time. A chill had gone through me when the last tile clinked into place above my head. Cracks between the tiles admitted slivers of light. Except for the sturdy ladder, the cramped space consisted of floor-to-ceiling shelves filled with bins of scrolls. Voices sounded above. Scraping sounds. Papa trying to explain himself.

A sickening thump. Papa fell, blocking out the already scant light. He didn't move. I hated myself for not crying out to him. Instead, I covered my mouth with both hands, my body shaking. I feared Papa was dead, or worse, dying and in pain.

Here in the wide expanse between cities, I stared up at the sky. A swath of stars so thick it formed a white band of light. I felt exposed in the meadow, even in the trees.

"I was trapped under the t-tiles. I just waited and waited. I feared the soldiers would return at any moment. They would take Papa or find me or burn down the house." I expected to die down there. Burned. Or suffocated. I shuddered from shame and trepidation that I still struggled to grasp.

Some houses did burn. Ours was spared. Perhaps they didn't have enough magical flames for our clay home. I never knew.

"I realized that the scrolls P-Papa hid were dangerous, but I never d-dared ask about them." *And I might never have a chance to talk to him again.*

Instead of hugging me, Rubia leaned forward, eyes glazed over, deep in thought. Was she reliving her own day of the raid? Or had she moved onto the plan to embed me into the castle?

Rubia might be able to plan, but she couldn't fix everything. She couldn't repair my mind, the memories that suffocated me. No amount of planning would make my night terrors go away. It wouldn't magically heal the scar on Papa's face. Nor would my stutter go away. Just like my great aunt, Zalmoxis saw fit to curse us both.

I put my hand on Rubia's back. "These nightmares... they're not your fault."

She whispered in Getaen, her voice rough. "If my family had any backbone, they would've forced the true heirs to return. By stopping the curse, they would've stopped the raid. I curse Odon and his cowardly heirs. I will never be feeble like them. Because of their weakness, I lost my husband and child."

I jolted upright. Rubia grabbed my shoulders, her eyes glinting in the embers of the fire, but from tears or from rage, I couldn't tell. "My husband. My child."

Rubia had been married? Had a child? I thought I knew everything about her, but I knew nothing. I opened my mouth, but the words stuck. Like my tears, they were locked away.

Rubia stood up. Her wool cloak draped over her shaking fists. Without a word, she fled into the darkness.

"WE ARE ALMOST TO PATRIDAVA," Constantin said, shifting in his seat. "Patridava takes trade seriously and sends out soldiers to clear out the forest of brigands along this main road."

Rubia smiled at the older man. When the farmer turned back to the road, she muttered under her breath in Getaen. "That's why I selected it, you miserly know-it-all."

With each passing day, Rubia's patience grew thinner. From the dark circles under her eyes, I judged she was not sleeping well. I dreaded going to sleep each night, knowing I would awaken with horrible dreams, screaming for help. But every time the sun went down, exhaustion lulled me into sleep's loving embrace.

Other wagon wheels creaked, and unfamiliar horses neighed. I tipped my head up. A caravan of traders pulled onto the Emperor's Highway from a side road. It was one of several roads that had merged with the highway over the last two days, but this one was by far the busiest, sending clouds of dust into the air. Dirt settled into every crevice of my skin, under my nails, and up my nose.

The sun was high, beating down on us. Sweat poured down the sides of my face, prickling between my shoulder blades. As we drew closer to the city, Patridavan Thorns directed the travelers.

"Ah, the blessed guards of Patridava. They're the reason the forests around the city are not teeming with vermin. You may drop your hoods," said the farmer.

Were the soldiers looking for the daughter of a scholar in Moesia? A young woman about my age with golden eyes?

Rubia dropped her hood, and I dared do the same. My sweat-damp hair plastered the side of my face. Rubia and I inspected each other. She pursed her lips, and I giggled. If she was any reflection of me, we looked far worse than street urchins from the Fissure. Dirt caked Rubia's face, only interrupted by crusted lines where beads of sweat had streaked down. Wet strands of hair stuck to her cheeks and forehead, and the top was ratted like a nest.

I combed my fingers through my hair, trying to untangle some of the knots while I inspected the valley. The forest had been cut back for a half a day's travel in all directions around the city, revealing the Dacian River which had grown wider each day. Several fields had already been harvested, and some were turning yellow, ready for the scythe. Along the side of the road, young girls sold flowers.

"There are benefits to living in the shadow of the Emperor. No one dares invade, and they can be bold in their growth," I said in Getaen. We had fallen into the habit of speaking in Rubia's native tongue during our conversations. Rubia had decided it was safer for everyone, including the farmers.

"We were never invaded in Moesia either," said Rubia, her voice flat. "Except by the Emperor's Capidavan troops. Here in

Patridava, his presence is woven in with the people like two lovers holding hands."

Papa had always said this city was too close to the Emperor; it was like getting too near the sun. Dangerous. The people of Patridava would be loyal to the Emperor, not Moesian women on the run. We needed to be cautious.

Constantin had told us, repeatedly, about the virtues of Patridava. Apparently, the city's complex water system enabled the local Clovers to farm vast tracts of land, and the surplus was sold in other cities like Moesia. I imagined those farmers grew wealthy in the process.

"Each street there sells a different item," Constantin said.

"There are merchants in Moesia and every town I've visited," Rubia said.

"Not like this. Patridava is unlike anything you've ever imagined," Constantin replied.

I wiped my hands on my dress, cringing at Constantin's insinuation that we hadn't seen much of the kingdom or had small imaginations. True or not, his chatter had soured Rubia's mood.

Constantin pivoted, speaking more to his son than to Rubia and me. "Patridava is fascinating and beautiful in its own way. But I couldn't leave my little valley for a hectic city. It's a nice place to visit but not to stay."

After I'd heard Constantin and Marcus arguing at the river, I wondered how I hadn't noticed the tension between them earlier. Marcus sat next to his father, only speaking when necessary. And on the rare occasion Marcus spoke to me, Rubia would send me to fetch something. Or she would ask Constantin a question, and then we would have to listen to his stories for hours. It seemed that Marcus' few words irritated her even more than the old farmer's never-ending tales.

I did agree with Constantin that Patridava was fascinating. While Moesia was dense with most of the homes in the Commons an arm's length away from each other, our hill seemed small compared to the sprawling valley that gently rolled out as far as I could see. Field upon field stretched out, dotted with farm buildings and smaller barns and animal coops. Beyond the fields, Patridava's stone wall hid the city from view. The wall was about the same height as Moesia's but much longer, stretching for miles in either direction. My heart fluttered with anticipation.

The soldiers and other travelers paid us little mind as we bumped along the road. As we neared the gate, Constantin pulled to the side of the road and stopped.

Marcus hopped down from his seat and helped Rubia from the back of the wagon. She thanked him and discretely checked the gold nugget still hidden in her belt. Marcus reached up to take my hand, to steady me. My fingers were sticky from apple juices and sweat. I didn't want to touch his hand so I jumped down from the wagon instead.

I had practiced what I would say several times last night when everyone else was asleep. "Thank you for safe passage."

"Even from a miserly old farmer?" Marcus folded his arms across his chest.

His words punched me in the stomach. He knew Getaen. Or at least enough to understand Rubia's comment about his father. Marcus had never hinted that he knew what we were talking about. Rubia was paying Constantin and didn't hear Marcus throw her own snide words back at me.

"I... I." I stammered. "Rubia didn't mean... "

Marcus ground his teeth. How many rude comments had he heard over the last seven days? More importantly, what had we said about the key and the curse within his earshot? Marcus spun on his heel and stomped back into his wagon.

Constantin turned and tipped his hat to both of us. With a snap of the reins, the farmers moved on.

I stared after the wagon, regrets piling up.

"He hates me," I muttered. It was partially our fault that Marcus and his father had tension between them. If Marcus hadn't tried to stand up for us at the river, maybe Constantin wouldn't be so hard on him.

"Don't feel bad. You were a distraction from whatever silly concerns that boy had on his mind," Rubia said, stretching.

I blinked. "Distraction?"

"I suspect he feels rebuffed, my dear Nicoleta, and doesn't know how to handle it very well." Rubia rolled her eyes and started walking to the city gate.

"I'd prefer he didn't think I was stuck up." I was exasperated, thinking about my sticky hands, disgusting cloak, and sweaty hair. I never had a chance to rebuff him. We hardly spoke. No, it was because Marcus had understood our rude comments. And he had defended us and was reprimanded for it.

Rubia started walking to the massive gate. "Why do you think Constantin balked at taking us when he saw you? Inside Moesia, you are a pretty young woman. But outside, you are unique, eye-catching." Rubia shrugged. "We can't waste our energy worrying about the farmers. You have too much to prepare for. And although they were sufficient escorts, they had ears, making it very difficult to talk."

I debated telling Rubia that Marcus understood some Getaen. But, we'd been careful to have our treasonous conversations in private. Hadn't we?

I chewed the inside of my cheek. "Rubia, there's something I should tell you about Marcus."

"Nikka, most of your friends were born in Moesia and will die in Moesia. For you, it's rare to meet someone and then let them go. Marcus is an autumn leaf already fallen away, to be blown about wherever the wind sends him. You are the seed meant to start a new tree."

"But —" I started.

"Listen, Marcus is dangerous." Rubia clenched her fist and took in a sharp breath. She shook out her shoulders and dusted off her skirt. When she spoke again, she'd calmed herself down. "Let's take our opportunity to get a hot meal and a comfortable place to sleep."

"And a bath," I added.

What did she mean, 'Marcus is dangerous?' I was itchy and longed to wear something that wasn't crusted with my own sweat, so I let her comment about Marcus go for the moment; I would definitely be asking about it later.

The long days of bumpy riding had taken their toll. Rubia limped a little heavier, and it took her longer to warm up her muscles. It would be good for both of us to get a few days of rest. Ahead, the crowded gate loomed.

Marcus and his father had already disappeared into the throng. I wished I could explain to the farmers that I struggled with my speech. I was sorry I seemed like a snob.

No. I could've told them all along. I was a coward. How could I expect to find Papa and a descendant of Odon if I couldn't even be honest about my stutter with random farmers?

Rubia pulled a clean cloth from her satchel, wiped the dirt from her face, and then handed it to me. It was no use trying to get cleaned up, but I shook out the cloth and followed Rubia's example.

"I'll apologize if we see the farmers in the city," I said. "I'm sure they thought I was rude."

"Patridava is one of the largest cities in the kingdom. If you do see them by some miracle, it's best to pretend we don't know them. The less they're associated with us, the safer they'll be. That's the best thanks you can give them."

We took our place at the back of the long line to the gate, behind a wagon filled with crates. A woman riding a horse clopped up behind us. She dismounted and held the horse's reins. A shiny leather scroll bag stuck out from under her half-cloak, and a short blade strapped to her belt flashed when she moved. She wore a pinned scarf, neatly tucked into her camasa, indicating she was married. A welcome breeze blew, but the woman grimaced, covering her nose with a gloved hand, turning her face up and away from us.

I was in awe. This woman traveled alone, knew how to use a blade, and didn't stink up the entire area doing it.

"How long will we stay here?" My stomach twisted at the thought of Rubia's plan. I wanted to get to Capidava and find out what happened to Papa. But when we arrived, I would be separated from Rubia. For all I knew, she was my only surviving family.

"If all goes well, we'll leave tomorrow morning," Rubia said, interrupting my thoughts.

Tomorrow? Our night in Patridava would be the one place where we had access to a roof, bed, bath, and warm food. Once we reached Capidava, Rubia would leave me and attempt her mission to tell the High Judge the secret of the True Key, secure me a place as a scribe's assistant, and find out Papa's fate.

The plan seemed reckless, but she would dig in her heels if I pointed out the flaws. I shuddered, regretting my promise not to complain or beg Rubia to change her mind. But I *had* promised, and I could handle this like the grown woman she needed me to be. I had a small hope that there was something she wasn't telling me. A piece of the plan that would make everything fall into place.

Today, Cassus and Odon found an injured fledgling in the gardens. Cassus cared for it all day, finding little worms and bugs for it to eat and keeping the dogs away. Cassus was clearly sad when the ouzel flew away and Odon teased him for it. I reminded them that their mother always appreciated a tender heart. I wish Hanna were here to see them now. She'd be impressed by the young men they're turning into. Cassus always asks for stories about her, but I don't know much besides the little things I saw her do for others. No grand tales of adventure and battles like their father.

In court, I now stand on the left side of the Emperor, which Dragan hates though he still sits at the right hand, the most trusted position. He's appalled with a Getaen in the court. When the princes are in attendance, Odon rolls his eyes and Cassus makes faces at me when he thinks no one is watching. I do my best not to smile. The Emperor's Warlock must at least appear fearsome. I look forward to when the bird returns to Cassus' favorite climbing tree. I Bound it to return to that tree every season.

— VAHID, WARLOCK TO EMPEROR TRAJAN CARACALLA

CHAPTER

EIGHT

GETAEN BATHHOUSE

Past the gate, Patridava buzzed with energy. We crossed a circular, open cobblestone area wide enough to fit a dozen wagons side by side with room to spare. Teams of horses pulled wagons around, most of them exiting the circle and continuing up the main road. Under my feet, the entire area was made of stones, meticulously set in an ornate spiraling pattern.

Whips snapped, wheels crunched against the stones, and people called out to one another. After four days on the quiet road, all the noise was a shock. Throngs of people bustled around with heavy baskets on their backs, carrying root vegetables, kindling, hay, and more.

"Hurry along!" the woman behind us in line shouted as she mounted her horse.

Rubia glared at her, but grabbed my arm and pulled me away so the fast-moving crowd wouldn't crush us.

On the right, a cobblestone road, wide enough for four wagons skirted the inside of the city wall. It was crawling with Patridavan Thorns in their green half-cloaks. Nearby sat a large building integrated into the side of the stone wall. In the open space in front of the building were two platforms: one smaller than the other. On the large platform stood a tall whipping post with a chain attached, and four sets of stocks, one occupied.

A guard exited the large building. He moved with more rigidity and discipline than I had seen from the Thorns in Moesia, his back straight as an arrow and eyes as sharp. The guard scowled at the man in the stocks. I pitied the embarrassing fate of the criminal, with spoiled food stains on his pants, face, and hands.

Rubia nudged me and I followed her gaze to the center of the circular cobblestone square. On top of a stout column, a statue of a man on a horse towered, three times as tall as any man. He wore a flowing cape, sword at his hip, and a regal crown on his brow. The statue looked down upon the people as they wove around him.

"Emperor Cassus Caracalla VII, our ruler, I assume. He should be known as the Lilac Emperor," Rubia said. Her voice wasn't loud, but it dripped with malice.

"Hush!" I looked around, but no one was listening to the wretched-looking women.

A little further, a narrow, dirt-packed street broke off from the main road, only wide enough for hand-held carts, likely leading to the lower houses. Straight ahead, the widest cobblestone street of the three cut through shops and taverns.

It wasn't long until the stream of wagons slowed. Only two wagons could fit at a time because merchant storefronts and buyers overflowed into the street. We passed several wagons, but the woman with the shiny leather scroll bag rode ahead of us. She maneuvered her horse through the crowds and disappeared around a corner, the fastest traveler on the road.

Throngs of city dwellers bustled through, pushing aside travelers: Laborers going about their work for the day; beggars with their cups sat as close as they could to the wagons without getting crushed. Wealthy merchants, low-born Poppies, foreigners, and everyone in between mingled on the streets. A Lazican from the East with an ebony complexion called out with a deep, rich voice about openings in his inn. Like the other nearby buildings, it was made of wood with a thatched roof, but it had glass windows with red curtains, fringed with gold. Near the front door were bright, blossoming flowers. If Otho hadn't insisted on triple the price for our passage, we might have been able to afford a night in the inn with the pretty flowers.

We walked through the wide, stuffy street until we reached an area of vendors, touting their wares. Many wagons pulled off into the inns' yard or stopped behind the tents lining the road where they loudly traded. Vendors sold barley, wheat, and oats — all different grains.

We turned onto a street lined with ambrosial flowers. It felt like I was walking through a rainbow of blooms. Otho's words about how each street only sold one item made sense now. Would there be a street with fruit vendors where Marcus and Otho were selling tomorrow?

Rubia found a Getaen woman who agreed to guide us through the city, hungry for news from Moesia.

"Do you have news of anyone from the River Lands? Has anyone from that area settled in Moesia in the last year?" she asked.

"None that I know of, I'm sorry, but Moesia isn't what it used to be after the plague came three years ago." Rubia patted her shoulder.

As we zigzagged through winding alleys, Rubia and her new Getaen friend laughed, slipping into thick southern accents. They spoke faster and faster, using slang and phrases I didn't know.

We stopped in a part of town with crooked buildings and

crumbling facades. The Getaen woman pointed out a tavern with an inn above. Rubia offered her a copper bit, but the stranger refused, sharing a quick embrace instead before departing.

Inside the tavern, the stuffy air made it difficult to breathe. Wafts of barley bread, onions, sweet corn, and garlic made my stomach growl. Forks clinked against stoneware and mugs thumped on the wood slab tables, conversations flowing faster than the ale in the lilting Getaen tongue. The crowded room was filled with ruddy patrons, their uncovered heads a range of hues from ash blond to bright copper, to deep red.

Rubia wove her way to the counter and spoke to the barkeep in her native tongue. "We'd like a meal and a place to sleep for us two."

While they spoke, I tried to be invisible. Despite the fact that I looked similar to some travelers in the room, many eyes were on me. I was a little too tall with bones a little too big. My features not quite dainty enough, nor my eyes quite blue enough. My tan a little too deep and my hair a bit too brown. Under my cloak, I hugged my small satchel next to my body. I was either too Dacian or not Getaen enough. Rubia handed the barkeep three bronze bits, and he gave her two bowls of soup, two rolls, and two large mugs of ale.

The barkeep pointed out a man in the far corner. The man had thinning hair and a smattering of tiny red dots on his cheeks. Rubia nodded and made her way to open seats near an unlit fireplace. As we sat, I opened my mouth to ask about the man in the corner. Rubia shook her head. I ate my soup in silence.

Had food ever tasted so good? The barley and corn soup was just like Mama used to make. Memories of her warmed me more than the soup.

Before I'd finished, Rubia spoke. "I need to speak with someone before we leave. Don't move."

Where would I go?

She threaded between the tables to the man with red speckled cheeks in the corner. Alone, surrounded by Getaens, the back of my neck pricked. I squirmed at the thought of so many eyes watching me slurp the last of my soup. I felt like a lonely tumbleweed lost in a vast desert of strangers. Not soon enough, Rubia returned for her cloak and scarf. She signaled for me to follow her. I slipped my barley roll into my satchel, and we made our way through a doorway in the back of the tavern.

There was a small, open courtyard where the back of several misshapen buildings met up. I followed Rubia into a shack that looked like it would fall over at the slightest breeze.

"You mustn't speak. You have a Dacian accent. Here in Patridava, Getaens stick to themselves. Their accent is less tainted," Rubia growled under her breath. "I'm sure the tavern keeper charged me more than the other patrons."

We stepped into the open doorway of the shack. The floor sloped downward into the ground. Unease crept over me. The darkness and earthy aroma surrounded me, seeping under my skin, reminding me of the pit in Papa's study. I forced myself to follow Rubia into the cavern. The rock underfoot was slick and steep; the rough stone walls became increasingly uneven, jagged edges slicing past me. As the temperature dropped, the humidity rose. I caught a whiff of rotten eggs. I was almost grateful for the noxious distraction. Beads of sweat rolled down my neck and back. My limbs tightened, and I struggled to keep up. Rubia continued on in stubborn silence into the darkening tunnel, not seeming to notice my alarm.

In my mind, I was back in Moesia under the terracotta tiles. I grabbed the craggy wall, stony edges digging into my skin, reminding me I wasn't helpless under tiles in Moesia. I couldn't catch my breath. The walls were closing in, crushing me, trapping me. I turned to escape from the suffocating memories.

Rubia gripped my shoulder. "Look, there's a light ahead. You can go to bed now, but you'll feel better after a bath."

Not far ahead, a warm light flickered. I wouldn't let my irrational fear rob me of the bath I'd looked forward to for days. I shakily followed Rubia down the tunnel as it curved to the right and revealed a fire torch. The light calmed me a bit if I didn't fixate on the way the fires made ominous shadows dance against the walls.

We approached the old woman who sat nearby, and Rubia spoke in Getaen. "We are staying in the inn, here for our allotted baths."

"You have good timing. Usually there is a long wait. Many travelers come here from the surrounding inns and much further. This is healing water, untouched by Zalmoxis' curse upon our lands. It is the best water in all of Patridava." The old woman's voice quivered as she boasted.

I cringed at the proud language, much the same as I'd heard from the street merchants on the way here. In Moesia, we knew Zalmoxis as a vengeful god. We avoided speaking his name, hoping to be forgotten.

Down the corridor, the water splashed and words echoed. Children giggled, and a woman's voice carried, chiding someone for taking their sister's sandals. The heavy sulfur in the air stung my nose. I hoped I'd get used to it soon. A moment later, a woman with wet hair and two children scurried past us. The two children stopped poking each other long enough to nod in greeting as they passed us.

As Rubia and I descended the path the family had come, the tunnel curved again, blocking the old woman from view. The corridor widened and ended in an uneven circular room about five paces wide. Two blue-hued luminaries reflected off the shiny black stone. In the center of the floor was a bubbling abyss, a bathing pool.

Rubia stripped off her dirty shoes and socks and set her cloak, belt, and satchel on top of her shoes, wearing only her chemise.

"You go first." She waved for me to enter the pool. She stood in the mouth of the entrance, her back to the water as she combed through the tangles of her hair. "Put on my extra chemise when you're done."

My fingers trembled as I stripped off my sweat-stained clothing and stepped into the water. From the center of the pool, I could touch the edges on either side. The bottom was uneven and surprisingly deep in one spot; deep enough for me to submerge my shoulders. The water was warm and bubbled, a luxury I'd never imagined. I forgave the pool its rotten egg smell, took a deep breath, and closed my eyes. I plunged my head into the water, running my fingers through my hair, rinsing away the last week's sweat, grime, and uncertainty. I would've stayed in the pool all night, but I didn't know how much time we were allotted. Rubia would make me eat apples for another week straight if she didn't get her turn.

I forced myself out of the relaxing pool. I rummaged around in Rubia's satchel, pulling out her clean chemise.

"Done," I said, evaluating the hem of the chemise. It fell at the middle of my shin, scandalously high. Plus I didn't have a towel, so the chemise soaked up every drop of water on my body and then clung to my skin. Before I could pull my long dress over the top, Rubia tugged it from my hands.

"Don't bother with this. Comb your hair." She pointed to her comb in the open doorway.

I grabbed the comb and worked it through my knotted hair while Rubia bathed. I stared at the scant light from the old woman's torch bouncing off the far wall. It was trying and failing to hold back the oppressive feeling of the cave.

The old woman echoed down the corridor, "People are waiting! Finish up!"

I cringed. Rubia had only been in the bath for moments. I should've been faster. Rubia shouted back that we paid for two baths, not one.

"Your time is up!" the old woman insisted.

Water splashed behind me as Rubia got out of the bath. I'd only combed half my hair when Rubia spoke.

"I'm done."

I turned to see Rubia with my wet clothing in her hands. My heart swelled with gratitude. Somehow she'd managed to wash herself and at least rinse out my chemise, dress, and aprons.

"Oh, Rubia... " I didn't know how to thank her.

The old woman barked, and her shadow fell larger as she marched toward us. Rubia didn't seem to be in a rush, pulling her dress over her wet chemise.

"We were told a quarter hour," Rubia said, barely raising her voice.

Wearing just Rubia's too-short and now damp chemise, I wrapped my putrid unwashed cloak around me as best I could. Fortunately, I wasn't in Moesia where rumors would run wild, disgracing Papa.

Rubia was still tying her cloak around her neck when the old woman lumbered into the bath, picked up the wet clothes from the ground, and shoved them into Rubia's hands. I snatched up the two satchels and my boots and edged toward the exit.

The old woman waved her arms, shooing us out. Rubia grumbled, but I was happy to escape the underground cavern.

When we turned the corner, a green apple sat on the old woman's chair. Behind the chair, waiting next in line, was

Marcus. My jaw dropped, and I pulled my cloak tighter around me with one hand, dropping one of the satchels. Marcus leaned over to pick it up but paused, his gaze shifting to Rubia. Even in the dancing orange firelight, I could see his face flush almost as hot as mine felt.

Rubia stood taller, and Marcus stepped back, politely giving me a chance to gather up my satchel, which I appreciated all the more when my boots also slipped from my fingers as I reached down to pick up my bag. I hugged my things to my body, flustered.

"Marcus." Rubia nodded an acknowledgment before brushing by him.

"I-I... " The words stuck in my throat as a realization and sudden horror washed over me. I must look a fright with half my hair combed out, half still in tangles, wearing a scandalous tiny shift, and wreathed in the scent of sulfur and my putrid cloak. Not to mention my inarticulate stuttering and staring.

Rubia returned, grabbed my wrist and pulled me away, breaking me from my trance. Head down, I scurried behind Rubia, not looking back. When we were outside in the court-yard, the late afternoon sunlight burned my eyes, and I was grateful for it. The weight of the cavern lifted from my shoul-ders, but something else settled in its place.

I glanced over my shoulder at the shack hiding the dark corridor to the bath. My insides soured with embarrassment. Just hours ago, I'd have given away my hot supper for a chance at apologizing to Marcus or Otho. Now, I'd rather crawl into a hole and die than face either one of them again. But as Rubia said, Marcus was a leaf. An autumn leaf that would flutter away, my missteps with it.

I swallowed and hurried after Rubia to a side stairwell on the outside wall of the tavern. Rubia led me to the third floor. There were about fifty thin mats scattered all over the floor and thin ropes crisscrossing the room, just high enough to hit my forehead.

A dozen women were in the room, and I was relieved to see no men, other than the youngest boys holding the hands of their mamas. There were several open windows, no glass, with a welcome cross breeze.

I dodged the ropes as we made our way to two empty mats together along the far wall. Rubia flung my wet dress, aprons, and socks over the nearest rope, which worked as both a partition and a way to dry clothing in the breeze throughout the night.

I situated my clothing so it wouldn't dry too wrinkled. I ran my fingers over the silk ribbons on my aprons. They would be stained, and I'd probably never completely rid them of the cloak's stale tobacco malodor. But still, they were clean. Rubia had let me enjoy a simple moment of peace in the bath. She always looked ahead. How could I doubt her? She would overcome our challenges. She always did.

I remembered her considerable, gruesome losses.

Rubia lost one child, and she won't risk losing another.

A wave of emotion overcame me. Tears welled in my eyes. Rubia patted my back and guided me to my mat. She walked over and whispered to a girl with fire-red hair, not much younger than I. Rubia returned, sat down, and took the comb I still clutched. I hadn't even realized that I'd had it. Rubia resumed combing my hair where I had left off and hummed a lullaby.

The melody stirred a memory loose. Rubia had sung to me, possibly every night, for moons after the raid on our house. She had explained that Papa's aunt stuttered and either it would pass, or I'd learn to speak around it. She had shown no sympathy, other than the fact that she sacrificed her nights to be at my side. I appreciated that she didn't pity me. She stood by me, especially when Papa had withdrawn. Now she was determined to find me the apprenticeship I was destined for since the moment Mama had laid the orb in my hand. Rubia had expectations of me. Hopes.

But all I had were doubts. Fears. The tears burned my eyes, and I tried to blink them back, but instead, one trickled down my cheek. I'd never done anything without Rubia, not really. And now she'd planned to leave me. Abandon me as Mama and Papa had done.

"You haven't had a chance to mourn your papa," Rubia said softly.

I clutched my knotted stomach. I was crying about her plan, about being ripped apart from the last person who knew me. Knew Mama. An unwelcome tinge of guilt that my tears were not all out of worry for Papa wrapped in with my sadness. I desperately wanted to find him. But I wasn't mourning Papa, not yet. I clung to my hope that he was alive. But if finding out his fate cost me Rubia, was it worth it? I wiped my tear. It was Rubia I mourned.

Growing up, Rubia had always been a part of my life, part of our family — a fractious second mother to me. A firecracker and yet a stable force in my life. Understanding why she hadn't selected me as an apprentice lessened the pain of her rejection. She had said there was something else I was meant for, greater things. It was all true. But, I would give it all up. I'd give anything if it meant I could get Mama and Papa back. If I could keep Rubia.

As my tears rolled down my cheeks, Rubia hummed and combed my hair. It had been almost a week since I'd seen Mama's blue vision. So many things had happened since then. I had held my emotions in, not knowing what to do with them, but in a quiet room, I couldn't fight them any longer. The anguish, all twisted up inside me started to unravel and release from every pore. Rubia didn't try to hush my tears or console me; instead, she continued to hum while she braided. The girl with fire-red hair brought a cup of steaming hot water to Rubia, a puzzled look on her face before she made her way back to her mat.

Rubia's humming didn't stop as she pulled wrapped up herbs from my satchel and a mesh cloth from hers. She steeped the herbs in the hot water. From the soothing scents of the chamomile and valerian root, I knew the concoction: sleeping draught. I pulled the cup close to my chest and let the heat sink into my fingers. I gulped it down, knowing blessed sleep would soon take me away from the agony of consciousness.

The room grew fuzzy. I tried to focus on Rubia as she organized our sparse belongings. Her eyes widened. Something was wrong, but the tea softened the edges of my alarm, pulling me to sleep. I blinked, trying to keep my eyes open. Rubia was speaking to the girl with the fire-red hair.

My eyes fluttered as Rubia disappeared down the stairs. I was alone. I wasn't angry or frightened. The tea saw to that. It was a mere notation in my mind. Our last night of peace together, and Rubia had already abandoned me. I was asleep before the tears dried.

The Emperor asked me to curse Dragan. Trajan's gaze pierced me, attuned to the smallest lie. So I told him the truth; I had no love for Dragan, but I wasn't an assassin. He demanded I show loyalty to him and his sons by doing as he bid me. I gritted my teeth and nodded.

Dragan is as sharp as ever, which I think concerns the Blood Emperor. Instead of Dragan, I suspect the Emperor desires a Patridavan at his side. Patridava is a small farming town, but that will change. A road is being built from Dacia to Patridava and beyond, far beyond, bringing trade and fortune into the kingdom. It was Dragan's idea to build the road in the first place.

I dread creating this curse and the inevitable wedge it will create between myself and everyone else in Rupea Castle. No one likes magic, especially dark magic.

In preparation, I researched ancient northern curses and learned something shocking: Getaens are descendants of those hermits in the northern mountains. Why didn't my Norte master ever mention this? We could be distant blood relations. The thought is simultaneously intriguing and sickening. I've never met a northerner who wasn't prideful, cold, and cruel.

CHAPTER

NINE

BIRTHDAY GIFT

Rubia shook my shoulder gently. Bleary-eyed and groggy, my dreams of Mama slipped away. Her words escaped me, like fire smoke curling the sky, though I remembered the sad look in her eyes.

Rubia checked over her shoulder and crouched next to me. "Everyone is sleeping during the thieves' hour. But walls never sleep."

Stars glittered against the black night sky through the open windows.

"Are we leaving under the cover of d-darkness?" My tongue felt even more thick and useless than usual. I pushed myself up onto my elbows and tried to calculate how much sleep I'd gotten, but my mind refused to do the simplest math. The vestiges of the sleeping draught still tainted my mind.

"We need to do some trading at sunup before we leave for Capidava." She took my hand and pulled me into a seated position. My dress hung next to us, giving us a little privacy.

I yawned and tried to force my brain to work.

"Today is your birthday. It's your sixteenth year under the sun," Rubia whispered softly, and I strained to hear her.

117

With my mourning over, I had planned to spend a carefree birthday with Papa, eating sweet rolls glazed with honey and butter and making wishes. Instead, I was running to the capital, in the desperate hope of finding Papa or, at least, information on what had happened to him.

Rubia pulled a lump wrapped in cheesecloth from her satchel. She untied the string and sprinkled a grainy substance around us. At the sight of it, all longing for sleep melted away. This wasn't Healer magic. It was Sonus magic.

"I traded a sleeping draught for this powder from the Sonus I met in the tavern yesterday." She sprinkled another layer of the sandy substance around us. The dust particles tickled my throat and smelled like charcoal.

Rubia had planned ahead for this conversation. While I was slurping my soup, she was negotiating with the ruddy-cheeked man from the tavern. I sat up straight, facing Rubia, a thrill welling inside me. What she was about to say was important enough for Rubia to acquire this protection circle — no one outside the circle would be able to hear our words. I helped her push the sand on the smooth floor into an unbroken, curved line around us.

"I have a present for you. Your mama made me swear to keep the pendant until after the danger of the plague passed and to wait until your sixteenth birthday to tell you the truth of the orb." The expression on her face was hidden in shadows, but her excitement was tangible.

In Mama's blue vision, she mentioned some things would have to wait until I was of age. Did she mean sixteen? Today? My heart thumped.

"Of course, you found out more than was intended before you turned sixteen." Rubia peeked around my hanging dress before slipping off the gold necklace. "But now, we'll make it official."

My heart pounded harder against my ribs.

The gold shimmered faintly in the starlight. She held out the necklace, the pendant trembling at the end of the chain. Electric energy pulsed.

I tilted my chin, and Rubia slipped the necklace over my head. The pendant rested heavy on my chest. I wrapped my fingers around the uneven orb. It was comforting in a strange way; the last gift Mama had given me, was now returned. At the same time, doubts wriggled inside me. How would I be able to continue Mama's work? Rubia only had mere days to teach me what she had taught Mama over the course of years.

"Things are finally as they should have been." Rubia sounded lighter. "I will tell you something as you've proved how responsible you are. I didn't want to carry the pendant these last three years. However, I honored Leila's wish to withhold as much burden as possible until now."

I leaned in, hanging on her every word.

"It's tradition for the younger Guardian to keep the pendant with them. Usually the two Guardians are a parent and a child or grandchild, at least a generation apart. The healthier, younger Guardian to carry the pendant, and the older, wiser Guardian to guide the way. Your mother and I were close in age, only ten years apart, but she was my only option. And she carried the weight of the responsibility as well as anyone I've known."

Rubia chuckled.

"Why laugh?" I asked.

"Prejudice. We find it everywhere, in time. We often look at those above us in status, but if we look around us, at ourselves, we find it there, too. I'm laughing at my hubris. The folly of my family." Rubia sighed. "We let ourselves believe that because of our magic, because we were deemed by some long-dead, ruthless dictator to be Getaen leaders. That we were the only ones worthy of guarding the necklace. But your mother did more to uncover the heir of Odon and the secrets of the key than anyone else. With your father, a non-magical Dacian, they found things lost to us long ago."

Rubia took my hand in hers and kissed my knuckles. My heart softened at her tender gesture, and I squeezed her hands in return. She continued in a whisper, "I'll be your guide as my grandmother was for me. Finally, things are back in the natural order. Not in the tradition my family turned it into but the way Guardianship was originally intended — protection of the key and the heir by any two people who put the needs of the kingdom before themselves."

Rubia released my hand, her voice lowering. "There is something I need to ask you."

A cool breeze brushed against my bare arms and face. I gripped the sphere around my neck, something solid and grounding.

"When you were twelve and took the oath, we never explained what it meant. And although it saved your life, we never asked you if this was something you wanted." She took a deep breath. "Now that you know the truth, is this a path you want to take?"

What option did I have now? Mama hadn't wanted this path for me, but in giving me the orb, she traded her life for mine. Rubia had agreed to the Guardianship because she wanted to protect me, to save me as she hadn't been able to do with her own child. But what did I want?

Rubia turned me around and loosened the braid from the night before, giving me time to think. The stars had started to fade from the sky as it turned from inky black to a deep blue.

Did I want to give up my last connection to Mama? Did I want to continue her work? Beyond that, was I the best person to be a Guardian? Here, surrounded by Getaens, Rubia could find another Guardian more capable than I.

"You gave me the necklace out of urgency. Would you have selected me to be the Guardian if not for the plague?" I asked. Rubia hadn't chosen me to be her Healer's apprentice, and this was much more important.

"When the Lilac Plague came to Moesia and we were trapped, your Mama had to choose. Giving you protection from the plague would also weigh you with a Guardian's responsibilities. Or to leave you free but vulnerable to the horrible disease." Rubia gathered the top layer of my hair and braided it into a crown around my head, leaving the rest to fall in soft waves. "But you've always been a daughter to me. I won't deny that you becoming a Guardian was what I'd always hoped."

If I'd had wings, I didn't think they could lift me any higher than her words. I relished every syllable, letting them wrap around me.

I ran my fingers over the grooves of the pendant. As much as Rubia's admission stitched together part of my heart, I knew she was right: I hadn't chosen to be a Guardian. I had merely obeyed Mama, repeating her words in a moment of panic, not knowing what they meant for her or for me.

Could I give up the Guardianship now? I could stay in Patridava. I knew enough of the Healer's trade to make a living. In a few years, I could return to Moesia. With a little hair dye, I could live near the uncle I barely knew and start a new life.

But I couldn't simply abandon Papa and start a new life as if he were already lost. Nor could I ever rest knowing I'd let Rubia carry all the risk alone. Another part of me was curious about the heir and excited to walk my parents' path. Hadn't they inadvertently been training me in research and language all my life? Who else could Rubia find and train before the scrolls were all transcribed? Rubia only had a small window of opportunity to secure a Guardian within the castle walls.

Whether or not I wanted to be a Guardian, the task had fallen to me; I was determined to honor Mama's memory, Papa's quest, and Rubia's stubborn courage by accepting the role of Guardian.

I stood up. The pendant nestled against my chest as if it had always been there. The weight of it meant much more than simply wearing a valuable trinket. It meant sweeping away the last illusions of hiding in the cracks of society as a Healer. No secret visits to my uncle. No more faint dreams of a husband and family. Yet, as I pulled my dress off the rope and tugged it on, still cool and wet, I didn't feel nervous or alone. For the first time in years, I had a purpose, a reason to live for something greater than myself. I straightened my spine and drew a deep breath.

Rubia dressed silently, then scattered the protection circle with her foot. She watched the room like a hawk as I folded my extra pair of clean socks in my satchel next to the remaining rolled herbs.

I held the orb in my hand, wondering at the power of the warlock who created it so long ago. Did he suspect that greed would eventually destroy the accord between the descendants of the Blood Conqueror?

The questions drove me. I wanted to uncover the secrets of the plague. If I could discover the treasure's location and pass on what we knew of Odon, that would be a great legacy. Even if I didn't find a true heir in my lifetime, with Papa's scrolls gone, just recording what he and Rubia taught me would be an accomplishment. Hiding that information away inside the bowels of the Emperor's castle, the last place the Emperor's soldiers would think to look — now that would be quite the feat. Eventually, someone would put all the pieces together and stop the plague. With every fiber of my soul, I hated the plague. I couldn't think of anything I'd want more than to help stop it.

I closed my eyes and silently promised myself to see this through until my last breath.

I modified the curse incantation to my own liking: a blend of ancient Getaen and modern Dacian. Time consuming, but I wanted to be sure it worked correctly, and I wouldn't test the condemning words on anyone else.

I accompanied Dragan to interrogate a prisoner. In the dungeon, I grasped his arm. I've never placed a curse on a person before. It worked better than I imagined. Dragan huffed through his gritted teeth to tell me what a rotten Get I was and how I'm just a foolish pawn in the Emperor's game.

The Emperor was angry I left Dragan alive in a pit, but when I explained the curse, he laughed and congratulated me on my ingenuity. Since then, I've been included in more of the Emperor's collusions.

Odon and Cassus are still studying with their uncle in the west. I hope they'll be proud of my increased standing when they return.

—VAHID, WARLOCK TO EMPEROR TRAJAN

CARACALLA

CHAPTER

TEN

LILAC HORRORS

A crowd of people, wagons, and horses amassed around Patridava's northern gate. The sun's first rays promised another sweltering day. Vendors lined the opposite side of the square, already calling out tantalizing descriptions of the dried goods they sold and the benefits for travelers.

My cowl hung behind me. Half my hair was braided and out of my face, and the rest bounced in waves against my back. My dress was almost dry despite the more humid air in Patridava, and I relished the clean, coolness of it as I brushed past wagons, stalls, and people. The orb was hidden under my apron and dress. The key felt natural, like it was always meant to be there.

Rubia spoke with yet another merchant preparing to leave.

"Two women are too much trouble, especially two exotic beauties such as yourselves," said a merchant wearing a tall velvet cap. The back of his wagon was filled with wooden crates, and he was accompanied by two men with thick necks, stubble, and blades. He studied us and shook his head. "I recommend you travel with the Emperor's official seal or paid mercenaries to protect you. The roads surrounding the Capidava are not like Patridava. They're crawling with thieves, and I cannot risk inviting an attack."

His warning held no menace. Still, he turned his back to us and continued to check the straps holding the boxes fast.

Back home, I'd been 'that motherless girl with a cursed tongue and a suspicious father.' It was odd to hear strangers describe me as a beauty but also a little exciting. Outside of Moesia, I could be anyone.

Rubia curled her hands into fists and turned to scour the area for another face she approved of. This was the third merchant who'd turned us away. The first caravans of the morning were already leaving for Capidava in the soft dawn light.

"The caravans in front have the Emperor's seal. They'll travel the fastest, straight through to the capital in two days. But their cargo is much more precious than any money we give them. We must settle for a slower, yet still well-protected caravan." Rubia stood on her tiptoes, scanning the merchants."Go wait for me near the sisters minding that dried meat stand." She pointed to the outer edge of the crowd, furthest away from the main gates. "Let me try asking without you lurking nearby and see if our luck improves."

I slid past people to the outskirts of the throng. The spiced meats made my mouth water. I nibbled on my barley roll from the night before. Rubia's flowing dress and aprons swished between wagons and merchants, and then she was gone.

While I waited, I thought back this morning; we had left the inn when the dim shadows of the pre-dawn still dulled the vibrant colors of the Getaen district. I had followed Rubia through the narrow streets. The cool air prickled my skin through my damp dress. I welcomed it after the sweltering heat of the last few days.

Rubia rapped her knuckles on a colorful door. A young boy

with white-blond hair resembling Rubia's invited us inside. The cluttered room smelled of rosemary and elderberry. With the door and windows shut tight, a bluish light came from a dozen glowing luminary orbs placed around the room. The orbs had hundreds of floating white sparks inside, darting around in a random pattern. I had never seen so many luminaries in one place, but I shut my gaping mouth, copying Rubia's serene expression.

Narrow shelves lined the walls, filled with concoctions for sale. A doorway to the back room was partially covered with a heavy curtain. Patterned rugs led to the rear wall where a balding man sat on a blue floor cushion with his legs crossed. His robe wrapped across his chest, and his belly sagged over the belt at his waist. His trousers were loose, and he wore nothing on his feet.

I'd met Protectors, but after many of them died in the plague, I doubted their efficacy. Rubia had scolded me, saying I shouldn't scoff at things I didn't understand.

Rubia pulled out an orange vial from her satchel, and the Protector leaned forward, saliva on his lips. When he turned to me, his cheek twitched.

"Remove your shoes and lay down." He gestured to the rug in front of him, then to the boy. "Hang that cloak outside."

The young boy who had allowed us entrance snatched my cloak with a crinkled nose and disappeared into the back room. I settled myself on the soft, thick rug, wondering what Rubia had bargained for. From the back room, the young boy brought a bowl of water and a clear vial of liquid and placed them next to his master. The Protector chanted and set the vial in my hand. The glass vial swiftly heated, and the Protector's brow rose.

I sat up on my elbows and watched the Protector pour the vial's contents into the bowl. Upon contact, the water inside swirled into a vibrant scarlet. The Protector's smooth chant hiccuped before he continued, dipping his fingertips into the mixture.

Rubia nudged my leg, and I lay back down.

"Her body is overwrought, on the brink of malady." The Protector spoke over me. "You didn't mention she would be in this condition. I can protect her flesh and sinew, blood and bone, or mind. Which would you like to fortify?"

"She's a healthy young woman. And for an orange-sting potion, you'll protect all three, or we'll be leaving." Rubia clutched an orange vial in her hand.

I rolled my lips together. Orange-stings were prohibited.

"My Protector's skills are the best in the valley, and I don't wish to be taken advantage of. But as you've traveled a long way and your orange-sting looks sufficient, I'll be generous and protect two," the Protector countered.

"If you can get a better sting potion in all of Dacia, then you're welcome to it." Rubia stood.

I moved to follow her, but the Protector put a hand on my shoulder. "Let's not be hasty. You're already here, and I'd not like to waste my time."

Rubia looked down her nose at him. "Give her your highest quality protection, and this orange-sting is yours."

"I swear it," he said.

Rubia sat next to me, and I lay back down. The Protector tapped his fingertips against my forehead, leaving a smear of water behind. The mood in the room changed from discord to tranquility as the Protector repeated the tapping on my wrists and fingers. With every touch, heat flowed through my muscles. My mind cleared. His hand hovered over my torso and tightness I hadn't noticed before unwound. I closed my eyes, relaxed but alert, listening to the lyrical chanting and sensing the light pressure from his fingertips on my heels, toes, and behind my ankles.

Rubia squeezed my hand, and I opened my eyes. Had I fallen asleep? The boy and the bowl were gone, replaced by my worn leather cloak. The Protector sat on his cushion, one of Rubia's orange vials tucked into his belt.

"... so much emotional turmoil," the Protector was saying. His spell was placed on me, but the Protector only spoke to Rubia, his hand caressing the orange vial. "It's draining her physical strength. To keep her body healthy, she must rid herself of emotional distress."

Rubia merely thanked him, but her face was cold as stone as we made our way to the street of merchants selling root vegetables. I popped the last bit of my roll in my mouth and internally scrutinized the Protector's last words. As if just taking all my worries and tossing them away from me was that simple; I brushed off his advice. But between his magic and my uninterrupted sleep, my stride lengthened, and my mind was clearer.

While Rubia bartered packets of herb medicine for tubers, a familiar voice pulled me out of my thoughts. "I'll trade you a basket of apples for four rations of dried meat."

I turned to see Marcus an arm's length away, carefully pouring a bag of apples into a basket that two girls held up for him, sisters, most likely. He looked refreshed from the night before, his clothes somewhat cleaner. He wore his wool cloak and a wide-brimmed hat. The older sister handed him skewers of meat with a smile while her little sister, not even old enough to wear a double apron, twirled her hair with her fingertips, giggling at nothing.

My mouth went dry, the bread forming a ball of mush against my tongue. At least I was fully dressed. Reflectively, I pulled my cloak tighter around me.

Marcus put the meat in his satchel and thanked the sisters.

I turned my back to him and took two steps away.

"Nicoleta?" Marcus said.

The ball of bread-mush in my mouth seemed to grow too big to swallow. Here was my chance to say something, to try and explain my rudeness, but instead, I just stared up at him as he walked over to see me, my mouth stuffed with food.

"I wanted to apologize for... ah... for last night. For catching you... unaware," Marcus said. Was that a blush on his ears? "I hadn't expected to see you in the bathhouse. I mean I'm sure you take baths. I'm sure Getaens are normally clean." He stumbled over his words and scratched the side of his clean-shaven face.

I wanted to be irritated by how he divided Getaens from Dacians, but I felt a little sorry for him blundering through his words like a new foal trying to walk.

"Have you... found passage to Capidava?" Marcus cleared his throat and looked over my shoulder. He wanted to change the subject. Thank goodness.

I shook my head and awkwardly tried to chew the bread in my mouth.

"I told Rubia last night that you'd have trouble finding someone to go with. Where is she?"

I raised an eyebrow but pointed to the crowd where I'd last seen Rubia. When did Marcus talk to Rubia about our travel plans to Capidava? I was with Rubia almost every moment, and they never discussed the next leg of our journey. I chewed the bread more, hoping I could just swallow it like a normal person.

"I was thinking, it might be better for you two to split up into different caravans," Marcus said.

I scowled, remembering his father's annoying habit of assuming we wanted his advice. Obviously we knew what dangers were lurking. I wanted to tell him as much, but between the wad of bread and my stutter, I held my tongue.

"Our wagon's over there." He pointed to the south side of the crowd. "Let me speak with my father, and I'll be right back." Marcus turned and jogged around the growing crowd.

As soon as Marcus left, I chewed my bread quickly like a slovenly boor, swallowing even less daintily. The older sister at the meat stand gave me a disgusted look, and the younger sister snickered and made grunting noises like a pig. My face burned, and I stepped further away from their table, ignoring their faces and their tempting meat skewers. The breeze shifted bringing me the smoky scent.

No! I'd rather starve than ever trade with those two. My traitorous stomach growled louder.

I wanted to find Rubia. As busy as the Moesian gates were in the morning, they were a trickle of water compared to the roaring river of commerce in Patridava. If I moved, Rubia might not find me for hours. Where was she? It sounded like Marcus had a plan. As frustrating as Marcus could be, I trusted him. As long as we budgeted for Otho's prices, we could weather a few more days of apples and tall tales.

Finally, Rubia elbowed her way through the crowd and beckoned me. "I may have found us safe passage to the capital. I met a Getaen assistant to a wealthy merchant from Capidava. The merchant is returning home with goods from the Getaen Sea, sailed here from the East, beyond Dacia. The goods are worth a small fortune, so he has an army of mercenaries. He also travels with the Emperor's seal. The assistant said several Getaens work on the crew, and we would be safe traveling with them. He's agreed to an introduction to his employer, Master Elek of Capidava. If Master Elek is amenable, we shall leave here within the hour."

"We may have a better option." I tugged Rubia's sleeve before she rushed away. "Instead of riding with strangers, we can ride with the farmers who b-brought us this far."

"But they don't have mercenaries or the Emperor's seal, and this Master Elek has both. Besides, Otho said many times they're headed east then home for the fall apple harvest."

"Marcus is d-discussing options with his father. B-Besides, they have Velos, the fastest horse north of Capidava." I snickered at my own joke.

"Don't be ridicu —" Rubia's gaze focused over my shoulder. "Marcus, nice to see you again." She bowed her head slightly.

Marcus inclined his head politely and gave me a slight smile before focusing on Rubia. I was perplexed at his change. He hardly spoke or smiled anywhere near me the entire trip from Moesia.

"I've spoken with my father. He has a clever idea for how we can travel safely to Capidava. You'll need —"

Rubia held up a hand and cut him off. "You've done so much for us already. I appreciate the offer, but I can't possibly ask this of you. Besides, we can't afford to pay the triple rate... Again." Marcus winced slightly, but Rubia didn't seem to notice and continued. "We have made other arrangements that will be safer for us and for you."

A shadow of disappointment crossed Marcus' face, but he quickly recovered. "We may be making a trip to Moesia in the early spring. Might I see you both while I'm there?"

My stomach twisted.

"With any luck, we'll be back in the Moesian Commons by then," Rubia lied.

I hadn't let it sink in that I would never see my city's beautiful hill again. I slumped. Was this how Mama felt when she had been forced to flee from her childhood home? But my family wasn't in Moesia anymore. Family is home. My family was Papa and Rubia. There was nothing but ghosts and memories for me in Moesia.

I took Rubia's hand. Before I followed her into the crowd, I looked back over my shoulder at Marcus. I wasn't sure I wanted to ever know why Rubia thought Marcus was dangerous; I didn't want to taint this last memory of him. I tried to memorize the arch of his brow and the exact color of hazel in his eyes in the morning light.

"Thank you," I mouthed more than I said.

Before he could respond, people passed between us and swallowed us up in the crowd.

"When did you and Marcus talk about our trip to Capidava?" I asked.

"Last night after you fell asleep." A large man bumped into Rubia. She frowned but pressed forward.

"Why did you leave me alone?" I was practically helpless after drinking the sleeping draught. The thought of being completely unguarded sent a shiver through me.

"You were safe. I spoke with Marcus mere steps away from the inn. It was a mistake to divulge our plans to the farm boy. I'll have plenty of time to tell you all about what happened while we're on the road to Capidava." Rubia tightened her grip on my hand as we wove through the thickest portion of the crowd. "Pull up your hood."

I covered my hair just before we stopped in front of a tall, wiry man with wisps of short gray hair. Tattoos of Getaen symbols wove up his muscled arms. Even without them, I'd have known his heritage based on his sunburned skin. The small brand on his neck made me shudder. The mark of a slave. He may have risen to the status of assistant to a powerful merchant, but he was not free to choose his destiny. How much protection could he really offer us? He gave a respectful nod to Rubia, but there was a slight hesitation when he looked at me before he gestured for us to follow him around several wagons marked with the Emperor's symbol.

Despite my discomfort, I was impressed with Rubia's

resourcefulness. The Getaen slave stopped next to a man with his back to us. The man was much smaller than the Getaen, with narrow shoulders and a slim waist. He waved one hand in the air, heavy gold rings on every finger. The feather on his velvet hat extended six inches into the air, and his tidy, coal-black hair was cropped short underneath. The Getaen slave tapped the ringed merchant on the shoulder and whispered in his ear. The man turned and studied Rubia, not seeming to notice me. Even though he was a short man, he was still a head taller than Rubia.

"Let me introduce you to Master Elek of Capidava," the slave said.

Rubia gave a stiff bow, her words pinched. "We are seeking safe passage to Capidava. We have a gold nugget, pure quality, of weight twelve, in exchange for transportation and protection."

I gripped my satchel tighter. Rubia planned to barter the gold nugget? Our expenses to Otho for seven days to Patridava paled in comparison to what Rubia was offering for this two-day leg of our journey. That would leave us with only two bronze bits once in Capidava.

"We?" Elek ripped his eyes off of Rubia and noticed me. His entire countenance changed. He smiled, but it was oily, and he lifted both hands in the air as if to celebrate seeing a long lost relative. He stepped forward and grasped both my hands in his.

The Getaen slave folded his arms and frowned at the back of his master's velveted head.

Master Elek let go with one hand and yanked back my hood. "Tell me, what is your business in the great city of Capidava?"

Everyone spoke to Rubia, my elder, not me. But Master Elek was my superior, so I responded.

"We travel there to seek my P-papa," I said.

"He is a scholar in the capital at the Emperor's request," Rubia said. It was a good lie with a thread of truth.

Elek's smile didn't falter. His gaze made me squirm; his grip on my hands grew tighter. "Such a fine treasure as this young woman will be difficult to protect. As you know, the forests around the capital are crawling with vermin. Men with the worst of intentions."

The slave shifted his weight uncomfortably.

"Fortunately, I have men who I pay well to protect my valuable items." Elek dropped his hand from my hood to my neck, and my skin crawled where his soft fingertips grazed as they traveled down to the chain of my pendant. My instincts screamed for me to run, but my muscles wouldn't respond. I stood frozen in place.

"Even this gold trinket would be worth something to a thief." Elek's eyes narrowed. He raised his voice to his slave, speaking without taking his eyes off of me. "We must be ready to leave shortly. If Andre isn't here, we'll leave him. I don't care if he's the Emperor's mistress' cousin. He'll find his own way home."

Rubia's hand closed around my upper arm. "Your words are wise, and I take them to heart. I now realize that traveling to Capidava is a fool's errand."

Rubia pulled my arm, but the merchant's grip tightened, sending shooting pain through my fingers. "You wasted my time? I think not. This young woman will accompany us."

Rubia reached into her satchel. "For your trouble, I will pay you the gold we agreed upon."

Elek barked a laugh, but his eyes were dark. "You think one gold piece would buy even a hog a trip to the capital? Women like you must pay a much steeper price."

Elek nodded to his Getaen slave. The slave's face was filled with disgust, but he pried Rubia's hand off my arm. Panic rose into my throat, trapping my words. I twisted, trying to escape Elek's grasp. Rubia struggled against the slave, staccato southern curses spewing from her mouth.

The merchant dragged me a few steps away; my world was being ripped apart. This couldn't happen. I was being kidnapped in broad daylight in the busiest area of the city. I wanted to cry out despite the risk the Thorns might be on the lookout for the daughter of a treasonous scholar, but in my rising panic, my stutter rendered me mute.

Master Elek pushed me against his carriage.

"My tenants will thank you." The merchant's words poured over me. "They will be pleased that my taxes are so light this year. Pretty girls are worth three times as much toward tax levies."

Someone shuffled in the carriage behind me. Hands gripped my shoulder.

"Get her in the carriage!" Elek spat.

I was yanked up, the unseen hands digging into my shoulders and arms. The backs of my legs scraped against the carriage foothold. No one seemed to notice my distress. But the pain in my calves seemed to jolt me; I thrashed, trying to escape. The hands tightened.

The slave threw Rubia to the ground. Rubia cried out. Glass shattered. Orange dust filled the air. Rubia vanished into the crowd. People near the dust covered their eyes and cried out in pain. For a moment, the grip on my shoulders loosened. I took the distraction Rubia provided and leapt away from the carriage, pushing past the oily merchant. There was a tug on my sleeve; the material ripped, but I didn't slow.

The string of my cloak tightened. Sharp pain shot across my neck. I was jerked back. I tugged at the string on my cloak, fumbling to undo the knot. The tie snapped away and I fell forward, skidding along the ground. My pulsing blood pounded in my ears with each heartbeat. Rubia was nowhere to be seen.

Elek jerked me to my feet and spun me around. My cloak crumpled around me, tangling my feet. I shrunk away. He caught my pendant in his fist. The delicate chain snapped. The key was in his hand, the gold chain swinging between his fingers. The merchant's face was purple with rage. He took a step toward me.

"The Patridava guards will arrest your mother for witchery and —" Elek stopped short. His face contorted.

My pendant fell from his grip and landed at my feet. He looked at his hand, eyes wide. His palm and fingers were grey. His hand started to whither, the skin becoming twisted and diseased to the wrist.

Elek stumbled back. His wild screams pierced the morning air like a hunted animal.

I snatched up my pendant and darted into the crowd. Avoiding the area contaminated with bright, orange dust, I circled toward the meat vendor table, desperate to find Rubia.

Cries emanated from the area affected by Rubia's orange-sting, but the merchant's high-pitched screams carried louder than all the rest. I had almost been trampled before when the plague had broken out in Moesia. This time, I used my elbows and kept my feet under me, moving through the uproar. Vendors, merchants, and servants at the edges were straining to see the source of the trouble. Several Patridavan guards with their green cloaks dove into the crowd, hands on their sword hilts, shouting for people to move aside. My heart pounded against my ribs as I fought my way through, hunched down, hoping to avoid attention.

"Nicoleta!" Rubia called from behind me. I spun around. We grasped each other's wrists. Rubia pulled me to the edge of the crowd, not far from the table where Marcus had traded apples for dried meat earlier. We crouched down behind a wagon laden with boxes of wool.

Rubia's fingers fumbled at her cloak's knot.

I put my shaking hand on hers, trying to stop her from giving me her cloak. Nervous energy made it almost impossible for me to speak. "Patridavan... g-guards... looking f-for... you."

"Everyone's attention was on me when I was struggling with the Getaen slave. They saw me throw the orange-sting. I'll never be able to get through the gates today." Rubia threw her cloak across my shoulders. "I'll return to the inn. They'll protect me. We need a place to hide you."

She poked her head over the wagon before crouching back down.

"I can't... I can't... " My breathing was shallow, and I struggled to form words. My skin crawled where Elek touched me. The edges of my vision started to blur. I frantically rubbed my wrists as if I could wipe away the touch of his hands.

Rubia slapped me across the cheek. I gasped, rocked back on my heels, and stared at her.

"Don't let an obstacle like that vermin merchant keep you from seeing your ultimate goal, Nicoleta. You have much to accomplish. This is just a hiccup. Rise above it!"

My cheek smarted. Rubia was right. I needed to be strong if I expected to ever make it to Capidava, let alone find a way to stop the plague.

Some merchants were closing up their shops. People were still shouting. Some had been hurt in the chaos. They were afraid. They'd been attacked. Patridava was one of the most heavily protected cities in the kingdom, but Rubia had risked an uproar to help me escape. I put my hand on my stomach, willing myself to calm.

Rubia closed her eyes, mumbling and shaking her head as she thought through our options. "We must separate. Immediately. With no friends to hide you here, it's only a matter of time until Elek has the Patridavan guards turning this place inside out for you. Obviously, he can't admit he tried to kidnap you. He'll say you stole something from him and demand compensation."

She paused, eyes darting back and forth across the sky, deep in thought. She lowered her gaze and focused on the road to the east. "Run to the eastern gate. I noticed local villagers using it to access the fields. There will be plenty of wagons headed that way this time of morning. Once out of the city, you'll have to skirt the fields and make your way back to the Emperor's Highway." She rummaged around in her satchel. "If you cannot find safe passage, hide in the woods until I pass by in two days. Two days. You've seen the risks of making a poor choice."

She pressed the gold nugget into my palm and slipped an orange vial into my satchel. "Just hold your breath and throw the vial on the ground if you need a diversion. If you get to Capidava before I catch up, find an inn near the Getaens. I'll find you."

Words failed me. Rubia acted more frightened for my safety than her own despite the fact that any witnesses would describe her as the attacker. I wrapped my arms around her neck. She hugged me back so hard it hurt my ribs.

"I'll be fine." I was glad my voice sounded more confident than I felt.

"Go, my daughter. Go!" She whispered as she shoved me into the street just ahead of a crowd of women pushing vendor carts away from the chaos. I was hidden from view from the crowd of merchants and the Thorns at the gate.

I wrapped my arms and Rubia's cloak around myself. The shouting behind me faded as I turned the corner and walked down a side alley. I paused, not able to see over the many buildings. Navigation on the Moesian hillside was simple. The Patridavan Valley was disorienting; it was like trying to find my way in a bowl.

I remembered Rubia's advice about hiding amid the farmers' wagons. I could follow them straight out of the city. I hurried back to a main road, shaking my head, frustrated with my mistake. Every moment mattered when it came to escaping a city.

I bit my lip at the memory of trying to escape the Lilac Plague in Moesia. We had been too late, the city gates closed, and it cost Mama her life.

My heart thumped. Should I run? Would that draw too much attention?

I placed myself among the wagons, horses, and farmers leaving for the fields. Two Patridavan guards on horseback pounded up the street. I couldn't take my eyes off their green cloaks and stern faces. They thundered past as they raced to the north gate. It wouldn't be long until the entire city knew about the attack and closed *all* gates. I had to get out before they questioned Elek, or I'd be swept up in the merchant's web of lies. We'd come so far; I refused to be caught now. Especially after Rubia jeopardized her own safety to help me escape Elek once already.

I picked up my pace. The initial rush of energy I'd felt earlier waned. Elek might appear around a corner, pointing me out with his ringed fingers. I shoved my pendant and its broken chain deep inside my satchel, out of view.

A horse clattered down the road, gaining on me. Was it a guard rushing an order to close the eastern gate? Not daring to turn back, I started running. What if it was Elek's slave? Would he try to kidnap me again?

I ducked into a narrow alley, hoping the horse and rider would pass by. Instead, they sped down the alley after me. The horse stopped and boots slammed onto the cobblestone street. I dug my fingers down into my satchel, clutching the orange-sting. I whirled to face my pursuer.

"Nicoleta." Marcus stood holding Velos' reins.

I had never been happier to see his face.

"Need an escort now?"

I couldn't tell if he was trying to be sarcastic or sincere. I didn't care. I wanted to say I was happy to see him, but it came out as a cough as I nodded frantically. The woman I'd seen yesterday on the horse had quickly maneuvered through the city to her destination. If I ever needed a horse, it was now.

Marcus slid his foot into the stirrup and mounted in one swift, sure motion. He slid back behind the saddle.

"Dagger." I held out my hands.

Without question, he handed over his blade.

Holding my apron aside, I slit my dress from knee to hem before giving back the blade. I put a foot in the stirrup and clasped his waiting hand. It was warm and strong, callused. He pulled me up in front of him. My skirts bunched up around my thighs, exposing my bare calves and ankles, even with the new slit in the front. At the moment, modesty was the least of my worries.

Marcus held one hand on the reins and the other firmly around my waist. The horse bounded out of the alley and onto the main cobblestone road. I gripped my satchel with one hand and the pommel with the other, trying to keep myself on the speeding horse.

As much as I wanted to see where we were going, I kept my head lowered, hoping people wouldn't be able to identify me later. It would put Marcus in even more danger if he were associated with Rubia and me.

Marcus navigated easily around the wagons in the street, but with every passing moment, I worried the city officials would close the gates and conduct a proper search. What would they do to us? What if Marcus was caught helping me? I gripped my satchel tighter, willing Velos to go faster.

The road curved, and the eastern gate came into view. My heart soared.

Marcus slowed Velos to a trot. Guards stood near the open gate, wagons still freely traveling.

"What is your business out of the city?" a guard asked.

I gripped my satchel until my fingernails turned white. Freedom was only an arm's reach away.

"My cousin is an apprentice Healer. I'm escorting her to Moesia to treat sick relatives," Marcus said.

"Healer? My wife has a cough. Anything for her?" the guard asked.

I wanted to kick him and ride away. Instead, I sunk my hand into my satchel, past the orb and vial, and found Rubia's wrapped herbs. I forced myself not to check the street behind me. I grabbed yellow grass and sage and thrust them toward the Thorn. Any moment, I expected the distant sound of soldiers on the cobblestones.

"S-steep these in b-boiling water... in w-water... " My stutter was thick. A flush raced up my chest to my neck. Not only would the guard remember me, but this was also Marcus' first time hearing my stutter. What would he think? I forced everything to the back of my mind except the words. "... in w-water to d-dilute... " My face contorted as I struggled to form the sounds. I hunched away from Marcus behind me. "... the tea."

"Nervous?" the guard asked, his hand sliding to his sword.

"She has a twisted tongue," Marcus replied, taking the herbs from my trembling hand and shoving them closer to the guard.

I gripped the pommel. Marcus was either not easily pulsed, or he already knew. Had Otho told him?

"Cursed tongue." The soldier spat on the ground. I flinched at the harsh words. I'd heard it whispered behind my back but never said so brazenly. Despite being high above the guard on a horse, I felt small as an ant.

Marcus pulled the herbs back a little. "We can keep the herbs if you're too good to take free medicine from a Healer."

Forget the insult. Let's go! I wanted to scream.

The guard glowered but took my herbs and waved us through.

As Velos trotted through the gates, relief flooded me. Marcus sped his horse to a gallop down the road between fields. I straightened my back and gripped the pommel. I couldn't let a Thorn's words rattle me. Things would only get more difficult for me in the future. I needed to be fierce, like Rubia, with skin like boiled armor where words wouldn't even leave a scratch, let alone a painful gash.

Over Marcus' shoulder at the Patridavan gate, figures in green arrived on horseback. Within moments, the gates started to close.

I let out a nervous laugh. This time, I hadn't been trapped inside the city to await disaster.

Odon came to me, asking for an amulet for a court noblewoman. I was happy for him until he explained the amulet should burn her skin whenever she blushed — to train her to only have eyes for him. I protested, pointing out that sometimes people flush when they're embarrassed, nervous, or ill.

He pressed a dagger to my throat and threatened me if I didn't comply. He's threatened other court officials but never me. I was stunned into silence. Assuming that was my sign of submission and agreement, he shoved me against the wall and left. I created the amulet and mourned for the Lady, but even more for my stupidity for thinking of Odon as a brother.

Would Cassus have defended me? The hollow feeling in my heart tells me he would not. They are much changed after returning from their training with their uncle. There are no traces of their mother's tenderness.

Odon apologized later, but I'm still wounded. The Lady will still suffer. I can't help but pity her inevitable confusion when she takes sick with fever and the amulet burns her flesh. Furthermore, Odon has learned nothing. He will make future demands, more threats. Either it's always this way with brothers, or perhaps they are no brothers of mine.

Last night, I dreamed of Getae. The smiling faces blurred by quickly. Laughter and sunshine beat down on my pink skin. Someone invited me to sit in the shade and sleep during the hot afternoon. I hadn't felt that content in a long time — at ease in my own skin. But the air grew too warm. I couldn't reach the shade. People beckoned me to join them, but with every step, they grew further away.

I woke in a cold sweat, awakened by someone in my chambers. I called out a spell, and thank the stars I didn't kill her right there. Next to my bed was warm water and mint leaves. The young servant fell to her knees and apologized. She'd heard me struggling in my dreams and brought me something to drink.

I apologized, which she readily accepted. Sanaz introduced herself as a new servant in Rupea. I didn't know what to say. Just hearing a kind voice took my breath away.

— VAHID, WARLOCK TO EMPEROR TRAJAN

CARACALLA

ELEVEN

MARCUS' AGREEMENT

Caravans trundled in the opposite direction, toward Patridava. I wondered how frustrated they'd be when they arrived at the closed gates. Few travelers were coming behind us, only those traveling around Patridava on their way to other provinces.

We still traveled in the relative safety of the valley, the city walls out of sight behind us. Before Patridava, I'd traveled with Marcus for almost a week, hardly speaking. And we fell back into the same habit.

I practiced talking to him in my mind.

Thank you for helping me.

Thank you for finding me and taking me out of the city just in time.

Thank you for not *turning me over to the guards for the terrible crime of buying a cloak that contaminated the entire area around me with decades-past-stale smoke.*

Marcus dismounted Velos, and I slid off the horse, onto the dirt road next to him.

My hip ached a little where I'd landed on the cobblestone street when I struggled against Elek. Given how hard I'd landed,

I expected to be painfully stiff. But although I could feel the tenderness, I felt surprisingly strong.

"Are you all right?" Marcus asked. "You can ride Velos."

I shook my head. Velos had galloped since leaving Patridava, and the poor horse was breathing hard.

"My legs are just s-stiff." I slipped over a few words. "I'll be fine."

Pain didn't register when I was trying to escape Elek's grasp. Everything had been a blur of terror and energy. Now I took inventory of my clothing. The right side was dirty and frayed. When Elek grabbed my cloak and I'd fallen in the square, I must have landed on my right side. When I'd slid on across the cobblestones, my dress tore in places, yet my skin was barely marred.

My hands stung. I pulled them close, inspecting the damage.

Marcus took my bright red hands in his, his brows furrowed. His rough hands emanated the heat from the day. My heart thumped, and I pulled away. Noticing my startled face, Marcus cleared his throat and tucked his hands behind him.

"Ah, sorry. I shouldn't have grabbed your hands like that. I just didn't realize you were injured." He took a step away from me.

I cupped my hands together, pulling them up to my chest. Behind us, a wagon wheel creaked, and distant voices echoed. Traveling slower meant we'd meet up with riders coming up behind us, and I wasn't ready to engage with strangers.

"Well, Velos needs to rest," Marcus said. As he pulled the reigns, his cloak shifted revealing his papa's guild pin.

I followed Marcus into the forest. Not far from the road, we passed a large pile of burned brush and tree limbs.

"Who did this, do you think?" I asked, pointing to the charred pile. I'd seen several in the valley already.

"The Patridavan Governor takes the safety of these roads very seriously," Marcus explained as he led Velos along a game track. "The Governor directs city taxes to road crews who clear brush and burn it. Soldiers monitor and free the roads of thieves and menacing wild animals in the area. The cleared brush makes it difficult for thieves to hide."

"And for... and for us, too." I glanced over my shoulder. The road was still completely visible.

As we walked, the sound of the rushing water intensified, and the foliage grew thicker. I scanned the area for movement but saw only leaves fluttering and two birds swooping from tree to tree. We passed through an opening between bushes and found ourselves on the rocky banks above the massive Dacian River.

Even this late in the summer, the river was still wide and swift. I imagined in the springtime, it would rage, filling up the entire riverbed and engulfing all of the smooth rocks on the steep embankment.

Marcus dropped Velos' reigns near tall grasses at the edge of the water line. While Velos grazed, I sat on the rocks and checked my hands. I expected to have dozens of tiny pebbles and bits of dirt embedded into my palms, but it looked like they were simply dirty and flushed red; instead of injuries shouting for my attention but felt only tired and shaky.

Marcus's shadow fell across my hands. He handed me his waterskin. "The water will do you good."

"Thanks," I said flatly. His constant advice about the most basic things irritated me. I lifted my bruised water gourd for him to see, already filled from the city well this morning.

He turned to leave. I knew he meant well and had probably saved my life in Patridava, so I forced myself to speak.

"I appreciate your concern." I flushed with embarrassment and took a breath. "I just wanted to rest for a moment."

Marcus was quiet as he studied my face. Would he give me more ill-considered advice or tips on how to not stutter? Or worse, accuse me of a tongue cursed by Zalmoxis?

"May I sit with you?" Marcus asked.

Rubia's words echoed in my mind: *Marcus is dangerous.*

But he'd been nothing but honorable, if a little cold. I waved to the spot next to me. The simple act of letting Marcus sit next to me, close enough to smell the fear sweat that had dried on my skin and clothes, was an act of trust. We were alone for the first time. What if he decided to hurt me for disrespecting his father or for not talking to him for days? Marcus was bigger and stronger than I. My thoughts flashed back to Elek's clammy hands gripping mine, and I shuddered.

"Are you feeling well?" Marcus looked into my eyes. He'd never done that before. I told myself he would never act like Elek, would never lay his hands on me in anger.

"It's nothing." I broke eye contact and looked away. My feelings stormed inside, and I wanted to keep everyone away, including Marcus. Still, he'd helped me, and I was grateful.

I repeated what I wanted to say several times in my head, but it was difficult to concentrate between the stinging on my hands and the butterflies in my stomach.

"Thank you..." I said.

"For sitting with you? It's the least I could do." Marcus tried to finish my thoughts.

I shook my head. "Thank you for getting me out of the city." My rehearsed words sounded flat, not filled with the gratitude I felt.

I watched Marcus as he idly plucked stones from near our feet and tossed them into the river. Beads of sweat had formed on his brow. I savored the heat from his body next to mine. Despite Rubia's words, I trusted Marcus. Without her watching my every move, I was free to stumble through my words and make mistakes. What harm could there be in trying to be honest, not about the Guardianship but with who I was?

"I never would've made it out of P-Patridava alone. Why d-did you help? I thought you hated me?" I spoke unrehearsed words.

"I didn't hate you." Marcus shook his head. "I thought you were a rich snob looking down on us mere farmers."

Yes, I was the daughter of an Azure scholar while he was a farmer. But that was before Papa was imprisoned, which was far more than a blemish on the Aurelian name. I hadn't dared ask Marcus if he owned land or was owned by it. And he wasn't base enough to share it, though his clothing was a little too fine for a Poppy. Either way, if Papa was accused of treason and I was a fugitive, I didn't know what that meant for me — certainly nothing good. My stomach twisted. At best, according to Rubia's designs, I would be a servant, a Poppy, tied to Rupea Castle. I suspected that would place me far lower than Marcus. In Elek's hands, I would have been a slave, the hot brand on my neck. I winced.

Marcus paused his stone throwing. "I assumed you were someone you weren't. I'm sorry."

His words about my apparent snobbery hadn't offended me. The thought of a brand terrified me.

"On the trip b-before, from Moesia, I'm sorry I was quiet. I had things to say, I just... " What reason could I give for my aloof behavior? I found him annoying and intriguing at the same time. But I had a million other things on my mind. And I liked that he thought I was a normal girl whose face didn't scrunch up when she tried to speak.

I tried to smile, but it felt false. I glanced at Velos who seemed well rested and was contentedly munching grass. I was anxious to get moving again.

"Rubia explained some things last night," Marcus said.

"Why did you meet with her?" I sat up straighter, suspecting that Rubia never planned to mention their meeting.

"After you left the bathhouse, I noticed something glinting on the rocks, right where you were, um, arranging yourself. I knew whoever it belonged to would be frantic about the gold. So I waited outside the bathhouse with it. Sure enough, Rubia returned, a wild look in her eyes." He grinned. "I think she felt like she owed me a conversation."

Marcus picked up a flat rock and sent it skipping across the river's surface, and I imagined his arm wrapping around my waist again. *Don't be ridiculous!*

Marcus held out another flat rock to me, his smile turning playful. I took the stone and flicked my wrist, happy it made a respectable four skips across the surface before sinking into the water.

"Rubia explained you had something weighing on your mind. She said not to judge you too harshly because there were things about you I didn't know."

Yes, that I'm a half-Getaen Guardian on my way to infiltrate Rupea Castle and discover my treasonous Papa's fate. Oh, and don't forget: I need to find the heir of Odon and stop the plague.

"I wish you would've just told me about your stutter," Marcus said.

I swallowed my laugh and pathetically covered the resulting snort with a cough. Of all the things Rubia was alluding to, my stutter was not one of them.

"Did Rubia tell you about my s-stutter?" I asked, trying to sound casual.

"No, she kept things brief." He chuckled.

"Sounds like her." I pictured Rubia with her lips tight, giving Marcus the minimum time she felt she owed him. Marcus hadn't known about my stutter until he'd heard it at the gate. I never would've guessed that he was reacting to my stutter for the first time. I chewed the inside of my cheek.

Marcus was a good liar.

Marcus looked at me. "She said you were a loyal, kind person."

At his words, it hit me: Rubia had given me a chance to escape while she stayed behind. Yes, I had known her plan, but only now had my mind quieted to let it sink in. "That wasn't supposed to h-happen."

"I'm sorry I wasn't closer," he said. "To help. When I came to look for you, you were gone. And then I saw the orange cloud, and... I knew you were both in trouble."

I shot to my feet, rubbing my arms. My fingers found the rip in my sleeve. The entire seam was torn from the top of my shoulder, across the front, and to the armpit. Only a few stitches were still intact. Three years of embroidering and a greedy merchant destroyed my dress with one violent yank. Even if I stitched the sleeve back together, the repairs would be a constant reminder of what happened in Patridava.

"Do you want to talk about it?" Marcus asked.

Elek's face flashed in my mind. I closed my eyes and put the heels of my hands to my eyelids, trying to wipe the memory away. How could I tell Marcus I was almost kidnapped and enslaved? I was humiliated, terrified, furious.

"It's fine. We don't have to talk," he said, his voice soft as if settling a skittish animal.

I opened my eyes. Marcus had taken a step back with his hands out. Velos was a few paces behind him.

Voices sounded over the river, and we both spun toward the noise. The birds had fallen silent. People were coming closer. Not up the road, but up the river bank.

Grasping the gold nugget Rubia gave me, my only resource for food, travel, and safety, I held it out to Marcus in my open palm. "Are you willing to earn this honestly and take me to Capidava?"

"Don't ask me to take you to Capidava," Marcus said, his voice tight. "Ask me to take you back to Moesia, instead. Anywhere else."

I shook my head. There was nothing for me in Moesia. "Either you take me to Capidava, or I will go alone or wait for Rubia." The gold nugget glinted in the sun. "If you won't take me, I'll understand. We can part amicably."

"Guards heavily patrol the entire valley." Marcus stepped back, grabbed Velos' reins, and led the horse up the steep embankment as if ending the conversation.

I scrambled up the rocks, away from the river. I had a sinking feeling that Marcus would wave goodbye and wish me luck. It was too much to hope that he'd take me through thief-infested terrain to the capital.

Marcus mounted Velos. "You'd never survive out here for two days, waiting for Rubia, with the guards patrolling."

I sucked in a breath.

"I can't have that on my conscience." He held out his hand to help me up. "I'll take you to Capidava."

SWEAT DRIPPED DOWN MY BACK, the sun at midday. Marcus and I walked more than we rode, not wanting to overtax the horse that would take us the two long days to Capidava. Road dust coated the bottom six inches of my ankle-length skirt. With only my satchel and Marcus' two saddlebags strapped to Velos, we passed lumbering caravans on the road north. One of them had twenty wagons strung together with mercenaries strategically placed in front, back and, I guessed, hidden inside. They were armed, and the scars and wary looks told me they'd seen plenty of blood. But the focused mercenaries didn't frighten me — it was those who seemed to look through me like I was dead that sent a chill down my spine. I wondered what would be worse, traveling with mercenaries or meeting the bandits the mercenaries guarded against.

When we'd traveled before, Rubia had successfully directed all questions to Otho who had eagerly obliged with long-winded stories. I'd heard all about Otho's adventures and only now realized he'd not told us much of substance. I knew he was a guild farmer from his pin and that they lived in a valley in the north. But I'd have to reference a map, which I didn't have, to locate Rodnic. I knew Marcus was Otho's son, but I didn't know if they had other children. The only conversation of real significance, I'd overheard by accident by the river. I had no idea what was really important to Marcus or his family. The old man was more secretive than I gave him credit for.

"When you came to find me in P-Patridava, what was your p-plan? You were headed east then home, but now you're taking me to the capital. What did your father have to say about losing his r-revenue for the late summer?" The sun sapped too much of my energy to care about my stutter.

"It didn't take me long to convince him." Marcus walked on the other side of Velos, but I noticed him touch the guild pin.

"Your father agreed to ab-bandoning your route to help a stranger?"

"Yes. My father is a shrewd businessman. You've seen that side of him. He has a family to support, but even if we weren't around, he'd still do it. He loves farming, and he loves the sound of coins when they stack up."

"I recall his love of coins." I was still annoyed with him raising his rates when we were clearly in distress. Still, I knew Marcus didn't approve of his father's mercenary bargaining practices.

"My father saw an opportunity to give two wealthy women from Moesia a trip to Patridava. But what really interested him was the fact that you were so jittery. He was going to take you anyway because he likes company. That you were in obvious trouble only increased his interest and gave him all the more reason to bring you with us."

I frowned. Rubia and I were running for our lives, and Otho found it entertaining. Not only that, but he'd charged us triple for his own amusement.

"I thought you were going to say he felt sorry for us."

Marcus shook his head. "I didn't like his tactics, but I must respect him. For all he knew, Rubia was a Lily trying to avoid paying taxes to the Emperor."

If that were only the truth.

"My father didn't think that it would cost you so dear. His heart isn't as cold as the coins. You should see him around my sisters. He dotes on them all, but especially the oldest."

"Why is that?" I gave Velos a grateful pat, despite the sweat on his flank. The longer we walked, the hotter the day grew, and the wilder the forest became. The burn piles were further apart and the undergrowth was less maintained.

"Well, she's clever, beautiful, and hard-working. She's unlikely to ever wed."

I cocked my head to the side. Why would this eligible sister not wed? And why was Marcus comparing her to me?

"When my sister, Mara, was young, she was thrown off a horse. She was knocked unconscious and broke her arm. Mara was a distance from the house, and confused, she wandered off in the wrong direction. No one found her for hours. By then, her arm was beyond repair. It was amputated below the elbow. Velos is the only horse she's comfortable riding now."

That was why Otho didn't want to part with his horse for the Emperor. Because of his daughter.

"The men in our village decided long ago she wasn't a practical choice for a farmer's wife. It is a physical job filled with mending, baking, milking, tending to children, and a thousand other difficult tasks. They judged her without giving her time to learn to work around her missing arm. You should see her now, Nicoleta. She's amazing. You'd love her. She's smart and learned to do everything from thatch roof repair to baking the most amazing apple crumb pie."

Marcus meant for his words to be kind, but they wrapped around and crushed me. It was good his sister was able to adapt, but not everyone could learn to work around their imperfections. I tried to make my stutter go away, and it wouldn't. I would never have a silver tongue, never be able to speak my mind on an impulse. I detested when Rubia or Papa suggested that I could.

I slowed my pace. Marcus was just like everyone else, thinking my stutter was something I could overcome. Another encouraging little speech. Another person telling me that my stutter would make me a stronger person. But I hated the stutter. I *was* the stutter.

"Nicoleta?" Marcus turned, realizing I was stalled behind him.

I wanted to scream in frustration.

"I need a b-break." I backed toward the edge of the highway. I'd had nothing but space for years, and suddenly I had no privacy, not even to check my body for scrapes and bruises after my scuffle with Elek.

"You just said you didn't want that last caravan to overtake us. Something about creepy and —"

"Y-you're just l-like... " My face contorted in the ugliest way, but I didn't stop. I pushed through. I wanted Marcus to see the true me, to be disgusted. "Just l-like, Rubia!"

"Your mother?"

"She's not my mother!" I screamed. I stormed away from him, past an overgrown pile of brush. Brambles tugged at my skirt, but I ignored them. I couldn't get away from Marcus fast enough. I was not like his sister. I was just me.

At the river, I plunged my hands into the cold, soothing water. My frustration threatened to boil over into tears, and that made me even angrier. I wasn't sad. I was mad. I couldn't talk to anyone the way I wanted to. Why had Zalmoxis cursed me?

I splashed water on my face, letting it trickle down, soothing my burning forehead and cheeks. Marcus sat next to me. His hand went to rest on my shoulder, but he paused before touching me and pulled back.

I took a deep breath. Marcus had tried to connect with me by telling me something honest about his family, and I had exploded. I was behaving like a child. Mama and Rubia had been right not to trust me with the orb sooner. I pressed my hands deeper, letting the chill waters run over my skin, calming me.

"I'm sorry. I have no excuse. That anger is from something else. Not you," I said, my voice barely above a whisper.

"I'm glad you let down your walls," Marcus said. "My sister's challenge is highly visible. She can't hide from hers like you try and hide yours." He cleared his throat. "Like I hide mine."

"You have struggles?" I thought of his perfect life: two living parents, neither with treasonous backgrounds, his perfect voice, no terrors in his dreams, and wanted by his guild. I lifted my hands out of the water and pressed them against my face, welcoming the cold.

"Everyone has challenges, Nicoleta. Everyone. We can never judge someone's whole life, all their challenges, by how they look on the outside." Marcus paused. "And perhaps a flaw in one person's eyes is actually a strength. Perhaps that unique thing is what makes that person *them*. And they just need people to accept them as they are. Perhaps people need to embrace what makes them different."

My stutter — could I accept it? The idea was novel, but it struck true.

"Hey!" Marcus laughed and flicked water on me, taking me out of my reverie.

I shied away, surprised. Marcus was always reserved. And now what was this? Silliness?

I didn't like the way I'd been acting — brooding, cold, and focused on my burdens. I wanted to start over and accept Marcus' goodwill. My burdens, the orb, Papa, all of that would not simply vanish because I let myself relax and enjoy a moment in the afternoon sunshine.

I leaned forward, refilling my gourd. With a sudden twist, I splashed him with ten times the water he'd flicked on me.

I laughed and jumped to my feet, hoping to avoid retaliation. "We should go. Caravans and all."

"Of course you say that now." He had a mischievous glint in his eye I'd never seen before. "Come on, Velos." He jogged over to the horse. "You've had enough grass for now."

We walked back to the road, and I couldn't help staring at him, seeing him differently. Now what was he? A friend?

As a child, I had friends in Moesia. The plague took too many people, not caring about age or status. I started taking care of Papa, and my stutter shut me away from others — an invisible wall I couldn't break down.

Marcus caught me staring at him. I blinked and looked ahead.

"I'm hungry. Want to eat while we walk?" he asked.

"Good idea." Though Rubia still had our fish and vegetables with her. Fortunately, there were late summer berries and broad-leaved spectus plants along the side of the road. The berries were delicious. I hated the spectus' bitter roots, but they'd store in my satchel for days.

Marcus held out a skewer of spiced meat to me.

I didn't know what to say, but my mouth watered.

"It's not fresh apples or oats, but it'll keep your strength up. Consider it part of the deal. We'll travel the rest of the day by foot until we reach the watering hole at the edge of the Patridava Valley late this afternoon. We should arrive in Capidava the day after tomorrow."

As Marcus placed the skewer in my hand, the heat from his fingertips buzzed up my arm. *Marcus is a necessary travel companion. No distractions. No distractions!*

I bit into a piece of meat and savored the taste. When Marcus bought the meat this morning, I never would have guessed that I'd be eating it.

"How did you know how to find me in P-Patridava? A-after the attack?" I asked.

"I had quick words with my father and took Velos. I recognized Rubia's shawl over her head as she was leaving the area. She told me where you were headed. Once I had her safely back to the outskirts of the Getaen community, I rode to find you."

"I've b-been worried sick about her, w-wondering if she got away."

Marcus winced. "I should have mentioned that earlier."

"Yes, you should have told me sooner, b-but i-information gets mixed up when you're in a hurry," I said, repeating what Papa had told me so many times in his painstaking research.

"At least I earned Rubia's trust in the end," Marcus said.

"What do you mean?"

"She went to great lengths to keep us apart for the entire journey. Didn't you notice?" Marcus shrugged. "Even when I was your only option from Patridava, she still hesitated. Why is that?"

"Don't read too much into that. She is c-constantly moving and likes to keep me b-busy as well." I left out the part about Rubia thinking Marcus was dangerous. She was a paranoid mama sometimes, and Marcus had never shown a sliver of a dangerous side. "B-Besides, why would you care? You swore not to speak to me."

"That was when I thought you were a snob." Marcus waved his hand and did a grand bow.

I laughed. *Look at me now, as fancy as an urchin from the Fissure.*

Marcus changed the subject. "The watering hole will be busy. It's on the border of the Patridavan Valley, and most everyone stops there, traveling both north and south. There is a large concentration of thieves after the watering hole. That's where we'll need to be cautious. Most of the traffic has merged on the Highway, and it's ripe pickings in the unpatrolled forest."

I dipped my hand into my satchel again, feeling for the orb. Rubia would expect me to put the key first. It was easy to travel with Marcus, and he had been honorable, but I couldn't completely depend on him. He didn't know what was at stake. I had to think ten steps ahead like Rubia.

Marcus strode with a calm confidence. I wanted to place all of my faith in him, but Rubia hadn't, and I couldn't either. I dreaded talking to other merchants; I didn't want to have another Elek incident. Still, at the watering hole, I had to be on alert for other options.

Sanaz revealed she is half-Getaen. She colored her hair dark brown in hopes of finding work at the castle. She said it was a relief to tell me. She has felt so isolated and alone, and she hasn't even been in Rupea Castle for a year. She doesn't know how I've survived.

She confessed the Getaens hate me for serving the Emperor, and yet they also hope that I'll find a way to make their lives better. At first, it hurt to be despised by a people who I've always cherished. They don't know me. But Sanaz has softened my pain, helped me feel more connected to my people.

Though I know not how to accomplish their hopes, I do know I must live for something beyond myself.

— VAHID, WARLOCK TO EMPEROR TRAJAN CARACALLA

TWELVE

THE WHITE CLOAK

I savored the last drops of water from my gourd and wiped my brow. How much further to the watering hole? The highway grew busier with every road we passed, side roads that led to other provinces around the kingdom and beyond. Since leaving Moesia, the visceral new sights, smells, and sounds had awakened a part of me. I understood more of Mama's excitement in planning each excursion. Though fascinating as it was, my worry about Papa never left the back of my mind.

Pounding hooves sounded behind us, traveling fast. My chest tightened until they thundered by. It was two riders on horseback with no visible cargo except for the swords and daggers at their hips.

I struggled to decide how much to divulge to Marcus. He and I needed to quickly part ways in Capidava. As a friend, I didn't want him caught up in our trouble. But what information could I share with someone Rubia deemed 'dangerous?'

Marcus spit out the mint leaves he'd been chewing on and pointed ahead. "Up there is the watering hole. And more importantly, the official end of the Patridavan Valley and the Governor's protections."

A wagon poked out from the thickening forest. As we drew closer, I spotted several more. Horses neighed, and people's voices rang out. As much as I longed to rest, part of me dreaded converging with a crowd of people.

"Bring me the tin cups!" Someone instructed in a brash, reverberating voice.

"I'll wait here amongst the wagons." I pulled up the hood of Rubia's cloak. "I'll be out of the way, and it'd be b-best if people didn't see me talking to you."

"Try to stand where we can at least see each other," Marcus said.

I waited on the outskirts, watching travelers rearrange and secure their supplies in the back of their wagons. It was difficult to see through the trees, and I lost track of Marcus. I moved toward the river, attempting to keep him in sight. I also wanted to investigate my options for traveling north. Around a few more wagons, the forest opened up a bit. Either the Patridavan Governor kept this area clear of underbrush, or it was trampled by too many feet.

A wide stream fed into the Dacian River, the current wild and fast where they joined together. The water cut downstream past large boulders and rippled past me. Part of the river spun out, creating a natural pool, easily accessible to horses. Upstream of the pool, travelers filled their water containers and washed their faces. I counted two dozen horses and more than fifty travelers.

I'd hoped to see more plants to eat on the journey but found nothing. Deeper in the forest, travelers secured tarps and blanket rolls. I hesitated to dig around where strangers set up camp.

Some of the strangers were engaging in conversation,

shouting over the sound of the river. But most were like Marcus, silently going about their business. I searched for a trustworthy face, but I didn't see a spark of warmth among the rough travelers.

The longer I scanned the area, the more wary I became. There were few women in sight, while mercenaries and merchants were thick. I headed back to where Marcus left me.

Halfway back, I paused. I was alone for the moment except for a couple of horses. I pulled up the back of my dress and inspected my legs. Given how hard I had hit against Elek's carriage, I expected to have purpling bruises. Instead, I found only slight tenderness. Checking over my shoulder, making sure I was still alone, I pulled my dress up further, inspecting my thigh. One spot was red and warm to the touch but otherwise uninjured.

A sneeze nearby caused me to drop my hem. I clutched my satchel, one hand closing around the orange-sting inside. I scanned the wagons until my eyes settled on the finest carriage I'd ever seen, covered with an impractical satin canopy. A woman with delicate features and golden skin leaned forward into view. Ignoring me, she leaned out the window as a servant came bustling over. The woman's glossy, chestnut brown hair didn't reach her shoulders. Her dangling earrings grazed her bare collarbones. Her sweeping neckline not only showed her collarbones but half her shoulders as well. I'd never seen clothing or hair like hers, but most interesting was the wide, stiff band she wore against her forehead, almost like a crown. The beads glinted in the sunlight, and several small feathers adorned the side.

When the servant moved away from the carriage door, I noticed a circular seal with a crest and crown emblazoned in gold. The Emperor's Seal.

I stepped back, feeling exposed. What if she'd heard what

had happened to Elek? Had other merchants made it out of Patridava, before the gates closed, who knew about the *incident?* Marcus and I had traveled quickly but by foot most of the way. Word of the magical attack might have arrived before we did.

I took a breath and told myself that any of the merchants who left before us, wouldn't have noticed us. The gates were probably still closed from this morning's incident. Even so, I slunk behind a nearby wagon. The carriage door slammed, and I peeked around to see a wiry man dressed in black. I sucked in a breath. I'd seen that clothing one time before. In the raid. He marched straight toward me. I huddled down and pressed myself against the wagon, the vial slick in my damp hand, waiting for him to pass by.

The black-clad guard stopped in front of me. For an agonizing heartbeat, I waited for him to pull out his sword.

"Lady Katalin would like to speak with you," the man said. This close, I noticed the edge of his sleeve was trimmed the color of blood orange.

"M-me?" The only noble I'd spoken to before was Gallus. And that didn't go well. *Please let this be a mistake. I can't talk to a noble. She is more likely to remember me. What if she knows Elek?*

He continued, his voice raised. "Hurry and stand up, girl. The Lady has asked to speak with you."

I wrestled with my mind; the primal part of me screamed to curl up into a ball. The other part of me recognized that disobeying a noble had consequences. That was the last thing I needed. I forced myself to release the orange-sting inside my satchel, wanting to save it for future perils. I strained to straighten up, determined to get this over quickly.

The guard marched me back to the carriage with the imperial seal.

"A walk will do me good," Lady Katalin said. The man

opened her door, and she descended with a flourish. I wanted to stare at the feathers in the band across her head, but I kept my gaze down. She beckoned for me to join her.

I'd walked all day, and my legs ached, but I stayed silent. *I am not memorable.*

"It feels nice to stretch one's legs, doesn't it?" she said, her feathers bobbing up and down as she walked. She lifted her vibrant dress so it wouldn't drag, showing too much leg and ornate shoes that would cause a blister after walking from here to the watering hole and back.

"Yes." Best to keep my answers short and agreeable.

Lady Katalin looked only a few years older than me, but an air of nobility radiated from her every movement.

"Are you traveling from Patridava?" She managed to look down her nose at me, even though I was taller.

I clutched my satchel tighter and followed Rubia's example of staying close to the truth when possible.

"Yes, my lady. We are traveling to the capital."

The Lady sniffed and lightly touched the side of her nose, which irritated me because I'd just bathed yesterday.

"Very good. I was traveling to a city in the east, Burridava, but I was turned away on the road. The Lilac Plague struck. I cannot believe I wasted two days on this wretched road to visit with the master of their trade guild, only to be sent back as if I were some... messenger." Her sharp voice was laced with annoyance. "And if the Guild Master dies, it will delay our trade deals for moons. I won't be able to report success to the Emperor until next spring."

A shock went through me. The plague was two days from here? Memories of the Lilac Plague in Moesia flooded my mind. The wasting away, the blisters. Mama assuring me I was immune. I'd delivered water to everyone I could. Day and night, day and night. My parents had sequestered themselves. *That* morning, so deceptively beautiful. The one where I found boils on Mama's face, her fingers tinged grey. Her screams with each bursting blister, her nails clawing the air. With the sleeping draught and pain remedies, she only moaned.

"I had hoped to salvage the trip with a visit to the Governor of Patridava." Lady Katalin's words blurred.

There were a few moments when Mama seemed to recognize me. She had reached out to me with her frail, gray hands. I couldn't touch her because the delicate boils covering her body threatened to burst with the slightest brush. The sadness in her eyes had taken my breath away. It gutted me that I couldn't hold her hand or even braid her hair. She tried to speak — even her throat was blistered. I sang her Getaen lullabies. My voice was clear. And I was grateful because those songs were the last thing she heard. Even now, my throat grew thick as I remembered her feeble attempts to smile, trying to bring me comfort despite her agony. No one should die that way.

"But I hear the Patridavan gates are closed. Is it true?" Lady Katalin frowned.

"Excuse me?" I could barely process her words, memories of the plague fighting for my attention.

"Patridava. The gates. Are they closed? Did a witch attack?" Her words were clipped.

I gripped my satchel strap harder, my fingernails digging into the palms of my hands. She wanted gossip? I roiled inside. How could she be so calloused about the plague? All she saw was her mild inconvenience, not people's suffering. The families torn apart. The heartache that would never heal.

I was rooted to the ground, my hands balled into fists around my satchel strap.

"Why are you stopping?" She pursed her lips. "Come along," she added as if I were a misbehaving puppy.

I forced myself to put one foot in front of the other. Lady

Katalin's fine brows pulled together, making her look like a child about to throw a tantrum. I shoved aside my thoughts of the plague. I could never help the people who needed me if I displeased this noblewoman and ended up in the stocks, or worse.

"The gates were closed. B-But will likely re-open soon, my lady," I cleared my throat, giving me time to think through my next response. "There was trouble at the gate with a merchant."

I was pleased with myself for not stuttering bad enough for her to notice.

"A merchant? No, no. It couldn't be from a merchant. You must have heard the rumor from a low-born source." Her animated hands cut through the air. "I heard it was the plague or the work of a witch."

We circled around and headed back toward her carriage. I focused on the seal on her door, willing an end to the vexing conversation.

"You were inspecting this area. You seem an observant girl. A girl like you would have to be to survive, I suppose." She touched my ripped sleeve and then rubbed her fingertips together like she was trying to get the residue of the lower classes off of her.

I'd forgotten about the rip of my sleeve and the tears in my dress. Lady Katalin probably assumed I was an abused slave, obedient only to a whip. I promised myself never to look down on a slave the way this woman looked at me. Lady Katalin's eyes tactlessly searched below my ear for the slave's brand. For the first time today, I was glad my sweaty hair was down, obscuring her view. Let her wonder all she wanted if I were a slave. She couldn't know unless she demanded it. And a lady like herself would never deign to ask anything about me. I inwardly smiled at my small victory.

"It's not the plague, I can assure you." As I said it, Elek's gray hand flashed into my mind. I felt uneasy at my own confident, reassuring words. His injury did come from the orb, and it had warlock magic I didn't yet understand. Inexplicably, Elek's hand did appear like it had been struck by the plague.

"Quite." Lady Katalin's shoulders relaxed. "Patridava is a clean city. The Lilac Plague falls upon dirty, lowborn towns, of course. If only you would keep yourselves clean, you wouldn't bring it upon yourselves. There's a river right over there, and you can't be bothered to bathe. It is fortunate you have others overseeing the Kingdom on your behalf."

I clenched my teeth, listening to the filth that poured from her lips as if anyone had done anything to *deserve* the Lilac Plague. I itched to pull out the orange-sting and throw it at her. I needed to resolve this conversation before I was tempted to waste Rubia's potion on someone so worthless and condemn myself in the process.

"I'm sure the P-Patridava guards will let you in when they see the Emperor's Seal," I said. "The city hasn't been hit with the p-plague. And it wasn't a mage's f-fault the gates were closed."

Lady Katalin closed her eyes and shuddered. Under her breath, she complained, "Those Getaen witches are savages at heart. Dark witches. I cannot believe the Emperor still keeps them at his side."

My insides twisted at the thought of blame being placed on Rubia. How dare anyone refer to her as a dark witch? Clearly, this woman didn't understand magic. It was a tool to be wielded by those who studied it.

"It *was* a merchant who caused the scuffle," I repeated, frustrated she wouldn't believe me.

I looked straight ahead at her carriage, envisioning it enveloped in fire, burning to the ground. Perhaps with her inside.

"Did you see the scuffle yourself?" Katalin asked.

My mouth went dry. The Lady was powerful. If she suspected I was lying, I would be in grave danger. At the same time, I didn't want to place myself at the scene.

A hand touched my arm. My heart leapt into my throat before realizing it was Marcus. He led Velos by the reins behind him.

"Can I help you, my lady?" Marcus said, with a deep bow.

"Lady Katalin." She introduced herself with a demure nod. She did a subtle movement with her fingers. Near her carriage, her guard had his hand on his hilt, but he stood still.

When Lady Katalin looked up at Marcus, her eyes sparkled. She glanced at the guild pinned on his camasa then up to his face. Rugged travel suited him, making him even more handsome and slightly dangerous looking.

"Marcus Constantin of the Rodnic Valley," he responded. Without a wagon, he looked more like a mysterious man of means rather than a farmer.

Lady Katalin leaned forward, her eyes meeting his. His hands could easily wrap around her tiny waist. Facing each other, they looked like a natural fit. Marcus was just tall enough that her head would nestle on his shoulder nicely.

My stomach lurched. How could I think Marcus would be with anyone as horrid as this vapid woman? Even if she was impressively gorgeous and rich and noble. Katalin's perfect rose-colored lips curved into a smile of such coquettish perfection I knew I was awkward and doltish next to her.

"Constantin." She tested Marcus' family name on her tongue. "Your servant was most helpful in conveying information on Patridava. I am a trade ambassador to Emperor Cassus VII. I was traveling to Burridava but was diverted away by peasant rumors of the Lilac Plague. So instead, I decided to visit the Governor of Patridava to discuss extending a trade route and, of course, sample the most delicious tarts. His clever wife instructs the kitchen staff to create them in the shape of a frog." She licked her lip like a cat at a bowl of milk.

I wanted to smack her, but Marcus' face brightened at the words "trade route." His hand dropped away from my arm just as another of the Lady's well-dressed servants appeared. He led two matched bay geldings into the traces of the lady's carriage and started fastening them in. They were easily fourteen hands high and so dark they were almost black.

"Interesting," Marcus said. "I would like to discuss more, but I understand you're in a hurry. You'll be traveling in the dark, arriving in Patridava well past midnight."

I inwardly groaned. Couldn't he just get this conversation over with so we could leave this infuriating place?

"I, too, would love nothing more than to continue our discussion." Lady Katalin waved to her black-clad guard, who rushed to her side. She whispered in his ear, and he marched back to the carriage.

"If you visit Capidava, please stop by my estate in the Rose Court," Lady Katalin said as her guard returned, handing her a white fur cloak. "This cloak will grant you access through all the gates. More importantly, while you don't have the Emperor's seal, you may have mine. I dare say it will protect you for this dangerous leg of the journey."

She held out the cloak, and Marcus took it. Her hand rested on his forearm for too long before she slid her hand down, across his fingers. She then pointed at the crest on the cloak, a circle emblazoned with a fox on the front, the same blood-orange color of the trim on the guard's sleeve, and gold leaves filigreed around it.

"This is too generous. I cannot accept," Marcus said.

Lady Katalin ran a finger over her silken hair and batted her long eyelashes. The afternoon sun beat down on us, but she didn't break a sweat.

"I'm lending my seal in exchange for the information on Patridava. You may lend my cloak to your servant. It is wise to protect your *belongings*. Return it to me in Capidava at your convenience." She smiled before sauntering back to her carriage.

I clenched my jaw, afraid if I opened my mouth that I would stutter through a tirade of insults. How did Rubia ever manage to hold back her biting tongue? I ran my fingertips across the misshapen orb at the bottom of my satchel. With the stakes this high, Rubia would stay silent.

Skin of armor. Like the Patridavan guard, I couldn't let Lady Katalin's words hurt me. They definitely couldn't stop me. Suffering the plague was much worse. I tempered myself.

Still, I hoped Marcus would correct her. I was paying *him* to escort me. As far as he knew, I was an Azure. Not his servant. Certainly not a slave.

Marcus mounted Velos, folded the white cloak, and laid it grandly in front of him. Lady Katalin stared out her carriage after him, fanning herself delicately. She didn't even look at me, her full attention on Marcus. He didn't scoot back for me. Marcus clicked his heels against Velos' sides, and rode back to the highway, leaving me to scuttle behind him.

I POUNDED my fist into my thigh. How could I have thought Marcus might be a friend? I was a fool. As long as he delivered me to Capidava, that's all that mattered. He only rode Velos briefly before walking next to me again, but it was too late. He'd revealed a side of him I wished I had never seen.

I was a dirty, tired wretch while Lady Katalin was a Rose, as she so astutely pointed out. Well, she may have been on an errand from the capital, but I was on a mission set seven generations ago by a warlock and the Blood Conqueror. I would not be shaken.

Marcus was a means to an end. I wouldn't ever see him again after tomorrow night. The orb, the treasure, the curse — as a Guardian, untangling these were more important than my hurt or Lady Katalin's barbs. They were definitely more important than fickle Marcus.

Marcus walked next to me, leading Velos, but we seemed further apart than ever. I stewed, and every moment stretched uncomfortably, seeming to last for days. Not even birds dared to break our crushing silence.

"We should make camp for the night," Marcus said. "There'll be little traffic here from the north. Most people will go straight to the watering hole when they're this close. Not many thieves around here either, so close to the resting spot where travelers could band together."

Marcus guided Velos off the road and into the forest. "Tomorrow, we will watch for travelers also headed to Capidava. We'll find an amiable group to join."

But what if no friendly caravan arrived? I wanted to ask. Friends seemed unlikely after what I saw at the watering hole and in Patridava. And what would we do if Elek and his army of servants, slaves, and paid mercenaries caught up to us? Even more, I wanted to ask Marcus why he was helping me at all.

My body ached for sleep from walking most of the day and carrying my satchel and water gourd. I couldn't afford to waste the remaining sunlight by collapsing as I longed to. I had to search for edible plants. I found only more bitter spectus. I yanked the plant by the base, the roots not wanting to be wiggled free. In the end, I won. I didn't recognize most of the plants this far north, giving me few options to forage. The delicious carrots and turnips of Patridava sounded perfect right now.

"I'll take the first watch tonight," Marcus said. Was he trying to seem generous after how he acted with Katalin? Or did he not think I was suited for the task?

I snatched the white cloak off Velos and stomped over to a fallen tree. The temperature dropped fast when the sun dipped below the horizon. I threw the cloak on a bed of moss next to the tree, plopped down, and leaned back on the rough bark.

"You probably shouldn't get that dirty," Marcus said.

"Someone as fine as Lady Katalin has many b-beautiful cloaks in her collection, I'm sure." I wondered if Marcus would catch my double meaning. A vision of Lady Katalin and Marcus standing toe to toe popped into my mind. "You're considering r-returning this to her?"

I focused on the silhouette of the tree branches above his head, knowing I was acting callow. Part of me hoped Marcus was as repulsed by her as I was. But she only showed him her beauty, her wealth, and a touch of kindness. Of course, he would be flattered.

"I haven't decided." Marcus threw a saddlebag on the ground near me. "You handled her well, by the way. I would've been rattled if someone thought I was a slave. With your appearance, I'm not surprised she came to that conclusion. When it comes to people in power, it's better to let them keep their assumptions. Let their prejudice work to your advantage. I followed your lead. We kept to the story she'd already written about us in her mind. I bet she couldn't describe you now if she tried." He actually grinned as if being forgettable was what every young woman longed for.

I swallowed, still looking at the treetops. He seemed sincere, but how could I be sure he had only been playing along? Lady Katalin's interest in him seemed sincere enough, and I'm sure it was flattering, especially for a farm boy, to have a Rose flirting with him. I hoped the white fur was already stained underneath where I sat.

"She seemed eager to give you quite a r-reward for returning her cloak even if it was ruined from keeping your *b-belonging* warm at night." I was glad I kept the hurt from my voice.

Marcus shrugged. "I thought we could sell it when we get to the capital. You'll need a place to stay and food to eat while you wait for Rubia."

I poked my fingers deep into the luxurious cloak. That was a good idea. Why hadn't I thought of it?

Marcus furrowed his brow. "Wait, I thought you and I were playing into her assumptions together." He cocked his head to the side, "You thought that I was —"

"Y-you d-didn't say a w-word since the watering hole, until just n-now." I offered as proof of his cold attitude.

"There is no such thing as an uncomfortable silence." Marcus threw his hands in the air. He spun around on his heel and dug through the other saddlebag, pulling out the tool for Velos' hoof.

A flush burned up my neck. I still felt angry and hurt for his perceived slight, but now I also felt silly and humiliated that I had misunderstood so badly. How could I keep getting situations so wrong? I had trusted Rubia's instincts for so long that I no longer relied on my own. Marcus had earned my respect in so many different ways, and yet at the first sign of a rebuff, I put up emotional walls and sent arrows over them at the one friendly person.

While Marcus checked Velos' hooves and brushed her down, I pulled out my water gourd and took a long drink.

I let the sound of the river wash over me, hoping to clear my thoughts. I'd been emotional ever since I'd seen Mama's blue vision. Losing Papa, gaining the responsibility of the key, realizing Rubia was planning to offer me up to Rupea, and the best-case scenario was that I'd be selected for a scribe apprenticeship in the castle where I needed to find out more about the treasure the orb opened. Not to mention the enormous task of finding an heir of Odon, which my parents hadn't been able to do in a lifetime although they were much more knowledgeable. And until all that was accomplished, the plague would rage.

It was too much. I had to get control of myself. I slowed my breathing, and tension drained from my muscles. How could I make decisions that impacted so many people if I couldn't be logical? I had to be tougher, smarter.

"Marcus, I can't read your mind." I started with the obvious. My words were calm and slow as I articulated what I needed to say. "You're already doing so much for me, and I a-appreciate everything. Truly. But, right now it would be helpful if you could communicate your thoughts." A bit of the tension in my neck eased.

Marcus stood up and brushed his hair out of his face with the back of his wrist. He dropped the brush into a saddlebag and came to sit on the moss next to me. In a low voice, he said, "Nicoleta."

A strange thrill ran down my spine to hear him whisper my name.

"My sisters complain that I'm always in my thoughts. It's a habit of mine. But if it'll help you through your difficulty, I'll do my best."

Difficulty. The word was woefully insufficient.

"I don't know why exactly you're going to Capidava. You've never been specific, and I've never asked. But I know you're carrying a heavy burden," he said.

"Thank you for not pressing me for details. Honestly, I'm not handling the p-pressure well." If only he knew some of my petty concerns and inner turmoil when I should be singularly occupied with finding my papa and the heir.

"While we're being honest, I didn't tell you the whole truth about the bathhouse in Patridava," Marcus said.

I pulled my knees up to my chest and wrapped my arms around them. "What do you mean?"

"I don't normally stay in the Getaen part of town. I hoped to see you again at one of the Getaen taverns or inns. I didn't feel good about the way we'd parted. I was unhappy with some of my father's decisions, and I redirected my frustration toward you. When we left you by the gates, I was hollow inside. I needed to apologize." Marcus plucked a blade of grass and rolled it between his fingers, releasing a faint, lemony scent. "I didn't expect to see you at the bathhouse, especially not... " He trailed off and then cleared his throat. "Everything happened so quickly I didn't have a chance to talk to you."

"I was hoping to see you and a-apologize, too," I said. "I wanted to be friendly, but —"

"But you stutter." Marcus finished my sentence.

I held out a hand. Hiding who I was from Marcus only led to frustration. "Don't try to speak for me. I know you're — I know you're trying to help. But, just give me a m-moment."

His eyes widened. "I'm sorry. I'll never do it again."

I let a smile bloom on my lips. "Thank you."

He tossed away the grass from between his fingers and his shoulders relaxed. I let my chin rest on my knees, and for a blissful moment, I was at peace.

A breeze rustled the leaves, breaking the quiet between us.

"I should —" Marcus moved to stand up, and I lightly tugged on his cloak.

He sat back down, and I pulled my pendant from my satchel. Before we plunged into the forest, didn't Marcus deserve a warning about the orb at least?

I rolled the orb around in my hand, thinking through what I could say.

I held up the pendant but out of Marcus' immediate reach. "My travel has everything to do with this."

~

Marcus waited patiently while I gathered my thoughts.

"This orb is d-dangerous to touch for anyone who isn't b-bonded to it. It's imb-bued with magic. Unfortunately, a merchant in the square g-grabbed it." I took a deep breath, steeling myself. As deep as the secrets surrounding the orb were, I'd rather divulge my treasonous accusations of a usurper than what happened with Elek. What Elek had done wasn't my fault, yet a taint of shame swirled in my confession.

"The merchant had... intentions." I fiddled with my fingers. "He r-refused to let us go."

Me. He refused to let me go.

"Rubia smashed one of her stinging vials on the cobblestones." Once I started with the story, the rest of it sputtered and spilled out of my mouth. I told him how I'd pulled away, only to be yanked back and nearly choked by the ties of my cloak.

"And he broke the chain of my mother's necklace."

The chain had fallen off my pendant, probably somewhere in the bottom of the bag. Someone who didn't know the orb as I did might think the flat area and other misshapen bumps were from abuse over the years. But, for being made of soft gold, it never scratched or dented. Per the scroll Papa showed me, it had always looked like this. Only the deliberately carved symbols on the surface marred its lumpy, satin appearance.

"The pendant damaged the merchant's hand, perhaps beyond repair. I'm sure he'll want revenge." The image of Elek's shriveled, grey husk of a hand blazed in my memory. I didn't understand it myself, so I didn't mention those details.

A tiny bit of the weight on my shoulders lifted. It was a relief to finally tell Marcus the truth, or at least part of it.

"Rubia created the magic in the necklace?" Marcus asked.

"No. A warlock did," I said. "A very powerful one."

And it was created almost two hundred years before Rubia was ever born.

"If Rubia created the orange-sting, she's proficient with Healing as well as inflicting pain," Marcus said. "It was dangerous of her to reveal she had the potion, let alone hint at the possibility that she had made them."

What would Marcus say if he knew I had another one in my bag? Beyond that, he didn't seem to grasp that the pendant I held was much more powerful than a vial of orange-sting. If the True Key could topple an emperor as the scrolls foretold, it had more power than a thousand orange-stings. *My pendant.* The idea felt comfortable, and that comfort frightened me a bit.

Marcus unstrung the leather strip in his lower sleeve. "Until you return home and replace the chain, you can use this to carry the pendant. It's sturdy, anyway. Now you'll be able to find it with ease whenever you need it."

I smiled, warmed by his kindness. We were friends, I told myself. I slid the golden orb onto the rough leather string and held it up.

"May I?" Marcus held out his hands to take the ends of the string and tie them around my neck.

"Be careful not to touch the pendant." I reminded him, handing it over.

His fingertips brushed my hands, and my breath hitched as he took the leather string from me. I inclined my head, lifting my hair to bare my neck for him. I was grateful for the growing darkness to hide my blush. His arms wrapped around me for a brief moment, and then the pendant lay against my throat. Marcus' fingers worked at the back of my neck, tying the knot. It was as if Marcus had broken the invisible wall between us. I had traveled with him for a week, but in the half-moon light, right next to him, his smell of sweat, earth, and mint made my heart thunder against my ribcage.

"There." Marcus laid a hand on my upper back, signaling he was done.

I tucked the pendant safely away under my dress and turned to face Marcus. I hoped he'd be staring at me like he stared at Lady Katalin, but he was gazing at the stars.

"That doesn't answer why you're going to the capital,' he said.

I didn't know what Rubia had told Otho or his son, but I was sure she either lied or was vague.

"My papa is in Capidava." *I think.* I decided simple truth was best.

"You're going to meet him or *find* him?" Marcus asked.

I rolled my lips together. Between him understanding Getaen and his keen observation, he'd figured out more than I expected.

"If he were able, he'd have traveled with you to the capital," Marcus said.

I decided to continue being honest even if not completely open. "Yes, I'm going to find him. Or find out what happened to him."

"And about my outburst... Rubia not being my mama." I rubbed my palms against my dress as I gathered my thoughts. "Getaens don't have a rigid view of family. It's more about who you select to be your family than it is about who you share b-blood with. Rubia didn't give b-birth to me, but she's always been a mama to me even before my mama d-died." My voice cracked. "The p-plague."

Marcus shifted but didn't interrupt.

"My mama was the logic, and Rubia the passion. Rubia can d-dance longer and laugh harder than anyone I know. She lived through the p-plague, and she was different after, but she's always p-protected me, in her own way. At the same time, she expected me to accomplish d-difficult things." I scrunched my dress in my fist. "I shouldn't have said she wasn't my mama. That was d-disrespectful of who she's been to me all my life."

Marcus was quiet for a long time. I thought perhaps he had forgotten I was even sitting there before he finally spoke again. "I heard what Lady Katalin said about the plague. I wish I would've gotten back sooner. Her words were cruel. Most everyone has lost someone to the Lilac Plague."

Marcus picked at a rock in the dirt and tossed it. "It hit our valley when my father was young. He lost everyone in his family except his father and an older sister. It was before I was born, but my grandfather still has nightmares about it. It's strange. Because of it, our valley is young. There are few people older than my father in our town. The survivors carry invisible scars."

"Everything changed," I said. "P-parents who'd lost children grieved while they took in orphans. Masters had lost apprentices. Bakeries had no bakers. There were more needs piled up around me than I could p-possibly meet in one day." My words seemed inadequate to describe the destruction.

Marcus nodded. "I think that's why my father still travels with me, even on short trips, when he'd rather be home. He's afraid to leave me in a town where the plague breaks out. I remember how vibrant Moesia was before the plague. When the plague broke out, Papa skipped Moesia that season. He does things like that, believing he'll be able to protect me." Marcus' chuckle was dark and mirthless. "As if one could be protected from the plague."

A shadow crossed my heart. I could help protect people from the plague. I *would* help stop the plague.

"Lady Katalin said that the p-plague broke out just two days from here." What was happening in their city right now? Panic. Sequestering. Soon enough, they'd be crying over their dying loved ones. I shuddered.

Marcus pulled himself closer and put his arm around me. He'd never touched me without a purpose, from riding Velos to handing me food. His arm was welcoming and heavy, grounding me. I leaned into his shoulder, and we looked up at the stars. I blinked, refusing to spill tears.

"I can't believe how wrong about you I was," Marcus said.

"You're not the most talkative p-person. What was I supposed to think of you?" I blinked again. I wanted his comfort, his assurance that everything would be all right. I clutched one hand at the pendant under my dress. "I'm surprised you thought me a snob. My hair was so sweaty it stuck to my face under that d-disgusting hood. I'm sure that cloak stank up the whole area."

"The whole valley." Marcus laughed, and I elbowed him in the ribs.

Marcus put a hand on my face, meeting my gaze.

I closed my eyes and breathed him in. His hand was rough, but I didn't care as it moved from my cheek to my hair and down my neck. I wanted to escape and fall into the oblivion of the moment. I tilted my face up to his and felt his breath on my lips.

But how could I sit here, romancing in the moonlight? People were dying, and I should be protecting them.

I pulled away.

He's dangerous. Rubia's voice came into my mind. Like the tail end of distant thunder, rumbling deep inside my chest, I realized what Rubia meant. The revelation wasn't startling, but it shook me all the same. She'd seen our potential feelings all along. That's why she kept us apart.

"Nicoleta?" Marcus caressed his thumb across my cheek.

I longed to forget the reasons I was running. Couldn't I steal a sliver of happiness? I almost reached for Marcus' shoulder to pull him back toward me, but Lady Katalin's words echoed in my mind. The plague was consuming Burridava.

My burdens clung to me, not letting go from my mind, no matter how much I wanted them to. I leaned back and looked down.

"Marcus." My heart ached. I would never know what it would be like to have Marcus visit me in Moesia. I pushed away the illusion that we could be anything more than momentary acquaintances. Nothing existed in our tomorrows. "I can't... I'm s-sorry."

Marcus drew his hand away from my neck. Immediately, I missed his warmth. But it was more than the physical sensation; the feeling between us grew cold.

"I'm sorry, too. I thought... nothing. I should let you sleep." Marcus shot to his feet.

Heat rushed into my cheeks. I longed to wrap myself in Marcus' embrace, but I couldn't get lost in a chasm from which I might not want to escape.

I'd told him so many secrets, but not about the heir and stopping the plague. I was sure Marcus knew there was more to my story, that I was holding back from him for a reason. But everyone even associated with the necklace was either dead or being hunted. If I explained more, I'd only make things worse for Marcus, burden him with dangerous knowledge that wasn't truly mine to share. How could I do that to him? To his family?

"I — I —" I stumbled, not knowing how to fix the rift my secrets had caused. My concern about Burridava, my trepidation about finding the heir.

"We have an early start. Try to get some sleep." Marcus moved to Velos in the semi-darkness.

"Marcus, wait," I called.

He turned to me, his face hidden in the shadows.

"If there was a chance that you could stop the p-plague, what lengths would you go to?" I knew he would see it as an impossible question; still, I wanted to hear his response.

"I would go until I couldn't take another step or another breath." Pine needles crunched under his feet when he shifted his weight. "Anyone in the kingdom would give up everything to see the Lilac Plague end."

His words struck me as hard as any of Rubia's slaps. I would give up anything, too... even him. We stared at each other, but I couldn't read his face in the shadows.

"But it can't be stopped, Nicoleta. Whatever you're planning, walk away." His voice was rough, almost desperate. "I'll take you back to Moesia, and I won't charge you a thing. There's nothing anyone can do."

Anything I said would make things worse between us. I stared at my hands in silence, my blood pumping so hard they were trembling.

I curled my hands into fists and stared up at the night sky. The stars winked above, and I wondered if Zalmoxis was laughing at my impossible tasks.

The High Judge passed a law on behalf of the Emperor today. There is a new tax on all magical products and treatments. Sometimes I wonder if Zalmoxis conspires against Getaens. Sanaz doesn't ask me to speak to the Emperor on the Getaens' behalf, which I appreciate. Though, I see the disappointment in her eyes when I do not.

— VAHID, WARLOCK TO EMPEROR TRAJAN

CARACALLA

THIRTEEN

MIDNIGHT RIDE

Mama reached toward me. I stretched, trying to grab her hand, but it got further and further away. She wasn't moving; I was sinking. An earthy aroma surrounded me and darkness fell. I was in the cavern below Papa's study. The tiles above me were gone, but the walls began to close in. I cried out for Mama, but she wouldn't look at me. I leapt and grabbed a hold of her hand, but it wasn't her hand. Every finger had gold rings adorning it. Thick rings with jewels. The hand withered. I screamed and tried to jerk away, but the grotesque fingers lengthened and intertwined with mine.

My body convulsed. I thrashed my arms, trying to escape the withered hand, but it seeped into my skin, burning it.

"Nikka!" I heard my voice from afar as if from under water. "Nicoleta!"

Cold air enveloped me. I fluttered my eyelids, and shapes and shadows swirled around me.

"Nicoleta, it's me," Marcus said. "You're dreaming. It's all right."

I gulped for air, brushing off my skin. "It's on... it's on me. It's —" The words died on my tongue. The ringed fingers vanished with the rest of my nightmarish sleep, though the burning sensation on my hand lingered. I breathed hard, sweat beaded on my face, yet I shivered, goose bumps rising on my arms.

"I heard you thrashing. Are you well?" Marcus asked, his hands still on my shoulders.

I rubbed the palms of my hands together, erasing the residual burning sensation of my nightmare. I wanted nothing more than to lean into Marcus, but I refrained. If I turned to Marcus for comfort, alone and under distress, I would regret it later. He didn't deserve to be used, and I didn't want more guilt when the sun rose.

I turned to the stars for comfort, but they were starting to fade.

"S-sorry to frighten you. I'll be fine." I forced a smile as he handed me my water gourd. "Y-you should rest. You let me oversleep as it is."

Marcus rose stiffly, lumbered to his blanket roll, and collapsed with a sigh. "Wake me when the sun comes up."

Moments after his head hit the mossy ground, his breathing deepened into a rhythmic pattern. I wiped the sweat off my face. My hair was a tangled mess. What did Marcus think when he saw me thrashing in my sleep each night?

I chided myself for fussing about my hair. It was the least of my worries. The guards were likely scouring Patridava for Rubia and me at this very moment. And the plague was bearing down on Burridava. The worst of the damage wouldn't be over for a few weeks. Only then would families know who would live and who wouldn't.

Sometime during the night, Marcus had pulled the fur cowl over my head, keeping me warm. Still, a chill ran down my spine, and I tucked my knees into my chest and rocked back and forth on the ground. I couldn't shake off my dream. The hand. The plague.

I pulled out my pendant and rolled it around in my hand. But what could I do? Rubia had a plan. I hated it, but it was our best option. Or was it?

I loosed the braid that crowned my head and combed my fingers through it, snippets of last night's conversation floating into my thoughts. I was always more emotional when I was tired or stressed. Now awake and rested, I was invigorated. Focused. Last night, Marcus said something in passing, probably not even thinking twice about it.

Anyone in the kingdom would give up everything to see the Lilac Plague end.

He echoed my own thoughts. But, would I give up everything? I'd clung to the hope that I would be reunited with Rubia after she spoke with the High Judge and I was an apprentice. That hope held me back. I had to let the illusion go. The stars twinkled as I allowed myself to acknowledge the truth: Rubia wasn't counting on reuniting with me after she confronted the High Judge.

Strangely, instead of sadness, I felt a weightless clarity. I hadn't wanted to see the truth for days. Rubia knew her value to the Emperor was only as good as her information. Once scribes and clerics scoured the scrolls, they'd burn them and her. And if Papa were kept alive that long, he'd be silenced then, too. All their deaths would be for the dream of successfully seeding me as an apprentice scribe. As years passed, I would secretly record everything I knew, find a new Guardian, and locate the treasure.

The stars twinkled, oblivious as I let my thoughts settle. I sat up taller and gripped the pendant. Rubia, my Rubia who I'd always admired for her ability to plan ahead, was blinded by the death of her child. She was desperate to keep me safe. She thought by dying, she could save me. But the chances of me accomplishing the tasks she had listed were almost none.

I gulped my water, a daring idea stirring. Why cower in some hope that, as an apprentice, I could find the long-hidden treasure? Why scrounge together scraps of information when Papa and Rubia had likely taught me more than all the clerics knew combined?

There was a chance I could stop everything before it burned. I jumped to my feet, the idea in my belly growing. After the fight with Elek and the long day of travel, I should have felt sore and stiff, but I felt fine. I sent silent gratitude to the Protector and his tapping fingers as I stretched, letting my muscles warm up from sleep. It snapped my mind into sharp focus. I could stop the plague from killing everyone it touched. Stop the burning, starting with Papa and Rubia.

I paced by Marcus, and a twig snapped under my foot. He snorted and half-opened his eyes.

"Just me. Sorry," I whispered. He rolled over and dozed back to sleep.

My mind buzzed with my new plan, and I had no one to share it with. I knelt next to Marcus, the line of his chin and curve of his brow hidden in shadows. He'd honored everything he promised.

I couldn't explain my reasons to him. His honor would compel him to journey with me all the way to the castle doors. Right into the wolves' den. Because of my bond, the orb protected me. But not Marcus. Only an immoral fool would lead a friend into danger.

The forest was quiet as I braided my hair in a low, simple bun. I needed to switch Rubia's plan so instead of revealing the truth to the Emperor, I revealed it to someone else. Someone who could protect the truth, and themselves, with titles and armies.

It may or may not be the High Judge. I'd have to discern the best person when I arrived at the castle. Or perhaps it would be multiple people. Yes, multiple witnesses would be best — the pressure on them would be much greater. No one would want to be the person who let another noble's child die in the plague because of their blind loyalty to the illegitimate Emperor.

I inspected the sky and estimated the sun would rise in less than three hours. This was the thieves' hour, the best hour for sneaking anywhere, including through a forest.

A few feet away from Marcus, I brushed away damp leaves and picked up a stick. I scratched into the dirt "Velos boarded in Capidava", circled it, and rammed the stick into the dirt, like a flag with no banner, so Marcus would be sure to see the message. Velos had two saddlebags. I left one for Marcus with all his food next to the words I had written.

I rummaged around in my satchel, finding the pouch from Rubia with the gold nugget, and set it in Marcus' bag.

I knelt next to Marcus, my lips near his ear, and whispered. "I have something important to do. If I live through the next moon, perhaps one day our lives will cross paths again."

He couldn't hear me, but I felt better explaining.

Marcus would be angry with me. I didn't want to lose his trust and friendship, but if that was the price of saving the kingdom's people, I was willing to pay it. Something had changed inside me. I would even give up my opportunity to find out what happened to Papa if I must. The plague was a terrible scourge on our kingdom that had to be stopped.

I picked my way across our campsite to Velos. I'd seen Marcus tend to Velos for days. I heaved the saddle onto the horse and attached the saddlebag. All the while, I rolled my seedling of an idea around in my head, and it started to grow. It relied on people who feared the plague. Marcus had said himself that anyone would give up everything to stop the plague. I knew he was right. I simply had to find the right people in the same place.

I could do this.

The powerful nobles would rally, wanting to stop the plague. They just needed to know the facts. I pressed my thumb on Lady Katalin's cloak's emblem and suppressed a laugh. I brushed off the idea that my giddy feeling inside was based on vindictive spite. Turning Lady Katalin into an unwitting aid to grant me access through all the gates of Capidava, including the Rose Court, was a necessity, not reprisal.

I unhooked Velos' reins and led her away. Velos neighed but followed me, tempted by the grass I'd gathered and held just out of her reach. Marcus could travel to Capidava on foot in two days. With one rider, Velos could make it to Capidava before the next nightfall.

I brushed against evergreen branches, releasing the scent of pine. I took a deep, cleansing breath of the crisp, night air. Droplets of dew fell on the fur of the cloak.

Near the road, dry twigs crunched under my feet. A chill settled around my shoulders. Velos pulled back, not wanting to continue.

I stroked her mane, brushing away my doubts at the same time. "I trust that you're everything Otho bragged you were."

Her ears pricked up, and she snuffed, a puff of air floating in the silver moonlight. I put my forehead on hers, calming us both. I led Velos onto the Emperor's Highway.

As we walked, I began unraveling conversations I might have with the nobles. I'd get tongue twisted if I didn't memorize points and counterpoints. Soon enough, stars faded, and crickets quieted. Travelers and bandits would both be waking. The soft dirt along the side of the road muffled our movements, and I was attuned to any discordant sounds.

Rustling in the bushes startled me. My heart thumped. I slid my foot into the stirrup, mounted, and quickly settled myself. I took the reins and tapped my heels against Velos' flank. Whether it was human or critter, I didn't care. The noise signaled it was time to ride fast and hard to the capital.

The white hood fell back, the wind stinging my face, weaving its tendrils through my hair. We flew down the road, faster than I'd ever ridden. My seed of a plan grew. I'd bring the powerful together. I could do this. I'd reveal the truth. Capidava would rise up and demand a change. No one wanted to see their children die. My mind cleared of everything except for brisk morning air and freedom. Hope bloomed in my chest.

This was possible. For the first time in generations, there was a chance to stop the Lilac Plague. My lips parted and curved into a smile.

The Emperor forbade me from marrying. My commitment is to the kingdom, and my attention is not to be divided, or so the Emperor demands. It seems he plans to isolate me as he did the Queen. I must keep my temperament neutral towards Sanaz, the same as I do for everyone. My friendship will only put her at risk, not just from the Emperor but others as well. Getaens see me as a traitor for my complicity in the Emperor's capricious actions, especially heavy taxes on magical products.

— VAHID, WARLOCK TO EMPEROR TRAJAN CARACALLA

FOURTEEN

THE THIEVES' HOUR

Velos' hoof falls were loud, announcing our arrival. If I rode by thieves just waking, I hoped they'd be too off guard to act. Sweat darkened Velos' flank, but I sped her further, wanting to gain distance before the dawn broke.

The forest on either side of the road was dense and wild, muffling even the rushing of the river. Pale pinks and oranges bled into the sky, visible through the branches and the treetops looming over me.

Around a bend, I caught a glimpse of a caravan along the road. I pulled back on the reins, and guided Velos in a small circle in the road, backtracking a few paces to keep us out of sight.

The travelers must have stopped for the night and were now preparing to leave. By the orientation of their wagons, we were traveling in the same direction. If I traveled far enough behind the caravan without them spotting me, the caravan would draw the attention of any thieves, and they wouldn't notice me.

On the other hand, I couldn't travel too slowly. I needed to make Capidava by nightfall. If this caravan was slow, I'd have to ride around them, but this time when I passed a caravan, I'd be alone.

I dismounted and grasped Velos' reins, taking a few tentative steps forward. I ran my fingers over my necklace, thinking. I needed more information.

I guided Velos off the highway and onto a narrow animal track into the woods, the forest pushing up against the trail on either side. It zigzagged toward the water, as most animal tracks did, but still generally headed north nearer the caravan. If I could spy them breaking down camp, I could learn about them and then decide if I wanted to approach or travel faster alone.

Each tree felt like it had eyes staring down at me. Every step was a game to see if I could avoid crunching dry branches or leaves underfoot. Velos wasn't playing along.

As I drew closer to where I estimated the camp was, a branch broke nearby. The back of my neck pricked in warning. I couldn't see further than five steps in any direction. I paused, dread making my footsteps heavy.

The normal sounds of horses neighing and clinking of plates gave way to sudden shouts. My heart jumped into my throat. Screams and the crashing of metal rang through the forest. Velos neighed and jerked her head from side to side. I scanned the dense forest for any sign of movement. Men shouted. There was trouble between the merchants, or with thieves.

"Easy, Velos. Easy, girl." I loosened my grip on the reins and patted her side. I forced myself to take a deep breath.

More metal on metal clanged, and Velos jerked her head up, ears back, poised to bolt. This was a terrible idea. I was alone with a horse that barely trusted me. If I went back now, could I beg Marcus to forgive me? I shook out one of my hands. No, it was as dangerous to go back as it was to move forward; I was too deep into the forests of Capidava now.

I took another deep breath and pulled one of the bitter roots out of my bag. Velos eyed me warily but eventually was tempted by the root. I coaxed Velos forward on the path. The sounds of metal stopped, but shouting replaced it. The words were muffled, and I strained to hear them.

Velos grudgingly followed the root in my hand, her ears still perked. When we reached a shallow stream, I opened my palm and let her gobble up the food. Velos bobbed her head up and down, finally daring to take a sip of the water.

Perhaps traveling deeper in the forest would be a good option for a single rider until I could get past this caravan. Between the river and the sun, I could guide myself north.

The clanging of metal rang again. I jumped. Velos popped her head up from the stream, water dripping from her mouth. The fighting was closer this time. There was a cry of pain and Velos skittered.

"Shhh, shh, girl," I spoke softly, forcing myself to stay calm. I patted her neck.

Velos snorted but settled. Beyond the trees, a deep voice sounded, carrying through the forest. "The Emperor shall hear about this. He values trade. Commerce means money. Money means a full treasury. He will double the guard and clear the vermin from these woods."

Laughter was followed by a baritone voice. I couldn't hear most of what he said, but I did hear, "Emperor Cassus... " And, "... looking for it!"

It? What was "it?" I wondered.

A third, more nasally voice spoke up and all I could pick up was "gold," or perhaps it was "sold."

The deep voice sounded again, his voice more angry than

frightened. "We don't have such a trinket. As you can see, none of us are southern merchants and we don't trade in gold."

I held my breath.

The baritone voice responded with what sounded like a monologue, but all I could pick out was "... in Patridava."

My hand shot to my pendant. Gold trinket. Patridava. Looking for *it*?

I fought the urge to run and instead crept ahead on the path. There was no way I would try to join this caravan; I had to sneak by.

"I am loyal to the Emperor. I don't fear rabble of the woods." The man with the deep voice had a touch of disdain. "There was a strange event in Patridava. Elek Moldva of Capidava was attacked and suffered a serious wound to his hand. He's nursing his wound in his carriage and will relay his incident to the High Judge when we return. Now that you understand we travel to Rupea, let us pass in peace."

My stomach dropped. There was a shuffling of bodies and indistinguishable voices arguing. How had Elek traveled so quickly? I thought through the possibilities. With his status, he could have received permission to leave Patridava soon after the gates closed. Maybe even before. His hand looked like it was affected by the plague, yet the guards had let him leave. As a noble, no one questioned him.

I clenched my jaw, stewing. When my family was desperate to leave Moesia, we had no signs of illness, but no status. We lacked the Seal of the Emperor. We were trapped, and Elek hadn't even been quarantined.

The shouts grew louder. The baritone man spoke again, his voice louder this time. "Elek's assistant is available for questioning."

My breathing grew rapid. Velos softly bumped into me from

behind. Was the assistant the Getaen slave? Would he describe Rubia? Me?

More voices argued, but I couldn't pick out the words. The deep voice sounded again. "The assistant will have to do. Elek's carriage is putrid. He's been ignoring an infection that has festered. Not even an entire lilac bush would cover the stench."

My hands were clammy. I tugged on Velos' reins and we pushed ahead. I needed to reach Capidava before the caravan. How much could I accomplish before Rubia and I would be described and hunted? I'd be right in the belly of the very beast looking for me.

Elek had all the pieces of information; he just needed to connect them: Rubia, me, the plague, the orb. *The orb.* The bandits were looking for it specifically. Someone was hunting for the True Key, likely willing to pay the bandits to find it. Who sent them?

My urge to flee only strengthened. I wanted to find Rubia and hide until the sensational nature of Elek's news faded. But the plague was raging, hurting people every moment I delayed.

Velos and I accelerated our pace as the voices faded in the distance. The sun was fully up in the cloudless sky. Another animal track led close to the road. I swung up onto Velos and blazed back onto the Emperor's Highway.

Velos quickly began to sweat, but I rode hard. I needed to make it to Capidava before sundown. Velos was capable of a demanding pace, every bit as strong as Otho had claimed.

My heart sunk a little more, thinking about Marcus awake and angry with me. This wasn't fair to him, but he said himself he'd do anything to stop the plague.

As Velos and I followed a gentle curve in the road, a mountain range came into view with a sprawling city clinging to the sides of the nearest peak. The mountains surrounding it loomed like an army of white-capped defenders. It was Capidava, lush and green, like nothing I'd ever seen before. The dense, terraced dwellings were carved into the ivory granite walls of the mountain.

My plan had been nothing but a distant dream until now. As Velos' hooves pounded over the highway, foreboding encroached on my soul like a dark shadow. I steeled myself for the risks I was about to undertake without Rubia guiding me or any allies to turn to.

The white cloak flapped wildly behind me as I leaned into the wind. The words started to form in my mind. The truth that needed to be said.

This was much bigger than ignoring my elders, traveling without an escort, or borrowing a horse. I was about to force myself onto the stage of the kingdom, speak in front of Capidavan decision-makers, and make them believe me.

ACRES OF SLASHED forest surrounded Mount Capidava. The smells of burned grasses and tilled earth greeted us as Velos galloped out of the forest and into the open. I pulled her to a trot, and she shook her mane, revealing the dark sweat on her coat. We'd arrived sooner than I'd expected. The summer sun was low in the sky, saturating the earth with a final blast of heat before the end of the day.

"Almost there, girl. Do you see it?" I said.

At the top of the mountain, Rupea Castle stared down the Emperor's Highway, inspecting every soul. Gleaming turrets and crisscrossing walls emerged as if carved out of the mountain itself. A roaring waterfall pounded down the mountain's east side before crashing to the base, forming the great river that flowed south to the Getaen Sea.

A wall wrapped around the entire perimeter of the mountain's base, wide enough for the horses and riders patrolling on top, and was dizzyingly tall. Massive twin wolves, carved from glistening white granite, sat on their haunches, guarding either side of the wide gate. The closer I came, the more I was dwarfed in the shadow of the beasts. Next to them, even mounted on Velos, I was unable to see over a single paw.

Two guards stood at either side of the open gate, questioning visitors one by one. Grumbling travelers, horses, and creaking wagons waited their turn as the sun beat down without the protection of the forest. I mimicked the lone female rider I'd seen in Patridava as much as I could. I dismounted and slung the white cloak over my arm and stood tall, pretending I often traveled alone.

I checked over my shoulder as a caravan emerged from the forest. Elek's caravan couldn't be here so quickly, but with every new arrival, the chance of gossip from Patridava increased. Sweat trickled down my back. My leather cloak was gone, and my hair was now wrapped into a simple knot. Still, if anyone paid close attention, I'd be revealed as one of the troublemakers in Patridava.

I held my head high, positioned my cloak to hide the worst tear of my sleeve, and practiced what I would say to the Thorns.

I sipped the last of my water. My gourd shell was soft and bruised, ready to be discarded. I wouldn't have money for a new one, which wouldn't matter.

A girl with a basket of carrots stared at the stained yellow embroidery on my sleeves, identifying me as Moesian. I rolled my lips, forcing myself not to be wistful for days past. I had to count myself lucky in one way; I had seen the world beyond the walls I was born behind. And now I needed to embrace Capidava as my new home as Mama and Rubia had done in Moesia.

The guard spoke to the traveler in front of me. His quick

words and harsh accent reminded me of the soldiers in the raid. My grip on the fur cloak tightened.

"What is your business in the capital?" a guard with beady, black eyes demanded. Despite his tone, I relaxed a bit seeing his green cloak and attire matched that of other city guards, not of those who raided Moesia. Not like Lady Katalin's mercenary.

"I have a cloak to return to Lady Katalin." I showed him the white cloak, now marred by moss chunks and evergreen needles in the fur.

A wrinkle furrowed the guard's brow. "Lady Katalin asked you to return this?"

I squeezed Velos' reins in my hand, but I spoke my practiced words. "My master told me to return it."

Noticing our delay, the guard with a full beard next to him looked from the guard interrogating me to the cloak in my arms.

"Your master asked *you* to return Lady Katalin's cloak?" The bearded Thorn chortled. "More likely stolen."

The guard with the beady, black eyes frowned. "Show this cloak's seal at the upper gates. Do not be delayed or lose it, or you will be found and punished."

The bearded guard started to interject, but the beady-eyed guard stopped him, his words clipped. "Lady Katalin and her belongings are closely protected. No one steals the Vulpe seal and lives to tell the tale."

The bearded guard stiffened and quickly turned to the next traveler in the line.

The beady-eyed guard turned back to me, lowering his voice. "Discretion is required when it comes to the Emperor's Ambassadors. Go swiftly."

"I need to board my horse for the night first," I said.

He gave a curt nod, and I led Velos forward. I let out a

breath, my shoulders relaxing. I'd succeeded in my first hurdle, getting into Capidava without being arrested.

Inside the gates, the city was similar to Patridava in some ways. But surprisingly, the cobblestone square was smaller by half. The statue of the Emperor in the center of the square was larger, forcing travelers and merchants to squeeze around it. I wrinkled my nose at the stench of refuse, horse dung, and the miasma of human bodies permeating the air. Everything about the city seemed cramped and dirty.

Like Patridava, the right side of the square was set aside for criminals. A small wooden pavilion near the guard station held three stocks and a single wooden post with metal chains attached. I shuddered as I passed by the stocks, making my way to a row of shops.

I was quickly lost in a ravine of stone and wood looming on either side, stretching into the sky. Between the structures, precarious, narrow walkways crisscrossed overhead. I gripped the cloak tighter as I walked until I found a friendly face.

"Is there a Getaen boarding inn?" I asked a woman.

"I'll have my boy take you there. It's a fine place for room and board for your kind." The woman turned to her son. "Take this woman and her horse to the Desert Charm Inn."

"Thank you for your kindness," I said.

She waved me on and turned back to her washing.

The boy led me up winding streets, too narrow for wagons. The tall structures at the base of the mountain were compacted so close together that a blade of grass couldn't grow between them. Nor could the sun penetrate down to the cobblestone path to dispel the shadows.

As imposing as it was, Capidava had an energy and rhythm all its own. Children scurried by me carrying baskets or an evening bucket of water; a candle maker dipped a last round of wicks.

"Have you heard about a sickness? A plague?" I asked the boy. I wondered if they'd heard about the plague in Burridava.

"Lilac Plague?" He visibly paled. "Mama says that if we appease Zalmoxis, we will be protected."

I wanted to ask how the people of Capidava appeased a god, but he was already nervously biting at his fingernail, so I didn't press him further.

"There is the Desert Charm." The boy pointed to a building teetering to the point of collapse. It was made out of stones that look like they were set a thousand years ago. The inn wasn't built into the stone wall, it leaned against the mountain, looking like a tired old man about to give up the ghost, the structures on either side propping it up. I opened my mouth but then closed it again. I had to be about my business. Hopefully, it would stand for one more day.

"Thank you," I said. I wished I had a bit to give him, but the only thing I had was my gold chain, which I needed for Velos.

The boy lingered. I dug around in my satchel, pushed aside my spare socks, and pulled out the herbs. I ripped off a strip of my already torn sleeve and rolled up yarrow, elderflower, and peppermint. "Steep this in hot water this winter for anyone with a fever."

The boy nodded and scampered away.

I only had one of Rubia's magic-infused packets of medicine but I knew the recipes. My medicine was still far more effective than none at all.

I tied Velos outside the inn and went in to find the tavern keeper. Here I was not the daughter of an Azure Dacian scholar but a lowborn outsider. In front of the building, people stared at me while they ate bowls of soup, sweating despite the shade from the surrounding buildings. Inside, the inn was crammed with people. Not a spare seat, room to stand, or air to breathe. I realized why people were sitting outside to eat.

I squeezed through the patrons, trying not to gag from the overwhelming odors. The barkeep was a tall woman with blond hair cascading in curls down to her waist. She had large, blue eyes and eyelashes stained with charcoal.

"Another round, Raye," shouted a man with dark red hair.

The barkeep poured him more ale and turned to me.

"I'd like to board my horse," I said, keeping the white cloak low enough that she couldn't see it over the counter. Compared to the attire in this room, the cloak looked pristine.

"And a room for you, young lady." It was more of a statement than a question.

I shook my head. The walls looked like they might collapse at any moment. "I'd like to b-board the horse for five d-days." I pulled out my gold chain. "The horse is p-property of Marcus C-Constantin, and he'll be coming for her."

Knowing how quickly Marcus found me in Patridava, I was sure five days to find Velos would be more than enough.

"I can board her for four days and no more. And that's doing you a favor." Raye, the innkeeper, looked at the tear in the shoulder of my dress. Her voice was more practical than compassionate. "I can see you're in need of a kindness."

I didn't know if she was showing me kindness or robbing me.

"Four, but give the horse extra rations tonight. She saved my life." Rubia would be happy I at least tried to negotiate.

The woman had a hint of a smile on her lips. Was she impressed that I pushed back? She plucked the chain from my hand. The chain Papa gifted Mama. I took in a sharp breath, not realizing how difficult it would be to part with it.

"Borshe, tend to the young lady's horse out front," Raye called to a broad-shouldered man carrying a tray of empty mugs. "And give her extra rations."

The barkeep flicked a strand of blond hair from her face. "A bowl of soup? It comes with boarding the horse."

I shook my head. "Give it to Marcus when he arrives."

The aromas of Capidava had snuffed any appetite I'd had, and I was anxious to escape the stares and suffocating heat of the inn. Besides, I couldn't waste the hours that Velos had gained me by lounging about enjoying a bowl of soup.

Back outside, I hid the Vulpine Seal in the folds of the white cloak. No need to announce to everyone exactly where I was going. With any luck, no one would ever connect me, Nicoleta Aurelian, with Lady Katalin. My Lilac appearance would be the disguise I needed. I sucked in a breath and prepared to do something I'd never done before: trespass.

I tugged at the fur on the cloak. *And I'd steal.*

I wouldn't be doing this in just any peasant home, either. It would be at an estate in the Rose Court.

The High Judge passed another law. All magical Getaens must register with their local officials. Not just the successful creators of magical potions who've set up shop in Patridava but every magical person. This means that even if a Healer's only clientele is their family, they still must report. Even a Seer, if one were to be found, would need to register.

— VAHID, WARLOCK TO EMPEROR TRAJAN CARACALLA

FIFTEEN

WHAT A MYSTIC SEES

I pressed through the streets, Lady Katalin's white cloak on my arm. I stayed to the busiest roads that wound uphill, hoping to keep clear of the seedier portions of the city. It wouldn't be long until gossip flowed from lips to ears of Elek's attack by two witches, one who happened to match my description. I kept my head down, but the white cloak practically screamed for attention.

As I brushed past a group of girls not much younger than me, one reached out and tugged the cloak. She had shocking blue eyes and wild flowers braided in a crown around her head. I scowled at her, wary despite her curious eyes.

She released the cloak. "Soft as a new babe's bum."

Her friends laughed as I hurried on.

Two mounted Thorns trotted by, one after another, through the narrow street. The last thing I needed was to be questioned by the city watch. I ducked in among the locals and pressed myself between two rickety vendors' stands, keeping my back to them as they passed.

The sun slipped further down as I progressed up the mountainside. Musical notes from guitars thrumming and a smooth fluted melody carried through the cobblestone street. The street widened into a small, busy courtyard. Laughter and chatter mixed with the smells of bread, barley, and something tangy I didn't recognize. The square was surrounded by a two-story high wall created by a series of half-dome circles. Attached on the far side was a massive stone building with people visible through the large open-air windows. Families and young couples thronged the area. Many held thick slices of bread or mugs of beer with foam slopping over the side. Several children held sweets partially wrapped in paper. Vendors lined the periphery of the square, happily trading food for coins. I remembered celebrating the Spirit Fest as a child, but not after the plague. Every single person in Moesia had wiped ashes on their face for years. Remembering the spirits of our ancestors was too fresh, too painful to properly celebrate. My sullen attitude clashed with the vitality of the festival unfolding in front of me. Still, I was curious.

Many women wore their hair short, cut off at their shoulders like Lady Katalin, though their clothing wasn't as fine. They wore layers of beaded necklaces, embroidered scarves, silver charms, and piles of flowers in their hair. The men wore clean camasas with wide belts, fitted trousers, and tall boots.

People with simple clothing, like Marcus, mingled with others in silks and soft hats. Dark skin, pale skin, and every shade in between. Though, the dirty, ragged people of the city I'd seen below were noticeably absent.

I was alone and travel-worn, but with some mending and flowers, I could blend in. I hadn't felt this way since leaving Moesia, and the idea comforted me in some small way.

The music changed, and several girls squealed. The crowd backed away from the center of the square. Six smiling young women, hair piled with ribbons and flowers, danced into the open space and slid bells on their wrists. I made my way through the crowd as the music grew louder and faster. The women twirled and swayed to the music, the bells on their wrists ringing through the air, mingling with their laughter. I paused, mesmerized by their colorful skirts and tinkling wrists.

A couple next to me smiled at one another, their fingers intertwined. The edges of my innocent wonder frayed. The couple were lost in each other as if the world around them had ceased to exist. I'd seen that look between my parents. Hated that I had seen it between Lady Katalin and Marcus.

A pit formed in my stomach. I brushed my fingertips across the leather string around my neck and shook off my thoughts of Marcus. I couldn't afford distraction with a city dying and Elek closing in behind me. I turned to flee up a side street when a woman's words caught my attention.

"I hope these young ones never learn the meaning behind the dance." The woman leaned her head against the man's shoulder.

"Don't fret, my pet. With the sacrifices, Zalmoxis will pass us by, as he has for fifty years. The young will never know every chime of the bell represents a life snuffed by the Lilac Plague."

The man noticed my eavesdropping and glared. I darted to one of the many archways, away from the heady smells and the distracting music. Near the exit, a subdued group of people with white hair and almost translucent, alabaster skin stood out. I'd never seen anyone from the far north, but I'd heard stories of them, the magical people who rarely left their solitary mountains in the Norte Kingdom. According to Rubia's telling of ancient lore, the Getaen people split from their icy northern roots and migrated to the warm sea a thousand years ago.

I only caught glimpses of the northerners through the moving crowd as I raced up the side street. I had to make it to the upper wall before sunset. Not only was it easiest to hide in long, dark shadows, but it would be disastrous if I was arrested after curfew, still in possession of Lady Katalin's cloak. Before dark, the cloak was my access through the gates. After dark, I feared, with a few questions from the Thorns, that the cloak would become my noose.

ALTHOUGH THE MOUNTAIN WAS STEEP, the valley below was difficult to see. Occasionally an alley would line up just right and I could identify markers on the horizon or catch glimpses of Rupea Castle above; with these markers, I guided myself through the city. My calves burned after my many days of travel and the afternoon of hiking up the steep Capidavan mountainside. At least, the temperature was dropping to a comfortable degree.

The cobblestone road split, leading to an area of homes and fewer businesses. The front of each home was made out of wood but appeared to burrow directly into the mountainside. Compared to the Moesian Commons, the structures were cramped together, but they were well maintained with robust herbs in pots.

Two houses down, a grizzled man sat on a stool, smoking a pipe outside his door. He watched me with little interest as I continued up the street.

A slim woman with milky eyes sat on the ground with her back against a wall. A scarf was pinned over her gray and white braided hair. Simple rivers of green embroidery ran down the outer sleeves of her dress. She was clean and her clothes neatly mended except for her socks. They were worn thin and bare in many spots from the dirt-packed road.

"Come. Come, child. Let Mystic Marianna tell you your fortune. What is a copper bit compared to knowing what Zalmoxis has in store for you?" she asked. For a woman who appeared to be blind, she seemed to look directly at me.

"I have no money," I said. Rubia had explained long ago that fortunetellers were all liars, but seeing the calloused soles of her feet stirred me. "But I can trade you."

I sat next to her, resting my legs and pulling out the socks Rubia had washed in Patridava out of my satchel.

"I'd like directions to the entrance for the upper wall." I put the socks in her hands, immediately comfortable in her presence. "I can give you these. They'll keep your feet clean and warm."

The blind woman was silent, staring straight ahead as her fingers inspected the socks. They weren't silk or even soft wool, but they were sturdy and clean, thanks to Rubia. I'd eventually find the upper wall on my own, but with the sun low in the sky, the fastest route would be helpful, and the old woman seemed harmless.

"Meager gifts that cost the giver much are to be cherished. Thank you." Marianna put my socks on her feet right over the dirty ones she already wore.

"I will give you something better than directions." Her voice was raspy. "I have information to impart, girl."

Her milky eyes seemed to penetrate through to my soul. The intense lines of her face drawn around her lips and eyes told me she was not a simple, idle fortuneteller.

"Almost fifty years ago." Marianna's voice faded, lost in thought. "Has it really been that long?"

She gazed at unseen memories I could only guess at. After a moment, she continued. "My little brother and I were both sickened with a plague."

"The Lilac Plague?" I asked.

Her wrinkled skin had a few divots that could've been scars left by the plague.

"The Lilac Plague." She repeated my words and spat on the ground. "Those were the early days. A lovely name for such an abhorrent disease that lay waste to my town. I caught a fever like many others. But like too few, my fever broke, along with my blisters. I assumed my blurry vision was a temporary effect. When I learned my brother died while I was delirious, I was overcome with grief. My father didn't even know where my brother was buried; he'd been sick at the time the body was taken away. Probably tossed into a mass grave." She had little emotion to her voice; the stories had lost their sting.

Memories of the plague and the never-ending cries of anguish came back, threatening to rip open my healing wounds.

"I'm sorry to hear about your brother. I lost my mother to the plague three years ago." I fiddled with the pendant.

"Then you know what many don't. After the plague, the emperor's soldiers come, demanding a levy to protect and restore the town. My father gave all he had to keep us from the brand." A bitter laugh escaped her lips, the first emotion I'd seen from her. "Little good it did us in the end."

She lifted a gnarled hand, brushing aside her braid, revealing a small brand on her neck. A triangle with a slash through it. I recoiled from the slave mark, clutching my pendant tighter. The ghost of Elek's hands sent a chill down my spine. That could've been my fate.

"The next year, my father's new wife sold both my sister and me. I'll never know if my father gave his blessing. I like to think that he didn't even though I know we were too much a burden to keep. I was fourteen and my sister almost sixteen."

My fingers dug into the white fur of the cloak draped over my arm. Would Papa ever be desperate enough to sell me? No, he'd thrown me in an underground cavern and allowed his face to be sliced, never revealing where I was. My heart despaired, heavy for the woman, her fourteen-year-old self, sent away, alone.

Marianna smiled, showing several missing teeth. "Don't be too sad. It was the best worst thing that could've happened to me."

I stared into her milky eyes. How did she know I was saddened by her story? I hadn't made a sound.

"My father's wife sold me before the blindness was too noticeable, so I gained her a few coins before I was tossed into the bowels of the Rupea to help in the kitchens. My sister was untainted from the plague, a beauty. My last memory of her is emblazoned into my mind; we were children in the foreign city of Capidava, somewhere in the lower district, when we were torn apart from our frightened embrace. Me, thrown back to the gritty floor. I will never forget her screams."

Of all the phrases I'd prepared, I wasn't equipped to respond to such a wrenching tale. The plague was the tipping point for a boulder that ran down the hill of this woman's life, smashing everything in its path.

"Each day I worked in the kitchens, my vision grew worse."

A colorful butterfly caught my attention, and I noticed the front of the houses reflecting shades of pink in the setting sun. I needed to be on my way. Dusk was the most difficult time for the eye to see, the perfect time to wander the Rose Court.

Marianna continued, "An aging witch heard about me. She offered me a trade. My remaining eyesight in exchange for my freedom. I agreed and she bought my freedom from the emperor."

"So you were blind but free?" I said, hoping to spur her to the end of her story. Though I enjoyed her company, my time was running short.

"Not precisely. I see differently, and in colorful ways I don't even think the witch expected. A side-effect of her magic, I suppose."

I wrinkled my nose. Was she a charlatan? Rubia never mentioned magic like this.

"You've recently battled, but your body wasn't terribly harmed because of… ah, a Protection spell. A powerful one. Be warned, the magic in your body is almost extinguished. It burns hot and fast through your body." Marianna tapped her chin. "You are a vibrant soul, filled with an intensity and meaning. Your heart emanates a great purpose. A royal purpose?"

I touched the necklace meant for the royal descendant of Odon. That was true. Perhaps there was more to fortunetellers than Rubia knew.

A little girl with long, dark hair walked up the hill toward us with a jug of water on her shoulder. The old woman smiled at her from a distance.

"Thank you for sharing your story." Still, as heartfelt as it was, I needed directions. I stood to leave, but Marianna's spotted hand reached out and grabbed my arm.

"Wait. The story was the history you needed to understand these words." Her voice cracked.

I knelt back down, anxious to continue on my way.

"I tell everyone my story, hoping a few will hear me. When I was young inside Rupea, where the women prattled about hearsay and distant news, the rare occasions the Lilac Plague consumed a town caused a shock to us all."

I held my breath, already knowing and dreading the conclusion she was drawing out for me.

She continued, "Already this year, there have been two villages reported destroyed by the plague."

"Burridava?" I asked.

The mystic shook her head. "Burridava as well? Too close, too close." Her grip tightened, "Every year that passes, the plague increases."

Her milky gaze pinned me, but I didn't shrink away.

"It's only a matter of time before the plague returns to where it started, no matter how many sacrifices these fools make." Marianna spat on the ground again.

My mouth gaped. "The Lilac Plague has already been in Capidava?"

"This is where it *first* appeared. Most of the slaves taken in the following years helped rebuild this very city."

The little girl stopped in front of us. "Omi Marianna, it's time for supper. Let me help you get cleaned up."

"Ah, Annuska, my granddaughter." The old woman beamed at the little girl who refilled my gourd with fresh water.

"As one goes through the long dark night that inevitably comes for us all, one must struggle to endure until the dawn." Marianna gazed adoringly at the girl. "Joy is like the sun's rays, no one beyond its reach unless we keep to the shadows of sorrow. Stand in the light."

I helped Marianna to her feet. Rubia might be too harsh on fortunetellers, but they were certainly less than straightforward.

Was she right about the plague increasing in strength? Was it possible the Warlock not only created a curse that would last hundreds of years but one that increased in power over time? The idea sent a shudder through me. He intended to wipe out the entire kingdom if the rightful heir wasn't on the throne.

The mystic shuffled inside, her shoulders rounded, chattering with her granddaughter, leaving me in a state of upheaval. The plague had to be stopped and fast.

The little girl re-emerged and skipped to my side, jolting me out of my thoughts. "Omi asked me to guide you to the upper wall."

In this winding city, a guide was far better than verbal directions. Little Annuska took my hand in hers and led me back down the hill... and to an impossibly long, steep stairway I never would've found on my own.

At the top, after skipping two steps at a time, I rested my hands on my knees, sucking in breaths of air. The stairway led up to a wide, flat path that wound around the mountain in either direction. Across from me, on the far side of the path, was a wall covered in miniature climbing roses. I'd made it to the upper wall.

"Left to the Lilies. Right to the Roses," Annuska had instructed.

I turned right and soon spotted two guards in pressed, green cloaks next to a gate. I marched up, trying to look more confident than I felt. I'd been through so many gates I was already prepared with my words.

"I'm here to deliver this cloak to Lady Katalin." I held it out to the older guard whose glib smile displayed a cracked front tooth.

He looked at the tear in my sleeve, and I chided myself for not re-braiding my hair while I was listening to Mystic Marianna. Too late now. I threw my shoulders back and showed him the seal on the cloak, the fox encircled with leaves.

"Who gave you this cloak?" Cracked tooth demanded.

"Lady Katalin herself." I was glad my voice didn't quiver.

He put his hand on the hilt of his sword and gestured for me to enter.

After I passed, I heard the younger guard jest. "An imbecile looking for reward."

The cracked tooth guard responded. "No one leaves the fox's den without receiving their due."

There is a deep pain in my left leg. I haven't told anyone, not Sanaz nor even my brothers. I wonder who has gotten close enough to me to curse my body. I don't trust any Healers.

— VAHID, WARLOCK TO EMPEROR TRAJAN

CARACALLA

CHAPTER

SIXTEEN

CLEVER AS A FOX

Past the upper gate, the road was still steep, but everything else was different. Expansive, manicured estates dotted the mountainside around me, each one larger than the last. Smooth, pearly stone exteriors reflected the bright orange and pink sunset colors in their glass windows. Fruit-laden trees and delicate flower gardens were pruned to perfection. On the rocky outcroppings, not grand enough for estates, sculpted evergreen trees clung to the rocks.

The estates were imposing, but nothing compared to the castle looming above them all. Rupea Castle stood vigil, a statement of power that had only been defeated once, by the Blood Conqueror himself, in ten thousand years. The roar of the waterfall only added to my awe. Past the mosses and even pine trees that were showered in a constant mist, the waterfall crashed into a deep abyss beyond the cliffs.

I gripped my necklace as I checked the crests of each estate. In the lustrous territory of the Rose Court, I felt like a rat that had been let loose in the kitchens.

Blind Marianna had seen beyond my outward appearance. She was right about the Protection spell. I wasn't sure about my

229

vibrant soul. However, what she said about the royal purpose of my heart... that, I understood. The key I clutched was connected to both an important *and* a royal purpose: stopping the plague by a true heir. Her words reinforced what I needed to do, strengthening my resolve to see my brash plan through. I wanted the true heir on the throne.

To force Cassus' hand, I needed the nobility to know the truth. The Roses must find the true heir. Why else did the nobility have their titles and power if not to help those in their kingdom? After all, their wealth was built upon the stooped backs of those who toiled in the fields and the kitchens.

As I checked the crests, I passed a few servants going the opposite direction, carrying baskets or notes in their hands. Interestingly, the road was twice as wide above the upper gate but with far less traffic.

Nearby, a door opened, and a man and woman emerged, followed by a younger woman who looked enough like them that I was confident she was their daughter. Her head was a mass of bouncing ringlets. I stood afar, in the shadows as they descended the steep, grand front steps. A pair of thick men with full-wrapped, knee-length fotas pulled up to the fine mansion house with a two-wheeled carriage in tow. The sleek, polished, wooden carriage had a tall back that partially curved around on the sides but was open in the front. I'd never seen anything like it. Nor had I ever seen a man in a skirt, and their bare chests were all the more peculiar. The lower portion of their legs that I could see looked like massive tree trunks.

The man helped the woman into the fine carriage, and their presumed daughter climbed in after them. The two men pulled the carriage up the mountainside, across the smooth cobblestone road. I stood transfixed until the carriage was pulled out of sight, stunned at the indulgence of the Roses.

I continued to inspect every crest as the main road cut

around the mountain. The castle was getting closer, and the pink mountain had turned to blue in the pre-darkness, the long shadows fading into the evening, but I still hadn't found Lady Katalin's estate. Lights flickered in some windows, identifying which homes were occupied. Despite my burning muscles, I pushed harder.

Two more times, I hid while lavish carriages were pulled up the hill. The road narrowed and sliced into the side of the mountain before wrapping in a tight curve. The next estate sat at the pinnacle of the curve, boldly carved into the white rock, similar to the castle above. The carved spires of the estate jutted into the sky, the body of the mansion brazenly on the precipice of the mountain, defying gravity. My stomach tightened. Only the lower windows were lit — the servants' quarters. There were no houses across or adjacent, just cliffs, and jagged rocks.

I ran my hand across the crest on the gate. As I suspected, a fox surrounded by leaves.

Lady Katalin's fur cloak weighed heavier on my arm. I hadn't anticipated feeling so small, so impossibly unqualified to do this alone. Even from outside the gate, the view from the mountain was impressive. The treetops formed a lush, green blanket over Capidava. Beyond the trees to the south, Rubia was making her way to Capidava. To the east, Burridava was in despair: children crying, hoping their mothers would live through the night.

I tucked in my chin and pushed the metal gate, which swung open soundlessly. Instead of going to the front door and graciously handing over the cloak and leaving, I checked over my shoulder before heading to the servants' quarters. The servants' path was rocky and ran parallel with the wide walk to the main doors for several steps before quickly sloping down to the basement level of the home.

With Lady Katalin gone, I hoped that only the minimum

necessary staff would be on duty. Based on Lady Katalin's haughty air, I assumed her manse would be full of dark corridors and guest rooms, and from the look of the place, I was right. I needed a place to get cleaned up and couldn't afford an inn, but a noble's empty home was perfect.

Next, I needed to figure out how to meet with the nobles all in one place, including the High Judge. If I approached one person, they could brush me off. But a crowd... that would demand a deeper review of my statements. Perhaps I could attend the court. Anyone's trial would do, but I'd prefer to have Papa present as I explained the dire situation to the nobles.

I took a breath. One problem at a time.

The latch opened easily. At least the servants' quarters were unlocked. The door creaked. Inside, someone snorted. I jerked my hand back from the door. Clothing rustled followed by a deep snore. I peered into the room. A portly man with rosy cheeks slept upright in a chair, a bottle of wine precariously balanced between his fist and his lap. Next to him on a table were several unwashed dishes and a pot of soapy water.

I picked up a dry rag next to the pot and dipped it in the still-warm water. I scrubbed my face and hands, quickly turning the rag dark brown. I frowned. Any more wiping and the soapy water would be too dirty for even this drunken servant to miss. I needed a proper bath.

Not daring to close the creaking door, I tiptoed past the man, through the kitchen, to the servants' sleeping quarters. As I suspected, most of the servants were gone, probably enjoying their evening in Lady Katalin's absence. I slipped off my boots, carrying them in my hand, and crept up the stairs.

On the main floor, I found an expansive room for entertaining. My feet sunk into the deep, soft rugs. I passed plush chairs and unlit candelabras. On one side of the room sat a large instrument, taller than I was, with dozens of strings stretching from one end to the other. On the other was a massive fireplace. Through the tall windows, meager light was swallowed in the coming darkness.

I clutched the white cloak tighter. It was doubtful even Gallus, for all his high Moesian airs, had ever laid eyes on such extravagance. To live in such opulence was nearly beyond imagination. I cringed at the thought of Lady Katalin, someone surrounded by luxury, visiting our humble home in Moesia.

Past the massive entertaining room, a grand entrance led to a winding staircase. On the stairs, I felt exposed. The railing provided almost no concealment from anyone who happened to walk by below or above. I scurried up, alert for any sound.

On the second floor, I explored the rooms, looking for a way to clean up. In Moesia, we bathed outside, but Papa had explained that northern homes had baths inside because of the cooler climate.

At the end of the corridor, there was another winding staircase. The stairs were marble and curled upwards into darkness. I gripped the railing, growing more uncomfortable with each trespassing step. I ignored my unease and continued searching in hopes that Lady Katalin would have guest rooms equipped as Papa had described. On the next floor, the hall was lined with glass windows looking out over the dark forest. Stars twinkled in the dusky sky.

The thick rugs under my feet led to the closed double doors at the end of the corridor. The mansion sucked all the sounds of life away, leaving only a ringing in my ears.

My home was loud in comparison. Even in quiet moments, Papa's quill scratched on parchment, birds sang, and noisy children passed by. Lady Katalin's home was sealed off from everything, a refuge of silence.

The doors swung open to a circular room with the lingering scent of rose perfume. Directly across from the double doors, the room had five tall glass windows overlooking the forest. On the left was a large, raised platform bed suffocated under layers of blankets with fine lace edges. Across from the bed was a long couch in front of an empty fireplace. I absently laid Lady Katalin's cloak on the couch as I took in the rest of the room.

Next to the bed, shelves lined the wall, filled with bands like the one Lady Katalin wore, a collection of rounded fur hats, and matching muffs. In the center of the wall was a tall mirror with a thick gilded frame.

Opposite the mirror, wardrobes curved around the room, framing a massive vanity piled with delicate, cut-glass containers.

Above me was the most impressive feature in the room: a glass window placed in the ceiling. I peered up at the castle, a dark thumb blotting out the moon. The Emperor's presence bore down upon the house day and night.

I shrunk out of its purview over to the wardrobe.

Too tempted not to look, I threw the doors open. Inside, hung an array of elegant dresses. I marveled as my fingertips grazed the rich textures, ranging from silky smooth, to plush velvet, to lace.

"Excuse me, but trash belongs on the street, not in a Lady's bedroom."

I spun around and saw a young servant woman holding an unlit candelabrum. Her dark hair was pulled back, her face in the shadows. Her dress was stiff, hardly moving as she walked briskly toward me, a narrow fota apron tied around her waist with a thin belt.

My heart thrummed in my chest. My words stuck in my throat, but I was able to point to Lady Katalin's cloak, my excuse to be there. Though I was hoping not to need it.

The servant ran a hand across the fur cloak, quiet for what seemed to be an eternity as she inspected the seal. I was trespassing, and this cloak was the thread keeping me from the stocks. If this servant pulled hard, the thread would snap. I leaned back against the dresses.

"My apologies. I didn't realize a guest of Lady Katalin's was visiting." She gave me a deep curtsy before rushing to the side table and setting down the candelabrum. Closer to the window, I could see her unlined face in the moonlight. She and Lady Katalin had the same dark hair, brown eyes, and golden skin. Unlike Lady Katalin, this girl's youthful, round cheeks were dotted with freckles.

"I d-didn't... I came through... " I slowed my speech. "I'm Nicoleta of Moesia, here on an errand for Lady Katalin. I came through the servants' quarters so as not to disturb anyone. I didn't want to be a b-bother." I was glad I had washed my face in the kitchen although my stringy hair made me look like a street urchin.

"I'm Tulia. Lady Katalin requested your presence in her home?" Tulia picked up the cloak, inspecting it. Disgust flashed across her features, but she neatly folded the cloak without a word.

I wondered how she would clean it. Or perhaps she'd burn it. It was hard to say. I waited awkwardly, unsure what to say, hoping that Tulia would give away some clue as to what she expected of me or if she would throw me out.

"The gate guard instructed me to be discreet." It was true, but that wasn't my reason for sneaking through the house. "I'm returning the cloak on b-behalf of someone Lady Katalin entrusted it to." I tried to sound official.

"This way, please," Tulia said, leading me to the mirror in the center of the wall of hats. "A guest of Lady Katalin's should be treated like one."

Tulia pressed on the mirror and it popped open like a door. I followed, unsure of what she intended. My neck prickled in warning. Still, I needed to clean myself up.

Through the doorway was a smaller bedroom suite. A shaft of moonlight shown through a tall, narrow glass window that overlooked the forest.

"You'll find it quite comfortable tonight," Tulia said, lighting a candelabrum. "This was once the quarters for the Lord's assistant, never far from where he was needed."

A small fireplace backed up to Lady Katalin's massive fireplace on the other side of the wall. The bed was raised, like Lady Katalin's, but a simple wool blanket and a dark fur covered it, and a small table sat beside it. Near the window was a large tub with a fox statue on a pedestal next to it.

"My apologies. I didn't realize we'd have a guest, and most of the other servants are gone for the evening. I am, of course, happy to attend to you. Would you like me to bring you something to eat?" Tulia lightly brushed the side of her nose.

Abashed, I realized Tulia probably followed her nose to find me here. The quick rinse in the kitchen was like rubbing dust off a clod of dirt. My chest flushed.

"The road has been d-difficult these last few days. My caravan was attacked by b-bandits." My lie sounded confident. "I appreciate your Lady's hospitality. I'm also on an errand to Rupea Castle and must prepare quickly."

"The castle?" Tulia asked.

"I am here on urgent business. You have open court in Capidava, correct? I must be at the next hearing." I waited, hoping she would tell me which trials would be open to the public. Besides, as far as Tulia knew, I was here as an official guest of Lady Katalin. The Lady seemed important, and people didn't seem to question her actions. I needed that.

"You mean to go tonight? There is no court until tomorrow." Tulia barely hid the amusement in her voice.

"I saw many nobles going to the castle. I need to attend the trials. It's a matter of life and death." What amused Tulia so? My attending without a written invitation? My attending without an escort?

"The nobles are attending dinner at the castle. The Judge himself will be dining with them, so of course, there will be no court until tomorrow," Tulia said.

"Who is invited to dine at Rupea Castle?" I asked.

"The entire Rose Court and their esteemed guests. Of course, I can arrange to have you attend tomorrow. But not tonight. I could never have you prepared at this late hour." She hastily added her last words.

"I'll attend court tomorrow, then," I said agreeably. *And I'll attend dinner tonight, too.* I couldn't let my chance to study the Roses slip away. Learning more could make all the difference between failure and success. I needed to know what drove the Roses — what would spur them to action?

"I'll fetch you something to eat, and we can discuss court in the morning. I'll make sure you're on your way before sun up." Tulia edged toward the door.

"Tomorrow then," I lied. I took a step toward her before she could leave. I wouldn't be sleeping here tonight, but I still needed a bath. "Is there somewhere I can bathe tonight? I'd hate to ruin the bed sheets after your kindness."

My plan, for the most part, was still unchanged — use Lady Katalin's house to clean up and then on to the castle. All I had to do was wait until Tulia fell asleep, find something to wear, and be on my way. I could do this.

The servant hesitated before moving to the tub near the windows. "I'm happy to draw you a bath. I apologize for not offering it sooner."

I expected her to leave and fetch warm buckets of water. Instead, she walked to the fox statue beside the bath basin. She grasped one of the ears of the statue and turned it. Water flowed down the extended tongue of the fox and into the basin, filling it as if by magic. Steam rose from the water into the air.

Tulia noticed my wonder and smirked at the yellow embroidery on my torn sleeves. "I doubt they have anything like this in Moesia. The estates in Capidava have direct access to water inside the mountain. Lady Katalin's grandfather had water piped throughout the house. All the bath water is heated day and night over a fire in the kitchen; a servant is always attending to it. The family and their guests have hot water available anywhere in the house."

If your servant is a large man who loves wine, you may need to check the flames.

I dipped my fingers in the warm basin. I couldn't wait to tell Papa about this extravagance. The details of this contrap— My thoughts abruptly stopped.

A momentary lapse; I might never have the chance to tell him. I rubbed my tightening chest.

"I'll fetch you supplies. Leave your clothing and I'll wash them." Tulia pointed to a small rack near the tub. She lit a candle on the small bedside table. Her face was pleasantly bland as she turned to leave, not meeting my eyes.

Tulia closed the door behind her, leaving only a blank wall with no handle or visible hinges. I hoped she would be quick about her business. I needed to get this over with and pretend to sleep so she would leave and I could continue to Rupea. There was no turning back now. Furthermore, if I missed Court in the morning, there was a good chance my lies would catch up to me before I got another chance.

❧

I peeled off my clothing, including the pendant, and slipped into the warm water. The bath was a new kind of magic. Between the hot water, glittering stars outside the window, the candle's soft glow, and the scent of beeswax, I felt transported. I closed my eyes and submerged myself under the water, knowing it immediately turned from sparkling mountain water to a dirty pond.

The water relaxed my tight muscles and aches from riding. I closed my eyes, letting go of my frustration over not knowing how to act around Tulia. I had little experience with household servants. There were too many things I didn't understand about Capidava's Rose culture. Even Tulia seemed a bit closed-off, or perhaps that was just her nature.

When the door opened and candlelight flooded the room, I realized I had dozed off. The water was now tepid as well as murky with soap scum and dirt.

I poked my head up above the basin. Tulia set the lit candelabra on the side table and a nightgown on the bed.

"Would you like assistance?" She smiled, but her eyes were hard. In her hands were a jar and a linen towel.

I shook my head. "I just want to dry off, crawl into bed and sleep for a thousand years."

I was exhausted, but I had no intention of going to bed.

Tulia gave a curt nod then set the linen next to the basin on a small table and placed the jar on top of it. "This is to wash your hair."

"Thank you, Tulia," I said. Her kindness gave me a twinge of guilt knowing I would take a dress from Lady Katalin and leave before dawn. Still, it wouldn't be Tulia's fault I had Lady Katalin's cloak and therefore her supposed permission to enter the house. Besides, Rubia would steal a dress in a heartbeat if it meant saving thousands of people from a horrific death.

"I'll have these for you in the morning." Tulia plucked up

my dirty clothing off the rack. She leaned further down, near my satchel where I'd set the key.

"Wait!" Water flew as I jumped to stop her. "D-don't t-touch... D-don't touch the necklace." Water dripped from my hand, drenching the stone floor and Tulia's dress.

"I'm no thief." She frowned.

"No, no! Of course... of course not." Though gold was precious in Moesia and a hundred times more so outside our mining city, I kept those thoughts to myself.

"I would never lose your trinket, either. I'm just a servant but have my honor." Tulia reached for the satchel with the necklace on top.

"It will hurt you!" I blurted while flailing my arm to keep her away.

Tulia stumbled back, her brows drawn together.

I hooked the leather with my finger and clutched the pendant. I rubbed my eyes with my thumb and forefinger, deciding how little I could share and still sound truthful.

"This is an amulet. Cursed. It harms anyone who touches it who isn't Bonded to it," I said.

"I've never seen a design like it before; it's not much to look at, is it? Flat on one side with strange notches on the other. And the markings, are they Getaen?" It was the first time Tulia had even a hint of curiosity in her voice.

This was my chance to practice some of my speech out loud. Tulia would be a good example of how a Capidavan might react.

"It's actually why I'm here." I took a breath. "Have you heard of the Lilac Plague?"

Tulia's eyes widened. "Yes, of course."

"My mama was killed in the plague over three years ago. It devastated Moesia," I said.

Tulia tilted her head, her face softening.

"I'm here because this piece of cursed gold can help stop the plague. Forever. The pendant and information I have are key to unraveling a curse that was set into motion over two hundred years ago." I watched her as I spoke, and she finally met my eyes. "Can you imagine our kingdom without the p-plague haunting us?"

Tulia brought her hands up to her lips.

"I'm here to present this information," I added. I made a mental note to practice a bit more before tomorrow to completely erase my stutter before I interjected at court.

"Your cursed orb can stop the plague? That will be the biggest news of the century, and Lady Katalin isn't home. I'm sure she'd like to hear of this, first. Otherwise, she'll be at a disadvantage when she returns." Tulia tapped her chin.

I pursed my lips. That wasn't the response I expected. "I'm sorry if Lady Katalin is negatively affected while she's away from court, but it cannot wait. The people in B-Burridava are dying as we speak."

Tulia smiled slowly, a glittering expression in her eyes. Rubia had the same look right before she did something mischievous. Then Tulia's face fell, her eyes downcast.

"Oh, no," she whispered as she sunk to the bed, her hands gripping the fur blanket.

"What's wrong?" I asked.

Tulia jumped up and marched over to my clothing. "One rinse won't do. Change your water. Wash your hair and get out of the tub. Be quick. I'll help you get into Rupea."

She ran from the room, taking my clothing and slamming the door behind her. I puzzled over Tulia's odd reaction. At least she seemed to understand the gravity of my words. I hoped the nobles would be similarly motivated to rush into action. I fiddled with a chain at the bottom of the basin, releasing the water.

In the flickering candlelight, the squalid conditions of my travel swirled in the sullied water and disappeared through the hole in the tub. As it lowered, I inspected my body. I ran my hand over the red area on my shoulder that I had expected to be a deep purple. My hip was similarly unscathed after colliding with the cobblestones. Protections were officially added to my 'not swindlers' list. More importantly, I had escaped Elek without a brand on my neck.

I plugged the drain and twisted the fox's ear, sending a cascade of warm water into the tub. I twisted the fox's ear off. Then on. Then the other ear, sending cold water blasting into the tub. Then twisting the ears slowly, I controlled the amount and the temperature of the water as it fell. I left the stream at a trickle, wanting to enjoy the steaming indoor waterfall for as long as possible.

I opened the jar from the side table, and the perfumed contents mixed with the steam from the bath, infusing the room with the luxurious scent of roses. The concoction in the jar was both oily and gritty. Two hot baths were a luxury I'd never had, but instead of relishing it, I attacked my scalp with the fancy mix.

I scrubbed my nails, rinsed my newly rose-scented hair again, and climbed out of the tub. I dried off with the thin linen towel before wrapping it around my body and putting the orb around my neck. I felt around the doorway but could find no handle nor even hinges. I pushed on it, the way I'd seen Tulia do it, but it didn't open.

My heartbeat quickened. Where was Tulia? Had she meant to lock me in? Should I not have told her about the pendant?

I spun and marched to the window, hastily running my hand around the periphery. Even if I broke it and squeezed past the shards of glass, I would be greeted by a thousand feet of air as I tumbled to a rocky death below.

Elek's mansion was probably in these upper estates. I didn't relish the idea of escaping him only to plunge to my death at his feet. I tried not to picture him in his carriage, riding up the hill, his hand wrapped in a sling. I took a calming breath to stop my runaway thoughts. Elek's caravan accommodated many people at a lumbering pace. They would have to spend another night in the forest, just like Marcus. I paced the floor. But, if Elek's caravan pushed through the night, he could be in Capidava by morning, possibly attending the morning trial? Would the caravan be so bold?

The rustling of Tulia's clothing announced her as she rushed into the room. The flickering candlelight from her candelabrum reflected the concern in her wide eyes.

"I'm so sorry. I thought you were a thief." She was breathing hard, her face flushed. "It's happened once before. Some Lilac stole a Vulpe family cloak. Instead of using it for travel or trade, they made the mistake of returning it here, believing anyone with the cloak would be entitled to a night of hospitality. They were eager to see how a lady lives until they experienced the ruthless Vulpe house." She shook her head and refocused on me. "Once you started bathing, I sent for the Thorns at the upper gate."

No, no! I hadn't left my home, gotten attacked by Elek, abandoned Rubia, stolen a horse, betrayed Marcus, and narrowly escaped thieves in the forest to be caught in a net by Lady Katalin's servant.

Tulia grabbed for my arm, but I pushed past her. I had to escape before the guards arrived.

"Wait!" Tulia shouted.

"I should've known Lady K-Katalin would employ servants as horrid as herself." I fled from the guest room, still only wrapped in the linen towel. My face contorted; I was sure I looked frightening in the candled shadows, but I didn't care. I had to speak. "She cares a-about no one but h-herself and you're her m-mirror image."

"How dare you lump us together! I rushed to send word that it was a mistake, that there's no intruder." Tulia's nostrils flared, her voice growing louder with each word. "You're safe here for the night!"

I stopped, the linen barely secured around me, my dirty satchel in my hand.

"I'm not like Lady Katalin." Tulia's eyes bulged. "I believe you, your story. Don't accuse me of being like *her*. You know nothing of me."

The room fell silent except for Tulia's breathing. My shoulders slumped. We'd both lied. We'd both made assumptions. There was no point in pretending I would stay here for the night. At least I'd gotten cleaned up.

"P-Please return my clothing. I'll leave immediately." My voice was flat and unfriendly.

Tulia sucked in a breath, and her lips tightened. I inwardly groaned. What had she done with my clothing? She had said she would wash them.

"I burned them."

Sanaz worries about her baby. Will he have magic? And if so, can his magic be hidden? Whenever I see Sanaz's decorative marriage disks on her belt or rub her growing belly, I wonder what might have been if I'd ever told Sanaz about my feelings. I oscillate between happiness for her and heartache.

— VAHID, WARLOCK TO EMPEROR TRAJAN
CARACALLA

CHAPTER

SEVENTEEN

IN TULIA'S HANDS

Tulia sat me down on a tufted seat in front of Lady Katalin's vanity mirror, handing me a comb and instructing me to untangle my unruly hair.

"I knew Lady Katalin didn't send you the moment I saw the Moesian embroidery on your dress. No influence, no cloak. And, obviously, you don't have influence." She shot me a glance. "The cloak is a spider's way of bringing prey to her web. You were clearly not her target. I knew you'd be easy to subdue and take away to…"

"T-to the stocks." I finished her languishing sentence. The stocks would ruin any chance of the nobles believing what I had to say.

"Entering into the Rose Court without permission is a serious offense." Tulia searched through a drawer, producing a pair of scissors. "However, when you warned me away from the necklace and told me your story, I sensed your truth. Except, I'd already sent that lackey to fetch the guard."

"Is he a large fellow with a red nose? Fond of naps?" I asked.

Tulia raised an eyebrow and nodded.

"Then there's a chance he passed out before he ever made it to the guards," I said, half-jokingly.

Tulia rolled her eyes. "Kalman would roll down the hill to deliver the message if he needed to. I sent another servant to intercept the guards on their way up. I need to check to make sure it was done. In the meantime, finish combing your hair so I can cut it when I get back. I cut Lady Katalin's hair, and I'll admit that I have quite a talent with scissors. You'll look very high-hat with smooth hair. Ringlets would be better, but we won't have time for that."

"It's traditional for Moesians to keep our hair long. I don't want it cut," I countered.

"Yes, I'm sure you braid it in the summer and wear it long in the winter. Very practical, but it tips you off as lower class. You'll fit in so much better once it's cut." Tulia hastily organized the vanity top covered in little brushes, paints, and glass bottles.

Mama and Rubia had braided this hair many times. "I'm Moesian, and I'll keep my hair."

Tulia frowned.

"Isn't there a fashionable braid of some kind?" I hoped to find some compromise.

Tulia straightened and threw up her arms. "I'll think of something. I'll be back soon. Keep combing that mess."

After finishing with the tangles in my hair, I moved to the bed. I couldn't help but be drawn to the pale yellow clothing that Tulia had draped on Lady Katalin's bed: a chemise, dress, catrintas aprons, and marama. Tulia hadn't mentioned the clothing before she dashed away. I pulled on the snug chemise and waited for Tulia to return.

The chemise was made of the raw, nubby silk I had fawned over in Moesia. We had never been able to afford such a garment. Beyond the chemise, the dress was in a class all its own, as soft as rose petals and seemingly twice as delicate. It was embroidered with faceted beads from the shoulder to the elbow. At the elbow, the sleeve's sheer material billowed out before tying at the wrist.

Tulia burst in and dropped a pair of shoes at my feet as words tumbled from her lips, "Thank the stars, the guards were intercepted and sent back to the wall. I promised to do the dishes tonight to make up for the other servants' inconvenience."

"Thank you. I appreciate all your running about to help me." I didn't mention that had she not lied and planned to trap me in the first place, she wouldn't have to run back and forth and then do dishes. Instead, I skimmed my fingertips lightly over the dress. "This is too fine. What will happen when it goes missing?"

"Lady Katalin received these from an old beau. Or should I say a distant admirer who wished to be a beau. She never wears pale colors and had me stow it away. I doubt she remembers it exists." Tulia held it up to me. "Besides, it was never fitted or hemmed and is about your size."

"Are you sure?"

"Just put it on and be grateful," Tulia huffed. She stood back, watching as I picked up the dress.

I pulled on the yellow dress over my slip. The material was cold against my damp skin, but it dropped around my body like a cloud. It swished across my legs like smooth water with every step I took. The hem grazed the rugs, my toes just peeking out under the bottom.

Tulia buttoned up the back of the dress before turning to the double catrintas aprons. They were slightly darker yellow with an intricate embroidered swirling pattern. Tulia deftly tied the shiny ribbons, fastening the apron on each side while I held up my arms.

"You almost look like a Lily in this." She laughed, and then it abruptly turned into a snort. "Don't tell anyone I said such blasphemy. Oh, and nobles never refer to themselves as Lilies or Roses; that would be uncouth. To them, Dacia is split into nobles and peasants. There is nothing else."

"Interesting," I said, running my hand down the apron. "This is such a gorgeous shade of yellow."

"Citrus. It's citrus. Never yellow," Tulia corrected.

She directed me back to the stool, and I watched in the mirror as Tulia swept pieces of my hair into large, smooth loops.

"Dab some of that powder on your face." She pointed at a jar on the table.

I reached for a brush.

"A large brush." She redirected me as her fingers moved through my wet hair.

I dipped the brush in the powder and put it on my face.

"Pat, don't slather. You're not a market busker!"

I tried not to cough as the powder stung my throat with each pat.

Tulia's nimble fingers stopped, and she looked at me in the reflecting glass, the flickering candlelight illuminating both our faces. She braided and then looped a strand of hair just like Mama and I had done for each other all those years. I blinked back emotions that threatened to melt my resolve. Did she know the Getaen traditions? Was she manipulating me?

"Do you really think you can succeed? Trying to stop the plague with your trinket?" She paused her work, her face falling. "I have old clothing you can have. You can try your luck on the streets of Capidava. Better yet, go to my old master in Patridava. My family has served his for generations. With a note from me, he would take you in, treat you well. It's a better fate than what I fear is in store for you if you go through with whatever dim-witted plan you've concocted." Tulia was direct, but there was no barb to her words. Her offer was sincere.

"I'm sure your master would make for a safer fate, but I have to do this. I-It could stop the plague," I said.

Tulia tugged my hair again, tight enough to make my eyes water, her gaze turned back to her task of looping and smoothing the strands with her fingers. "I knew you'd say that. And as much as I fear the plague, I have other reasons for helping you." She braided another strand as she spoke. "Lady Katalin ensnared my old master. My service is part of his blackmail payment to her each moon. I am separated from my family. I've only seen my little brother once in over a year when he traveled to Capidava on an errand with my master. He's growing up, and we barely know each other anymore." Tulia's face was tightly controlled, but her eyes glittered with fury.

"Besides, I don't believe that Zalmoxis blesses the lineage of the great Emperor Trajan Caracalla and curses the rest of us." Tulia's voice was a mixture of bitterness and sarcasm. "Zalmoxis is a god. All humans are weak creatures in comparison, emperor and slave alike. He curses us all the same."

Tulia finished pinning my hair in quiet contemplation before she began her endless discourse about the rules of the court. My head swam with minutia, but I focused when she got around to talking about the Judge.

"If you're going to find the High Judge, he will be in the dining hall. Emperor Cassus rarely makes an appearance, but just the possibility of his presence keeps the nobles coming every night." She patted the top of my head, signaling she was done with my hair.

I leaned forward, not daring to touch her masterpiece. Normally, my Moesian braids were functional, but Tulia's creation was a magnificent bungle of twists and loops. Though some of the pins jabbed uncomfortably in my scalp, I admired her handiwork. Several of the braided looped pieces hung low enough to brush my neck, hiding Marcus' leather strap which held the orb.

"If the Emperor is there by chance, do not approach him unless invited. It will be seen as aggressive, a possible assassination attempt. You could be killed on the spot."

Tulia spun me around and picked up a small container off the vanity. She dipped her pinky finger into a red substance and dabbed it on my lips. This close, I guessed Tulia was possibly thirteen or fourteen. Like me, she was torn from her family and forced to grow up too quickly. Only, Tulia was a servant, working long, hard hours. My complaints about caring for Papa and our home seemed insignificant and empty.

When finished, Tulia spun me around to the mirror once again. I looked like an exotic noblewoman visiting from a faraway kingdom. Fortunately, there were no bruises or scrapes on my arms to be seen through the sheer lower sleeves.

Tulia put her hand on her hips. "If you'd let me cut your hair and wait until tomorrow, you'd turn a head or two. However, like this, you won't be humiliated."

I was speechless at her kindnesses. Tulia picked up the scarf, revealing another item below it, a yellow velvet pouch that closed with a pull of a thin white cord. She wrapped the scarf around my head and shoulders. I blinked, realizing she hadn't asked about the red mark on my shoulder, and I was grateful. I didn't want to think about Elek, much less talk about him.

Tulia handed me the pouch. "This purse will have to do. It's been in the closet since falling out of fashion, but Lady Katalin would notice anything else missing.

"It's lovely," I said.

"It's a decoy. Put anything of real value in the hidden

pockets of your catrintas," Tulia poked at a hidden compartment in my apron.

The only things I had left were a few herbs and the orangesting. I stowed the herbs in the purse and slid the vial into my apron. The material was thick enough to disguise the tiny bulge near the side seam.

"Thank you," I said. "I don't know how to ever repay you."

"You're leaving the fox's den but going into a wolves' lair. Don't think a noble woman's fine dress and a potion will protect you. They won't. You must be careful. There are many intricate rules of the castle. I'm afraid you won't last through dinner."

"With all you've done. I'll dance in and out without a hitch," I said, confidence in my plan growing.

"No jewels, feathers, nor hat, with frightfully long hair and only the illusion of curls. We'll have to hope they believe your Getaen traditions are quaint rather than offensive." She sighed and handed me a pair of flat-soled, black satin slippers. "These are my best shoes and my gift to you - a good luck charm."

Tulia stepped back and inspected me. A tiny smile threatened.

"I'll never utter your name, of course," I said, not mentioning how tight Tulia's shoes were on my feet.

"Of course. It will save me the trouble of denying I've ever seen you. The stocks would be the least of my troubles if Lady Katalin discovered I assisted you in impersonating a noble." She grabbed my hand, pulling me out of Lady Katalin's room.

"You'll need to dispose of my satchel." My satchel looked indecent for a rat to live in, yet I'd clutched it as a lifeline for days.

I pulled out the only remaining proper Healers' packet. "This tea will put anyone into a restful slumber. It must be steeped in hot water to activate the effects of the herbs. It's not much, but please take it as a gift for all you've done for me."

She grinned. "I have just the person to —"

Her words were cut off by a pounding on the door. Tulia's face fell, and she darted to the top of the grand staircase. The portly servant staggered toward the door.

I pulled Tulia's arm and we darted away from the open staircase to hide.

Kalman's words were slurred. Before he could open the door fully, guards stormed into the house.

"Drat the competence of the Thorns. They must have decided to investigate anyway." Tulia pointed down the hall that led away from the grand entrance. "At the end of this hall is a narrow door. Take the stairs down to a servants' washroom. You'll find another set of stairs to the servants' quarters. I must get back to Lady Katalin's room and clean up. Remember, you were never here."

I pressed the sleeping tea herbs into her hand. "If someone comes asking for me, please don't, p-please don't tell him where I've gone. It'll be b-better for everyone."

She gave me a quick nod and shoved me down the hall before dashing across the open stairwell back to Lady Katalin's room. My heart thumped as I fled, not daring to look back. The velvet purse bobbed against my wrist.

My satchel. I hoped Tulia could dispose of it quickly as she arranged the room to look as if no one had ever been there.

I had no idea how long before the soldiers charged up the stairs. I lifted the hem of the dress higher, running as hard as I could to the end of the hall. I found the narrow door, threw it open, and scurried down the stairs to the washroom.

I wasn't sure why I desperately had to tell Tulia not to send Marcus for me. It was safest to push everyone away. Or was it something else?

In the washroom, I slipped and caught myself as I pivoted to the next flight of stairs. I rushed to the lower level, my feet flying.

Perhaps I wanted to believe Marcus would come for me, despite my betrayal. In some recess of my heart, I could believe he felt the same spark I did, and the only reason I never saw him again was because I'd instructed Tulia to keep my disguise a secret. Ending our barely-friendship would be my choice. And I would never have to face the consequence of his bitter feelings, or worse, his apathy.

At the bottom of the stairs was a small room with shelves of clean clothing and linens. Which way to the kitchen? Blood pulsed in my ears in the darkened hallways, half expecting a Thorn or a servant to jump out and grab me at any moment.

I followed a flickering light to the empty kitchen. The pot of water and dishes still waited to be cleaned. My clothes, embroidered with the yellow of Moesia, had been haphazardly thrown on the fire, suffocating the embers. With the poker, I jabbed at the clothing and tossed on kindling to stoke the flames. The evidence of my former life along with Elek's attack would burn, leaving only dust and ashes.

Behind me, someone shuffled and let out a loud belch. Not waiting to be found, I ran out the same door I'd entered through; it was still open a crack, but it squeaked a bit as I slipped through. I listened for the soldiers. Muted shouting sounded from deep within the house through the open main entrance. But I saw no green cloak Thorns outside.

The only way out was to walk past the front doors to the main road.

My stomach twisted, and I wanted to vomit. Everything was moving too fast. The toady servant was probably in the kitchen now. I couldn't go back inside. The only way out was along the exposed pathway.

I took a breath, threw back my shoulders, and forced myself to walk the servants' path, ignoring the weakness in my knees. I was grateful for the nighttime cover, but my yellow dress was like a balefire. My skin prickled, waiting for someone to spy me from a window or walk out of the mansion.

I turned onto the main road and picked up my pace. Behind me, wheels creaked on the cobblestones. I picked up my pace, not turning around. Had they seen me exit Lady Katalin's estate? The path cut through the mountain, walls of rock on either side. There was no place to hide. The road curved up the mountain. Soon I would be out of sight of Lady Katalin's house. The wheels grew louder. I turned my head away, hoping they would pass by without giving me much notice.

I had no such luck. The carriage stopped alongside me.

I received a strange visit tonight. Odon's young mistress came to visit me after dusk. She is engaged to a nobleman, per Emperor Trajan's command. She asked me to create another amulet for her beloved fiancé. I was stunned to discover the amulet didn't burn her except for when she was getting sick. She thought the amulet was a kindness from Odon, a warning to allow her time to procure medicine before the fever took hold, possibly saving her life.

Her words astonished me; it seems that she cares for the man she's engaged to, yet the amulet only burns her when her body temperature begins to rise in response to illness. I vaguely recall being worried, when I created the amulet, that every time the wearer was ill, this amulet would cruelly burn her. I inspected the markings on her amulet again, realizing the symbols, while cold and unchanging and carved into metal, could have more than one meaning. The bonding I created was impacted by something beyond the words and the symbols: intention. What a revelation!

My excitement turned sour; it was another insight my northern master had never divulged.

— VAHID, WARLOCK TO EMPEROR TRAJAN
CARACALLA

EIGHTEEN

INTO THE WOLVES' LAIR

"Hello, there," a man called out.

I steeled myself before facing the carriage, not sure what to expect.

The man seated in the open carriage might have been considered handsome except that his ridiculous hat looked too much like Elek's, including the large, bright feather extending from the top.

"I find it to be a lucky day when I meet a guest of our great city, especially one as lovely as you. You shouldn't be walking like a pauper. Let me give you a ride," he said.

One of the well-muscled men pulling the carriage opened the small door for me to step inside.

I had no idea what was proper to say, so I said nothing. I simply nodded, imagining that I was a haughty noblewoman like Lady Katalin who nodded as if she were a cat with something up her nose trying to sneeze. I seated myself in the carriage next to the strange man.

"I'd heard Getaens were friendly." He laughed as the carriage jerked forward. He gestured to the pillow I was leaning back on. "No pillow between us? How scandalous."

Embarrassment burned up my neck. Did he think I was flirting with him? I was double grateful that the dress had a high cut that both hid the pendant and my blush. I yanked the pillow out from my back and shoved it between us.

"Please, allow me to introduce myself. I'm Lord Jovian," the man said.

"I'm Nicoleta of Moesia." I tried to smile, but something about him made my skin crawl. Perhaps it was the way his eyes traveled my body as if it were new territory he intended to map or the way he lounged in the carriage, careless of clothing that cost more than most families made in a year.

"Who has the pleasure of your company in our fine city?" Jovian asked.

"I'm here to assist in translating scrolls the Emperor recently acquired," I repeated my practiced reason.

Lady Katalin's estate was near the top of the mountain, so it didn't take long to reach Rupea Castle. As we traveled, Jovian made polite, if invasive, small talk, practically shouting over the roaring waterfall. He tried to tease out who my 'people' were and if I had any sort of 'attachments.' I made agreeable sounds and nodded, hoping I would seem more aloof rather than awkward.

The road widened into a square, large enough to fit hundreds of people. Massive fire pits lined the perimeter, lighting the area. Even from the carriage, I felt the warmth of the flames. Polished carriages lined one side of the courtyard with the burly men loitering nearby. One of the men opened my door, and I escaped before Jovian could pry further.

Nobles strolled at a leisurely pace through Rupea's doors.

"Well, young scholar, as you have been invited by the Emperor," Jovian said as he strolled around the carriage. "I would be honored to have you join me this evening."

I wanted to wriggle away but left to my own devices, I had

as much chance of wandering into a closet as finding the dining hall. Following tactlessly on Jovian's heels would only raise his suspicions that I wasn't the dignified guest I pretended to be. I took a deep breath, plastering a serene look on my face, and allowed Jovian to take my elbow as we approached the castle gates. The looming white granite walls were imposing, even in the moonlight with the dancing orange flames. As we drew closer, I realized the guards flanking both sides of the castle's entrance didn't wear green cloaks. Instead, they wore the same black attire as Lady Katalin's guard. The same black clothing as the soldiers from the raid. A chill ran down my spine. It took all of my self-control to put one foot in front of the other.

"This way, young lady." Lord Jovian shifted his hand onto my back. I tightened my grip on the velvet pouch.

Several of the Thorns' hilts glinted in the firelight. One bounced on his heels, and another's mustache twitched as they scanned the nobles while they passed by. I blinked, willing myself to traipse past them as the other nobles did.

"A moment, my lady." A guard held up his hand as I approached the entrance.

I realized almost too late that the *lady* was me. I stopped and forced myself to give him an indignant glare.

"I do not recognize you, my lady. May I inspect your invitation?" The guard's words were courteous enough, but his manner was cold and impersonal, matching his eyes. Like the other Thorns at the entrance, green edged the bottom of his sleeve.

"This is a guest of the Emperor's," Lord Jovian said, his hand slipping further down my back.

A flush burned up my chest. I had never said I was a guest of the Emperor. Lord Jovian had assumed it. But now, I was caught in the lie by omission. I was alert for any opportunity to part ways with the man who'd leeched onto me.

"And do you need to see my invitation, impudent fellow?" Lord Jovian huffed.

"No, of course not, my Lord Jovian." The guard's eyes narrowed, boring through my thin lie. "I had not been told the Emperor invited a guest to the castle tonight."

"A bit of a misunderstanding, I fear. In truth, I'm here at the request of another noble, not the Emperor himself." I had hoped my appearance as a noble would be enough, but clearly, I would need a name. I couldn't say Lady Katalin; it would put Tulia in even more danger. Though loathed to utter it, I knew only one other noble in Capidava. "I am Lord Elek's guest."

The soldier's penetrating stare moved to Lord Jovian before returning his focus to me.

"Lord Elek is in Patridava. There is some rumor that he was injured there." The guard moved his hand subtly closer to the hilt of his sword. If I had been in my normal Moesian attire, he would have already chased me away or beaten me for my impertinence. But dressed as I was, the guard refrained.

I put my hand to my chest in mock worry. "He was injured? How shocking! We met through the Duke of Patridava. His wife throws the most lovely dinner parties." I was disgusted with my lies, but I'd rehearsed several versions of them. "They serve the most delicious tarts in the shape of a frog."

I hoped I remembered Lady Katalin's bragging correctly. Who would want to eat frog-shaped tarts, delicious or not?

"Do you expect Lord Elek will be delayed long? He was very interested in my translation skills." I continued to feign concern. "He said there have been some developments and I might be of some use. I left for Capidava right away before Elek was finished with his business."

I never thought I could turn the horror Elek had unleashed on me to my advantage. I pictured myself throwing my orange-sting at Elek's feet. Oh, it would be so satisfying.

"I don't think we need to delay any further." Lord Jovian sniffed.

The guard straightened taller, his shoulders back. "My apologies for your delay. Would you care for an escort to dinner?"

I expected Lord Jovian to object as he had already offered to escort me, but instead, he said, "You may guide her to my table as Lord Elek is away."

Lord Jovian turned to me. "I have some business to attend to, but I will dine with you shortly."

I suppressed a genuine smile at my change of fortune. Instead, I gave a polite nod. I would be led straight to the dining hall instead of blundering around the castle or having to arrive with Lord Jovian.

"I'll take her." A voice sounded from behind me.

"Of course, sir." The guard puffed out his chest.

On my right, an older guard with broad shoulders approached and held out a hand to show me where to go. "This way."

His high cheekbones, faded strawberry blond hair, and almond eyes were Getaen. I struggled to hold in my questions in front of Lord Jovian and the other guard. The Getaen guard led me through wide double doors and into a hall parallel to the front of the castle. "May I introduce myself? I'm Jamil of the Emperor's Own."

A small gasp escaped my lips. I didn't know what the Emperor's Own were exactly, but the way the guard deferred to Jamil and his all-black sleeves indicated he was important. Rubia had said there were precious few Getaens in any position of influence in Rupea. My heart soared at my good fortune. "You... you're Getaen?"

Jamil raised a brow. "Are we not all Dacian?"

His walk was the stiff march of a soldier. Did he see my

comment as an insult?

"Indeed we are all Dacian. My mother hails from the *very far south* of Dacia." I grinned.

Jamil's gate had an almost imperceptible hitch. "I suspected as much, yet I don't often see a Getaen dressed in fine silks."

I don't often see dresses this fine at all, I thought.

Jamil's pockmarked face signaled he had survived the plague. I had never seen any living soul with such ravaged skin, however, he was likely once a handsome man. With the white in his hair and the wrinkles around his eyes, I guessed that he was Papa's age, but with his scars, it was difficult to tell.

"I didn't expect a *southern* Dacian to be in the Emperor's Own," I said.

"Nor did anyone else." He lifted his chin. "It will be good to have a Southerner in the court tonight."

Our footfalls echoed across the endless hall that gradually curved out of sight. Above us, there was no roof, only the starlit sky. We passed regularly stationed Thorns and braziers burning high until Jamil turned and entered through another set of double doors, passing yet another set of guards. It was like going from night to day. The floors were shiny, veined marble, reflecting the light of the artful luminaries. Sturdy alabaster pillars held up the vaulted ceiling.

"How did you say you met Lord Elek?" Jamil's voice was casual, but I suspected it was a subtle interrogation.

"Why do you ask?" Rubia would be proud that I'd answered a question with another question.

He cleared his throat. "No reason. It's simply unusual for a young woman to travel alone, especially after coming to Lord Elek's... attention."

I could only imagine that both nobles and servants of the Rose Court well knew of Lord Elek's disgusting behavior. This Getaen soldier wondered why Elek considered me worthy of presenting to the Court. I had to be of some strategic value to him. My skin crawled at the prospect of being of value to Elek in any other way.

"I'm a translator. I've come to present information to the High Judge," I repeated my oft-practiced line.

"You translate text between Getaen and Dacian? Is that so difficult?" There was no mockery in Jamil's voice.

"More difficult than you might expect. A Getaen text might mention 'the rich love of the sea.' A Dacian might assume the deeper meaning is any valuable goods transported on the sea. But a Getaen is probably referring to salt, because it preserves, or even algae, because it feeds." I tapped my chin, thinking. "Or they might be referring to their homes. Some Getaens migrate with their families and animals. Depending on the clan, their home might be near the sea where they barter for that season. A northern Dacian might not have the context or understanding to make the correct translation."

"So now that you've explained, I'm sure I can translate, too," Jamil said.

"Well, that's the simple —"

His lips twitched into a smile.

"Oh, you do have a sense of humor!" I hadn't been with someone who seemed to understand me since leaving Rubia. His presence was immediately comfortable.

"I'm from Moesia. My name is Nicoleta." I wanted to confess to him about my journey, but like Marcus, it would only put him in danger. I was here to speak with the most powerful people in the city, not drag this man down with me.

As we continued, the sound of flutes and strings filled the air. I chewed the inside of my cheek, wondering where I would sit or what I would do. If the Emperor was there, I'd stay only a short amount of time. The last thing I wanted was to draw undue attention before the open trial. Tulia had confirmed the

Emperor didn't attend common trials, so I had little concern he would overhear my argument there.

"Are you ever stationed in the dining room?" I hoped Jamil would tell me what to expect when I arrived. Any shred of information helped me plan my words.

"Sometimes, yes. Normally, I could stay close to the room if you requested, but tonight I'm unable to do so. I have other business to attend."

The music grew louder, followed by polite laughter. With every step, I was closer to the wolf's den. But if there was even the slightest chance I could end the plague, I'd have to risk getting eaten alive.

"Another duty?" I asked, keeping myself distracted.

"Yes, I'm checking in on the Emperor's latest fascination. I feel sorry for the fellow. A widower — lost his wife to the plague three years ago," Jamil said. "Apparently, this scholar might be able to decrypt information the Emperor's been after for years."

The air was sucked from my lungs as if I'd been punched in the stomach. A scholar? He was talking about Papa. He had to be. Papa was here. Not just in Capidava but in Rupea Castle. Was he close enough that if I cried out, he could hear me? Was he down this hall? Was he hurt?

I was next to a Getaen who could help me find him. A Getaen I'd felt comfortable with.

Jamil continued, "It would be nice not to have to bring back every scrap of parchment or scroll we find for a change."

I forced myself to breathe, torn between wanting to run and scream. This Getaen took part in raiding desperate cities like Moesia. No, I couldn't be fooled by his Getaen heritage. He wore the Emperor's black. Had he watched as Papa's face was cut? Had he held the blade?

The guard stopped next to the open double doors, music, delicious aromas, and chatter pouring out of the room.

"Are you all right, Mistress Nicoleta? You're pale as the moon,' the Getaen raider asked.

"A s-scholar?" My hand clenched at my stomach.

"Yes. In fact, when you said you were a translator, I thought you were going to say Lord Elek had requested you verify his work. Seems he's in need of some assistance." The guard tilted his head.

Could he hear my heart pounding? I was sure anyone could hear it, except for the music. All I needed to do was request it, and this man would take me to Papa. Even if Lord Jovian came looking for me, raising suspicions, even if my identity was uncovered at the wrong time, my chance to plead with the nobles gone, I still yearned for Papa.

Papa would want to see me one last time, but I knew he would want to save Burridava more. If I reunited with Papa, any guard, scribe, or servant in the room could too easily discern we were family. It was risky to appear to Papa without warning, without a plan. If I were discovered to be anything other than a noblewoman here at Elek's invitation, I'd be condemning myself and any city the plague touched in the future. I clenched my hands into fists, feeling torn in two.

BEFORE I COULD CHANGE my mind, I thanked Jamil and pivoted to the dining room filled with a hundred noble wolves ravenously consuming bits of meat, gravy, fruits, and all manner of foods piled high on platters. I hovered in the doorway, staring at the center of the raised dais. Behind the long, imposing table sat a massive golden throne.

On that royal seat, Emperor Cassus Caracalla VII sat,

holding a pheasant leg in one hand while his dark eyes scanned the room. Growing up in Moesia, I was used to seeing gold, but the sheer amount took my breath away. Cassus VII peered down upon the gathering with an austere power that only one who could kill with a mere snap of his fingers could muster.

Could I avoid his attention, or should I leave now? Plenty of bright colors, feathers, and distracting designs could camouflage me while I studied the nobility and snuck some food before finding a place to sleep.

"Right this way." A servant gave me a courteous smile and led me forward.

Out of the corner of my eye, I saw Jamil disappear, along with my chance to see Papa. My heart tightened, but I strode behind the servant, my chin up. Wolves could smell weakness miles away.

The servant guided me to the far side of the room. Lord Jovian's seats were some of the furthest from the Emperor's table, probably not good for Jovian's courtly ambitions, but it suited me fine. Out of the Emperor's direct view, I could be discreet. The wall nearest the table was floor-to-ceiling windows with a magnificent view of the night sky and flickering lights from the city below.

The servant indicated for me to sit and said loud enough for the closest nobles to hear, "Welcome, Nicoleta, translator and esteemed guest of Lord Elek."

Intruder. Impostor. I slid into my seat, trying to keep a serene look on my face.

Below the dais, the tables formed a massive square except for a wide opening where nobles and servants could pass to the inner seats. Jewel-colored cloths draped the tables, the surface littered with platters, plates, and goblets. Roast fowl, warm bread, apricots, plus a dozen things I didn't recognize teased my senses.

On the tables and the floor danced reflected circles of light from above. Massive chandeliers hung from the ceiling, mystical blue-hued light reflecting off thousands of crystals. Beyond the lights, the ceiling was made of stone, glass, and lead.

I had expected the Emperor to dress like Elek, but Cassus VII was the merchant's opposite in many ways. His somber clothing was fine and well-tailored, but the cut was practical. No gold ringed his fingers, nor were there jewels across his chest. He only wore a simple gold circlet upon his head.

A stunning Getaen woman perched on the seat to the Emperor's left. She had glossy, dark red hair pulled to one side and held with a jeweled comb. She wore a simple, emerald dress complimented by dangling earrings that grazed her bare collarbones. She would have looked gorgeous in a muslin sack. She gazed out at the crowd with a mischievous twinkle in her eye while she delicately sampled from a plate of grapes and cheese.

On the Emperor's right was an older adviser with sharp features and graying hair. The adviser scowled at a portly lord who was seemingly oblivious that his glass of wine was threatening to spill into the adviser's lap.

Directly in front of me was a large silver plate, two spoons and a dull knife on my left, an odd utensil on my right, and a frighteningly large, jagged knife at the top of my plate. My stomach growled, but the surrounding chatter and music drowned it out.

"... and my merchandise has not arrived as it should have. I'm telling you, Lady Domitia, the forests must be cleared of the riff-raff. Don't you agree?" A round-faced man next to me spoke to a severe-looking woman across from him. He picked up the edge of the table cloth and wiped the dribbles of wine from the corner of his mouth.

"Yes, yes, indeed. Shameful." Lady Domitia's tone was dismissive as she plucked food off the raised platter abutting my silver plate.

My mouth watered, the delicious smells making my head spin. My impulse was to grab all the food within reach and shove it in my mouth.

The music ended, but the room still thrummed with conversation and laughter. Three musicians sat at the base of the Emperor's dais. A jester stood up and juggled in the center of the floor. The redheaded woman gave the performers an encouraging nod, which wasn't much, but it was more than they received from anyone else.

I copied the severe-looking Rose, Domitia, and plucked a pheasant leg and a thick slice of warm bread. The difficulty would be in pacing myself like a lady. I lifted the meat to my lips, but before I could take a bite, Lady Domitia asked, "And why are you visiting Lord Elek?"

The pheasant in my hands teased my senses.

Did the nobles know of Elek's particular appetites? Did they think me a paramour or a conquest? The round-faced lord next to me paused his complaints to listen.

"I'm a translator here to offer my assistance with a matter of importance to the kingdom," I said. I took a bite of the food before the lady could ask me another question. The sweet meat melted in my mouth, a hint of rosemary and thyme mixed with the juices.

Lady Domitia's nostrils flared. On one hand, I didn't want to irritate the nobles, but on the other, I couldn't yet reveal too much of my purpose.

The music started up again, and the three musicians danced in the center of the room. Several people started clapping as soon as the music began. Even Domitia's face softened, and she started clapping along.

I ripped off a small piece of bread with a shaking hand. My stomach protested, but I forced myself to chew slowly.

"Did you arrive today? Did you see any trouble on the Emperor's Highway?" The round-faced man turned to me and pressed a stubby finger against the table.

I took my time swallowing. "With thieves? Yes."

"You see?" he cried to Lady Domitia who was ignoring him in favor of the music. The nobleman turned back to me. "What caravan were you with? I have a shipment of rugs I was expecting."

I stalled, forming a response while drinking from my goblet.

"There were many goods. But I didn't pay them much attention." I took another small bite of bread, hoping he would talk to someone else and leave me to eat and observe in peace.

"You must've noticed the Emperor's Seal on the wagons. Lord Elek wouldn't send a guest with just any caravan. Didn't you notice anything of note?" His voice strained over the music, and his face grew redder with each word.

"I made my own arrangements," I said.

The nobleman's face turned cold, and his beady eyes peeked from under his bushy brows.

The noblewoman across from me stopped her clapping and coughed a reminder. "Lord Porcius, my dear, this is my favorite song."

It struck me that he did look rather like a pig. Pig Porcius.

"Lord Elek asked you to be his guest, and you made arrangements without his guidance?" His piggy nose wrinkled.

A laugh sounded behind us. "A Southern woman after my own heart."

I turned to see the beautiful Getaen woman in the emerald dress standing behind me. The pig-faced man shot her a nasty look before turning away.

The noblewoman took a bumbling drink from her goblet

while the Getaen woman glared at the back of Porcius' head. After an uncomfortable silence, the noblewoman across the table reached over and stroked the pig-man's hand. "Dance with me, darling."

Her lips were pursed, but her eyes pleaded for him to do as she asked.

Lord Porcius' lips rolled in, forming a straight line, seeming to suck in the words he wanted to say. It was a strange sensation to see a Getaen with such power over Dacian nobles.

The pig-man stood up, adjusting his leather belt under his ample stomach.

"Lady Essa." Lord Porcius gave the Getaen woman a shallow bow before marching away. The noblewoman slunk away to meet him, joining in a dance I'd never seen. Would Lord Jovian return and ask me to dance? I shuddered at the notion.

To my surprise, Lady Essa sat down in Lord Jovian's empty seat.

"Who are you?" Lady Essa leaned forward, her voice low. "Why are you here?"

"My name is Nicoleta. I was requested to clarify documents the Emperor recently took into his possession," I said.

The musicians broke into a song I'd heard many times:

And the two brothers were both strong and sure
But Odon was foolish and wanted a war

"Rumor is, Lord Elek invited you as a... translator," she said and gave me a knowing look.

A group of ladies passed by, and Lady Essa sat up straighter and feigned a smile.

The musicians sang as their fingers moved deftly over the chords.

Cassus the First saved us on that dark night
With his will and his might, he won the just fight

When Odon was bested, he ran and was heard of no more

How many people had heard this song? The lie perpetuated since Emperor Cassus III.

"Getaens are not welcome here, even an educated Azure. Elek would never have invited you," Essa whispered, her fake smile still firmly in place but her eyes serious. "Your lies have granted you access to the heart of the castle, but they will carry you no further. Tell me quickly. What are you doing here?"

"I intend to translate the scrolls. I b-believe they have… " I stopped before my face contorted. How could I explain to a woman, obviously a favorite of the Emperor, that I mean to overthrow him, that it was the only way to save our people?

"The scrolls have information to stop the p-plague." The words I'd practiced refused to flow. My hand was wet with sweat on the strings of the velvet pouch.

I could see over Lady Essa's shoulder as Lord Jovian strolled in.

I locked on his face, smiling wide so Lady Essa would be alerted to his arrival. I didn't want Lord Jovian catching her unaware.

Lady Essa reached out and grabbed my hands, her voice barely a whisper, "You are in danger. Find Jamil, the guard who escorted you. He will meet you outside the doors, and you can disappear."

The jolt of her warning ran through me. I pressed my false smile wider at Lord Jovian. I squeezed Lady Essa's hands as he approached.

"Essa, how lovely to see you visiting with Lord Elek's guest," he said.

Lady Essa stood up, meeting his gaze. I didn't realize how tall she was before, but the two were nose to nose. She gave him a cold smile. "My lord, you seem to have forgotten that the

Emperor saw fit to grant me a title. Do not address me so familiar again."

Jovian's jaw clenched. The other nobles pretended not to listen, but no one spoke nor ate as they waited to see what Lord Jovian would do.

Finally, he cleared his throat, "Ah, yes. Do accept my most humble apology, *Lady* Essa. We are so very unaccustomed to people such as yourself in... society."

"Change can be difficult, my lord, even after two hundred years. Getaens have adapted and learned to make the best of it. Eventually, you'll learn to do so, too." And without a further word, Lady Essa sauntered off. Behind Jovian's back, she gave a slight shake of her head to the adviser on the high table next to the Emperor.

Lady Essa and the adviser had noticed me. Surely the Emperor had as well. I needed to extricate myself and find a place to think, and hopefully sleep.

Lord Jovian plopped down in his chair. "It seems you were attacked by the Emperor's mistress while I abandoned you. A pity her new station didn't come with better breeding."

Lord Jovian gulped down nearly half a glass of wine. "Getaens. Uncivilized, the lot of them. My sincere apologies."

I frowned.

"Not you, of course. I'm speaking of the witches the Emperor has surrounding him. You look positively Eastern, if I were to guess."

I gritted my teeth and smiled. He knew I was Getaen. Furthermore, I didn't want to erase the Getaen part of me. I loved it. Anger flared inside me, but I extinguished it. I couldn't help those around me if I hated them.

Lord Jovian scooped food from the platters and started eating and pointing out different individuals of the court, laughing about gossip I couldn't begin to follow or muster the energy to care about.

Lord Jovian blabbered on, an apple in his hand. How different it would have been if Marcus were beside me. We could comment on the ludicrous fashion, impractical shoes, and rich foods. If only I had someone I could trust like Mama trusted Papa — someone to share ideas with. They had made each other stronger.

"What is on your mind?" Lord Jovian grinned. "You've been pensive, but just now, I glimpsed something behind your facade."

I blinked. "Oh, your apple. It brings back memories."

"Apples?" He turned his attention to a halved apricot and popped it into his mouth. "I'm quite fond of these."

I suppressed a grimace. Apricots were common in Moesia. What was he implying? I glanced at the doorway. Jamil waited on the far side of the corridor beyond.

Lord Jovian laughed, his mouth open, remnants of chewed apricot in his teeth. I moved to stand. Without warning, he slammed his fist on the table. "Such an entertaining woman you are, Nicoleta. Dance with me!"

He stood up, his hand held out.

"I don't know this song." The slow Dacian ballad was yet another thing to add to my long list of things I didn't know.

"Come, come. I'll teach it to you." Lord Jovian grabbed my arm. I just had time to slip the strings of my purse around my wrist before he pulled me into the center of the dance floor. I fumbled along, trying to follow his scant instructions. Was he drunk? The moments stretched on before the tune abruptly changed to a popular Dacian dance.

Lord Jovian groaned, but the music was sweet relief to my ears. A song I knew! As I pivoted to prepare for the dance, I noticed the lead musician nod at Lady Essa.

The song required more touching, which I normally didn't notice. But every step toward our partner offered Lord Jovian's hands a chance to ooze over my body. In the dance, we changed partners every sixteen beats. The other lords' touches were restrained and proper, only lightly skimming my side, in stark contrast to Lord Jovian's heavy hands.

Jamil's face was like stone as he followed my movements around the room, just outside the doorway.

Normally I would excuse myself, but Tulia warned that it was customary for a noblewoman to wait to be excused from the dance floor. A proper gentleman would notice a woman's needs and respond without her asking, Tulia had said.

It was a ridiculous nicety that I immediately hated.

"The wine has made me dizzy, I'm afraid." I couldn't think of a stronger hint.

The song ended, and Lord Jovian laughed, ignoring my comment. Obviously, Tulia had never met a *gentleman* like Lord Jovian. Despite Jamil's accidental confession to being a raider, I preferred his company to Jovian's.

"I'm tired from my journey." I tried again.

An upbeat Gatean song began, and Lord Jovian pulled me close. "You can depend on me for support."

This song hadn't been played in Moesia since the plague.

"I don't feel well." I was about to push away when movement at the high table caught my attention. A Thorn spoke to the Emperor. The Emperor left with the guard through a side door, and whispers began in earnest.

"I regret, I must leave you." Lord Jovian puffed out his chest.

"Such a shame." Relief washed over me. Not only was the Emperor gone, but Lord Jovian would be, too. Now was my opportunity. "Before you leave, I would appreciate you showing me who the High Judge is."

He paused, his eyes darting to the doors where several other nobles were making a hasty exit. "Of course. High Judge Vasile was seated next to the Emperor at the high table."

The entire table on the dais was now vacant.

The grey-haired man at the table was the High Judge. I assumed he was an adviser, but it was the very man Rubia had intended to speak to.

Fortunately, Vasile hadn't yet left the room. He was speaking to a nearby couple. He wore layers of fine clothing, a thick gold chain connecting his short dinner cloak across his shoulders. Several black feathers adorned his deep brown cap. As if sensing my gaze, he looked at me before excusing himself and striding over.

"Who is your lovely guest?" Vasile asked Lord Jovian.

"Ah, High Judge Vasile!" Lord Jovian clapped his hands together. "This is Nicoleta of Moesia, here to translate ancient text for the Emperor."

A chill ran down my back. I'd only mentioned I was translating scrolls, not that they were ancient. My fingers flexed. It wouldn't be a stretch for him to assume the text was ancient. Still, his introduction seemed oddly specific.

"A mysterious guest of Lord Elek is one I must meet." High Judge Vasile loomed over me, his hand extended. His voice was pleasant, but my stomach twisted.

I placed my hand in his, and he guided me to the periphery of the dance floor. Lord Jovian couldn't disappear fast enough. I didn't miss him.

"I apologize for Lord Jovian's behavior. I'm afraid he's a bit too much like his uncle. Clever with trade but doesn't understand the intricacies of the Rose Court." He placed his hands respectfully behind his back, guiding me through the first steps of the song. Within a few beats, the movements of the dance flooded back.

"Look at them, scurrying like rats to their little spies to find scraps of information on what the Emperor needs. They wish to wriggle their way closer to the throne." Vasile said as two more lords and the severe-looking noblewoman from dinner bustled from the room. Vasile shrugged. "But you'll notice the most respected nobles remained behind. The key to climbing in the Rose Court is never appearing like you're trying too hard."

I'm not here to climb, I'm here to sway.

We moved past each other, in step with the music before pivoting and coming face to face.

"You're a translator. Tell me about your work?"

I was confident that Vasile would respond to any hint that I wanted to be excused. I could leave now. But Rubia had hoped to meet with the man right in front of me. Perhaps this was the better opportunity. A bird in hand is better than two in the bush, Rubia would say.

I gave a slight shake of my head to Jamil. My conversation with the High Judge could last the entire song and beyond. Besides, how long could Jamil linger outside a room where he wasn't stationed before being questioned?

Jamil frowned and ran a hand through his hair, seeming to hesitate. I returned my attention to the High Judge. It was a risk to talk to anyone without the nobles as witnesses, but had the Getaen slave in Patridava had a chance to help us without his master present, I believed he would have tried. Vasile was away from the Emperor. I wouldn't confess everything, but if I wanted to test the sympathies of the High Judge, this was my chance.

I took a breath and peeled back the first layer of the true reason I was in Capidava. "I have seen scrolls I believe will be of great interest to you and the nobles of the Rose Court."

~

The High Judge pivoted, facing me. "We already have many scrolls and scribes. We even have a resident scholar from Moesia." His face was serene.

My stomach lurched. Did he suspect I was the missing daughter of the kidnapped scholar? I had mentioned I was from Moesia, but I'd kept my last name hidden, and Moesia had almost a hundred thousand citizens.

Still, I'd come too far to be prey in Vasile's trap.

"Your scribes don't know the scrolls as I do. Few understand the intricacies of both the Dacian and Getaen language better than me." I narrowed my eyes. "And the only brilliant scholar who's studied the scrolls since before I was born would never willingly reveal their secrets."

I pivoted and spoke with conviction. "I will."

The High Judge skipped a step in the dance before quickly regaining his composure.

This man was Rubia's hope for compassion and honest assistance because his blood carried some hint of Getae. Of course, after what happened in Patridava, I couldn't count on that. Still, he was the Emperor's right hand, influential and clever enough to ascend to that position. And the touch of his hand didn't make me want to shrink away. I peeled away the next layer of truth.

"The plague has spread to Burridava. I know how to stop it. I know how to stop the plague forever. To do this, we need the cooperation of the Rose Court," I said.

As we circled the room, many finely dressed nobles whispered behind their lace fans, their eyes boring into me, the newcomer in the yellow gown. Jamil was gone, and there were no friendly faces.

"How can the scrolls help stop the plague?" Vasile asked.

"The plague is a curse created by a warlock at the request of the Blood Conqueror." I stepped in time with the music though as a child I danced barefoot, not in tight slippers.

Vasile shook his head. "Emperor Trajan Caracalla built this kingdom. It is his legacy. Why would he lay plans to destroy it?"

"He feared his sons would tear it apart. He demanded an oath where they would *trade* seats on the throne after five generations. After another five, the lines would intermarry and share the throne through blood again." My rehearsed lines flowed from my lips, the secret truths anxious to be known. "Odon wasn't a traitor. He was only trying to protect the true heirs of the throne — his descendants."

One of the musicians near me hit a sour note. Vasile grabbed my arm and led me away from the dancers, lingering by the vacant dais. His face was stern, but his voice faltered. "Odon was a traitor and a coward. He fled and was never seen again."

"Without Odon's blood on the throne, we're all destined to be destroyed by the Lilac Plague. You know I speak the truth." I wanted to grab Vasile's shoulders and shake him.

"This isn't a safe place to discuss your claims." He guided me toward the double doors through which I'd entered.

He's nothing but a tool of the Emperor, a voice inside me warned.

"You speak treason. I can't be bothered with this nonsense," he growled as we neared the doors. "Just go while you can. I suspect Lady Essa arranged to have you safely escorted. I'll not tell her that you spurred her kindness by attempting to smear the name of the emperor she protects."

I had several speeches prepared but hadn't expected to be thrown out as a mere nuisance.

"I know this information is o-overwhelming. You're the one p-person who —"

"Leave now," Vasile said, a shine of sweat forming on his

forehead. "You have until dawn to leave Capidava or be arrested as a traitor and rebel. Take this as a generous gift, one rarely given to Getaens. Don't throw it away."

He snapped his fingers, and a Thorn moved toward us. I lurched away, putting Vasile between the guard and me, drawing even more attention to our conversation. If I left now, I'd never be allowed back inside.

"I've given up everything to p-present this i-information to the courts. I will speak s-so the nobles will remove the emperor and replace him with the true heir who can stop the p-p-plague." I drew my hands into fists, forcing each word out.

A servant muttered about my cursed tongue. The guard grabbed my shoulder, but I resisted and took two steps deeper into the dining room. Vasile had essentially banished me from Capidava. There would be no court for me tomorrow. This was my only opportunity to deliver my message.

I took a deep breath and recited my memorized message. "There is a key that will stop a curse, stop the *plague*."

The music crashed into discordant notes followed by silence. The dancing stopped, and everyone turned to face me.

I continued, this time recalling my memorized lines. "Only the true heir can wield the key. Otherwise, whoever touches it will die."

The guard's still hand grasped my shoulder but didn't move to force me away.

"Lords and Ladies of the Court. My name is Nicoleta Aurelian. I'm the daughter of a scholar who has studied the curse for almost twenty years. Using his research along with an artifact passed down by Emperor Trajan Caracalla, we can stop the plague from killing another person. Our kingdom will be saved!"

Vasile's shoulders slumped. The nobles muttered amongst themselves.

"Are we to listen to the shrieking of a Getaen peasant?" Lord Porcius shouted. "We of noble birth and blood know what's best for our kingdom. Throw the impudent creature out."

A plump woman wearing a necklace with a teal stone half the size of my fist stepped forward. "Let her speak."

Pig Porcius shouted again. "Just because your filthy son died of the plague is no reason for us to heed this nonsense, Lady Tyne."

Lady Tyne lifted her chin. "You're just upset my son didn't want that swine daughter of yours. He was as fine as crystal spring waters from the mountain itself. We all know it's rubbish that the plague only kills the lowly."

I broke in before the pair could bicker further. "This curse was set in motion over two hundred years ago. It was only to be unleashed if an oath was broken. The necessary path is difficult and frightening, but the other option is death by boils and rotting flesh."

I stood tall, finishing the piece of my speech I'd worked the hardest to perfect. They wouldn't like the rest of what I had to say. But this was my last chance to convince them.

"I, like you, was raised with the notion that the Lilac Plague is a curse from Zalmoxis. But that's a lie. He lets the plague rage, but he didn't create it. It was created by a warlock seven generations ago in this very castle."

The nobles gasped. Several ladies covered their mouths with their fans. But many others whispered to each other, jabbing their fingers toward me.

"A plague cannot be created," Lord Porcius spat. "Think of the power that would require; think of the permissions that would have to be granted!"

"It was created at Emperor Trajan Caracalla's r-request!" I paused only a heartbeat, gathering my thoughts. "After he conquered the Getaens, he turned his focus inward. He knew his twin sons would vie for the throne of his kingdom. So instead of r-risking the kingdom he'd won in the b-blood of b-battle, he forced an agreement between Cassus and Odon. Cassus' line would rule for five generations. Then to Odon for the next five. This was their oath."

I stuttered a small amount, but I knew my information was more important than my words. I moved my gaze from Vasile's reddening face to the rest of the room. "We can't go back and save those who've already died, but you can save many in the future by forcing Emperor Cassus VII to honor the oath that should have been kept by his father."

Several nobles grumbled, but others leaned back or cocked their heads as if contemplating my words.

"Blasphemy!" A nobleman with a green hat jumped to his feet. "Emperor Cassus' line is blessed by Zalmoxis."

No one is blessed by Zalmoxis, I thought, but I didn't have time to be distracted by philosophy.

"The curse began when Cassus VI took the throne!" I said. "What more p-proof do you need?"

The room erupted.

"She fabricated this story because she knows that's when the plague first appeared. If the plague started in the third generation, she'd say that is when Odon's descendants should've been on the throne." A woman with a maroon hat standing next to Lord Porcius spoke up. "This is not proof, and certainly not an excuse to let such treason be spoken in the very heart of Rupea Castle."

"What more do you need?" I quaked. "When the true heir uses the key to open the treasure, the curse w-will be lifted."

"Why have we never heard or seen a key?" Lady Tyne asked. Several others nodded as if in agreement. I brightened at the thoughtful question.

Thundering footfalls from heavy boots sounded down the

hallway behind me. How many Thorns were coming? How did they arrive so quickly? I was running out of time to convince the nobles to fight against the plague by finding the rightful heir.

I brushed my hand past the hidden vial of orange-sting in my apron. Now was not the time to attack and run. Instead, I yanked my pendant from under my dress. Blood roared in my ears as I clutched the uneven orb in my fist. Rubia had never planned on revealing the True Key. But there was a crack in the noble's resolve. I could sense it. They only needed proof.

"This is the True Key," I shouted and held up the pendant for everyone to see.

Vasile practically choked as he sucked in a breath, but I quickly continued. "It was created by the Warlock himself." My voice was loud and clear. "I'm a mere Guardian for the key, meant to deliver it to the true blood heir, to a descendant of Odon."

Many nobles gaped, but others leaned forward inspecting the golden orb in my hand.

Green cloaks flooded into the room with Lord Jovian in the lead. He pointed at me. "This woman is an impostor."

My stomach dropped. I glanced from him to Vasile who wouldn't meet my gaze.

"Do not touch the orb itself!" Lord Jovian said, full of self-importance. "She attacked my uncle with the orb in Patridava. I suspected it long ago, of course."

He puffed out his chest and spoke to the nobles, ignoring me. "My uncle has just arrived and confirmed my suspicions."

I ground my teeth. Jovian was Elek's nephew. Zalmoxis must have been delighted and amused, knowing I was caught the moment I mentioned to Jovian that his horrid uncle had invited me. He knew his uncle would have deemed an Azure too far beneath him to even converse with me, let alone invite me to stay at his estate as a guest. To the likes of Lord Elek, I was only worth as much as he could sell me for. I was a fool to let Lord Jovian keep me in the dining hall while arrangements fell into place to have me captured.

"Wait." A short, thin man with a beard stepped forward, curtailing Jovian's momentum. "You said your pendant is a key and it opens a treasure. Where is this treasure and what's inside?"

Soldiers stood at the doorway. I guessed I only had moments before they would drag me away.

"The location of the treasure is unknown, but it's of great worth. The treasure is likely still in Capidava. The emperor knows wh-where it is; I'm sure of it," I said.

Lord Porcius stepped forward. "So we are to believe there's a missing treasure? A warlock who created a curse that will only be lifted if the throne switches to the Odon bloodline? And that mangled pendant is some mystical key?" He slammed his fist into his hand. "Preposterous!"

The guard's grip on my shoulder tightened.

"Cor menus!" I shouted the words I'd heard from my parents. I was grateful the phrase came to me. "It means 'true blood heir,' and until there's a true heir seated on the th-throne, we're d-doomed."

The short man stroked his beard, examining the key from a distance.

"All part of her elaborate tale. This woman is nothing more than a Getaen witch, cursed by Zalmoxis with an evil tongue." Lord Jovian forced a laugh and waved with a wide sweeping motion like a stage performer unveiling a wonder.

"What did you hope to accomplish by this simple ruse?" Vasile's face hardened, and he took a step back, leaving me completely open for the guards to grab. My heart sunk.

No! Vasile had chosen to stay under the thumb of the Dacian Emperor.

My fingers gripped the pendant tighter and faced the nobles. "This pendant is the only key that can stop the plague. We must protect it!"

Surely some Roses would fight to save the key. It meant saving themselves and their children. I could wrench free of the guard's grip on my shoulder and thrust the key in their faces. However, that would make me no better than the emperors.

A few nobles exchanged pointed glances. Others looked at me with pity in their eyes. Most shouted angrily, accusing me of treason.

None stepped forward to say they believed me. Instead, guards grabbed my arms on either side.

A soldier stopped in front of me, thick leather gloves on his hands, no color on his sleeves: Jamil. His face was grim as if he didn't know me. He held out his hand for the orb.

"Careful!" I clutched the leather near the orb, not letting it swing toward him. Of all the people in the room, he knew the agony of the plague.

"Touch the leather string... the leather string only." My face contorted, but I had to warn them all. "The orb is d-dangerous."

I didn't know if Jamil believed me or Lord Jovian, but the Getaen guard didn't allow any of his flesh to touch the orb as he took the key and dropped it into a small bag at his side.

"Noble lords and ladies, you must r-rise up and speak. Y-y-you each have spies in the court, s-small armies to command," I fought with each word as my pulse quickened. "C-coins in your f-family v-vaults, you must work t-toge —"

"Take this tongue-twisted vermin to the stocks," Vasile commanded. "She will be on public display until her trial."

A hundred pairs of eyes stared at me, judging me. The guards dragged me away as the room erupted in cries of mockery and anger. I came to reveal the truth, but I had only condemned myself, Papa, and anyone else they discovered associated with me. I'd taken a chance, believing, hoping the nobles would rise to the occasion. How could they not see the foolish, shortsightedness of their decision?

I felt naked without the orb around my neck. I had failed Rubia and Papa. What would Mama say if she knew I'd lost the key — the very item she'd given her life to entrust me with? My chin fell to my chest.

Vasile rasped in my ear as I was towed down the hall. "Your trinket has eluded the Emperor for many years. Who would've guessed a Getaen impersonating a noblewoman would deliver it directly to us." He rubbed his brow. "I almost let you go, assuming you were an innocent child here to beg for your father. I underestimated you. I will not make the same mistake twice."

Zalmoxis, what have I done?

I'd committed treason, with the emperor's most loyal as witnesses.

The impudence of the official who dared to ask me why I hadn't reported to the local office on my magical work! I am the Warlock to Emperor Trajan Caracalla. My work for the Empire is not subject to petty taxes.

Fortunately, Cassus found me in my foul mood and asked me what was wrong. When I explained what had happened, Cassus laughed. I didn't think it was funny and told him as much. He told me I was getting too serious in my old age and promised to take care of it. I'm only ten years older than him, but I feel much older.

That little scab of an official should be dismissed. I could complain to the Emperor, but he's catching up on affairs of the kingdom after his bout with illness. The princes didn't comment on their father's changed disposition, but it's clear to me this illness has made him keenly aware that his time before Zalmoxis grows shorter every season.

— VAHID, WARLOCK TO EMPEROR TRAJAN

CARACALLA

CHAPTER

NINETEEN

A SACRIFICE

The stocks had been a vague, distant threat. As Jamil dutifully checked my shoes, the terror of being on display hit my stomach like a stone. A thickset fellow with a sneer, rummaged through my velvet pouch and clothing, throwing my last herbs on the ground and completely missing the orange-sting hidden in my apron pocket.

Four guards threw me on a wagon bed and drove to the lower portion of Capidava in silence. What would become of me? Painful possible consequences vied for my attention, making my muscles freeze up with dread.

I didn't struggle as the guards hauled me onto the platform for display. Urine lingered from the previous 'guest,' and I regretted all the food and drink I'd indulged in at the castle. The night had grown cooler, the darkness only pushed back by torches near the main gate out of the city.

"Traitor." A drunken man stumbled past me.

My wrists and head were secured in the stocks. The thick metal cuffs made it impossible for me to slide my hands out of the holes. I started to hyperventilate; I counted as I breathed, ignoring the guards as they gathered off to one side.

291

My vision blurred but still, I could see someone hand Jamil a small scroll with an official-looking wax seal on it.

"Captain Lucius has assigned you to stand watch." The guard's voice was hard, yet with a hint of pity.

As the guards prepared to leave, the sneering one lagged. "Jamil has finally shown the captain his true colors. A desert viper can never be tamed."

"Shove off, Commodus," Jamil said.

"I hope it's not too much for you to handle this little girl," Commodus snorted before his footfalls retreated. "She's tied up, but take care. I hear Getaens are witches."

I strained to peer around but could barely lift my head. I had to rely on my hearing and, unfortunately, my sense of smell, alerting me to horse manure and fetid human musk.

A few drunkards wobbled across the square. One stopped at the statue of the Emperor, and I had the pleasure of listening to the sound of piss hitting the base and running into the cracks of the cobblestones.

I didn't expect many travelers through the main gates until sunrise. My trial couldn't begin until the courts opened up in the morning, at the earliest. Instead of arriving ready to declare the truth of the Lilac Plague, I would be on trial for treason.

At least, I wouldn't have to dread Elek's caravan passing by. He was already here, probably with a Healer trying to cure his withered hand. I inwardly groaned. Once Lord Jovian reported to his uncle, Elek would definitely attend my trial, adding a false assault to the list of charges against me.

On either side of the main gate into the city square, near the torches lighting the area, four guards stood watch. One called out, "What's yur wife ta think when she hears how the high an' mighty fall. A long ways from Emperor's Own to petty criminal watch, but what does you be expectin' from southern Get?"

My stomach twisted at the insult. How had Jamil gotten caught up in my disaster?

"His wife be dead, didn't you hear? But his pretty daughter is still alive and well. Perhaps we should stop by and express our condolences," another shouted. They all laughed. I smacked the back of my head against the wooden stock as I craned my neck up to see who was speaking.

"Oy, you lot. Get back to your posts, or you'll be expressing your condolences to a bunch of squirrels while patrolling the Emperor's Highway ten days from the nearest way station," a voice chastised down from up on the walls.

"Jamil," I whispered. "Any g-guard could've stopped me. Any n-noble in the dining room. Why —"

"Silence." His voice was a low growl. Anger emanated from his every pore.

I passed the time counting the stones at my feet and tried not to wonder what was in store for me. Punishment for stealing? For impersonating a noble? For injuring Elek? For falsely using Lady Katalin's symbol to access the Rose Court? For treason?

A juicy vegetable smacked into the side of my dress and slid down my leg. I guessed it left a lovely stain on its way down to my feet.

A dirty face filled with yellow teeth jumped in front of me. I gasped as a gritty hand clasped the stock, and the stench of alcohol filled my nostrils.

"Think a fine lady like yourself can take advantage of Emperor Cassus VII of Capidava?" The man's eyes were blood-shot, and his hair was so greasy I couldn't tell the color in the half moonlight. "Fallen from your perch, all high-hat, to end up down here with us scum." His speech was slurred. I didn't know if he gripped my shoulder out of anger or for balance.

"No touching the accused," Jamil said, but his words were grudging.

"I borrowed this dress. I'm a commoner, same as you. In fact, I'm Getaen. How many Getaen nobles do you know?" I asked.

He stumbled back and lifted his fingers as if to count, but they held a bottle. He lifted the other hand but seemed to give up. "Getaen. Getaen."

He mumbled, seemingly lost in thought. "Grandmama was Getaen. Black tattoo snaked down her back. Saw it once when I was a child and a Healer asked me to assist. Kept the water boiling, I did."

Jamil stood silently behind me. I couldn't twist around far enough to see him, but I sensed he was watching the exchange.

The drunk wandered off, still mumbling about his grandmama. How many more drunken visitors would I get before sunrise?

As the night grew colder, I hoped fewer locals would pass by. However, it seemed Capidava never slept. I tried to close my eyes and rest standing up to no avail. My back ached.

"Jamil. I'm s-sorry you got caught up in all this. It was unintentional, I assure you." I shivered in Lady Katalin's thin dress and Tulia's impractical slippers.

He made no response. I craned my neck up to see the guards by the gate, who occasionally snickered and pointed in our direction. My neck pinched with the strain. I dropped my gaze to the ground.

After hours of standing, deep pain burned through my back. I pressed my wrists into the stocks, attempting to alleviate the throbbing in my spine, but found only minimal relief. The sky was still a deep inky blue with stars and the waxing moon.

A man called out and rang a bell. My head throbbed with every clang on the brass.

"We must purge the wickedness from Capidava. When is the last time we sent a proper message to Zalmoxis? The plague will come unless we sacrifice as he demands. Merely burying treasures or sacrificing birds will not do," he shouted.

"Go home, Falad!" a woman shouted, as she trundled by with a three-wheeled wagon. Her dress grazed her shins above her ankles. "We don't want to hear your nonsense today or any day for that matter."

"The Lilac Plague will return to Capidava unless we do as Zalmoxis demands. We must send someone with a message to him!" the preacher shouted. "Cities that practice righteousness are spared. Those who are not obedient are punished."

Jamil grumbled under his breath. And I heard a few coughs and distant laughter.

"Then offer up your own loved one." The woman halted her three-wheeled wagon. "Stop bothering the rest of us."

Several other people muttered agreements with the woman.

"Even now, Burridava suffers under the Lilac Plague," the preacher continued. "They have not sent a message through righteous channels for over a decade. It is their fault this tragedy befell them."

I waited for the woman to berate him again, but she didn't. Instead, an eerie silence crept over the square. I lifted my sore neck. People were drawing closer to the preacher who held a bell in one hand and a torch in the other.

"The plague?" a young man asked.

The preacher, Falad, continued. "Sure as I'm standing here. And it has been five years since Capidava has sent a proper message to Zalmoxis. Only a worthy human sacrifice will do."

My knees buckled at his words, and the metal restraints around my wrists slammed into the stock, rocking the chains and sending a clanging sound across the square.

"We must do one again soon, or Zalmoxis will judge us next. I can feel it in my bones," Falad said.

At least a dozen faces were glowing in the light of his torch. The words Rubia spoke in the graveyard my first day out of mourning came back to me. 'Grief can make one do terrible things.' Like Gallus reporting Papa to the Moesian guard. These people were reacting out of grief, out of fear.

Would the truth of the curse dispel their fear or, at least, relieve them of the notion that murdering someone in some sort of futile attempt to stop the plague was necessary? My heart ached to witness the damaging lies spreading right before me.

"It is true. The Lilac Plague has struck Burridava." I said. "I traveled the Emperor's Highway and heard the news from a noblewoman."

"Hold your tongue," Jamil said, his voice pitched low so only I could hear.

"See?" A smug grin bloomed on the preacher's face. "Even the accused agrees with me."

Despite Jamil's warning, I continued, "Zalmoxis allows the plague to rage, but he didn't create it. A warlock did, many years ago. Human sacrifice will not stop it."

The nobles wouldn't listen to my speeches, but perhaps the common folk would. No one wanted to select a friend or family member to be sacrificed to Zalmoxis.

"This isn't a game. No need to rile the crowd." Jamil pinched my shoulder in warning.

"Don't listen to this girl. She is a criminal and a liar," the preacher said. "We all know the curse is from Zalmoxis."

"That's a lie." I raised my voice. "I've studied scrolls written b-before your grandfathers were b-born."

Jamil squeezed my bicep painfully. I let out a soft yelp.

"You'll make things worse," he said under his breath. "Stay quiet."

"What are you? A thief? A liar? We can't believe a word you say." Falad's smile turned evil in the dancing torchlight. It sent a shiver down my spine. He dropped his voice, but it was clear to everyone gathered. "Zalmoxis has a hold on your lying tongue."

Turning to the crowd, the preacher cried. "We should have a proper sacrifice right here. Zalmoxis would appreciate a learned soul. Someone from the Rose Court."

I sucked in a breath. I was an outsider. Someone they could easily hate. Easily sacrifice.

The people looked at each other, not speaking on my behalf. Their behavior echoed the nobles'. Even those who wouldn't harm me would stand aside and let the preacher do as he wished. I hoped that Jamil was more honorable than vengeful and would protect me if only to save me for trial.

The sky was lightening. I had to speak up if I wished to see the dawn.

"K-killing someone will not stop the curse. I'm telling the truth. Look at me! I was thrown out of the castle b-because the nobles... because they fear losing their standing. They choose p-power and influence over the lives of their own people." My sentences were more fluid than they'd been in years. I still stuttered, but I wasn't afraid to let myself speak. "The Roses and Lilies are afraid to do what it will take to stop the p-plague. But, it can be d-done, and I know how we can do it!"

The crowd quieted. I could sense they were torn between the familiar preacher's words of doom and the slim chance at hope offered by a stranger. My words had the benefit of truth. What would win, his fear or my truth?

"I'll stand with her." A winded voice called through the

darkened street. I recognized Mystic Marianna, and relief washed over me.

"Well, well, if it isn't the 'blessed' mystic." Falad's words dripped with sarcasm.

People rushed to Marianna and kissed her knuckles while the preacher glared, his lips curled.

Annuska trailed behind Marianna. She slipped over to me and whispered, "Omi came as soon as we heard a noblewoman was in the stocks."

Of course, a noblewoman in stocks would be a gossip-worthy spectacle.

"Does she come to see all the nobles in the stocks?" I tried to joke.

The little girl shook her head. "No, but then again, I never heard of one before you."

How many others would come to mock me? At least Marcus wouldn't get here until tomorrow night. He wouldn't see me humiliated. Then again, after what I had done to him, maybe I deserved it.

Mystic Marianna spoke to individuals in the growing crowd, asking how a mother or uncle was doing. Had they solved this or that issue with their crops? Had their fortunes come to pass? Many nodded, thanking her.

Marianna beckoned to an older woman still wearing her nightclothes and a hastily wrapped cloak. "Always the first to see if the rumors are true. Do not be embarrassed. Go and tell others to come and hear my words. I have a prophecy that came to me in the night that everyone should hear. Be quick and return."

It was as if Marianna had sent a lightning bolt through the streets. Falad demanded people to stay, but they scattered, excitedly chattering.

Annuska helped her grandmother to the edge of the platform. Mystic Marianna crouched in front of me so I didn't have to strain to see her. Though, when she spoke, she tipped her head to the side, looking past me to Jamil.

"You must let go of your preconceived notions, or you will only cause yourself pain. If you make the difficult decisions, you may find honor from an unusual source," Marianna said to Jamil. "These notions are keeping you from seeing not only truth but are also putting a wedge between you and someone you love. Your daughter, perhaps?"

Jamil said nothing, but the wood creaked under his boot as he stepped back.

"Convenient for you to reveal a dream the same night I am in the stocks," I whispered, despite the extra privacy from Jamil.

The mystic winked as around us shadows faded in the pre-dawn light. There was some mummery she was about to play out, and I was desperate to see if she could keep the people from swapping their rotten vegetables for stones.

The Emperor mustn't continue to avoid naming an heir to the throne. Though Odon and Cassus are amicable enough, they won't be when the crown is for the taking.

I expect the Emperor to call upon my advice any day now as to which son he should name as heir.

— VAHID, WARLOCK TO EMPEROR TRAJAN
CARACALLA

CHAPTER

TWENTY

THE BANDITS' PRIZE

The guards near the gate eyed each other nervously in the pre-dawn. A few children in their well-worn sandals stopped not far from me, whispering before they joined the swelling crowd.

Mystic Marianna entranced the locals with several predictions of their lives and unveiled a few harmless secrets. Another round of laughs and cheers went up when she predicted a pregnant woman's spirited child would run her parents ragged. The preacher skulked at the periphery of the throng, his arms folded.

"Addressing a crowd is inviting trouble," Jamil growled in a deep voice behind me.

"Then why d-don't you send them all home?" I might have been more patient in my response earlier in the evening, but not anymore. My teeth chattered, and I impatiently waited for the sun that I knew would burn my skin by the next nightfall. I rested my neck on the stocks, rocking it to the side, far enough that I wouldn't choke or cut off the blood circulation to my head.

"Now, before this old woman rests her weary bones, let me

303

tell you about the woman behind me in shackles. The one the nobles have chained." Mystic Marianna moved so I was clearly in view. Hundreds of curious faces peered at me. The mystic continued, "This woman is special. Possibly even chosen by Zalmoxis to change the fate of our kingdom. I have seen it written in her future, clear as anything I've ever seen."

"She said she knows how to stop the plague," called a woman, but I couldn't see who. My neck pinched sending a spasm down my back when I attempted to lift my head.

I'd never told Mystic Marianna I knew how to stop the plague. I'd only listened to her story. Yet, she gave me a confident nod, urging me to speak.

I took a deep breath and repeated what I'd practiced. Every nerve in my neck sent shooting pains through my head, arms, and back. I pushed myself to look up, to speak louder though my jaw was stiff. I retold the story of Emperor Trajan Caracalla and the oath between his twin sons.

"A 'cor menus,' or true blood descendant of Odon must claim the throne, or the plague will continue. Some of you with keen perception have already realized the p-plague grows more d-deadly every year. Eventually, it will come for us all." Now the people of Capidava were further witnesses of my truthful, treasonous words.

Marianna put a hand to her heart. It was the mystic, after all, who had warned me the plague was growing worse just a few hours ago. Only now, she knew why: the wrong royal descendant was on the throne.

A gate guard mounted a horse and galloped away up the main road, the sharp footfalls of the horse ripping through the brisk morning air. Mystic Marianna brushed a hand over the mark on her neck before clearing her throat and continuing.

"When I was a little girl, rumors of the plague came only

once a year or so. But how often do we hear of the plague destroying a city now?" the mystic asked.

"The plague is always destroying one city or village," a man shouted.

I rested my chin against the stock; the weathered wood grains a blur.

"And now, the Lilac Plague is in Burridava, only a four day's walk from here!" a woman shouted. "It even hit a mountain village twice in twenty years!"

I lifted my chin, my back wracked with spasms, but I was determined to speak. "The warlock who cast the spell also created a way for the true heir to stop it. The key unlocks a p-power great enough to overthrow the usurper. The nobles r-robbed me of the key."

The crowd rumbled as they argued and complained to one another. A few people cried out, wanting to see the key, railing against the nobles, and even shouting about finding a descendant of Odon. The boards under Jamil's feet squeaked as he shifted his weight.

Mystic Marianna lifted her hands, and the crowd silenced.

"This woman is in stocks now, but she is destined to save us. I See it. But she cannot do it alone!" Mystic Marianna's voice was firm, her grey hair rustling in the breeze. "The nobles reject her words because of fear. Do we fear?" She waited and a few people shouted back.

"No!"

Jamil took a step, siding next to me, his knees slightly bent in a protective stance. Two Thorns by the entrance had left their posts, edging toward the crowd, their eyes on the Getaen guard. From the corner of my eye, I noticed Jamil loosen his sword from his sheath. Did he expect the crowd to attack him, to try to free me, to riot? What had we started, Marianna and I?

The crowd rustled with palpable energy. I let myself be

swept up in it. Though I no longer had the key, I was still the Guardian. My hope was in vain, but I longed to hold the orb again.

"Will we allow the plague to consume us when we know it can be stopped?" Marianna cried.

"No!" The crowd's response grew more decisive.

The guards' hands were on their sword hilts, their backs taut. The fear of the preacher had been swallowed by the invigorated crowd. The air sizzled, like a storm before lightning strikes.

"Go, friends, and share all you've seen and learned today. Make sure every neighbor, every child, every stranger —" Marianna lifted her arm, and the crowd hung silent, breathlessly awaiting her next words. "Every soul should know this story and decide for themselves if they will join their voice with Nicoleta Aurelian's in the search for the blood heir to wield the key and stop the curse."

People rushed toward the platform, but Jamil moved to intercept them, his hand on the hilt of his sword. The mystic redirected the converging group back into the city. As much as my back screamed in pain, I managed to give grateful smiles and nods as the people called out encouragement to me.

My heart swelled at Marianna's intervention on my behalf. The mystic had appeared like little more than a lowly beggar, but my instinct was to sit with her, to listen. If I lived to see tomorrow, I vowed to start trusting my intuition.

Sunlight tingled my skin. I bottled up as much of the energy of the crowd and the comforting warmth as I could and locked it away inside me. I would need that inner fire when I was pursued with unbending, cold judgment at the trial.

The outer gate creaked open, signaling the start of a new market day. An early group of travelers cut through the dissipating crowd. I counted seven pairs of feet and two horses with them, no wagons. They must have traveled through the night, which was bold for their small group.

One of the voices sounded familiar. I craned my neck, peering up at the seven rough-looking men and women and two packhorses laden with bags. As they spoke, I placed the voice. It was one of the thieves from the woods yesterday. I nervously pumped my hands, trying to warm them. No wonder they could travel so boldly; the Emperor might own the land, but the thieves ruled the forests.

One of the bags on the back of a horse moved. It was a person. My fingers tingled. The memory of the thieves' metal swords clanging sent a chill down my back. At least I wasn't being carried like a sack of grain on the back of a bandit's horse.

Behind me, I barely registered horse hooves clattering down the road as I studied the bandit's captive. A petite person had been slung across the back of the thief's horse, tied to the saddle to keep them from rolling off. They arched their back.

Her face came into full view: Rubia! She was bound and gagged, still wearing her rough-spun clothing, embroidery on the sleeves. Her long, fair hair was a tangle of knots, but her blue eyes flashed defiantly as she glared from her uncomfortable perch. When our eyes met, her eyes widened.

My stomach dropped, and my hands jerked. Metal clanged against the wood as I instinctively reached for her. Jabs of pain shot through my bruised wrists. Jamil stepped forward and stood even with me as the thieves passed by. He looked from Rubia to me. I dropped my gaze to the ground. I hoped Jamil didn't realize that I recognized their prisoner.

"The Emperor's Own allows thieves with obviously kidnapped prisoners to stroll through the gates?" I said. I hoped to brush off my reaction as a person unaccustomed to seeing such a thing while another part of me wanted to see his reaction. Was Jamil the raider I feared or the man who tried to help me escape?

Jamil ignored me as black-clad Thorns arrived and dismounted.

"Commodus, back so soon?" Jamil said.

"As you're unable to keep this troublemaker from drawing a crowd, we've come to handle the girl. How useless are you, Get?" Commodus sneered.

Jamil paid no attention to Commodus' words. Instead, he studied Rubia again before scrutinizing me. I could practically see his suspicious brain connecting us.

Although the bulk of the crowd drawn by Mystic Marianna had already dissembled, some had dawdled, watching the guards. Several approached the stocks.

"When is this woman's trial? We want to attend," one of the men said, putting one boot on the edge of the stocks' platform.

"The trial is not set," Commodus said, taking a step toward the man.

The mood shifted as fast as a summer squall. I cringed, trapped between the thorns and the crowd.

"Trials are public; we will be notified," Mystic Marianna said. Annuska winced under her grandma's heavy hand as they quickly made their way toward the cramped platform.

"The Emperor will do as he pleases." Commodus stepped forward again, his hip near my head.

"The Emperor will sit on his throne and allow the kingdom to be burned to ashes rather than honor the oath of his ancestors!" I shouted.

Pain shot through my skull as something slammed into my head. I cried out, my eyes welling with tears.

There was a scuffle, and Jamil pushed Commodus away from me. Marianna shouted, warning the guards of the impending plague.

Rubia, who had been silent as a mouse, twisted her bound hands, bracing herself against the horse's rump to pull the gag down.

"I'm an innocent woman, caught up in these evil little tyrants' nets!" Rubia's voice cracked at first but turned to screams, grabbing everyone's attention. "Bandits in the pocket of the nobles. Nay, in the pocket of the Emperor. I'll make you pay if it's the last —"

Her voice was cut short by the sound of a smack as one of the bandits imitated Commodus, striking the back of Rubia's head with the hilt of his dagger. I gasped. Rubia's body fell limp. I hoped she was only stunned, not dead.

The sudden silence put a damper on the group on the platform. Rubia's outburst forestalled the impending brawl around me. Rubia had drawn attention away from me to distract Commodus. Despite the painful consequence, she still protected me.

The sight of her tied up. The sound of a metal hilt against her tender flesh. Her silence tormented me. My hands shook, the bruises of my wrist crushing painfully against the metal bands.

The guards fanned out, ignoring me, sending the remaining spectators about their business. Little Annuska's sandaled feet guided Marianna away, her grandmother still admonishing the guards.

"A strange bird, this one." The thief who struck Rubia cackled as they continued past me. "Said only two words, 'High Judge.' And now she starts bellyachin' bout revenge and all."

"Oh, our little bird will sing. The Emperor will see to that," another thief said. He laughed and reached over to tap Rubia's cheek. I wanted to rake my nails over his face.

The wooden stock creaked as it was lifted off my neck. Commodus straightened me up, and my vision blackened as my knees buckled, pain shooting through my neck and shoulders.

As Commodus transitioned me from the stocks to chains, I reached for my apron's secret pocket with the orange-sting. My stiff muscles wouldn't respond fast enough, and Commodus wrenched my arms in front of me. The shackles clanged shut. My empty hands tingled as blood rushed back into them.

I suppressed the tirade of vile things I wanted to scream at the thieves before they were out of earshot, but I knew any ounce of attention I gave Rubia would be noticed, especially by Jamil. She would only be pulled deeper into the mess I had created. I was sorry for the trouble I had caused Jamil, but it was nothing like the throbbing agony pulsating in my chest at the sight of Rubia's battered body.

My helpless fury needed an outlet. I pulled away from Commodus and shouted at the guards around me. "Why d-do you serve a corrupt e-emperor? He's a conniving man who'll claw at anyone to keep his c-crown."

Commodus raised his hand to strike me. Jamil moved to stand between us and spoke in a calm voice. "It is my honor to serve the kingdom and the ruler of it. Cassus VII is a good leader. He encourages free trade and has kept invaders from our land."

Jamil's serene demeanor only irritated me more as he restrained my movements as if I were a petulant child.

"After the plague in Moesia, the Emperor's soldiers d-didn't help us," I said, daring Jamil to contradict me. "They r-raided us. T-took children as s-slaves."

Commodus grabbed my arm, shoving me toward the wagon the soldiers had brought down the hill. "Back to the castle for you."

The four sides of the wagon were made up of bars as was the roof. Commodus yanked me forward to lock my chains to one of the half loops welded into the floor. Given the low height, I wouldn't have been able to stand even if I had been unfettered.

Jamil's hand under my elbow was the only thing that kept me from falling as Commodus pushed me from the other side. Though Jamil was helping me to hold onto what dignity I had left after a night in the stocks, I couldn't forgive him. Not for the scar on Papa's face, for the terror of being trapped in a tight, dark hole beneath the ground while soldiers ransacked our home, broke Mama's things, and stole Papa's scrolls.

"The emperor has no honor. And neither d-does anyone who serves h-him!" My face contorted as I forced out the words.

"See? Here you are, getting yourself into trouble again when you're talking about things your little low-born brain can't understand." Commodus spoke down at me, feet planted on either side of my body.

"Save your words. You'll get your chance to speak in your trial," Jamil said. He beckoned, and Commodus hopped out. Jamil closed the door, leaving me alone inside.

Commodus laughed as he sauntered over to his horse. "Bid the sunshine and the fresh air farewell, Get girl. You'll be in such a dank, dark hole, no one will ever find you again."

His words took my breath away. I assumed they were dragging me back to the castle for my trial.

Jamil's jaw muscles flexed as he looked from me to Commodus mounting his horse. Jamil's hands closed into a fist. "Zalmoxis seems to want to pull you down into his inferno of wild fury. Perhaps the orb has already cursed you; you just haven't realized it yet. I pity you, Nicoleta of Moesia."

Jamil climbed into the front of the wagon next to another soldier just as they snapped the reins, and the horses jerked me toward an uncertain fate.

The Emperor called his councilor, the High Judge, and me to his chambers, but not for advice. He unveiled his plan. It's unprecedented. What could we expect from the man who risked his life, his people, in bloody wars year after year? Now his greatest desire is to keep the kingdom intact. He anticipates the nobles and other kingdoms will pit his sons against each other until Dacia is torn apart. It would happen no matter who the Emperor named as successor.

He's naming Cassus the first Heir. Then Odon's descendants will inherit the throne in five generations. Trajan wants a provision in place in case Odon is not on the throne in five generations.

The Emperor has asked me to place a curse on the kingdom if the throne doesn't revert to a descendant of Odon. The High Judge objected, saying it was too dangerous. The Emperor scoffed saying his bloodline was stronger than mortals could comprehend. I told the Emperor that a curse of that size would need time to create. I also needed an object to connect it to, something that would last for generations.

While the Emperor procures the object, it gives me time to think of just the right spell for a task of this magnitude.

— VAHID, WARLOCK TO EMPEROR TRAJAN

CARACALLA

TWENTY-ONE

IN THE DARK

Jamil didn't speak to me as he led me from the wagon through a side entrance into Rupea. His lips were drawn tight, his eyes troubled. His fingers fidgeted with a dark cloth tucked into his belt. I breathed heavily, exhausted. Jamil gripped my upper arm, and I struggled to keep up with his brisk pace. When I lagged, Jamil gave me a shove, not hard but impossible to ignore.

Two guards grunted salutations as we passed a doorway. Inside, we plunged into near complete darkness. The cold air sliced through the fabric of my dress. I strained, trying to see, not wanting to slam into stone. Jamil seemed to know his way even without a torch.

"Stairs," he said.

I stumbled, missed a step, and fell. Jamil caught me and gave me a moment to scrape my feet against the stone floor. My toe found the lip of the step, and I ventured down the stairs. As much as I resented Jamil, I was grateful for his steady guidance on the poorly maintained spiral staircase.

At the bottom, we entered a silent corridor, the echo of Jamil's boots announced our arrival. As we walked, the ceiling grew shorter, and eventually, Jamil had to stoop to avoid hitting his head. The dank corridor sucked all the early morning's warmth from me, chilling me to the bone. At the top of the wall on my right side were small window slits, just large enough for a rat to fit through.

We stopped before a heavy wooden door set in a narrow hallway with a low ceiling. A small man with a trim beard waited at the door. In the dim corridor, his dark hair gleamed like obsidian. His skin was ghostly pale. Had he ever been exposed to sunlight? For a mole who worked out of sight, underground, he was finely dressed with tailored clothing and shiny boots, not like a guard.

"I have a prisoner to deposit per the High Judge's orders," Jamil said.

My stomach clenched. Were these cells where criminals awaited trials? Whatever I'd expected, it wasn't this.

The small man at the door gave Jamil a knowing look. "This lovely creature is a criminal they don't want on display?"

The mole-man opened the door, and muffled moans and shouts echoed up. My bowels soured at the pitiful sounds. Jamil pulled me through the door, and the floor sloped down. A circular grate of iron slats was embedded in the ground on my left. There was movement between the slats. I squinted and jumped back. Dirty, bone-thin fingers wriggled out from under the ground below, soft moans emanating from beneath the grate.

Jamil jerked his head back to the mole-man. Was that concern etched on Jamil's face? The room was full of shadows; it was hard to tell.

The mole-man strode forward without a second glance. "Move your fingers or I'll remove them."

Jamil tugged me past another grate on the floor.

"When is my trial?" A raspy voice called out, but no one answered.

The only light that shone into the wide hallway was from the slits on the upper walls, similar to the ones on the other side of the door.

The further we walked, the more the floor angled down, and the tighter Jamil's grip grew on my arm. The stench of human waste filled my nostrils, making me gag. The slits on the upper wall shrank away as we walked deeper until only bright cracks of light appeared on the wall, unable to penetrate the blackness of the cavern.

Jamil's pace slowed, as blind in the cavern as I was. His grip on my trembling arm grew painful. My breathing was shallow, and I could barely lift my feet. The mole-man stopped, and the sound of tinkling metal came from his waist. Something scraped across the floor. The mole-man handed something to Jamil, and the Getaen let go of my arm. I took a step back, reaching for my orange-sting. Between my trembling hands and shackled wrists, I fumbled for the pocket.

The mole-man grabbed my shackles, silent and swift in the darkness. With a twist, the metal bit into my wrists. I yelped, but the noise was drowned as metal screamed across the stone floor. There was a soft click, and the heavy weights around my wrists dropped away.

"Down you go." The mole-man pushed me toward the dark hole before I could reach for the orange-sting.

"There's a ladder. It's not what you'd refer to as sturdy." The mole-man's tone was indifferent.

An icy hand wrapped around the back of my neck and squeezed. I dropped to my knees at the edge of the hole. The unknown crevasse bludgeoned me with terror. I couldn't go into a hole, not after the raid, not after...

The mole-man kept pushing me down as I teetered on the

edge. The cavern reeked of despair. Frantic, I clawed at my apron pocket.

"Grab the ladder or fall," Jamil growled at me. "It's on the right."

The mole-man shoved me, and I lost my fight with gravity.

I reached out, and my flailing hand gripped the ladder, but the rung gave under my sudden weight. It cracked, a splitting sound, and suddenly I was on my back, pain entombing every fiber of my body. I couldn't speak. I couldn't breathe.

Jamil let several Getaen curses fly under his breath.

"I'm her warden now. She's not your concern. You can lodge a complaint with Vasile if you're unhappy with the way I treat my prisoners." The mole-man's voice was light, brushing off Jamil's words.

"And if she's injured?" Jamil asked.

I tried to force air into my lungs, but they wouldn't respond.

"I'd have a care about how concerned to be over a traitorous witch." The mole-man's voice turned cold. "Rumor has it the Emperor's Own is convening to discuss your conduct later today. Would be a shame if they heard you continued to coddle the very Getaen who got you into this spot of trouble. I'd hate to see you stripped of rank after all *you've* done to attain it."

Jamil was silent, his breathing heavy. The grate scraped back across the stones.

Inexpressible terror gripped me as the grate fell into place, trapping me, and extinguishing the already dim light. Jamil and the warden left, the echoes of their footfalls fading away.

I rolled onto my side, gasping to force small breaths of air into my lungs. My eyes strained to take in my surroundings. I pushed myself up. A sharp pain shot through my right wrist. I gingerly probed it. My wrist was already swelling. I must have landed on it when I fell into the pit.

The stench and the pain battled for my attention. My

stomach churned. I put a hand over my mouth, trying to keep what was left of last night's dinner down. I would have to live with whatever smells I produced.

Tears stung my eyes.

"What have I done?" I whispered.

I stepped back, hitting my head on a protruding portion of rough stone. I dropped back down to my knees, blinding white dots spinning in front of my eyes. I touched the back of my head, and wetness coated my hair and fingertips.

Was Rubia in another hole like this one? What would she say when she found out I had lost the True Key? My fingers ached to hold the pendant. The security of the key was ripped away after I had only had it a few days. No, I'd practically given it away. It was my mother's legacy. It was my responsibility, and I'd made a mess of it.

I should have followed Rubia's plan instead of risking everything before the time was right. I pounded my fist against my chest and bit back the scream that threatened to tear from my lips. I crouched to the ground, head down, my cheeks wet with tears. The darkness pressed down, weighing on me, drowning me. I tugged at the neck of my dress, gasping for breath. The suffocating truth of my situation bore a hole through me, swallowing me. This wasn't a holding cell for those awaiting trial. It was a dungeon for those already condemned.

I pressed my fingers harder against the jagged stones beneath me, trying to feel something real. The cold granite at my feet settled me. I had been robbed of my opportunity to speak in front of the people that Marianna had won over this morning.

This time, I didn't hold back the desperate, frustrated scream that poured from my lips. I had ruined everything. Another scream echoed back. Was it my own or a hundred tortured souls calling out in shared misery?

My ears rang, my scream vibrating my bones. The walls of the cavern closed in around me. I had been naive to believe the nobles would risk their hot baths, fur hats, and velvet clothing. But where would they run for comfort when their estates turn to ash and their feverish children writhed in their arms? Cowards. The plague didn't care about the length of your hair or the quality of your dress. It only sensed human flesh, and it ravaged whomever it pleased.

I ached for the wretched people dying in Burridava. Blistered, delirious, and withering away. I shuddered, remembering Mama's glassy eyes and oozing sores.

"I tried." My throat was thick, tears streaming down my face. "I did try."

I rocked back and forth, leaving my tears wet on my cheeks as I let the abyss swallow me. I wanted to give up. I wanted to let the terror and guilt suck me down into the sand until I couldn't think anymore. However, my mind trundled on and on, torturing me. What if the treasure was not in Capidava? What if the Emperor had it secreted away, buried where no one would ever find it? What if Odon's descendants had already been wiped out? Papa spent his life seeking them out with no success.

Even if we were fortunate enough to discover a forgotten child somewhere, the curse was veiled with generations of secrecy. What unknown criterion had the Warlock folded into the curse? If I had learned anything from Marianna and Rubia, it was that magic was as duplicitous as it was useful. No matter what people thought they were getting, the one who had the magic made the rules.

My pendant. My pendant. My pendant. I lost my pendant. The Emperor has the True Key. I told him what it was. *He has my key.* The words tumbled in my mind.

Again, I was trapped in a dark cavern. Helpless. Papa in need of aid.

My breathing grew shallow. I curled into a ball on the jagged rocks, cradling my arm to my chest, and wished for numbing, endless sleep.

I imagined the weight of the orb in my hand; the first time Mama gave it to me. I had worn the necklace, oblivious of the price Mama had paid for the protection it offered me.

In Burridava, people were blistered. It would almost be a gift for them to die rather than relive memories of the plague over and over again. If the people of Burridava saw me here, crying and alone, they'd tell me to be grateful I was away from the Lilac Plague. For now, I was out of its reach.

I moaned over an injured wrist while others were losing the battle for their life. How selfish of me to despair now? I rubbed my face and took a deep breath through my mouth. I couldn't stomach the stench of the pit.

Faint light teased at the slats of the grate. It was the only way to orient myself in the dark cavern, just like the light through the crack in the floor in Moesia. I bit my knuckle. I wasn't a helpless child anymore. I wouldn't huddle in fear, waiting for death.

I pushed away the terrors of the past. I remembered Mama, content in Papa's study, not on her deathbed. On Rubia's words when she handed me the orb in Patridava, not her strapped down over the back of a horse. I focused on the happy occasions.

Rubia had told me many times, 'A Guardian's path is a difficult one.' What would she advise me now? She certainly wouldn't let me wallow.

At the edge of my dress, I found a rip and tore the material into a long strip. Wrapping with my left hand was difficult; I had to restart several times.

"Wrap toward the heart." I reminded myself of Rubia's instructions.

After wrapping and securing the material, I rested my wrist on my left shoulder. I explored the cavern, feeling my way with my uninjured left hand and toes. The walls were uneven and rough. The irregular space curved with the stones under the castle, about ten spaces toe to heel at the longest points. No bedding, just stones and broken pieces of the wooden ladder.

How long would I be trapped down here? Days? Moons? I pushed those thoughts away, focusing on each heartbeat. I thought about Cassus VI who had allowed his greed to unleash the plague and Cassus VII who let it rage unchecked rather than give up the throne. Anger flared inside me.

My pendant. My pendant. My pendant. What would the Emperor do with it? He had three options: hide the pendant, destroy it, or try to use it.

I ripped off another strip of my dress, bunched it up, and held it to the cut on the back of my head. If the Emperor was a foolish man, he would destroy the key and with it, Dacia. In the short time I had observed him, he didn't strike me as a fool. Besides, anyone who held the throne was clever enough to plan a few moves ahead.

Even if Cassus hid the key, eventually, he would be curious. A man that powerful would not allow secrets that could dethrone him to stay buried for long.

One day, Cassus would try the third option; he would attempt to use the key. It would be disastrous, of course. Then he would remember me, the Guardian who could handle the key.

As long as he didn't realize Rubia was also a Guardian, the Emperor would send for me. I tucked in my chin and gritted my teeth. I would be ready.

Sanaz told me to follow my heart — if I don't want to create the curse, I should refuse and disappear. She hopes that in the inevitable wars between Cassus and Odon, the Getaens can reclaim their independence. But I know bloodshed isn't the answer. Sanaz was just a baby during the Dacian-Getaen wars, but the nightmares still plague me. I wouldn't wish that on anyone.

— VAHID, WARLOCK TO EMPEROR TRAJAN
CARACALLA

TWENTY-TWO

LAST CHANCES

Seventeen broth bowls later, Jamil came for me. In the constant gloom, I couldn't be sure if I had been in the pit for three days or three weeks. Soft light revealed the warden above, watching as Jamil pried open the grate with a metal bar.

"Stand back," Jamil said, and a rope ladder uncoiled into my cell.

I put Tulia's slippers back on. A rat had chewed through the side of one of the slippers as well as bits of the dress where I'd been hit with the rotten vegetable. I struggled up the ladder, my muscles weak, holding my injured wrist to my body. As I emerged, Jamil's eyes widened briefly before he regained his composure.

The warden inspected his nails as Jamil closed the grate behind me. I thought I would be happy to see anyone, even the odious mole-man, but instead, my dislike for him built inside me every moment I was in his presence.

Jamil tucked the manacles into his belt and took my upper left arm instead. Dim light trickled in through the narrow window slits as we walked. Moonlight, I guessed. As Jamil marched me upward, I counted the grates.

"Why am I here?" a woman cried out, her dirty fingers worming their way through a grate. "There's been some mistake!"

The heavy door in front of us grew closer. Only after we'd gone through it and left the mole-man behind did I breathe a little easier. The slits in the walls grew into windows; I squinted my eyes as I adjusted to the brightness of the full moon. The further we walked, the more uncomfortable Jamil looked. His stride grew longer, faster. As we walked through the corridors, servants and guards gave us wide berth.

"Wh-where are you taking me?" My voice cracked from disuse.

"To get you cleaned up," Jamil said. "You're wanted for further questioning."

"You don't have to squeeze my arm in your grip of d-death," I tried to cover my fear with sarcasm.

"I trusted you before, and look where that got me."

"A-as luck w-would have it, I have answers to share." I didn't care if I stuttered in front of Jamil. He already figured Zalmoxis cursed me, so why hide it?

"It took me years to be accepted into the Emperor's Own, the only Getaen to rise so high. Then, along comes a forlorn young woman in noble clothes with a story about being a trans-lator, and I trust her, delivering her right to the feet of the Emperor himself so she can spew treason in front of all the nobles," Jamil said. He slowed and made a sharp right turn, down another corridor.

"I'm sorry." I realized his sleeves had a strip of green mate-rial along the wrist. I inwardly groaned. "I didn't mean to get you —"

"Save your apology for Irena." Jamil cut me off. "My

daughter had her own dreams and plans. Now she dare not show her face past the upper wall for fear of the names she'll be called."

We made a sharp turn and picked up our pace. I stayed silent. Everything he said was true. I had taken advantage of his trust and ruined his career and, apparently, his daughter's future as well.

Jamil pushed open a door and marched down a hallway. Light flickered, and wafts of bread made my stomach rumble. The kitchens were mostly empty, but the few servants there didn't bother to hide their reactions as we crossed the room. A thin young woman, holding a broom, coughed so hard I thought she might damage her lungs. An older man covered his nose with a kerchief. Shame heated my cheeks.

Jamil approached a portly woman with her hair pulled up into a tight bun on top of her head. "Madame Palanka, do you have a —"

She waved her arms in front of her face. "Yes, yes, just a moment."

Madame Palanka rushed out of the kitchen and returned quickly with a thin towel and a bucket. "Can I never get my work done? First that rapscallion Commodus and now you."

"Commodus?" Jamil said, his face darkening. "Where?"

"Enjoying third helpings of dinner, I'm sure." Palanka pointed down the hall. "I told him I'd bring it to them, but he doesn't listen to me. Fool idiot with a sword thinks he can swagger around *my* kitchen," She muttered.

"Once the girl is cleaned up, I'll take care of Commodus." Jamil motioned for me to exit the kitchen into the courtyard beyond. "Let's get this over with."

"Now, now, Jamil, you don't mean to stand there while this waif of a girl is washin' herself." Madam Palanka crossed her arms, bucket still in hand.

"I can't just leave her. She's more trouble than you'd think." Jamil crossed his arms as well.

Madam Palanka raised an eyebrow. "Oh, aye, a right terror with 'er bunged up wrist. The wors' she could do is dirty your fancy uniform. Leave 'er to me. If she gives me any trouble, I'll give 'er a vicious poking with my spoon." She brandished a utensil at me.

Jamil heaved a sigh and went to the door. He looked around and then pointed to me. "There's only one way in and out of the courtyard, and if you give Madame Palanka a moment of trouble, I will let Commodus wash you. So behave, if that's possible. And no speeches."

I nodded vigorously as Madame Palanka took my arm and hustled me through a short corridor and arched doorway, out into the courtyard. We were outside the main castle, but a tall, curved wall enclosed the open space. I couldn't see out to the valley and orient myself. A water well stood in the center of the courtyard, and the moon hung overhead. I drew a deep breath of fresh air. Had I ever been anywhere more wonderful?

Madame Palanka slowly inspected my broken wrist. Her touch was almost kind. I held my breath, not quite understanding my instinct to wall off the feeling I felt for her. Gratitude. I couldn't afford to feel anything but the burning desire to retrieve the True Key.

"Well, I say this much for yer luck: at least the break didn't tear through the flesh. Though the bone's already mending crooked like, but I suppose that's the best you could do with just bits of fabric." She tisked. "Yer covered in dirt, lucky your scrapes aren't infected. Zalmoxis, your smell alone is fit to kill."

"I can clean myself up." I reached for the bucket, but Palanka huffed and spun it out of my reach.

"I've been entrusted to clean you up, and I shall be doin' just that for the safety of the rest of us. Wait right there." Madame

Palanka pumped the well. A cool breeze raised goose bumps on my arms as I watched cold mountain water fill the bucket. No more warm pipes or comforting bathing tubs for me.

Madame Palanka turned to me and, without even a word of warning, flung the bucket full of water at me. I stiffened as the frigid water hit me like a wall.

I stood gasping and shocked as Madame Palanka turned back to the water pump.

"So yer 'The Golden Protector?'" she snorted, pumping the water again. "Yer just a lass in a yellow dress, naught more than that."

"W-what?" I shivered, water pooling inside Tulia's slippers.

"Thought you'd be more impressive, 'tis all," she said.

The back of my neck prickled. I glanced over my shoulder at the doorway back into the kitchens. No sign of Jamil. Shadows flickered with the torch flames before bleeding into the cool moonlight of the courtyard.

"Best to hold still," Madame Palanka said.

I braced my injured wrist against my body as another bucket of ice-cold water hit me. Lady Katalin's fine gown clung to my body. I wrapped my arms around myself, trembling. After the dungeons, I was chilled to my core. Water straight from the bowels of the mountain stiffened my joints and numbed my mind.

Shouting erupted from inside the kitchen.

"Scrub yourself off." Palanka shoved a pumice stone into my hand before rushing back into the kitchen.

A laugh burbled inside of me, but my lips were too frozen to let it escape my lungs. What would Jamil think of the cook's laxity in the face of such a dangerous outlaw as myself? Best not to add to her troubles by mentioning it. Besides, I didn't want to test Jamil's threat.

I filled up the bucket and unwrapped my injured wrist,

tossing away the strip of material. I plunged my wrist into the frigid water. I bit my lip as I gently prodded my forearm. Four finger lengths above my wrist, there was a newfound bump in my once straight forearm. I closed my eyes and pushed away worries that fought for my attention, instead focusing on my gratitude for the freezing water and the bit of numbing relief it provided. I then soaked my hair, loosening the sweat and blood that had congealed it into one solid mass.

Jamil's voice carried outside, but I couldn't make out what he was saying. I tiptoed back into the corridor, my body shaking with cold, a trail of water behind me.

"You're no longer in a position to tell me what to do." Commodus' voice came from inside the kitchen. "Besides, your prisoner should be presented to the Emperor now. What are you doing with her here?"

"Imagine what would happen if Jamil delivered a prisoner straight from the dungeons? She's in no state to be presented to a shepherd, let alone to Emperor Cassus," Madame Palanka snapped. "Besides, the Emperor has sent for his dinner. I'm sure he won't be meeting with anyone 'til after he's dined. He hasn't eaten all day. Now, if you'll excuse me."

I took a few steps back and held my breath, expecting Madame Palanka to reappear at any moment. Instead, I heard the clatter of silverware.

"Let me accompany you to deliver the food," Commodus said.

"And leave your charge unattended?" Jamil said, frustration in his voice.

Commodus sneered. "Oh, did I not make that clear? As your charge is so well mannered you trust her to bathe unsupervised, I'm sure you can manage her as well as deliver the old man to the royal library. Take her along for all I care. The scholar needs to get his nose back in those scrolls."

I hugged myself tighter, daring to tip-toe closer. Was Papa still in the castle? Was Commodus handing off Papa's care to Jamil?

"Remember to get the 'Golden Protector' to the Throne Room," Commodus said in a condescending voice as he retreated from the kitchen.

I wanted to leap back into the kitchen and ask about Papa. Was he nearby? But if Vasile hadn't bothered to communicate that the Dacian scholar was my papa, I didn't want to make it obvious. I picked up the worn linen towel inside the arched doorway and wrapped it around myself before entering the kitchen.

The room had been vacated, except for Jamil and a thin man next to him... *Papa.* My heart jumped into my throat and I leaned against the wall for support. Quickly feigning what I hoped was nonchallance, I spoke, drawing Jamil's attention.

"Is there anything clean I can wear?"

Papa's head whipped around, his eyes wide. His hand flew to his mouth, stifling a cry.

I held my wrist up to my shoulder, providing me with a little relief.

"Zalmoxis." Papa's hand clutched at his chest. I was sure I was unsettling to see, but I'd hoped Papa could pretend not to know me. I gave him a tiny shake of my head.

A young servant appeared in the hall, his shoulders rounded as he hovered in the doorway. Jamil ignored the servant, looking from Papa to me.

The servant cleared his throat. Jamil scowled then pointed to a neatly folded stack of clothing on the table behind him. "You'll change after I return to fetch the scholar. There's no other way out of the kitchens than by going right past me, so don't try anything foolish."

The moment Jamil followed the servant out of the room, I

lunged for Papa, embracing him with my wet arms, not caring that my wrist throbbed with the movement.

"Papa." I had so many questions, so many things to tell him.

"What are you doing here?" Papa whispered. "You should be in Moesia."

"Rubia —" Should I tell him that Rubia was a prisoner here, too? "I begged her to b-bring me to Capidava. I had to know what happened to you."

Papa released me. "My life's work was always going to get me into trouble eventually. I should've helped you make peace with that long ago. Then you would never need to come find me." He ran a hand across his bald pate and looked up at the ceiling. "I've made too many mistakes. Can you forgive me?"

"You p-protecting me from the raids, the d-derision of the kingdom, the r-responsibility of the orb until I was of age... everything?" My voice caught in my throat. *You never let bitterness sour your love for me when Mama sacrificed her life for mine.*

"The things I've discovered, the Emperor has laid most of them bare." Papa braced himself against the table behind him.

"You were doing everything you could to stop the p-plague. How can anyone fault you for that?" I hated seeing Papa torment himself.

"I've read additional scrolls since arriving, most of which I don't understand," Papa muttered. "If your mama were here, she'd help me make sense of things. Just having someone else to talk to who understands always helped."

"I'll l-listen." My jaw chattered, making my stutter worse.

"Nikka, I've been so turned around here, off my schedule, away from my usual tools. The records they saved are not organized sensibly."

I almost laughed out loud despite the situation. Back home, Papa knew where everything was in the heaps of scrolls and piles of artifacts in his office. But here, the Emperor's clerics probably made him sleep and eat at regular times, upsetting the natural rhythms of his genius. The scrolls were probably neatly placed where he could never find them.

"It's j-just as well." I took Papa's hand, preparing for my most distressing news. He should be aware of my mistake. "P-papa, I n-need to tell you something."

He looked down at me and waited.

"Rubia gave me the k-key. And I g-gave it to the High Judge." I inwardly cringed.

"What?" Papa paled, confusion etched into the wrinkles around his eyes. "Vasile?"

I nodded. "I thought if I just e-explained to the Roses and Lilies that —"

I dropped Papa's hand just as Jamil marched back in, a napkin in his hand. His eyes flicked over Papa. I realized, with horror, that Papa's camasa was wet across the chest and sleeves where I'd hugged him, and we had been standing closer together than mere strangers would have.

"Thank you for looking at my wrist." I gave Papa a subservient nod and stepped back.

Jamil dropped the napkin on the table next to me. It had a roll and meat inside. "First the clothes and now the food. It seems you have friends outside Rupea Castle who are eager to send the Golden Protector some gifts."

"The mystic?" I asked.

Jamil shrugged. "You've been hidden away for exactly two weeks, twenty days, and you're still as popular as ever."

Papa seemed to notice my yellow dress below the towel and ran a hand down his face. "*You're* the Golden Protector?"

Jamil put a heavy hand on Papa's shoulder, giving me a knowing look. "The scholar and I will wait outside the kitchen for you while you change."

Jamil squeezed Papa's shoulder. Papa winced.

Jamil must have surmised that the Azure scholar hugged me, a prisoner. Who would do that? A papa did. My knees were weak. Jamil knew.

"I'll be quick." Even if there were a way out and Jamil weren't holding Papa hostage, I wouldn't try to escape; I had to try and get the key back. The look on Papa's face when I told him the news of losing the key only strengthened my resolve.

Left alone, I set aside any lady-like decorum and gobbled up the food in the napkin like an animal. It had been twenty days since I'd had food that wasn't broth. The bread and meat felt like rocks in my stomach, unwelcome and indigestible.

I groaned, holding a hand to my belly. Water dripped from my hair onto the table, the floor. I toweled off while I made a mental list of herbal options to create a salve to speed the healing of my wrist. I found a knife and made slits in the linen towel before ripping it into strips. I had a long list of possible accusations, so shredding a kitchen towel and stealing a few herbs wasn't going to add much to my damning sentence.

I turned my attention to the clean clothes. I was humbled that Marianna would go to the effort of sending them. Even with her ability to See, she couldn't have known for certain that I would still be alive. All her efforts could have been for nothing.

I slid on the rough linen chemise and dress. I had never felt so grateful to be in something clean. The clothing was plain, lacking symbols or colors of any Dacian city. Tucked under the half-fota wrap skirt was a pair of sandals, scissors, and a note.

The clothing is given by many. The scissors are from me in case you change your mind about your hair.

My jaw dropped. Tulia? Finally, I laughed. The mere act of laughing brought more warmth to my soul than a day in the Moesian sun. I wasn't alone anymore. I straightened, standing taller.

With one hand, I shook out the neatly folded apron, and a

soft ping sounded against the stone floor. Thinking it was a small pebble, I almost ignored it, but I looked down. A glint reflected on the ground in the torchlight.

The fota slipped from my hands in a heap. I held a breath and picked up the gold nugget from the floor. I ran my fingers over the familiar shape of the piece of Moesian gold.

I danced around, not bothering to wipe the grin off my face.

Marcus had found Tulia. Tulia had ignored my last request and told Marcus where I'd gone. Together, they had plotted to send me the clothing. I didn't want Marcus to be caught up in my treasonous scheme, but still, I felt like I was floating. Who in the castle would Marcus trust in delivering this gold?

I WAITED in an antechamber while the Emperor finished his dinner. The anxiety of seeing Cassus mounted in my belly. I desperately wanted a distraction. The windowless room I was held in had two sets of closed double-doors on opposite walls. Six chairs and a narrow table lined one side, and a single magical luminary lit the room. Jamil paced the floor like he had while waiting for me to finish the poultice for my wrist.

Jamil had turned his back when I pilfered herbs in the kitchen. He had even scrubbed the dried blood and dirt from the back of my head, cleaning the injury from when I'd hit my head on the wall of the cavern. I wondered how many times he'd cleaned wounds as a soldier. Like Madame Palanka, he was surprised I didn't have oozing sores. I knew he was just getting me cleaned up for the Emperor, but something about him had changed since retrieving me from the dungeon.

Even with my brief wash, my hair was impossibly knotted. With no comb, the scissors tempted me, but Jamil had whisked the blades away while he was assisting with my preparations.

I refrained from running my hand down the apron to verify my secrets were still tucked out of sight. Tulia had again delivered an apron with a secret pocket where I stowed the orange-sting and gold nugget.

I had already tried to apologize to Jamil many times, but he brushed me off. Yet, with every footfall, he seemed to grow more agitated.

"How old is your daughter?" I asked, hoping to ease some of the tension.

"She's about your age. And twice as confident and loud about her opinions as you are." He snorted, still pacing the floor. "Irena certainly has opinions about the Golden Protector."

I cocked my head. "What does that mean? Golden Protector?"

"When the sun reflected off your dress and hair, you glowed. The guards had already been summoned, which is fortunate. There could've been an uprising."

I didn't know what to say, so I let the silence stretch out until Jamil filled it.

"Irena, she was there. She's upset with me. She believes you can stop the plague as you promised." He looked at my sandals, and his nostrils flared. While my dress sleeves and fota skirt were plain, the sandals had Getaen symbols painted on the leather strips. "She's always had a penchant for the protection circle on your sandal."

Had Irena gone against her father's wishes and helped procure this clothing?

"The symbol for salt?" I touched the center strap of my sandal, which featured one symbol: two crescents facing each other, one smaller and placed inside of the other. I hadn't thought much of them because sandals were very common in Moesia, but less so further north except for in the lower classes.

"I know the deeper meaning behind 'salt' because of Irena's

studies." Jamil folded his arms and scowled at the sandal. "It is symbolic of a parent's arms encircling their child."

It made sense that 'protection' and 'preservation' and 'salt' were related. Mama had often pointed out word correlations to me as a child. Though the true Getaen symbol was with the crescents nestled together, in the same direction. Whoever created this symbol was a fool. Unless the alteration *strengthened* the magic; then they might be brilliant. I hoped whoever was on my side was the latter.

Jamil fidgeted with the pommel of his sword. "Anyone caught trying to help or protect you will face the wrath of the Emperor."

A chill went down my spine. What did Jamil know that I didn't?

"Even if I suspected who sent this to me, their names won't cross my lips. I wouldn't wish the dungeon on anyone," I said earnestly. *Except for those thieves who assaulted Rubia.*

There was a crash in the hall outside the antechamber. I jumped. Jamil threw open the double doors into the hallway and rushed off, leaving me alone. I hadn't tried to run away from the kitchens. My freedom wasn't as important as stopping the plague. Still, I was surprised he left me unattended.

Several servants rushed past the open doors, but one slipped in.

The curl of dark hair, the slope of his shoulders, and his hazel eyes... in a heartbeat Marcus was at my side. Relief and surprise flooded me.

"We must leave before your guard returns." He gave me a nervous grin, guiding me to the door.

"How are you here?" I flushed, less from the possibility of escape and more from his proximity. There was only so much cleaning up a couple of cold buckets of water could do without a good scrubbing.

"It's a long story." Marcus looked at my bandaged hand and frowned. "Your fingers are purple." His hand warmed the small of my back as he tried to push me gently toward the door. "You're fortunate that's your only injury. When I heard what had happened, I wondered if you were still alive. I never should have brought you to Capidava. I knew it was too dangerous. I'm going to get you back home. I promise."

I dug my heels in, rooting myself in place. "I can't leave. The High Judge has my p-pendant." I put a hand to my chest where my orb used to rest and took a breath. "Remember when I asked you what you'd do to s-stop the p-plague? And you said you'd d-do anything?"

Marcus' eyes searched my face.

How could I make him understand when I never explained to him what the True Key was?

"I d-don't have time to explain." I said, "You just have to t-trust me."

"There are rumors about your abilities, but they make no sense. You can explain everything when we're safely away," Marcus said.

"You must go before you're d-discovered. If I run, my p-papa will get hurt," I said. "I won't l-leave him, and I have to try and stop the plague. No matter what it c-costs." *Even my freedom or my life.*

"A father would gladly trade his life for his daughter's," Jamil said from the doorway.

My hand flew to the secret pocket, my fingertips at the edge of the orange-sting.

Marcus spun around, putting himself between Jamil and me and pulling out his concealed dagger.

"Settle down there, boy. You're going to get yourself hurt." Jamil held his hand out.

"I'm leaving, and I'm taking Nicoleta with me." Marcus took a step forward.

Jamil closed the double doors softly, trapping us inside. "I'm not here to stop you. I'm here to help you."

"What?" Marcus and I said, almost in unison.

"My daughter has been trying to convince me all week. Those sandals are a message from her to me, not to you." Jamil ran a hand down his face. "The last two weeks I've wrestled with the idea that Cassus VII was never destined to rule, and my wife is dead because of his selfish choice."

Jamil's hand clenched into a fist. "I've heard many things in my travels, around campfires, from enemies' spiteful lips, and in darkened corridors. I assumed those rumors were lies. When I listened to your tale, the rumors I'd ignored bubbled to the surface. The puzzle fit together, as much as I didn't want it to. I fought against it, not wanting to believe I was serving the very man responsible for the plague. But I can no longer ignore your words and Irena's pestering."

Jamil took another step toward me. "If the usurper wants you dead, I want you alive."

Was Jamil claiming that the Emperor was our common enemy?

"I'll help you escape. I'll do what I can to track the location of the key inside Rupea Castle, and I'll keep an ear to the ground for the treasure it opens. You search the kingdom for this true blood heir." Jamil waved his open, up-turned palm as if sweeping me away from this tiny room and into the wider world.

I relaxed my fingers away from the hidden sting in my fota. All I had wanted was to discover Papa's fate. Once I'd spoken with him, allowing us both to say the things that needed to be said long ago, what was keeping me here? Finding the treasure, getting the key.

Jamil could track those items inside Rupea far better than I. My decision tore my soul to shreds: escaping without Papa or Rubia, or staying and trying to convince anyone to search for the true heir.

Jamil was right. Nothing would make Papa or Rubia happier than if I escaped, especially if I continued searching for the heir. I gave a hesitant nod. I could meet with Mystic Marianna and renew the search for Odon's descendant.

"The woman brought in by the thieves when I was in the s-stocks... " I began, not sure what I meant to say or how Jamil could help Rubia.

"I know," Jamil said. "Your reaction to seeing her gave you away. It won't be long until others notice as well. The Getaens who advise the Emperor are doing their best to protect her. But, they must tread carefully. I have some influence with them and will speak on Rubia's behalf. There's a chance the mages will claim her before Vasile connects her to you."

"And if he does?" I asked.

Jamil shook his head. "The sooner you leave, the better her chances."

Marcus put a hand on my lower back. "I'll take her through the servants' quarters."

Jamil shook his head and turned to me, "I have a better way, though you won't like it."

ALONE INSIDE THE DARKENED TUNNEL, I forced myself not to rush my counting. My heart thumped so loudly I feared it echoed through the dark, hidden corridors for any Emperor's Own to hear. While I counted, my fingers fumbled around the edges of the latch. On my tiptoes, I peered through a slit in the wall into the garden. The moon cast the manicured paths, flowerbeds, and trees into an array of gray tones. Jamil knew the weakest area of the castle, the Emperor's Garden. He had described how to find a crumbled portion of the wall in the process of being repaired.

The garden appeared empty, but I feared Commodus would dash in any moment. The best part of our plan was pointing the finger at the condescending guard. Commodus' eagerness to be seen by the emperor made him easy to exploit. Jamil had no difficulty convincing Commodus to be responsible for and deliver 'The Golden Protector' when the Emperor sent for me. And as we planned, Commodus had locked me in the antechamber alone to go shine his boots and likely brush his uniform; all it took was Jamil's disdainful look at Commodus' attire. Once alone in the antechamber, I had counted three stones over from the luminary. The passage was seamlessly hidden; not even a tapestry was needed to conceal it. I pulled the noiseless, narrow door open, reviewing the instruction Jamil had given me. Jamil looked a little green, revealing an entrance to the Emperor's Own passageways. He said not even Commodus knew their locations, but it was the only way to save the kingdom.

When I first closed the narrow door behind me and the crushing darkness enveloped me, I'd stood rooted in place, the terrors from the dungeon and under the tiles at home threatening. I forced my attention to the roughness of the walls and tracked my turns, trying to ignore my shaking hands and the cold sweat trickling down my back.

Staring through the slit into the garden, my attention was drawn by movement. A lone figure made his way from the corridor into the open grasses and onto a path. From his gait and silhouette, I recognized Marcus. He would wait for me at the wall, ready to help me over. I took a deep breath, nervous energy coursing through my veins, making it difficult for me to pull the latch and open the concealed door.

Along with moonlight, the sound of the rushing waterfall raced to greet me. The air was misty from water droplets. I stepped out onto moss-covered stones and pulled the secret door closed behind me. I didn't know how to secure it from this side, but I was sure Jamil would cover my tracks.

The tree Jamil described was easy to spot, even in the shadows of the night. It was the tallest tree with manicured bushes surrounding it. Fat pears hung invitingly from its branches. I would need food for the road. I wrapped my fingers around a firm yellow pear, but before it snapped free, I stopped.

The trip from Moesia to Patridava in the back of Marcus' apple-filled wagon washed over me. It felt like I had left Moesia years ago, not weeks. I had been full of fear, my focus on Papa the only thing that drove me. In seeking him, I discovered what it meant to be a Guardian of the key that could stop the plague. Stopping all the pain, the suffering — that was the most important thing I could do. But was leaving the best way? Or was it simply the least frightening?

The plague was speeding up, ravaging cities one after another, some more than once. Did I have the luxury of searching the kingdom for an heir? With the limited time the kingdom had, what chance did I have of finding any descendants of Odon? And if I did, what was the guarantee that the True Key would recognize that particular descendant as the true heir?

I released the pear. The delicate branch popped up and bobbled in the air. A soft volley of dewdrops splattered down like the first spring rains of Moesia.

I didn't want to travel alone, to be a fugitive. I couldn't go home, as much as Marcus was determined to see me safely there. I wanted to listen to Papa muttering to himself late into the night. What I wouldn't give to lay under a blanket of stars, listening to Rubia name common and rare plants. The thought of Marcus returning to see me next spring, to explore the promise I thought I saw in his hazel eyes — a future with a house of my own — but those things were never to be.

I had a sliver of a chance at stopping the plague if I stayed in Rupea, and my chances of stumbling into a descendant of Odon outside Rupea were far slimmer. If I stayed, I could urge everyone who would listen that we needed to find the true heir. Perhaps I'd even be able to snatch back the key. More likely, someone would drag me out of the dungeon when Capidava was in the grips of the plague, and they were finally desperate enough to search for the heir. I needed to be here.

My wrist throbbed, and I tucked it closer to my chest. The emperors were all fools. They couldn't outsmart this curse. A warlock, probably the most powerful Papa had ever studied, had created it. I pressed my forehead against the rough bark of the tree. A thought came to me, as if seeing the warlock in a new light.

I had always considered the warlock Dacian because he lived in the north and served the Blood Conqueror. But, of course, he was a magical Getaen. He lived with a foot in both worlds. Though I didn't have magic, I understood that part of him. Who would be more likely to understand the meaning of his Binding oath and the resulting curse if not me? Certainly not a Dacian scholar from the bowels of Rupea Castle. Perhaps not even Papa who was born a Dacian in the Dacian kingdom. Nor even Mama who grew up surrounded by fellow Getaens.

A breeze rustled the trees. Every passing moment made my time in the garden more dangerous. If he hadn't already, Commodus would soon discover I was missing. They'd turn the castle inside out looking for me.

I gripped a branch. I could run, but I wouldn't. The people of Capidava had shown they believed me. The Emperor feared how I'd turned them. Cassus had thrown me into a pit, hoping the commoners would forget about me. But the clothing on my back and the sandals at my feet were proof they supported me. Even Jamil, once one of the Emperor's Own, believed me. I not only had the truth but momentum on my side.

Behind me, at the wall, Marcus waited. Soon enough, he'd know I wasn't going with him. My stomach knotted at the thought of leaving him again.

I looked up at the castle, straining to see the tips of the spires as they reached toward the full moon. I pushed my shoulders back and marched straight back into Rupea. Few in the castle knew me, so if I moved with purpose, no one would give me a second glance, especially dressed in clean clothes. If I circled back to the main entrance, I could find my way to where I needed to be. Fortunately, the one place I wanted to be was the last place anyone would think to look.

I have had a lifetime of doing terrible things for the Emperor. Perhaps I can redeem myself now. I know Hanna would want me to find a way to protect others. I cannot turn away from Trajan Caracalla's arrangement between his sons; it is an opportunity to keep the peace between all the territories. But am I just keeping the peace now, only to create a curse destined to condemn the kingdom later? If only I could trust that the descendants of Cassus wouldn't be blinded by greed.

— VAHID, WARLOCK TO EMPEROR TRAJAN

CARACALLA

CHAPTER

TWENTY-THREE

STING AND BLEED

I marched down the hall, ready to confront Emperor Cassus VII. He needed me alive to manipulate the pendant; he couldn't risk killing me. Yet. And I'd already proved to myself that I could survive the dungeons. Any fear or doubts I had receded.

As more villages and cities succumbed to the Lilac Plague, the chances of the people overthrowing Cassus increased. If I survived long enough, I would need to be prepared with answers for them. I didn't know what those answers would be, exactly, but I would learn what I could. Not as a cleric as Rubia planned. Or exploring the kingdom as Papa hoped. Answers would come in snippets whenever the Emperor summoned me from the dungeons.

I passed a few guards scurrying around, but they paid me no mind. I picked up a tray with a plate of grape stems and a half-eaten shank of mutton abandoned in a smoking room. I carried it around, submissively averting my eyes from the guards' faces. Fortunately, the tray was easy to balance with one hand.

I turned the final corner, the entrance to the grand hall in sight. The Emperor would be finished dining, and the guards

347

would be scouring the servants' quarters and outside grounds for me. Muffled shouts sounded from the throne room.

Further down the hall was the entrance to the antechamber I had escaped from. Loitering in the hallway was foolish, but so was bursting into the grand hall without knowing who was there.

A snap sounded, followed by a strange, animal cry. There was another snap and another anguished scream. The snap was a whip; the scream was human. My stomach wrenched. Another snap and a strangled cry. Was it Rubia? No, the voice sounded nothing like hers.

There were no guards in the hall outside of the throne room. Had Commodus managed to convince them to leave their posts and search for me?

I set the tray on the ground in the hall and strode across the rugs to the closed double doors. Before I reached them, one of the doors swung open. Out charged a noble. I recognized the short man with the beard from my evening in the dining hall. He had asked questions and seemed to listen to my responses. He bumped my shoulder as he passed, his face clouded. He didn't utter an apology as he continued down the corridor.

I caught a glimpse of the room before a guard reached and closed the door behind the nobleman. Several nobles and their representatives lined the room despite the midnight hour. I hadn't heard them earlier from the antechamber. They must have recently convened. Or reconvened after the Emperor requested his late dinner.

I scanned the faces for Elek. Was he skulking amid the other high-hats? Had his hand healed? I drew my wrist against my body.

The crack of the whip cut, followed by a soft thud on the ground.

Barbarians. I didn't need to listen to more. I shoved against the door the noble had exited. It swung wide on its well-oiled hinge. I swept into the room, storming by the slack-jawed guards.

On either side, the nobles were a river of faces, fine clothes, and feathers in a riot of colors. Directly in front of me was the dais. The tables had been removed from it, and only the massive gold throne remained though Emperor Cassus was nowhere to be seen. Standing apart from the others, in front of the platform, were two Getaen women, the Emperor's witches, I assumed, and Vasile.

My attention was drawn to the figure on the ground. The wretched woman's body was crumpled at the feet of a guard holding a whip. Vasile stood between the Getaen witches and the ruined creature on the floor, his head jerking up to see who had disturbed the court.

The guard stepped back, leaving the woman struggling to support her upper body with her arms. Bile stung the back of my throat. The back of her dress was split open. A shock went through me as I realized the brown of her dress was dried blood. Her back looked like nothing I'd ever seen before, a butchered animal yet still alive.

Distressed by the swelling of her face and the dark bruises, I almost missed the blond of her hair. I gasped, and my legs buckled. The room spun, and the stone floor slammed into my knees. I vomited, coughing up chunks of the bread I'd just eaten plus the dungeon broth. My stomach heaved again.

Commodus yelled to a guard behind me at the door, but I barely heard him.

Rubia had always been a petite woman, but now her frame was skeletal. I rushed forward. She looked past me, unfocused. Before I could do more than drop to my knees at her side, hands pulled me back.

I thrust my hand into my secret pocket and took a gulping

breath. I threw the orange-sting on the floor. The grip on me released, and people yelped. I lunged for Rubia, dragging her as she whimpered, away from the poison in the air. I made my way to the antechamber double doors, struggling to hold my breath. I skirted the edge of the orange cloud hanging in the middle of the throne room, but still, my eyes and lungs burned. I pushed on the heavy doors. They started to open, but someone grabbed me. I twisted, clawed, and bit at my assailants but received a blow to the stomach for my efforts.

Two guards, their faces covered with scarves, pulled Rubia away. Her eyes fluttered half-closed and filled with tears.

"Rubia!" I yelled, reaching for her. My voice was drowned by the other frenetic screams in the room.

Another guard yanked me back, holding my arms behind me, sending shooting pains from my wrist up my arm and through my body. I screamed, trying to twist away to relieve the pain.

Rubia's guards wrenched her to her feet. She stumbled up, her feet uncoordinated.

Our eyes met. The world slowed, the moment feeling like an eternity. Rubia's eyes widened with recognition then sadness. We were helpless pawns. She had tried to protect me with her silence. A mother is loyal to her daughter. And I'd invalidated her sacrifice in a single foolish gesture, rushing to her side.

Commodus' mocking voice sounded in my ear. "You've caused a bit of trouble for me tonight. I'll make sure to return the favor."

An explosion of mind-numbing pain, a bright light, and darkness swallowed me.

～

ACTIVITY WHIRLED AROUND ME. I lay near the center of the throne room, my eyes smarting and tearing, my lungs burning. The orange-sting had mostly dissipated through retracted glass ceiling panels. Servants coughed as they fanned away the last stubborn fumes.

Past the glass ceiling, the dim stars were starting to die away. Less than two hours from dawn.

Commodus reached down and lifted me to my feet. My head spun, the knot where I'd been struck throbbed to the beat of my heart. My wrists had been shackled together in front of me, making it more difficult to get up, especially as the room dipped and spun around me. I'd never been on a ship, but if the description of seasickness matched the queasy loss of balance I felt, I never wanted to go.

"Welcome back, Golden Protector," Commodus mocked. His rough and heavy hand squeezed my neck, no doubt a reward for escaping him in the antechamber. I almost remarked on his shiny boots, but I bit my tongue. My true fight lay elsewhere.

"Where did you get the orange-sting? Did that traitorous Get give it to you?"

"Actually —" I watched Vasile by the dais as I responded to Commodus next to me. "— you did."

Commodus shook me slightly. "Liar."

"It's true. I had the orange-sting in my p-pocket, and you let me keep it in the stocks. I've had it the whole time." I grinned and turned to look up at him to make sure he saw it.

"Nicoleta Aurelian." The High Judge's voice was slightly raspy, but he stood tall and signaled the guards. "Glad you could join us. We were just discussing your purpose in Patri-dava and why you traveled to Capidava."

Rubia was sprawled on the stone floor nearby, her

breathing shallow, two guards looming over her, one of which was Jamil. I was grateful she wasn't forced to stand.

Jamil had one hand on his sword pommel; the other was clutched behind his back in a fist, his fingers white. He had gone to a lot of trouble to help me escape, only to witness me throw myself back to the wolves. I wished I could explain it to him, but I followed his lead and ignored him.

"Summon Master Elek," Vasile instructed a guard. "And then inform the Emperor that the trial for Master Elek's attackers is ready to begin.

I blinked several times. I had expected they'd taken me out of the dungeons to discuss their inability to use the necklace. Not discuss Elek. Did they not understand that people in Burri-dava were dying? During this trial, for Elek or not, I needed to make them understand the danger the entire Dacian Kingdom faced.

The lingering scents of blood and rancid vomit made me nauseous. I pitied the servant who had been assigned to clean up. Between Rubia and me, the room was a fine wreck. I wished I'd had something to feed Rubia. All I had was the gold nugget in my apron. I suppressed a wild laugh as I realized Commodus had failed to search me, and once again, I concealed something in my hidden pocket.

My throat smarted as I forced myself to take a deep breath and close my eyes, attempting to calm myself. Rubia's torture consumed my thoughts, clouding everything around me. I needed to keep my wits about me if I was to glean information from the court proceedings that would help me stop the plague. But I couldn't take my mind off the back of Rubia's stained dress.

I'd already memorized several phrases so they'd roll off my tongue, so I turned my thoughts to Vasile. It appeared the High Judge had already connected Papa, Rubia, and me. He knew I was a Guardian. But what didn't he know? What could I leverage? Did he suspect Jamil had helped me escape the antechamber? Did he know when the treasure was opened that it would have the power to topple a kingdom?

On the other hand, what did the Emperor know that I didn't? Where was the treasure hidden? Was it in Rupea Castle as Rubia suspected? Did the Emperor know what the treasure contained?

There was a murmur in the throne room. I opened my eyes as a warlock strode past the onlookers. He took his place on the dais behind the throne, gripping the top of it with his long-fingered hands. Although his hair was thinning, it retained its wheat blond color. The warlock's ruddy skin was wrinkled and spotted with age, but his blue eyes glittered with cruel intelligence as he looked over the room. A boy, who looked no more than ten, stood half-hidden behind the warlock. From his robes, which mirrored the warlock's, I assumed the boy was the warlock's apprentice.

Vasile mounted the dais and spoke in low tones with the warlock and a guard. On the floor in front of the dais stood the two Getaen women who had supervised Rubia's whipping. One old and the other young, they argued in the southern tongue.

"It cannot be undone, Pari," said the older witch. "Vasile's commanding it doesn't make it so." Her blue eyes and blond hair were faded like the flowers after too much Moesian sun. Shallow wrinkles lined her eyes, but her back was straight and muscles flexed in her forearms when she moved.

Lining the room was an ever-growing contingent of Roses and Lilies, each one dressed more opulently than the last. They chatted with each other, some even laughing. Without turning to inspect the onlookers, I couldn't see if Elek was in the audience. That was only some small consolation as the pig-faced Lord Porcius had placed himself where he could easily see my face. A few people in the audience wore simple clothing, setting them apart from the dazzling finery of the nobles. Some of the weight lifted from my shoulders knowing that commoners who supported me were here. I ignored Lord Porcius and focused on the faces that didn't scorn me. A woman winked at me and shifted her wrapped fota apron. Pinned to her hip was a yellow flower. It was a flash of sunny color; she covered it again, her gaze darting around the room.

Out of the corner of my eye, I spotted two guards at attention by the doors to the side antechamber. I was trapped and surrounded. The only way was forward, directly at the throne in front of me.

The main doors opened. Papa shuffled in, fidgeting with his camasa. The black-clad guard holding Papa had a gold pin on his chest. Commodus gave the guard a respectful nod. "Captain Lucius, sir."

Captain Lucius positioned Papa just off to my right and a little behind me. "No further trouble from the agitator?"

"No, sir." Commodus' tone was obsequious.

The room shifted their focus to Papa. Vasile frowned, and the warlock gave Papa a withering stare. But the witches didn't pay Papa any attention, instead eying me from head to toe.

"She wore the True Key without injury," said the oldest witch with the faded eyes.

"But, Ziba, how is it possible that someone with Getaen blood has it? And where did she get it?" Pari asked. She tucked a wisp of her strawberry blond hair away from her freckled face as she studied me.

"The True Key has been p-passed down for generations," I replied in Getaen. "There is much you don't know."

Commodus shook me. "Quiet!"

The freckled witch grinned at my words, speaking in

Dacian. "She'll have a hard time answering questions if she's quiet, Thorn."

Vasile's frown deepened, but he ignored Pari's words.

The older witch, Ziba, circled the guard and me as she inspected me. At her approach, the rustling in the room stopped. She was tall for a Getaen, but I was taller still.

"Have you been to the South?" Ziba asked in Dacian. From what Vasile had said, today's trial was about Elek. I guessed the witch couldn't ask me anything related to that *incident*. Why she was talking to me at all was curious.

I shook my head. "I was born in Moesia. I've never been south of there except to the nearby hills."

"You've seen magic?" Ziba asked, her faded blue eyes searched my face. "Learned its secrets?"

"Magic is not so uncommon in Moesia. Many Southerners live there," I said.

"What is your specialty?" A mischievous glint sparked in her eye. She wanted to know about the magic I held. I had none, but if Rubia hadn't revealed that, I wouldn't either. Not yet. I pressed my lips together, not taking my gaze off of her.

Instead of irritation, she gave me a knowing grin.

With a swish of silk on my left, people moved aside, allowing two newcomers to pass through to the front. Lady Katalin strode forward, her short, dark hair bouncing around her face, stopping when she abutted the dais. She looked refreshed like she hadn't just been awoken by a frantic representative alerting her to the trial a short time ago. The person next to her made my stomach drop. Marcus stood at her side in finer clothing than I'd ever seen him wear.

Before I could even so much as make eye contact with Marcus, the Emperor paraded into the throne room, Lady Essa at his heels. Cassus seated himself on the throne, his broad shoulders back, both hands resting on their respective armrests.

The room had already turned quiet, but now it became deathly so.

Lady Essa stood next to the Emperor. The southern witches and warlock bowed to the Emperor before Pari whispered in Essa's ear.

Emperor Cassus raised a finger, and Vasile cleared his throat.

"We are here to discuss the assault of Merchant Master Elek of Capidava," Vasile said. His voice was loud and carried easily throughout the room. "Your Highness, I present Elek of Capidava as a court witness."

My jaw clenched. Footsteps sounded, and Elek passed me without even a glance, but a cold chill ran down my back. A faint rotting smell wafted to me as he passed. One hand was pinned up in a satin sling, next to his body. With the other, he removed his feathered hat and dropped to his knee, bowing to the Emperor.

Emperor Cassus waved for the groveling man to stand. Elek stood, shoulders rounded, his chin down.

Vasile stepped forward. "Explain what happened to your hand in Patridava."

Elek fiddled with the cap in his hand. "I was doing my business in Patridava as usual. I kindly offered passage for a woman and her child to Capidava. Before we departed, I was attacked with Getaen magic. Many of my household are still recovering from damage to their sight due to the orange-sting."

I ground my teeth. Effects from the sting lasted hours, not days, as anyone present could attest.

Elek continued, "In addition, my hand was cursed. I am told I must amputate my hand."

"Why did they attack you?" Vasile asked.

"They meant to rob me, I'm certain, but my men chased them off," Elek said.

I clenched my hands into fists, glaring at Elek's back.

"We have the woman you identified as the one who used witchcraft." Vasile pointed to Rubia.

Elek turned, inspecting Rubia as she struggled to sit up, her dress in tatters. His eyes narrowed like a vulture, his lips curling.

"Yes, that's her." His voice was laced with acid. His disdain for Rubia when she was too weak to fight back made my blood boil.

"There is a rumor that she had a compan—" Vasile started.

"How d-dare you look at her?" I cut off the High Judge's words.

Vasile pivoted to me, his eyes narrowed.

"Because of your lies, this is her f-fate," I spat at Elek.

Commodus pressed his fingers into my arm, sending shooting pains down through my wrists and up my neck. I instinctively rose to my tiptoes. I raised my voice. "She did nothing to d-deserve this!"

"Nicoleta?" Rubia's unsteady voice silenced me. She glanced in my direction, not seeming to recognize me. My heart wrenched, wanting to be at her side, to sing and braid her hair like she had done for me when I needed comfort.

"Enough!" The Emperor spoke for the first time. He stared at me as if he could bore a hole right through me.

I held my breath. I needed Cassus to entrust me with the pendant. This was not the way to gain his goodwill.

Vasile cleared his throat and addressed Elek. "Did the accused have a companion with her?"

Commodus relaxed his fingers then tightened them again. I wriggled my shoulders, but he did not relent.

Elek gripped his hat tighter. "When we originally made our deal, I had yet to meet her companion."

"And how did you come to know she had a companion?" Vasile asked.

Elek looked up, his voice finding strength. "She claimed to have a child with her, but it was a lie. It was a young woman. When I discovered the disparity, I asked for higher payment for the increased risk."

The Emperor's shoulders tightened. The onlookers were silent, not even a foot scuffing against the stone floor.

"What was the payment?" Vasile asked.

"He wanted *me* for the p-payment," I interjected.

Elek protested. "Slavery is legal tender."

"Kidnapping is not." I wouldn't let Elek bury me in lies without a fight. I'd come too far to be hung for his deceit and greed. Commodus shook me; my fingers tingled as if someone was poking me with needles.

The Emperor stood, and Commodus straightened even taller. Elek's white knuckles clutched his velvet cap.

The merchant had filled me with terrors just thinking about how his skin felt against mine. And now he cowered before Cassus, not even a shell of what he had been in Patridava, yet sneered at Rubia. His true nature was revealed in how he acted towards those he considered below him.

This is what a coward looks like.

It appeared as if the mere act of not fleeing before the Emperor was taking every bit of strength he had. I let the vision of him burn into my mind. This is how I wanted to remember him. Weak. Pathetic.

"The young woman wore a golden orb around her neck." The Emperor's voice was low and sure. "You tried to steal it."

It was a statement, not a question. The Emperor snapped his fingers, and the warlock approached with a gilded box in hand. My necklace rested on purple velvet in the center of the open box.

I couldn't see Elek's face, but his body tensed.

The Emperor plucked the necklace from the box by Marcus' lace and held it in the air.

"You tried to steal a valuable artifact that belongs to me." His voice wasn't loud, but it unnerved me.

My mind raced. Elek's success as a merchant helped the Emperor fill the Kingdom's treasury. The merchant was one of his most important subjects. Yet it felt like Elek was here to be questioned rather than testify.

I remembered what Vasile had said about Elek, Jovian's uncle. It seemed he was not a favorite of the Rose Court. Perhaps because as a merchant, he was still a Lily, and the wheat was being separated from the chaff. Or was it possible that the Emperor believed me?

"It was a misunderstanding," Elek's voice trembled. "And for my effort, she cursed my hand, per my report."

I scowled. While the physical injuries from that day — the pain in the back of my legs and the welt across my neck — had healed quickly, thanks to the Protection, nothing could protect me from the fear that Elek's touch had pressed into my soul.

"The curse you claim this wretch put on you is one the witches had never seen nor heard of." The Emperor pointed to Rubia. "They questioned the accused days ago. There is no lying when under the warlock's spell. And no amount of future beatings has swayed her otherwise. This woman did not curse your hand as you claimed."

I glanced back at Rubia. She looked at the Emperor blankly as if trying to figure out who he was. Was she still under a potion's influence or disoriented from the pain of being whipped? It tore me apart to see Rubia this lost and helpless. That wasn't her. She was strong. Now I had to be strong for both of us.

"That woman is a witch like them!" Elek yelled. "Of course, they would—"

A flash of anger crossed Cassus' face, and Elek shut his mouth with a snap. The Emperor circled the merchant, lightly touching Elek's fine clothing, noting the gaudy gems accenting the collar. "You owe the Dacian Kingdom a great debt, Master Elek. Because you have been loyal to me all these years, I will give you a chance to redeem yourself."

Elek straightened, and he gazed at the Emperor like a dog hoping for a scrap from his master's table.

The Emperor held out the necklace.

The orb swung at the end of the leather, dangling in the air in front of Elek's face. Several nobles gasped.

"You may choose how to repay your debt. Forfeit all of your wealth to the kingdom's treasury or use this key to unlock an item of mine," the Emperor said.

Tension filled the air as everyone waited for Elek to speak. Lady Katalin pursed her lips, intent on Elek. I dared glance at Marcus. He was the only person not watching the exchange, his attention instead trained on me. Marcus gave a strained smile. If it was meant to reassure me, it didn't.

Marcus couldn't tell me everything would be okay. He couldn't try to return me to a life that no longer existed. Besides, he owed me nothing. And he could accompany anyone he chose. I tried to believe that, tried to not feel anything by Lady Katalin's hand on his arm.

"Touching that necklace is death, my Emperor." Elek's voice wavered. He glanced at the nobles around him, finding no assistance. Elek finally answered, his voice resolute. "I choose to forfeit my wealth."

"Captain, remove him from the room." The Emperor gracefully touched the jeweled hilt of his sword and gave a discreet nod I almost missed.

Before I could register what it meant, Captain Lucius stepped away from Papa and drew his sword. Elek turned as the Captain thrust his sword forward into Elek's midsection. Elek fell to his knees, blood dribbling down his fine, velvet jacket.

Papa jumped back, and my instinct was to do the same, but Commodus held me firmly in place.

The nobles around the room clutched their stomachs, eyes wide. Lady Katalin hid behind her fan though she peeked through the lace at the grotesque scene. Lord Porcius watched with calloused interest as Elek gasped for breath.

The merchant blinked rapidly, a slack expression on his face as Captain Lucius withdrew his sword. Elek choked, his uninjured hand touching his bloody vest, his eyes wide with disbelief. He mouthed something, but his words bubbled. Elek collapsed on his side, his mouth oddly open.

Vasile snapped his fingers, and the two guards from the antechamber door brushed by me to the merchant's body. The murder of Elek was a threat, not just to the other nobles but to me as well. With a nod of his head, the emperor could have anyone killed, and Cassus VII was in a cold, murderous mood.

My dreams have reverted to those I had as a child, of my time in the Sage Hills. In my dreams, many women care for me, and I can't recognize which one is my mother. They all teach me how to hunt, which berries to eat, and how to find water. In the morning, I grasp at the fading memories of several magical elders who taught me foundational knowledge for Binding before I was taken away.

Past faces, I lay awake at night trying to recall them. They comfort me somehow, like Sanaz comforts her baby boy. Perhaps my Getaen memories can help me navigate this great and terrible decision.

— VAHID, WARLOCK TO EMPEROR TRAJAN
CARACALLA

TWENTY-FOUR

WORDS OF POWER

A low hum from the nobles' whispered discussion started after the initial shock of Elek's murder. A servant scrubbed the marble floor at my feet, but the stain remained. Every dark spot on the floor, the floor I'd danced on, took on a gruesome new meaning.

My head and wrist throbbed, muddying my thoughts. The Emperor had killed the man who accused me. Was he displaying his power? Or making a peace offering? While the warlock whispered in the Emperor's ear as he sat on his throne, his retinue lingered within arm's length. The servant had no sooner exited the throne room when Ziba turned her pale blue eyes to me.

"Give her the key," she said, pointing at me.

The warlock and Vasile exchanged a glance. I had been waiting for this opportunity. Could they see the eagerness in my eyes?

"Did you hear the witch? Give it to her, Oslid!" Emperor Cassus snapped his fingers at the warlock. The onlookers stood silent.

The warlock stalked forward, the closed case for the pendant cradled in his upturned palm.

Commodus released my arm. It tingled as sensation rushed back to the limb. I wanted to kick Commodus in the shins, but with the pendant within reach, I controlled my impulse.

Over the warlock's shoulder, Marcus watched me, his posture taut.

With a gnarled hand, the warlock eased open the case, the orb glinting in the luminaries overhead. I wrapped my fingers around my pendant, and my heart seemed to expand in my chest.

Murmurs sounded from the nobles. Who had dared try the simple act of touching the orb in my absence? Getaen advisers watched intently. Ziba struggled to keep a smile from her lips. Lady Essa had been kind to me at dinner while staying composed as she was verbally attacked. Now her perfect brows were drawn together, a crack in her stoic veneer.

"A witch," Vasile said.

"The golden sphere harms those with magic the same as any other person of flesh and blood," Ziba spat at Vasile with hooded eyes. "As you have already witnessed."

I clutched the orb tighter, my already sour stomach twisting. Had a Getaen touched this willingly, or were they forced?

"As a Guardian, she protects the key, and it protects her in return," Papa said.

Commodus's fingers twitched on my shoulder.

Emperor Cassus leaned forward on his throne, not taking his eyes off me but holding his hand out to the warlock.

"The scroll," Oslid instructed.

Captain Lucius took a scroll from a leather cylinder at his hip. Keen nobles followed the scroll as he passed it to Oslid.

"My fool of a great-grandfather, Emperor Cassus IV, incorrectly believed that the curse was a lie. He decided to burn all records of it, parchment and flesh." The Emperor caressed the scroll in his hands. "This scroll was a fortunate find in a Getaen city two decades ago. One of the precious few I've been able to recover with any mention of the curse Emperor Trajan Caracalla requested."

I held my hands to my stomach and swallowed back the taste of bile. That scroll in the Emperor's hand must have been recovered in the raid on Rubia and Mama's clan before I was born, the same raid that killed everyone in the Sea Mist clan, including Odon's descendants and my extended family. Only one still survived, and she was broken and bleeding next to me. The Emperor did not so much as glance at Rubia as he prattled on about his and his father's endless searches for records about the curse, and their sacrifices to protect the kingdom. If his words were meant to make me sympathetic to his plight, they were hollow and displaced. Rubia would claw the Emperor's eyes out if she were lucid enough to process his laughable claims of protecting the kingdom.

Ziba cocked her head, studying me, but the Emperor was focused on Papa, giving him a meaningful look.

"Everything changed when we unearthed a cavern full of documents under our noses in Moesia just a few weeks ago," Cassus said. "We learned exactly what the key looked like, details on Guardians, Odon's genealogy, and many other details." The Emperor lifted the scroll. "However, this scroll predates those found in Moesia. This was written during the rule of Emperor Cassus III."

An original Guardian could have written it. Or perhaps been trained by them. I leaned closer, not wanting to miss a word.

Cassus continued, "Apparently, two siblings deserted into the darkness of the night with the True Key, only to be discovered three generations later in Getae."

The pendant's irregular edges dug into my hand as I

gripped it tighter. The descendants had not 'deserted' the capital — they had run for their lives.

"With the kingdom's safety at stake, you've certainly been slow in your interpretation. What is taking you so long, scholar?" the Emperor asked, his voice disconcertingly calm.

Papa's shoulders slumped. "A Getaen likely wrote this scroll, but telling a Dacian story. It's a difficult hybrid text and many of the words are unknown, could have multiple meanings, or were a mistranslation to begin with."

The faster Papa translated, the sooner they would no longer need him. Yet I knew the way his mind worked. He wouldn't be able to resist such a puzzle. If the work went slowly, it was because he truly struggled with the interpretation. I glanced back over, only to catch Lady Katalin whispering in Marcus' ear. I quickly returned my gaze to Papa.

Cassus extended a hand to me in a gesture of acceptance. "Young Aurelian, you misunderstand my goals, which is understandable, considering what my forefathers did. However, I do not wish to destroy the records of the pact made between Cassus and Odon but to bring them to light, to fulfill the bargain and end the treachery. We've made more progress on ending the plague in the last few weeks than we have in decades. I need your help."

Lady Essa leaned forward on her toes, seeming to hang on the Emperor's every word. Yet, his words perplexed me. He wanted to uncover the truth of the curse, but he raided homes to do it. He claimed to want to help the kingdom, but he made no mention of finding the true heir.

Papa spoke up, Captain Lucius still standing behind him. "That scroll was written by the first Getaen Guardian. The early Guardians were Dacian, which makes sense because... " Papa cleared his throat, thankfully noticing the Emperor's deepening frown as Papa was getting off on one of his scholarly tangents.

"From what I can tell, the Guardian was transcribing an oral history given by one of Odon's granddaughters who escaped — err, deserted — to the South," Papa said.

I glanced at Rubia, almost grateful she didn't understand their cavalier talk of her decimated clan. Almost.

"May I?" Papa gestured to the scroll. Vasile brought it to Papa, unrolling it.

"'Aureum lapis aquacum' is a line we saw repeated again and again in Getaen text from within the last fifty years. I didn't recognize it at first. The symbols are a combination of both languages, Dacian and Getaen, so they don't have a direct translation."

Papa tilted the scroll enough for me to see the text. I kept my chin down, not wanting to appear overeager as I scanned the symbols, trying to sort the partial curves and slashes into either Dacian or Getaen.

"Leila, my wife, translated it as 'the golden treasure.' In Getaen, 'lapis aqua' means water stone – something prized by desert travelers. To the clans, it would translate to 'treasure.' In Dacian, 'lapis aquacius' also literally means 'water stone.' but practically, it means something that seems precious but is ultimately worthless or even harmful – like a jinx or a curse. So this record implies what we've long suspected. The treasure is also a curse."

I strained to translate the symbols without moving so my shackles wouldn't clink against each other, alerting Commodus to what I was doing. I had read piles of mundane text in the past, but scrolls like this were almost sacred.

Papa pointed, drawing my attention to a particular line. "I translated this, 'cor capus och cor kapoi' as 'upon the head of the true heir or blood, shall fall the glory.'"

The warlock interjected. "This is a fool's errand."

The Emperor held up his hand. The warlock silenced, his

bushy eyebrows shadowing his eyes. I swallowed. Although emperors could rule through the might of their armies and the intrigues of court, a warlock could torture in a hundred ways, leaving no evidence behind.

"I've seen this next line many times, but a couple of the symbols are slightly altered. It looks like the Dacian symbol for blood, as in 'true blood,' as we've seen in the past," Papa said.

I tilted my head. Four extra lines overlay the Dacian symbol for 'true.' It was a Getaen symbol for 'heart,' which made sense. Of course, heart and blood would be connected somehow. The heart controls the blood.

Lower in the text, a symbol made me pause, sending a chill down my spine. It was the Getaen symbol for salt. Or protection. A crescent in the center and the outer circle, both facing the same direction, but the outer circle was almost closed like one more tick of the tool was needed but forgotten. Heart and protection. My mind whirled. It symbolized a parent almost completely wrapping themselves around their child. It was no accident. Certainty pierced me. The Getaen translator meant something by it.

A single word can change the meaning of everything.

The warlock who created the curse was subject to his emperor, but he had a mind of his own. A Getaen mind. The Getaen symbol for protection, representing family. He, of all the people in the court, would have a different interpretation of family.

I glanced at Rubia, my second mama, still dazed. She was like the circle, fiercely protecting me.

"Nicoleta Aurelian." The warlock spoke my name as if it left a bad taste in his mouth. "This will take much time to sort out. Your companion is no longer fit to be a Guardian. You must select someone new."

I stared at him. Words failed me. He knew Rubia was the other Guardian.

"I do not know the oath w-words," I said.

The Emperor looked at Lady Essa.

"Some truth, some lies," Lady Essa said.

How could I rip away the Guardianship without Rubia's consent? And beyond protecting the True Key, the Guardian was supposed to be the wise instructor.

"We have ways to make you recall the words. Even if you only heard them once, they'll be clear as a bell," the warlock said. The young apprentice behind him peeked over at Rubia. If the side effects were anything like what they did to Rubia, I wanted to avoid recalling anything by force.

"My Guardian hasn't finished t-teaching me," I said, stalling for time as I mulled the symbols on the scroll. It was indeed older, with an unusual hybrid language. But Mama had taught me both languages. Papa had always relied on Mama so maybe he'd missed some of the nuances of the Getaen symbols. Even I hadn't known the deeper meaning of salt until Jamil pointed it out. If only I could explain my intuition of the possible meaning of the text, Papa could help me put the clues together. I was willing to take my time and return to the dungeon. However, the faster I put the pieces together, the faster the plague could be eliminated.

"I will not B-bond the orb to another Guardian." I straightened. Rubia was in no state to perform the oath so they needed me alive.

The Emperor waved to the guards over Rubia. Metal rasped on scabbard, and a sword was at her throat with Jamil standing motionless behind her. His eyes were resolute. I knew he wouldn't risk stopping the blade against Rubia's neck. His goal was to keep me alive, not Rubia.

"If you kill her, I still will not B-bond the orb to another Guardian," I said. "Then I'll be all you have left to torture."

The warlock stepped forward. "The purpose of the Guardians is to protect the orb and the heir. You failed the heir but saved the orb. Now you will fail in that duty if you don't select another who is fit!"

"She's unfit only because you beat and poisoned her," I spat. "And the heir is lost only because of the murderous heart of Emperor Cassus VI."

Clothing rustled as the onlookers shifted. Lady Katalin pulled out her fan, pretending to cool herself while she whispered to Marcus.

I lifted my chin and addressed the Emperor directly. "You say you want to help the kingdom, to stop the plague. What have you done besides p-pillaging the clans, cities, and v-villages you claim to assist?"

I felt a surge of confidence with the pendant in my hand.

The Emperor raised an eyebrow and laughed. "You cannot fathom what ruling an empire entails." He spread his arms wide, his voice eerily quiet. "You think this is an easy task? Overseeing trade agreements, creating institutions of learning, keeping the roads safe from criminals, quelling arguments between villages, and keeping our enemies at bay?" His voice rose to a crescendo.

"The lies you tell yourself must be exhausting." My control slipped as anger coursed through my veins. "The forest surrounding your own castle is filled with more b-bandits than a d-dog has f-fleas."

Commodus smacked the back of my neck. I tripped forward before regaining my balance. "You r-raid towns after they are weakened by the plague you're too foolish to stop. Your people are forced to rebuild on the ashes of their d-dead. Orphans are forced into slavery in the name of t-taxes. How is this p-protecting your people?"

The perimeter of the room buzzed, but neither the Emperor nor I took our eyes off of each other.

"You are not the true heir. You're not of the line of Odon. You don't have a t-true heart." I spoke each word deliberately, letting them sink into every mind.

The Emperor's nostrils flared. Commodus squeezed my neck. The nobles were chattering, not bothering to whisper through their feathered fans. The woman who flashed me the yellow flower watched me with one hand pressed to her lips as if to stop herself from shouting in agreement.

The Emperor leaned forward, his words low, his face a calm mask. "I reach out to you in good faith, and you continue to rebuff me. We shall see where your arrogance will lead."

With a flick of his fingers, the room emptied. Only a handful of Roses and the Emperor's advisers remained to watch the spectacle. Lady Katalin remained, and inexplicably, so did Marcus. Her influence was even greater than I supposed.

High Judge Vasile wrung his hands as he waited for the room to clear. The moment the doors slammed shut, the Emperor turned to face me, fury etched in every line of his face.

A blood vessel in Cassus' neck pulsed, his face red. His voice was low and hard. "You will bind *me* to the key."

It felt like the air had been sucked out of the room. I couldn't breathe. Emperor Cassus would wear the pendant? It would protect him while his kingdom turned to ash at his feet. Commodus grabbed my arm and marched me to the dais, but my legs refused to work, and he ended up half-dragging me.

"I will never bind the key to you." I trembled, the links of the manacles pinging against one another.

"Cassus, my love." Lady Essa knelt at his side. "Let me do this for you. I fear the child will make a mistake with a word. What will happen to you then?"

"Do not fear. I will slay her myself before my last breath if she missteps." The Emperor stood, his gaze boring down on me.

The nobles were silent witnesses to Cassus' foolishness. If the Emperor killed me, Rubia would be the last Guardian, the last sentinel of hope against the plague.

"Why would you want to be a Guardian? It is a responsibility beyond running the kingdom, something you claim is already a heavy burden on you," I said.

Something about the scroll tickled the base of my mind, just out of reach. It was driving me mad.

"Some of us are born to rule, blessed by Zalmoxis. Others fight their way to the top, earning Zalmoxis' favor." Cassus' face was hard, his eyes dead.

"Don't —" Papa's words suddenly muffled behind me.

I pulled the key to my chest, the manacle falling toward my elbows, providing some relief for my sore wrist. Mama dreaded me having the responsibility of the key, but now I wanted nothing more than to keep it. This was my mission, handed down from both my mothers. After the Emperor killed Papa, Rubia would be next. What would that accomplish? I'd be the sole Guardian, and my family would be dead. And Papa and Rubia were the only experts on the True Key and the curse. Dacia needed them even if the Emperor didn't realize it yet. I had to be the one to give up my Guardianship. But that meant giving up my only bargaining chip, too.

Zalmoxis, curse me if I have made the wrong choice and brought the plague upon us all.

"Repeat after me," I said to the Emperor.

I closed my eyes and let the words flow:

To bind the key with your soul
Va poltim o kaga met ditaveshi
To imprint duty on your heart
Va skalm taut epi dabaveshi
Protect the key while it protects you
Mezenai to kagareshi mezenzai veshreshid
To strengthen your stride and to make plentiful/long your life
Va embalan naraveshi kai va emburim drigaveshi
To assist you in protecting the true blood
Va gherm veshidi mezenai to cor menus

The Emperor's hand trembled as I put the orb into his fist. The room was quiet as everyone seemed to hold their breath. But Cassus' fingers didn't turn to gray, nor did he cry out. Instead, a smile spread across his face.

"At last," he whispered.

I was an empty vessel; every purpose inside me crumbled to dust. I fell to my knees, staring at the dais but seeing nothing. Lady Essa let out a breath and followed Cassus back to the throne. He paused, considering the orb in his fist.

This close to the throne, the deliberate markings on the seat came into focus. Ornate patterns of swirls and dashes in ancient Getaen, the language of magic, similar to the key. On the side of the base of the throne was a spherical divot.

Energy thrummed through my veins. I had wondered where the treasure might be hidden. It had been in this room the entire time, in plain sight. The treasure was in the seat of the throne; the back and arms of the throne seamlessly incorporated the style.

"A necklace was passed down for generations." Emperor Cassus slid a hand into his vest and pulled out an ornate sphere.

He held it up for me to see. It was similar to my pendant but with more detailed artwork and glittering jewels on the surface.

Cassus stared at it with dark eyes. "We were told this would unlock the treasure for the right heir. My great-grandfather said it would unlock the treasure for the most fearsome heir. My grandfather told my father that meant the worthy heir. My father believed it meant the decisive heir.

"The key didn't work for me." Cassus rolled the bejeweled orb around in his hand before tossing it to the ground. It bounced across the floor and skittered to a stop. In the pre-dawn light, the dull rubies looked like dots of blood splatter. "It was a fake, a distraction by the children of Odon."

Cassus lifted the True Key to the light, examining it. "When my messenger brought me word of Elek's suddenly diseased hand and a witch, I suspected Zalmoxis was revealing the location of the True Key."

That's why the bandits were looking for the golden orb. The Emperor had sent them! I looked down at my shackled wrists, not wanting the Emperor to see my anguish. I'd delivered the key right to Rupea.

"Odon's line was entitled to the throne after the fifth generation," Papa said. "They are the true heirs, the true blood."

"If you speak again, scholar, I will be forced to cut out your tongue." The Emperor clutched the pendant tighter in his fist. "Essa, you will be the second Guardian now so you may assist me."

The Emperor looked at me. "Now pass the second Guardianship to Essa."

"What?" I forced myself to stand. How could he force the Guardianship from Rubia who had no mind of her own, thanks to him? Commodus grabbed me, pulling me back.

My papa spoke up, "Being a Guardian is a sacred responsibility, not to be frivolously given to your... lady!"

"Captain." The Emperor tapped his pommel as he had done before Captain Lucius murdered Elek.

"Wait!" I shouted. "You n-need... You need h-his knowledge!" I strained against Commodus to look at Papa. The pink scar pulled against his skin. I couldn't hear his screams again. I couldn't. I slowed my speech.

"The scholar is the o-only one that knows the s-secrets of the T-true Key." I could barely stammer out the words. I looked down at the Emperor's boots in a semblance of subjection.

"He can still work if he has eyes to read and hands to write." The Emperor's voice was calm, but menace tinged every word. "Captain, remove his tongue."

"If you cut out his t-tongue, you slow a-answers to o-opening the treasure."

Papa's chest rose and fell too quickly. His jagged scar stood out as a pale line on his dark skin. He would do anything to protect me, even give up his tongue.

"It is better to have a healthy Guardian." Ziba's words cut through the tension, her attention on me. I blinked, wondering if the witch meant that Rubia and the Emperor were both unfit.

Papa gasped behind me. I shut my eyes.

"Wait!" The word shot from my lips.

Along with giving up the Guardianship, I had given away any leverage I'd had against the Emperor. Now I would die in the dungeon without my Guardianship. When the plague continued, Lady Essa would understand the impending disaster and seek the true heir. She seemed to care for the Emperor, but she seemed to have empathy for others as well.

I bit my lip and nodded. The Emperor smiled, and Lucius shoved his sword back into the scabbard.

"Bring me Sonus dampening sand," I said.

Vasile raised an eyebrow, but the Emperor pointed at Oslid. "Fetch it."

Oslid's young apprentice scampered from the room.

"I must p-prepare her." I wriggled against Commodus, but he only loosened his grip after the emperor's signal.

I scurried to her side, my wrists still shackled. Rubia's wrists were bound and red where the ropes had rubbed them raw. I wanted to wrap my arms around her, but like when Mama had the plague, I knew my touch would bring more pain than comfort. Instead, I found a spot on her shoulder to rest my hand.

At my touch, Rubia's eyes sharpened a bit though her voice was ragged. "I'm all right. I'm all right."

My eyes welled up at her words intended to comfort me. She needed care, yet she still wanted to make sure my mind was at ease.

"Rubia... " What could I say? "I love you."

"I am fighting to stay, but I don't know if I can. The desert winds call me."

Jamil's leg twitched behind where Rubia was sprawled on the ground. I inspected her dirty hands, the skin stretched tight over the knuckles in some places and swollen in others. I set my hand so lightly on them that I barely brushed the skin. She gave me a sad smile.

"There is another who could be the Guardian. Like you, I think she lives with a soul on fire." I beckoned for Lady Essa to join us.

The Emperor handed Lady Essa the orb by the leather string.

"The Emperor's toadies." Rubia spat.

"This is Lady Essa," I introduced them as Oslid's apprentice returned with a bag. Oslid strode over, and I took the bag but otherwise ignored him. The warlock harrumphed and took a step back, though I'd hoped he'd turn tail back to the Emperor's side on the dais.

Essa got down on her knees in front of Rubia. "I'm Lady Essa Redvalley."

Rubia cocked her head to the side, her eyes unfocused again. "Of the Red Valley? I know that place."

I spread the voice dampener sands around Rubia, Essa, and me. I glanced at Marcus' blanched face, his lips rolled inward. I purposefully also looked at others in the room, though I ignored Porcius' smug pig-face.

I double-checked to make sure there were no breaks in the sand. Essa held the orb by the leather string, and Rubia's eyes widened. Faster than an owl diving for a mouse, Rubia snatched the orb out of the air and pulled it to her.

"Essa needs to be a Guardian," I said, my voice cracking. How could I get Rubia to give up her Guardianship? It was wrong to trick her, to force her to do it without her mind being completely aware. But Ziba was right, Essa was our best chance now.

"I will do everything in my power to help end this gruesome curse," Lady Essa whispered. In the dining hall, she was guarded. But now, Essa's face was open and earnest.

Rubia studied the sands on the floor then leaned toward me, her eyes imploring. "Nikka, am I so far gone? I can feel my life bleeding away, but..."

I sucked in a breath. Rubia was asking me if she was dying. I didn't know if it was the poison in her veins or the loss of blood, but she wasn't herself. She was confused and looking to me as her light in the darkness.

"It's time." My mouth was too dry to say more.

Rubia squeezed her eyes shut and groped out. I took her hands, surprised to realize they were not so much larger than mine anymore. As a child, Rubia seemed taller than mountains, her hands swift, strong, and full of Healers' magic. But now her hands shook in mine. Now I had to be the strong one.

Rubia's lips trembled as she recited the words to pass on the Guardianship; she didn't miss a syllable.

When Rubia's hand placed the orb in Lady Essa's fingers, Essa's eyes glittered with anticipation.

"I meant what I said. I want to end the curse." Essa stood, clutching the True Key.

Victorious, Lady Essa sauntered back to the dais and laid the orb in Emperor Cassus' hand. Their hands entwined as he stood. The muted light from the windows cast them into convoluted shadows, the treasure lost to sight behind them.

"Open the treasure; stop the curse." Rubia laid her head on my lap as the soldier next to Jamil kicked away a portion of the dampening circle.

Cassus put the orb in Lady Essa's hand, an eager gleam in his eyes. "Open the treasure, Essa. Do not touch anything inside."

They know exactly where the treasure is. Conflicted feelings warred inside me.

"The power inside can topple rulers," Rubia added.

I held my breath, but the Emperor was completely focused on Lady Essa and the True Key.

"Of course," Essa's gaze lingered on Cassus' eyes before moving to the side of the throne, to the cylindrical divot. The leather strap on the key swung as she moved.

Being a Guardian would not protect her from the power of the treasure. Papa had warned her. As if remembering his warning, she hesitated.

"Quickly," the Emperor's voice was hard.

"Essa," the warlock cooed. "You have many amiable qualities. If anyone can open the treasure, you can."

I had not noticed Oslid acknowledge the Emperor's companion even once in the throne room, nor had he used her title, so I doubted he believed she was terribly worthwhile. Even

Oslid's young apprentice's face scrunched up at the words of his master.

Ziba pressed her lips together. From the corner of my eye, I saw Jamil shake his head, looking imploringly at Essa, but everyone was fixed on the key, including Essa.

"If you want the treasure and are sure that Zalmoxis has favored you, then *you* should use the key." I taunted the Emperor, malice thick on my tongue.

Before the Emperor could respond, Essa gulped and pressed the key into the indenture, the flat side of the key facing out. She spun it around, trying to nestle the uneven surface perfectly into place.

"It burns!" she cried.

"When the key is placed correctly, the pain will end. Do not stop!" the Emperor shouted.

Essa fumbled, trying to shift the key, her hand shaking. The pendant flattened seamlessly into place. Essa withdrew her hand and jumped back.

"Did it work?" Essa trembled, her hand clutched to her chest.

For a heartbeat, I thought it did. But the key slipped out and pinged on the floor. Essa didn't seem to notice as she inspected her hand. Her eyes grew wide. Her fingers were gray, and the deadly color was creeping up her palm. She pulled her sleeve up and yelped in horror. We all watched as her hand began to wither, the gray continuing past her wrist.

She fell to her knees, shaking, watching helplessly as her hand thinned, muscles and sinews wasting away.

"Captain." The Emperor looked at Lucius, ignoring the distress of his beautiful mistress. "Essa does not have a worthy heart, it seems. But you are fierce and loyal. The pendant will work for you."

Lucius' face paled, and I saw fear behind his eyes. Pari

muttered an incantation over Essa as her face drained of color. I felt sorry for the woman who had fallen in love with a man who clearly cared nothing for her, who saw her only as a tool.

"Might I suggest having a previous Guardian try first? They have many years of training and were selected based on magic in their blood." Vasile pointed at Rubia. "That one won't put up a fight."

Jamil and the other guard lifted Rubia from my lap.

"Rubia's no longer B-bonded to the k-key!" I moved to block Rubia, "B-b-besides, only a t-true heir —"

Commodus wrenched my shackles, sending a shock of pain through my wrists.

"Even if she were still a Guardian, it wouldn't work," Papa added. "The wording has a double meaning. Not only does the line of Odon have the key, they *are* the key. *Cor menusreshi cor kagareshidi.* Basically, it means both — the true blood is the 'True Key' or 'the True Key is the true heir.' The syntax is... complex and self-referential."

The Emperor drew himself up, his fury directed to Papa, spitting as he shouted. "What are you blathering about?"

"It means that only the touch of the true blood will open the treasure," Papa clarified.

The Emperor smiled mirthlessly. "It seems like an excellent opportunity to test the veracity of your theory, my dear scholar," the Emperor said.

Essa's moans turned more frantic. Pari ripped Essa's sleeve. The gray disease was progressing up her arm. Pustules formed on her fingertips. I swallowed. The curse was progressing further, faster than it had with Elek.

Jamil and the other guard dragged Rubia toward the throne.

My pulse raced. I couldn't stand by and let them hurt her.

Rubia's head lolled, and a strange giggle rolled off her lips. "The key... it's very important. It's a secret."

Knowing Rubia, she would likely have volunteered if she'd been in her right mind. She'd do anything to stop the curse. But forcing Rubia to attempt to open the treasure like this disgusted me — it was murder.

The Emperor marched down the steps, his jeweled dagger in hand, his eyes on Rubia.

"W-wait." The word stuck in my throat.

The emperor grabbed Rubia's hand, the dagger poised above her palm.

I pushed louder. "Wait!"

The emperor looked at me, his face a mask. The tip of his dagger sunk into Rubia's flesh, a line of red in its wake.

"I'll do it." My voice was barely a whisper. "I'll attempt to open the treasure for you. Leave her alone. She's already been through enough."

Commodus' fingers dug into my shoulder, pulling me back. The Emperor raised his finger and Commodus stopped.

"I'll put the key into the t-treasure." I lifted my chin and looked straight into the Emperor's eyes. I knew it would kill me, but hopefully, it would prove to the Emperor, to everyone here, that whoever used the key had to be a descendant of Odon. I didn't trust the nobles to do anything; however, the Poppies that served them, Clovers in the fields, the Azures in the Universities — they might fight.

"Nikka." Papa's voice was jagged. "No. Look what it will do to you. Please, no."

"You and Rubia have knowledge I-I don't. Let this b-be my sacrifice. P-please." I turned my attention to the Emperor, my resolve firm. "P-perhaps the sooner the Emperor r-realizes he does need the heir of O-Odon, the sooner he'll search for them instead of allowing this l-lunacy."

Commodus shoved me forward.

I pushed back and held my ground. "I will do it on my own.

I swear I will put the key on the throne. Do n-not attempt to force m-me."

The Emperor nodded, and Commodus took a step away from me.

"Do not even consider touching the treasure inside. If you do, I will kill your father slowly while you watch. Then, I will kill your mother, also before your eyes." He wiped the blade clean. "You, I will keep in my dungeon as a pet until you die of old age." The Emperor licked his lower lip.

I raised my palms to the Emperor. The blade of his dagger made my nerves scream. I sucked in a breath. Each step I took to the throne seemed to stretch on forever yet was far too short. I was an impostor trying to insert the True Key into the treasure, just as Essa had been. Only an heir of true blood... or true heart could open the treasure. However, the Warlock interpreted that, I didn't know. I only knew that royal blood did not run through my veins.

The onlookers faded from my periphery as I focused on the throne. Rubia moaned. Instead of looking at the wreck of my second mama, I let my rage fuel my last few steps. I clenched my hand into a fist, knowing the drawing of blood was unnecessary. But it got Cassus what he wanted: a previous Guardian to volunteer — me.

I knelt beside the throne and stared at the orb before picking it up by the leather string. I knew its deadly power was there. Cassus drew up next to me. His bloodshot eyes followed my every movement.

Blood pounded in my ears. I tried to stop shaking. Sweat beaded on my forehead, yet my body was chilled. It occurred to me that I had never asked Rubia to help me make a blue memory. I shook off the pointless, random notion. There would be no one left to break it.

"Nikka, my child." Rubia's voice was never so soft. "You are my joy."

Tears blurred my vision, but I gave her a small smile. Captain Lucius stood next to Papa, his knife drawn and at Papa's side. Papa gave me a slow nod, his eyes comforting. We both knew his fate.

I ran my hand along the indents on the golden throne, my shackles clinking. Symbols of protection, heart, heir, and family were etched into the gold. Symbols etched by the Blood Conqueror's Warlock himself as he wove the magic into the treasure. I thought of Mama sitting on Papa's desk, laughing and eating her favorite cheese. We would be reunited again. I took strength from her memory.

The Emperor loomed over me, his feet apart, a malevolent snarl on his lips. "Let us see the Golden Protector open the treasure."

I took a slow breath, dangling the leather string between my fingers, steeling myself for the pain I knew would happen quickly. The plague would be unleashed into my body. I suppressed a shudder, wanting to at least appear strong for Papa.

With one hand, I snatched the orb. Pressed it into the indenture. I held my breath, feeling for every bump of the gold. I twisted, maneuvering the key. It wouldn't fall into place. I blocked away any thought of pain, focusing on the True Key and this strange lock. My fingers trembled. I shifted the key another degree. And another. The key dropped flush into place.

THROUGH MY PANIC, I registered one thing. There was no pain, no spreading gray, no blisters. I pressed my hand against the orb, holding it in. A click sounded from inside the treasure. My body buzzed in anticipation.

A flash of light. It seemed to go on forever, like the sun exploding out over the world. As if a twisted knot had finally unwound, I felt the curse release. A heartbeat later, a force blasted out from the chair, knocking both me and the Emperor aside. Tremors bucked the floors, rattling the chandeliers, but I couldn't hear the tinkling crystals. My ears rang.

Finally, the ground stilled. I scrambled back to the base of the throne, seeing the top of the treasure cracked open. The True Key had unlocked the treasure.

The ringing in my ears dulled. A woman was screaming. I blinked, seeing lights behind my eyes. There was a soft *thunk* and a groan near Rubia. A guard ran past me and knocked the Emperor away with a loud *thump*. The room erupted into shouts.

Dazed, I looked around.

One guard was crumpled on the ground next to a whimpering Rubia. Jamil was gone. Lucius lay stunned at Papa's feet. Marcus had his dagger pressed to Commodus' neck.

I blinked, trying to clear my vision.

The Emperor snarled, "You'll be hanged for this!"

I spun around. Jamil was wrestling with the Emperor, trying to keep Cassus from drawing his sword.

"Zalmoxis has not chosen you to be Emperor. It was all a lie. You should be the one hanged for treason!" Jamil said.

"Finish it, Nikka! Open the treasure!" Papa shouted.

I staggered as the realization hit me. In my hand, the True Key worked. The remaining crowd looked as stunned as I felt.

"The disease's progression stopped as soon as the key opened the treasure," Pari said as she tugged Essa's sleeve. Her words confirmed what I sensed. The oath was fulfilled.

I wanted to cry out with relief, but Cassus' string of vile threats and approaching Thorns stopped me. I couldn't let him get the treasure. There would be no stopping him from killing the people I loved. I lunged for the throne's seat. The entire top section of the seat had eased open. I wedged my fingers underneath and heaved off the top. Placing the key didn't kill me. Hopefully the actual treasure wouldn't either.

The walls inside the seat of the throne were etched with gold engravings. A massive crown and stone carving of a bird sat on a velvet cushion.

"No!" The warlock shuffled toward me. "You are unworthy!"

My hand shot into the box, slipped the crown over my shackled wrists, and yanked out the stone carving. I dashed to the back of the throne, putting it between Oslid and myself as Jamil struggled to pin the Emperor to the ground.

I didn't dare take my eyes off Oslid, but Ziba rushed up and pulled the young boy from the warlock's side as Thorns converged on Jamil.

Orange powder hit the warlock from behind. He cried out and fell to his knees, spitting Getaen curses. The small orange cloud enveloped him, Jamil, the Emperor, and the Thorns.

I jumped away from the stinging dust. The crown was heavy and awkward, dangling from my wrists. What should I do with it? It was meant for an heir of Odon's line. I had only wanted to end the Lilac Plague, yet now I held the treasure and could not risk letting Cassus touch it.

"Traitor! I will not just kill you, but everyone you care about!" the Emperor coughed.

A wisp of smoke curled up from the crown. Roses cried out and pointed, some pressing back toward the doors. The smoke expanded into a cloud, circling my hands, obscuring the crown and stone bird. My heart raced. The smoke enveloped me, obscuring my view of the gaping nobles. Was the curse about to strike me down? I had opened the treasure, yes, but I wasn't a true blood heir of Odon.

"Nicoleta!" Marcus called out.

Through the windows, the sunrise blushed corals and mauve across the sky. A calm sensation washed over me. I closed my eyes and relished the peace inside the cloud. If I was to die, I would do so knowing I had fought to save my people from the Lilac Plague and to stop the Emperor from slaughtering my family.

"No!" Cassus screamed an animalistic cry of rage. Something rammed into me, knocking me off balance. I fell forward, my knees hitting the dais stairs. I rolled down, hitting my shoulder and back. The crown and bird slipped from my grasp and spun away, out of reach.

The Emperor leapt from the dais onto the stone floor. He snatched up the crown and stone bird from the ground. Cassus' eyes sparkled with power; madness flushed his face. He cradled the objects to his chest as the curling smoke around the crown faded.

"I am the true blood heir! I *am* the key! No one could break the curse. Not my father, not his father before him. I was destined to be the true ruler of Dacia all along!" He shifted his gaze to me, lowering his voice. "And the one who opened the treasure will be my worthy bride, the Golden Protector. We, the only two who were powerful enough to control the —"

His eyes grew wide. He held out his hands, looking down at the crown and bird. The tips of his fingers turned gray. He stumbled backward.

"It can't be," he muttered.

The ashy coloring traveled up his arms. White blisters appeared on his fingers. The crown and carved bird clattered to the floor. Cassus fell to his knees and yanked up his camasa. The color on his chest faded from healthy pink to white to gray, spreading up toward his neck.

"No!" He reached out to the warlock and witches. Essa sobbed, still cradling her arm. The rest watched in mute horror.

Blister pustules formed on the Emperor's arms, his face turning gray. His eyes lost focus. He screamed and lifted his hands. His fingers grew darker and thinner, the flesh wasting away. He tried to shout, but his tongue was thick, his words unintelligible, his face swelling.

Commodus recoiled from the site, but Marcus ran to my side, dragging me out of the Emperor's reach. The Emperor collapsed, the blisters on his face bursting. A rancid smell permeated the air.

I knew that smell. The plague typically took several days to advance, but enhanced by the Warlock's curse, the Lilac Plague ravaged him like a lynx on a helpless rabbit. Cassus' hand turned to ash. No fire was needed to burn it away. My stomach churned, and I turned my head away, not wanting to see his body disintegrate. It would visit my nightmares forever.

"The Lilac Plague?" Marcus asked as he and I crouched together on the floor.

"Only an echo of it. The Lilac Plague is over," I said.

"The curse is lifted at last," Papa sighed, and I realized he was next to me. He looked to have aged a decade in the few weeks he'd been gone from Moesia. "I wish your mama was here to see it."

I glanced up at the Getaen advisers. Ziba raised her eyebrow, and a corner of her lip curled up. The guard next to Rubia groaned and rolled over, bumping into Commodus. He stopped moving when he noticed Jamil standing over him with a sword pointing at his throat.

Rubia lay on the stone floor, her chest rising and falling in a heavy sleep. Pari cradled Essa in her arms while Ziba made her way across the room, giving the Emperor's remains wide berth, before reaching Rubia. She opened one of Rubia's closed eyelids and put a hand on her chest, then nodded at me as if to say Rubia would be all right.

Next to the crown and bird was a pile of ash. Not even a scrap of the Emperor's clothing was left intact.

Ziba looked at me, a glint in her eye before whispering, "This isn't over for you, my dear."

The witch raised her voice. "Show us your hands, Golden Protector. Hold them up high for everyone to see."

My body screamed from aches and pains in every joint, but I held up my hands.

"The Golden Protector is not harmed by the treasure. She is the true heir." Ziba's lips quivered, holding back a smile.

The nobles gasped and whispered to each other.

The massive emerald on the crown winked in the light, abandoned next to the black bird inlaid with white marble. Before I had taken them to keep them out of the hands of Emperor Cassus. This was different. The plague was lifted. I had felt it the moment the treasure was unlocked.

"But I'm not of royal b-blood. I'm not even a Guardian anymore." I tried to stand, but the room seemed to dance. Marcus put a hand under my elbow to steady me. My gaze swept the room, looking for the laughter, the contempt I was sure I'd see on the faces of those gathered. Surely they knew a simple commoner such as myself, barely more than a girl, could never be Empress. Yet, no Roses objected.

Outside, the sun peeked over the sea of green, bathing the room in warmth. A key rattled against the ring as Jamil tossed it to Marcus. With a *click,* the shackles around my wrist dropped away. Jamil dipped his head as he swept into a small, stiff bow.

This was madness.

"I'm untrained and ill-equipped for the w-world of intrigue and p-power," I said.

"Which makes you the perfect ruler to usher in a new dawn. A new age of health and prosperity," Ziba said.

"Besides, I don't think anyone dares touch that throne now." Jamil winced, holding a hand to his side.

I couldn't deny the feeling I had when I held the crown for that brief moment. It had felt familiar, welcoming even — like sitting at Rubia's table, bathed in the scents of beans, barley, and garlic during the rainy season, Mama by my side, a friend spinning a tale, and Rubia laughing until she cried. It felt... like home, like I belonged. It felt right.

I leaned forward, my wrist and head throbbing. All the aches and pains that marred my body suddenly clamored for my attention.

I scooped up the bulky crown and carved bird.

Doubt wriggled in the back of my mind. Surely these items were meant for greater souls than I. I waited to wither or see if the ancient warlock had something different in mind for me.

Again a wisp of smoke appeared, turning into a cloud. I glanced at the pile of ash and held my breath. As the cloud grew larger, my fingers tingled. The room spun. Comfort rested in my heart. I closed my eyes and let the tingling warmth surround me.

The image of the symbols came into my mind, the crescents, and the magical Getaen wording. On the scroll Papa had tilted for me to see, the four extra lines symbolizing 'heart' overlaid the Dacian symbol for 'true.' It was there all along. The curse would break for either a descendant of Odon or for someone that the warlock deemed to have a true *heart*, someone he deemed worthy of ruling Dacia. Someone who put all of Dacia before themselves because they viewed Dacia as an extension of themselves, an extension of their family.

The Warlock had provided more than one way for the imperial line to change. As the prophecy had said, a true heir or someone of true blood could open the treasure. Blood, not in the way that northern Dacians perceived it, but in the way a Getaen child would have been raised; the Warlock cast the spell with two meanings in mind, right under Emperor Trajan Caracalla's nose. The Warlock understood the concept of a family community like I did. No wonder his spell made me think of Mama, Rubia, and the friends that gathered together. It was an echo of what the Warlock had felt when he created the curse. Under the reverberating warmth and love of the spell was a hollow aching of loss. My heart swelled, and tears wet my cheeks.

It might have been only a moment, or it might have been an hour, but the crown felt lighter, and the balance of the bird was different. I opened my eyes. The crown had transformed. It was now a circlet woven from dozens of delicate, burnished golden stems and leaves, punctuated with emerald gemstones. The stone bird had transformed into a short sword. The iron blade curved elegantly, and the hilt was inlaid with gold in an exquisite flower design. I inspected it closer to be sure — a canina flower.

My clothes were no longer the rough spun dress and leather sandals. The dress I wore was made of layers of gold silk, the sleeves embroidered with leaves and flowers from hem to shoulder, and emerald crystals stitched into the design. The cantrinta aprons were heavy, edged with soft velvet. As beautiful as the dress I had stolen from Lady Katalin's, it seemed common compared to this one. A deep green cloak, the exact shade of the Dacian flag, cascaded from the shoulders of my dress down my back. Two gold disks pinned the cloak on each shoulder. On my head, draped past my ears and shoulders, was a gold, lace scarf. I jolted — a pinned bridal veil. For a moment, I puzzled, but as if the Warlock whispered it into my ear, I knew what he meant by it. Now I was, in a way, married to Dacia.

I wriggled my fingers; my wrist was healed, with no bite marks on my arms. My aches and pains had been washed away.

Papa put a hand to his mouth, tears again brimming in his eyes. The remains of the Emperor were still piled on the floor, and Essa still moaned in Pari's arms. A lump formed in my throat, wishing the effects of the plague had reversed for everyone.

Ziba approached me and held out her hand.

I hesitated, not wanting to harm her, but she held her palm out confidently. "It's all right, Empress."

Empress, the word was strange to hear directed at me. I placed the crown in Ziba's hands, and she signaled to Marcus to open the doors.

Everyone from Lilies to Poppies poured into the room, including the woman with the yellow flower pinned to her skirt. Without waiting for their exclamations to end, Ziba thrust the crown into the air. The onlookers fell silent, gazing at me with upturned faces. The sun enveloped the space, sending light refracting off the shimmering silk, crystals on the sleeves, and the endless gold embroidery.

My limbs were light, my heartbeat steady as the room seemed to hold its breath.

Jamil was the first to drop to his knee, one hand protectively on Rubia's back. One after another, everyone followed, the Roses seeming to compete for who could bow the lowest. Marcus put a hand over his heart, his gaze upon me unwavering as he dropped to his knee and finally bowed his head. Only Papa stood at my side, blinking at the spectacle surrounding us.

I tilted my chin, and Ziba placed the crown over my pinned

veil. It felt as if a warm blanket were being wrapped around my body. A rush of emotion coursed through me; *the Lilac Plague ended at my hand.*

"You saved us all," Papa whispered into my ear before he dropped down to both his knees and sobbed at the hem of my skirt.

I've created the most binding curse in all of history, I'm sure of it. Though I created the spell weeks ago, I'm drained and wholly exhausted. Sanaz asks what I've done to myself. What she really wants to know is what sort of curse I created.

I simply tell Sanaz about my thoughts on a true heart. A true heart is brave in battles, like the Blood Conqueror. Loves others, like Hanna did and as Odon should have. To be as clever as Cassus. But most importantly, it means fighting for the people of the kingdom.

Sanaz begs me to fight, to heal. Her baby leans out of her lap and caresses my cheek. I smile at him, and Sanaz hopes I'm improving. She reminds me that I'm family. And I tell her, "I know. That's why I've done this — to have a legacy worth honoring."

My magic isn't replenishing. Somehow I imbued myself into the fabric of the lock and key. My penance for my foolishness and the horrors I've committed. I visited the treasure, and there was already an almost imperceptible strengthening of the spell.

I won't live long enough to know for certain if the curse will work the way I hope. It takes courage to have hope.

—VAHID OF GETAE

CHAPTER

TWENTY-FIVE

THE TRUE HEIR

I stood in the shadows, out of view of the crowd that had gathered from all over Dacia. I peeked through the curtain to the balcony. The courtyard beyond was filled with people. I had commanded that the upper gates be opened for everyone.

"People are coming from all of the surrounding cities. Every inn is full, so they're erecting a city of tents outside the main gates." Papa stood on my left. He was excited by the news, but it only made me more nervous for what was to come.

"Visitors are coming from beyond the borders of Dacia to meet the new Empress, Nicoleta Aurelian," Marcus added, standing on my right.

I knew they meant well, but the one I needed was Rubia. She would never coddle me. I had ordered the most capable Healers to see to her every need. They had hope that she would recuperate, but only time would tell for certain.

Marcus took my hands, sending tingles up my arms. I knew his gesture was only for support, nothing more. I didn't have time for it to be anything other than that.

"I'm E-empress now, so you have to tell me the truth. Who

are you really, Marcus Constantin? No mere farmer can tarry in a p-private trial."

He grinned. "You want to know that now?"

"Soon," I said.

I had a rush of things to do. It felt like I was trying to tame a waterfall while it crashed down upon me. Marcus seemed to understand that, encouraging me from a distance. Still, his mere presence was a distraction. The angle of his jaw, the way his soft curls brushed the nape of his tanned neck, the hazel of his eyes shining with fierce... *Stop it! Fierce protectiveness of his sovereign. Yes, that's what it was. For now.*

It had been two days since I put the crown on my head. I had changed out of the golden dress, fearing to ruin it before the official coronation celebration, and into a simpler, but still elegant gown. I had wanted to wash away any of the Emperor's ashes, to start my rule fresh and clean, both physically and symbolically.

I had spent all the previous day and night conversing with Jamil, Papa, Marcus, and the Getaen advisers, trying to absorb all I could about what I needed to do over the next few weeks.

I had sent for Mystic Marianna. I hoped she would agree to be an adviser. With her wisdom, compassion, and her ability to connect with the people of Capidava, she would be an invaluable ally. And I had already asked Papa to replace Vasile as my right hand, though Vasile would continue as High Judge, for now.

Everything was moving forward in a blur, but Jamil and Papa insisted I had to be bold these first few weeks. There would be anarchy if I didn't take a fair and firm hold of the kingdom, especially from Roses who might remember their own royal blood, no matter how diluted.

"It's almost time for your address, Empress Nicoleta." Jamil strode up behind us.

I bit my lip. I had a question that I had not had an opportunity to ask.

"I need to speak with Jamil in p-private for a moment," I said.

Marcus and Papa excused themselves before I turned to Jamil.

"I'd like for you to be the Captain of the Imperial Guard." After all his years of work and how I'd ripped that away, I wanted to repay him for risking his life and legacy for me.

Jamil coughed. "But I put you in the stocks. I threw you into the dungeon and left you there. I —"

I held up a hand, and Jamil's mouth clicked shut. I suppressed an expression somewhere between a smirk and shock. This would take some getting used to, though part of me already enjoyed the challenge.

"I need someone more loyal to the p-people of Dacia than to its ruler. I also need someone with good instincts. If you'll accept, I'd like to announce your p-promotion today," I continued. "We have a lot of work to do if you're up to the task. T-trouble seems to follow me wherever I go. There are already many who despise me and my d-decisions. I could use an honorable soldier like you guarding the kingdom and the throne."

Jamil shook his head. "Captain Lucius may not have come to your aid, but he is an honorable man. Give him a chance. In this time of turmoil, you would be wise to keep some things the same. If you would honor me, then do so by heeding my advice in this matter."

I would feel more comfortable with Jamil overseeing all the guards of Rupea, each city, and outpost. However, I could not deny he knew the guard better than I ever could. If I was to be a wise ruler, I must learn to trust in the advice of my counselors.

"I will take your advice, but d-don't think you're getting out of my service so easily."

Jamil raised an eyebrow but kept silent awaiting my words.

"I will re-structure the Empress's Own," I said. "You will be the head of my p-personal guard. You will work independently of the Imperial Guard, reporting only to me."

"As you command, my Empress. Restructuring the Own is wise as unfortunately, you already have many people who would like to take the throne. I'd like to select the guards myself." Jamil smiled, almost shyly. "With your approval."

"Of course." It still felt like I was a child playing make-believe; soon Mama would call me home, and my imaginary kingdom would vanish like mist under the sun.

Papa and Marcus hastened down the hall toward me. It was time to face my people. I turned to the open archway leading to the balcony and took a deep breath, reciting in my mind the words I had practiced all night. Marcus reappeared at my side, his presence a welcoming calm, simultaneously rousing butter-flies in my stomach.

"What if I stutter, and they b-believe I'm a fraud?" This was my first public appearance, and I didn't want the people to doubt me or have the impression I was weak.

I caught Papa shaking his head at Jamil, his face pale. He shoved his hand behind his back. Another issue must have cropped up. I'd have to deal with it after my speech.

Marcus squeezed my hand. "You'll go down in history as the woman powerful enough to turn a vicious emperor to ash with your touch, transform his throne into a crown with your blood, and banish the plague with your tongue."

I rolled my eyes.

"P-pari and Ziba know how to spin a tale," I said.

"Of course they do. They want a ruler with Getaen blood to take the credit for ending the plague." Jamil forced a laugh.

Something was definitely wrong, but I had to ignore it until after the speech.

Four more guards walked up behind Jamil, their freshly pressed half-cloaks clasped with ceremonial gold pins at their necks.

"It's time. Are you ready, Empress?" Jamil asked.

I took a deep breath. "Yes. Let's see if the people accept me."

A short man with a large chest walked up to me, his lips coated with a bright yellow substance. He made a deep bow before strutting onto the balcony. He stood on a stool, facing the crowd. In a surprisingly loud, deep voice he cried, "Empress Nicoleta Aurelian of Dacia, first of her name, daughter of Calvus Aurelian of Moesia and Leila of the Sea Mist clan."

My grip on Marcus' wrist was like a vice. The Sonus amplifier on the lips of the speaker practically made the ground shake.

"You stopped the plague and undid the curse. The people will love you." Marcus ran his thumb over my hands. "Lead the way, Empress Nicoleta."

I pulled my hand away and strode onto the balcony, which was draped with emerald velvet swags, gold ropes, and large bouquets at either end. There were so many faces looking up at me. All ages and races, from all over the kingdom.

Papa's whisper bounced off the walls behind me, barely loud enough for me to hear. "The true heir —"

A roar erupted from the crowd, drowning out even my own thoughts. They caught me off guard. The cheers grew louder and louder, reverberating inside me. I could see the faces of those closest to the balcony. They were weeping and waving at me. People tossed flowers and held their hands up in thanks.

When the cheers died down, I spoke to the Dacian people. My people.

"Seven generations ago, Emperor Trajan Caracalla

conquered the Getaen lands." I paused after each sentence as the crier repeated my words to be written and carried far and wide. "We have been as one people ever since. Our history has been darkened by the shadow of the Lilac Plague, a powerful spell enacted by the first warlock. He sought a peaceful transition from Cassus' line, but with his refusal to give up the throne, Cassus VI unleashed a curse upon his kingdom. Even during those dark times, we Dacians and Getaens have traded together. Bled together. And now we have come together to stop the Lilac Plague."

Cries of joy drowned out my words, so I paused and smiled, hoping I looked calm and regal, not like the simple girl I felt like inside. I focused on the face of a Getaen woman whose young daughter rode on her hip, her chubby fingers tangled in her mother's hair as she attempted to braid it. I swallowed a lump threatening to form in the back of my throat.

I did this for you so your daughter would never know the pain of losing her mama as I did. It made it easier to go on, knowing I was not just a ruler, but someone who suffered as so many others had.

"Trajan Caracalla's spell, enacted by his warlock, recognized me as the true heir. I promise I will serve the kingdom with all my heart, with all my strength, with all my soul. Long may Dacia live in peace!"

I took the gold pendant off my neck and raised it in the air. The morning light glinted off the misshapen sphere. A talisman fit for an empress such as I — unassuming but capable of doing so much good.

The people cheered, throwing more flowers at me.

They started chanting, crying out, giving me a new title.

"Hail Nicoleta, the Golden Protector, the Golden Empress!"

Jamil neared, a frayed note in hand. I smiled and waved at the people below, though I was anxious to see what the note said. I turned, catching Marcus pacing in the alcove. It was time to find out what they'd kept hidden.

As I strode from the balcony, Jamil smoothly handed me the note. The broken black seal made it easy to unroll.

Only a single sentence.

"A descendant of Odon has come forward from the Norte Kingdom — she is coming for Dacia."

Thank you for reading *The Lilac Plague*! I hope you love Nicoleta, her family, and Marcus as much as I do. The next book in The Unchosen series, *The Rose Court,* continues their story and delves deeper into court intrigue. Think it's hard to be born to the crown? Taking it from the bloodline and *keeping* it is even tougher! The political games are just getting started in Rupea Castle.

Download *The Rose Court* now!

To find out about new books, insider information, giveaways, and exclusive scenes, sign up for my newsletter at kristinjdawson.com!

Turn the page for a sneak peek at *The Rose Court*!

THE ROSE COURT
SNEAK PEEK!

CHAPTER

ONE

A BROKEN CHAIR

The council chamber chilled my bones far more than I expected with the leaves not yet turning color. Across the room, a prisoner held her shackled wrists on her lap, part of her stained sleeve pulled up onto her palm. She worried the edge of the cloth with her fingertips. She didn't tremble; I would have. High Judge Vasile's judgment would determine her freedom or condemnation. If the latter, the dank prisons in the stone underbelly of Rupea Castle would become her permanent abode — where rats ruled and humans wasted away.

The late Emperor Cassus VII had used the caverns to bury his own insidious offenses more than to incarcerate actual criminals. Something I knew from experience.

Jamil, the head of the Empress' Own, cleared his throat, pulling me out of my thoughts. No, out of my memories of being trapped under the grates of the dungeon. Jamil's scarred face and Getaen hair, red speckled with white, made others wary; but I trusted him with my life. He'd risked *everything* to help me and to overthrow Emperor Cassus VII. I followed

Jamil's gaze to Papa slipping into the room, a sealed note in his hand. I inwardly groaned. The constant barrage for attention drove me to finding new hiding places, but the make-shift courtroom proved unequal to the task, unfortunately.

Papa whispered, "An update."

The winged seal indicated the message came from my spy tracking the possible descendant of Odon, a potential heir to the Dacian throne. Although I'd been crowned, the formal coronation still loomed. The first full moon after the fall equinox, one moon cycle from now, this ceremony would signify the official beginning of my reign as Empress.

I cracked the seal and unfolded the message, making a crinkling noise. Ignoring Vasile's glare, I tilted the correspondence so Jamil could read along with me.

My contacts confirm Tatiana is the name of the one who claims to be the descendant of Odon. Still moving south, out of the northern Rodnic Valley. Still traveling with twenty. Per your command, we did not approach. Estimated arrival in three days. -V.R.

The initials stood for Valentin Rekine of the Emperor's Own elite; one of his personal, black-clad guards. No, the *Empress'* Own personal guard. He was following the heir of Odon and would be the last of my Own to return to the castle after Cassus' death.

The Imperial Guard near the prisoner studied the room, his gaze shifting to me when I crinkled the missive. The man had a distinct birthmark across one side of his face, the dark purple lesion covering his nose, one cheek, and neck, disappearing under his fitted camasa. He stood taller when our eyes met, giving me a respectful nod before turning his attention back to the prisoner.

Papa leaned in close to whisper, "Also, the witches are irritated. You missed your appointment with them again." Before I could remind Papa that I disliked the term 'witches,' he continued. "And Ziba, in particular, is losing patience. You've been ruling for nearly two moon cycles now, and she's grown tired of hunting you down so she can put a Protection on you. She said, if you die, it isn't her fault."

And she's one of my greatest supporters.

"I'm only trying to keep a kingdom from falling apart," I muttered. "I can't be everywhere at once." Part of me wanted to attend the trials to purge the horrors of the dungeon I'd experienced. Another part needed a break from the ever-present demands of the kingdom.

Vasile pursed his lips at our whispered disruption. He might run out of patience with my hovering, but he couldn't force me to leave. He couldn't even ask. An empress did as she pleased, something I struggled to navigate after a lifetime of accommodating others.

The prisoner stared past Vasile at the barred window behind the High Judge, or possibly at the blue sky beyond. Vasile delivered each question verbatim in a dispassionate baritone. His rigid adherence to the law was further supported by his extensive knowledge of it. He never wavered in his commitment to justice. He supported my proposed changes but urged for gradual steps over time. I admired his consistency and devotion to the law. Yet, I knew him from *before*.

He'd sent me to the stocks — a cowardly act. His refusal to try the True Key to stop the Lilac Plague revealed his inner nature; Vasile valued his position as the High Judge more than truth, the sanctity of life, or even what was right. I hoped his actions were out of some twisted loyalty to the crown. He'd never betrayed the last emperor, and I wanted to believe he'd be loyal to me as well. Indeed, thus far, he had been. I quickly learned that not every Rose or Lily, the nobles, would serve me as empress, but Vasile did. And I desperately needed a High Judge.

Vasile spoke his final judgment; "You have made reparations for your crime in the eyes of the Golden Empress."

I shuddered, knowing the implied meaning: the wretched woman had spent years in the dungeons when she'd been innocent all along. The prisoner's shoulders sagged as she let out a breath and gripped one of her chair's wooden spindles as if trying to steady herself.

While the black-clad guard unlocked her shackles, I moved toward the door. With several hours between trials, I intended to find Ziba.

"Oh, Zalmoxis," the prisoner cursed.

I spun as she collapsed into the chair, sending it clattering to the floor. Moaning, she flailed as if struggling to stand. I rushed toward her, but the guard reached her first.

The prisoner twisted and jumped at him, pressing her hand over his mouth and nose. He fumbled to push her off, and her worn dress ripped in the struggle. The guard slackened, his legs buckling, and then he crumpled to the floor.

Stunned, I froze, and Jamil bounded past me. The prisoner reached up, still clutching the edge of her sleeve, and lunged, scraping the material across Jamil's face. Jamil stumbled back, his movements jerky and disjointed.

The prisoner spun toward Vasile. The High Judge pressed his back against the wall, clutching the neck of his fine camasa tunic. Vasile's gaze flicked from the prisoner's hand to me. My stomach dropped as I spied her weapon. Carved and wooden, it looked like a piece of her broken chair. Vasile put his arms up just as she swung.

"For the true heir!" She hit him with a sickening smack on the side of the face.

Vasile's head spun, his body awkwardly following. And then he tumbled to the ground.

Jamil lunged drunkenly forward, swinging his sword, forcing the attacker away from Vasile. Horror snaked up through me, watching Jamil move like he was sleepwalking. He grunted and shook his head as if trying to keep himself awake.

"How are you still walking?" the prisoner snarled and then snatched Vasile's dagger.

Jamil's movements were painfully slow. She darted to Jamil's back, shoving him with enough force to send him toppling to the ground. Papa pushed me toward the door, keeping himself between me and the attacker.

My heart pounded against my ribs, but my feet were like lead. The prisoner slashed Papa's arm and wrested him away.

For a breathless moment, the prisoner and I stared at each other. Blood glittered on the edge of her stolen blade. Jamil struggled to his knees, but he'd never reach us in time. With a low growl the prisoner lunged.

I threw up my arms with a shriek. She grabbed my wrist and yanked me toward her. Off balance, I stumbled. The dagger pressed against my side. I tensed, waiting for the bite of pain. But she hesitated, her eyes reddened. A strange look passed over her face — regret, despair, rage? I couldn't tell.

"Forgive me," she whispered before she grabbed my hair and yanked. My head snapped back, my neck and chest exposed to her blade.

She gasped as her fingers jerked out of my hair, her body falling away. I stumbled into Papa behind me. The prisoner was sprawled on the smooth marble floor as her life pumped from her gaping wound. Jamil knelt on one knee, the prisoner's blood running down his sword. He coughed and wiped at his face, which was smeared with mushroom-colored poison. Strings of snot ran from his nose, and his eyes watered unceasingly. He gagged, and then with more resolve than I'd imagined possible, he staggered to his feet.

"My Empress," he croaked. "Are you all right?"

All right? Before me lay the prisoner in a spreading pool of her own blood, the injured guard, poor Jamil, and stunned Vasile. Behind me, my father grunted, likely tending his own wound. And I was the one person in the room left unharmed, only my hair mussed and dress stained. But... *all right?* My eyes burned with unshed tears, and a vice clenched in my chest. I wanted to weep, to hide, to run away and never hear mention of the palace again, let alone inhabit its long halls and cavernous rooms. But to flee would mean abandoning those who looked to me as their leader — Empress. Even now, Jamil, the leader of my Own, waited for my command.

"P-Papa, fetch Pari." Her Healer's skills were far beyond my own. "She cares for Rubia in the mornings."

Papa kept one hand over the blood oozing through his sleeve as he rushed from the room, alerting the guards outside the door. Jamil blinked rapidly, his face pale. I wasn't a magical Healer, but I rushed to the unconscious guard first.

I put my hand on his wrist as Rubia had taught me, finding only the faintest pulse. As guards rushed in, I used my marama scarf to wipe the mushroom-colored poison from his face. Jamil had received a lesser amount, and his regular Protections had likely spared him the worst of the poison's effects.

Vasile groaned and sat up. He put a hand to his head as another guard urged him to stay on the floor. I silently willed Pari to hurry.

"Nicoleta." I heard Marcus' voice a moment before he swept me up from the floor. The familiarity was a terrible breech in etiquette, but at that moment, I didn't care. I relaxed into his embrace, and the familiar scent of mint and hay enveloped me.

"I caught up to your father in the hallway," Marcus said as I pulled away. "He told me what happened," he added as his gaze roved over my features.

Tears threatened, and I started to shake. "S-she could have k-killed me. Why d-didn't she?"

"Who knows? I'm sure your father will find out who she was. Maybe that will tell us something about why she did this. Marcus put his arm around me, guiding me away from the mass of guards pouring in, though two of my Own stayed close. "You're lucky. There's not a scratch on you. Ziba's Protection is very strong."

"The prisoner didn't touch me. Not with the poison." She could have killed me with one swipe of her tainted sleeve. I had foolishly allowed my Protections to dwindle. "She was poised to stab me in the stomach but hesitated. Then she moved the dagger to my neck and hesitated again." I continued to shiver, and Marcus unpinned his half-cloak and wrapped it around me.

The prisoners knew I'd stopped the plague and commanded their retrials. So why would she attack me? "She said, 'For the true heir.'"

Marcus' face darkened, and the muscle in his jaw ticked.

"What is it?" I asked.

He remained silent, but the muscles in his neck grew taut.

But, I'd heard the whispers for weeks and could guess at his thoughts. "She's not the only one who thinks a part-Getaen commoner shouldn't sit on the throne."

"By Emperor Trajan Caracalla's decree, you are the recognized ruler. The spell he demanded be created responded to your touch and deemed you the true heir," Marcus said.

"You sound like Papa." I appreciated Marcus' attempt at reassurance, but Ziba's and Jamil's warnings suddenly became *very* real. I needed to accept that despite my good intentions and ending the corruption, a portion of my own people would rather see me dead than officially crowned.

Download the rest of *The Rose Court* and find out how Nicoleta navigates the thorns!

AUTHOR'S NOTE

This story was inspired by my husband's family lore about an ancestor who married below her status in 1788. As a punishment, her family took away her vast inheritance and said it would be released after seven generations had passed. Only then would her estate be distributed to her descendants. Of course, if there ever was documentation of such an arrangement it has long ago disappeared. No valuable assets have been doled out, nor do we expect a fat check in the mail. Even so, the story stirred my imagination: if someone really wanted to pass down a valuable asset after many generations, how would one do it? It is hard to predict future economies, the physical security of the document, and other legal matters. And then I started thinking if someone was holding those assets, how would they feel when the seventh generation got closer. Kind of like the steward who has ruled in the stead of an absent king for generations. One kind of gets used to the idea of ownership, even if it isn't technically theirs. Then I mixed in an emperor, magic, consequences and... voila!

This time period is inspired by the antiquity age, before

advancements in technology, art and wonder was lost to the dark ages. It lends to a magical realm very nicely. There are some obvious embellishments and twists to our real world — I wanted it to have a touch of the fantastical! I was purposeful in delving into ancient eastern European regions and people. The Dacians were a real people, also known as the Dacian-Getaens. They were known as fierce warriors, per the Roman records. They were the last people conquered by the Romans and the first area the Roman's abandoned. Because the area the Dacians, then the Roman's conquered was inhabited by several other groups over the last two thousand years, there are relatively few records remaining. Some argue that the Dacians were completely destroyed, but others in this region today still feel connected to their Dacian ancestors. To find out more about the real Dacian history (which is fascinating), including the very real Emperor Trajan (Roman), Rupea Castle (still standing), Moesia (actually was a country south of Dacia), and human migration, here are some resources I used that you might find helpful:

http://historum.com/ancient-history/84218-women-dacians.html

https://balkancelts.wordpress.com (technically more about the Theracians, but includes Dacian history as well.)

Also, there are many books about Dacians in your local library.

I wrote Nikka with a stutter because I've developed a small stutter as an adult, which is both fascinating and annoying. This was an excuse for me to learn more about myself, but I also always have the intention of writing characters with some sort of mental or physical struggle. Doesn't everyone have something they're battling? This makes it real. It's reflective of the world around us. Here are links to presentations and excellent websites on stuttering:

https://www.stutteringhelp.org/
https://www.stutteringhelp.org/content/joe-biden
https://westutter.org/

ACKNOWLEDGMENTS

Thank you to the beta readers and my street team! Many people read snippets of the story and gave me fantastic feedback. All your comments were gifts to me — your time, thoughts, and talents written in the margins of the page were much appreciated. Thank you! Shout-out to Emily Bradshaw & Drea Lee, who were there at critical junctures.

And an extra big thank you to my critique partners Polly Irving, Paul Tallman, and Sarah Shipley, who suffered through multiple story renditions. It was fun brainstorming my magic system and world, names for all the things (because... Raylene), and for your invaluable, personal insights on stuttering. (And a special thank you to Tina Tallman for being the most wonderful host in the world. Seriously. The whole world.)

Thank you to M.K. Martin — everyone should be so lucky to have an editor who is also their champion. Did I mention how much I love the language she created based on the actual languages of other nearby ancient city-states? Amazing!

Thank you to Jeff Wheeler, who looked at several of my stories and one day finally said, "This is the one." Then helped me in a million and one ways — I am beyond blessed to have you as a mentor. (No, you didn't ever agree to the position. Yes, you probably regret giving me your phone number because I text you about my milestones and whenever I'm wildly upset about things your characters do in your novels!) And to my friend, Raye Wagner, who sat me down and told me what was possible. And then rolled out the red carpet of information and said, "this way," so I didn't fumble along in the dark.

And thank you, Dawn Yacovetta, for proofreading! (Let it be noted that no editors touched the back matter — they cannot be held responsible for the crummy punctuation — ha!) And to Sue-Ellen Welfonder, who did a consistency pass and additional proofread.

Especially after writing this story with the themes of family and motherhood, I want to recognize my own amazing mom and all the women in my life: aunts, neighbors, youth leaders, and teachers who were like second mothers to me. I was fortunate to have the security of so many women who would have jumped into a fiery inferno and plucked me out.

To my husband, who told me it was time for me to change direction and focus on my writing. Cliff. Jump. Soar.

ABOUT THE AUTHOR

K. J. Dawson loves lionhearted, tenacious characters who step into their own adventure! She also loves chocolate, forests, and staying up too late — night owls unite! Kristin writes high fantasy with political intrigue, a bit of romance, and of course, magic. When she's not writing, toting her kids around to sports practices, or cleaning out the chicken coop, she's probably curled up with a fuzzy blanket and a book. Find her at: www.kristinjdawson.com

Also by K. J. Dawson

The Unchosen

The Lilac Plague

The Rose Court

The Canina Thorn

Stand Alone Fairytale

The Poisoned Prince

Fae Illusions of Trinth

Elven House of Ivy

Elven Council in Ashes (coming 2025)

www.ingramcontent.com/pod-product-compliance
Lightning Source LLC
Chambersburg PA
CBHW022036120726
47899CB00004BA/1182